Katherine Howell is a former ambulance officer. *Frantic*, her first novel, introduced Detective Ella Marconi and has been published in the United Kingdom, Germany, France, Italy and Russia. Katherine lives in the New South Wales Hunter Valley and is currently working on her third novel, *Cold Justice*.

www.katherinehowell.com

Praise for *The Darkest Hour*

'As with *Frantic*, I galloped through this book with my heart racing. Howell may have left the ambulance service but she can still drive a narrative at full speed with the sirens blaring. Pass me the oxygen, someone'
Sydney Morning Herald

'A quality crime thriller . . . emotion charged action . . . relentlessly fast paced'
Crime Down Under

Praise for *Frantic*

'In an assured debut Howell has created two sympathetic female characters and lives up to her title with plenty of lively action'
Sunday Telegraph

'Former ambulance officer Katherine Howell has written an adrenaline rush of a thriller . . . This is a book you don't so much read as devour'
Sydney Morning Herald

Also by Katherine Howell

Frantic

KATHERINE HOWELL

THE DARKEST HOUR

PAN BOOKS

First published 2008 by Macmillan an imprint of
Pan Macmillan Australia Pty Limited, Sydney

First published in Great Britain 2009 by Pan Books
an imprint of Pan Macmillan Ltd
Pan Macmillan, 20 New Wharf Road, London N1 9RR
Basingstoke and Oxford
Associated companies throughout the world
www.panmacmillan.com

ISBN 978-0-330-46240-2

1 3 5 7 9 8 6 4 2

A CIP catalogue record for this book is available from
the British Library.

Printed and bound in the UK by CPI Mackays, Chatham ME5 8TD

For Bronwyn, Phillip, Mum and Dad.

ACKNOWLEDGEMENTS

Thanks to:

Selwa Anthony and Selena Hanet-Hutchins for advice, enthusiasm and kindness, particularly during my own dark hours;

Cate Paterson and Kylie Mason at Pan Macmillan for inspired editing and comments;

Adam Asplin and Bruce Guy for answering my countless questions on police matters;

Ambulance friends Mel Johnson, Col Benstead, Allan Burnett, Jenni and Steve Flanagan, Garry 'Syd' Francis, Warren Leo, Justine Petit, Alan Smith and John Wood for all kinds of cheer squad work, including patience and good humour at photo shoots, and Graeme Strong, winner of the *Frantic* launch party lucky door prize;

The Mphil and sf-sassy groups, especially Graeme Hague and Kate Morton;

My family, especially my brother, Phillip Guy.

Most of all, thanks to my husband, Phil, for many things but especially his constant smile and positive outlook. Ditto to Ralph.

ONE

The wind howled between the buildings like a creature from an arctic nightmare as Lauren peered into the wreck, then turned to the cop beside her. 'He's dead.'

The cop gestured to the rescue squad. They'd all known, of course; when half the man's head was missing it didn't take a medical expert to figure it out. But waiting for a paramedic's say-so was just one way in which the services worked together, and Lauren liked it like that. This sense of professional courtesy was the same reason why she didn't get back into the ambulance but stayed out in the cold with the fire officers – who kept their hoses charged in case the crashed car burst into flames – and the general duties cops who were there to guide the patchy 2am traffic past the scene.

Lauren shifted from foot to foot, chin tucked inside her parka and hands deep in her pockets. Sydney winters weren't that bad really, but tonight that wind worked its way down her neck and up her trouser legs and eventually blew straight through her as if she wasn't even there. She left the lee of the ambulance and tried the shelter of the police rescue vehicle, then finally stood right up close to the fire truck, which was putting out heat from its pump-running engine.

Still, she ached from shivering by the time the police lifted the dead driver out onto the body bag and the government contractor's white van pulled into view. Freed from the possible need to transport the body, she said a quick goodbye and floored the ambulance over to Gilly's all-night café on Broadway.

With the precious coffee steaming in the holder between the seats and the heater whirring at top speed under the dash, she then backstreeted her way over to stand-by at Paddington station. This was the lot of the officer working single for the shift – you were prime choice if a body ever had to be transported and you got sent all over to fill in spaces when crews were busy. She didn't mind being one-out; it was better than working with some officer who was all pissed off about being dragged in from the western suburbs. Best of all, of course, was working with Joe Vandermeer, her shift partner for the last two years, but he'd called in sick tonight.

She kept the wheel straight with her knee for a moment so she could press her hands to the heater vents. With a bit of luck she'd get to stay at Paddo for a while, dozing in the warmth of the station, though the way the radio had been going off she doubted–

A man bolted from an alley on her left and she

grabbed for the wheel and hit the brakes. A thought flashed through her head – *this won't look good coming so soon after the accident with the bus, hitting a pedestrian, oh Jesus stop stop STOP* – as the weight and momentum of the ambulance kept it moving forward, but then the man was out of the way and running down the street. With her stomach at the back of her throat and the smell of spilled coffee in the air, Lauren hit the button to drop the window and yell at him, but then a second man shot from the alley entrance. He skidded into the gutter and fell over.

'Pair of idiots,' Lauren said, shaky from the fright. Hazard lights blinked as a car was unlocked down the street and the first man leapt inside. He took off, no lights. Lauren flicked on her high beams but couldn't make out the numberplate. The second man struggled to his feet and onto the footpath. Lauren assessed his stance and actions, then picked up the microphone. 'Thirty-four.'

'Thirty-four, go ahead,' Control said.

'I'm in Smithy's Lane in Surry Hills, needing back-up, please. Looks like I have a patient: a male with shoulder injury.'

'Don't know when I'll have somebody free,' Control said. 'I'll send the boys in blue your way in the meantime.'

'Appreciate it. I think this guy was up to no good,' Lauren said.

She drove to the side of the road, her stomach taking its time to settle. The young man sank back against the wall, his face contorted and his right arm clutched to his side. She pulled on gloves then got out with the torch in one hand and portable radio in the other. 'You okay?'

He was crying. She saw he was more a boy than a man. 'Don't call the coppers.'

'They might turn up.'

'Shit.' He pushed off the wall and started to stumble away.

'You need your shoulder checked,' she said. 'It looks dislocated, and it can keep popping out if you don't get it treated properly.'

'It does it all the time.'

She followed him. 'Let me help you.'

He muttered something she didn't catch. She glanced around for her back-up. 'What's the problem?' she said. 'Don't want to get busted for chasing that guy? You trying to mug him or something?'

'I wasn't chasing him,' he said. 'We were running away.'

'From what?'

He nodded back towards the alley. 'I'm not getting involved.'

He increased the pace of his shuffle. Lauren watched him go. To try to physically stop him was asking for a smack in the head. He was of sound mind, more or less; he could refuse treatment if that was what he wanted.

She went back to the alley. It was dark and the light from her torch was a narrow beam. She flashed it along the walls then on the ground, and spotted a man lying on the asphalt.

She played the beam over the motionless body. There was blood on his head. She glanced up and down the street but there was no sign of the cops. The area was empty, the glow of the orange streetlights cold and alien. She shivered in her parka. If she'd taken the body from the prang she'd be sitting in the morgue having a cuppa now instead of worrying about her safety in some piss-stinky alley. She shone the torch around the alley again, then started in.

Close up she saw two things: she knew who he was, and he was dead. Stewart Blake was a former schoolteacher, a convicted paedophile and murderer of a twelve-year-old girl, and his photo had been all over the news since his recent release from jail. Now his mouth hung open, and his pupils were fixed and dilated. The back and left side of his head were beaten in and dark blood pooled around him. Somebody had taken their revenge.

Lauren crouched for a token pulse check, then heard a slight noise further down the alley.

She whipped the torch beam around that way. The alley was silent. Cat, passer-by, killer, or another victim, not yet dead? Lauren crept along the cracked asphalt, torch out in front as if it could protect her.

The alley turned a corner. Lauren hesitated between a broken streetlight and the wall and shone her torch into the darkness. On her right a skip bin overflowed with builder's rubble, and beyond that a dented car with no windows, no wheels and no numberplate was up on broken concrete blocks. She listened, shining the light along the car's chassis, squinting at the dark shape that seemed to be hunkered down beyond it, then a groan from close by made her skin prickle.

She edged along the skip. The torch beam lit up two blood-spattered sneakers, then jeaned legs. When she peered around the corner of the skip she saw a man slumped against the wall, his hands clutching his chest. His eyes were squeezed shut against the torch-light but she recognised him just the same.

'Thomas?' Her stomach went into freefall. '*Thomas?*'

He moaned.

She kicked his shoe. 'Open your eyes.'

'Lauren?' Like he didn't know it was her. He cracked one eye open. 'Help me.'

His brown hair was shorter than when she'd last seen him, five years ago, but his Austrian accent was as strong as ever. There were specks and smears of blood on his hands but none on the shirt he was grabbing. 'Open your eyes,' she said again.

'Pain.'

'Bullshit.'

He grimaced. His forehead was shiny with sweat. 'Chest pain.'

In the distance a siren wailed.

His fingers pulled at the cloth of his blue shirt. 'Can't breathe.'

'Get up.'

'Heavy weight here.' He clenched a fist over the centre of his chest.

Was it Lauren's imagination or was he going pale? And it was a cold night to be so sweaty. He was describing all the right symptoms for cardiac pain.

'Man chased me.' Thomas rubbed the side of his jaw. 'Pain here too now.'

Lauren was torn. He really did seem to be in pain, and she should treat that, but the Thomas Werner she knew was not to be trusted.

'Once the police get here I'll help you,' she said. 'Okay?'

But his head dropped forward onto his chest and his arms slipped to his sides. She stared at his chest. He wasn't breathing.

She waited. If he didn't take a breath for three minutes, she'd know he wasn't faking.

But if he really was in arrest, each passing minute killed brain cells. Whatever he'd done here, she wanted him to face the consequences. She didn't want him dying and getting out of it.

She kicked him in the knee with the toe of her boot, then kicked him again, harder. He didn't move. She swore under her breath, and glanced back at the street where the ambulance was parked, where all her gear was. A fleeting thought suggested she just leave him there – her and Kristi's and Felise's lives would be so much the better for him being dead – but she knew what she had to do: confirm the cardiac arrest, call for back-up while running back to the truck and grabbing the defib and drug box and Oxy-Viva, then get back here and start saving the bastard.

She put the torch and portable radio down, squatted beside him and reached for his carotid pulse.

His arms came up and her heart jumped and her mind screamed *I knew it!* but there was no time to scramble away. He knocked her onto her back and threw himself on top of her. He wrenched a handful of her shirt and parka up under her throat, forcing her chin back, pressing into her neck. 'Go,' he said.

What?

She couldn't breathe or speak. She pushed at his shoulders but he only leaned further into her. She felt her ribs bending under his weight.

'Listen.'

His fist was so hard up against her chin she couldn't even nod. His face and the night behind it and the wall were disappearing in a swarm of white spots.

'You say one word of this and you and Kristi and the kid are in for it. Nod if you understand.'

He loosened his grip a little and she sucked in the cold night air and nodded.

'Even if they lock me up, I have contacts everywhere,' he said in her ear. 'I will get you.'

She could smell his sweat and the blood on his hands. She nodded again. He got off her, then grabbed her shoulders and roughly rolled her over. He pressed her face against the asphalt, his hand spanning the back of her head. 'Don't move.'

He gave her head a final shove then was gone. She heard his feet slap away down the alley. She lay spread-eagled, fighting back tears, the pounding of her heart seeming to reverberate off the asphalt, and her mouth full of the dull, sour taste of anger and hatred and self-reproach.

The siren drew nearer.

If the police found her crying, they'd know something had happened. She struggled onto her hands and knees, then hauled herself up against the skip and hung onto the lip, breathing the odours of cut wood and broken plasterboard. She looked down the alley but it was empty. The torch lay on the ground against the wall, its beam shining uselessly under the skip, and she grabbed it and turned it to the abandoned car. Had there really been something – someone – there? Was that who Thomas had said '*Go*' to? There was nothing there now.

The siren was close. Lauren picked up the radio and stumbled back along the alley. She stuck the torch under her arm and ripped off her gloves, stuffing them into her pocket. She touched her face, feeling for grazes that might make the police wonder. Her cheek was tender but felt intact, not even bruised enough to be noticed. She wiped her eyes on her wrist then shakily shone the light down onto her parka and trousers, brushing off dirt and sawdust. There were no rips, and any blood from Thomas's hands was invisible on the dark navy fabric. She couldn't see her shirt collar, but tucked it well down under the parka, then pulled the zip right up to her chin in case any bruising started to emerge on her neck.

The street at the end of the alley was lit with red and blue flashes, and a police car drove into view, its spotlight shining into the alley and momentarily blinding her. She flashed her torch off and on a couple of times, and walked back past the body without looking at it.

'Thirty-four,' she said into her radio.

'Go ahead, Thirty-four,' Control said.

'Cancel that ambulance back-up.' She took

a breath and tried to steady her voice. 'I have one patient code four. Police are on scene now.'

'Copy, Thirty-four. Call me when you're clear.'

She met the officers in the alley's entrance. She knew both by sight but not by name. They were young and blond.

'Body for you.' She was trembling. She shoved her damp hands into the back of her belt for support.

'You okay?'

He knows. But of course he didn't, couldn't. Lauren cleared her throat. 'The dead guy's Stewart Blake.'

'The child-killer?'

She nodded. The shakes were going, a little. This was how to do it. Concentrate on something else. Sooner or later they would ask if she'd seen anything, anyone. It would be okay. Tell the truth, just not the whole truth.

She pointed into the alley with her thumb, and they walked together, the cops with the barrels of their four-cell Maglite torches resting on their shoulders.

At the body the officers stared at the face.

'It's him all right,' the shorter cop said.

'No great loss,' his mate said, shining his torch beam straight into the dead eyes.

'No loss at all.'

The taller cop shone his torch around and down the alley. 'See anything?'

'Two guys ran out, that's why I stopped,' Lauren said. 'Young one, a prostitute by the look, ran down the street, and an older one jumped in a car and took off.'

'See the model, the plates?'

She shook her head.

'Hang around for the Ds, give a description of the men?'

She stuck her hands in her pockets. 'Sure.'

The officer looked at his shorter partner who was still staring at the body. 'Call it in, would ya?'

Lauren pressed her back against the ambulance while the police set up around the crime scene. She finished what was left of her coffee but kept the empty cup in her hand, something to hold onto. Her throat was sore but she'd climbed into the ambulance and checked her face and neck in the mirror, on the pretext of getting something out of her eye, and she knew she looked okay.

Five detectives, recognisable by their civilian clothes, stood on the footpath talking, then one came her way. 'Lauren, is it? What station're you at?'

She nodded. 'Lauren Yates, from The Rocks.'

The man scribbled in a notebook. 'I'm Detective Lance Fredriks. The officers said you saw two men running away?'

Lauren told the story. The detective's eyes never left her and she felt self-conscious about her words and the way they came out of her mouth. Did lies look different from the truth? When she described the young man as a little taller than her, about twenty, with dark hair and a limp, could the detective spot the misdirection? The last thing she wanted was for the young man to be found, because he might have seen Thomas or the dark shape, and then the police would come back to her with their eyes and their questions once more.

The other man who'd run out of the alley was easier; she said what she'd seen, which was close to nothing. Older, heavier, with a car. No way he'd be found, or come forward.

'You saw nothing else?'

'Not a thing,' she said, crumpling the cup in her hand.

The rest was the usual: come to the station in the morning for the formal statement; I'll be in touch if there's anything else. Lauren nodded and smiled.

'Thanks,' the detective said.

'No worries.'

Five months later, on a bright morning in early summer, the Coroner declared Stewart Blake's death a homicide carried out by persons unknown. The unsolved case would be relegated to a file drawer somewhere, to be taken out by an officer now and again, the pages flipped through, the cover signed and dated, then shoved back into the dark once more.

Her uniform damp with sweat, Lauren walked from the Glebe Coroner's Court past the media crews. She wanted to forget the whole thing, forget the way that one lie led to another, then another, and next thing you were holding the Bible and swearing and hoping like hell you could remember the notes you'd scribbled on the Gilly's paper serviette as soon as you'd left the scene about how you'd described the men you saw, because lies were harder to remember than truth. She'd studied those words for half an hour that morning then burned the paper in the bathroom, flushing the charred remnant and opening the window afterwards and watching the smoke blow out.

Felise had come in, nose wrinkled. 'Max's dad smokes in the bathroom too.'

'I wasn't smoking,' Lauren had said, reaching for the brush, smoothing it over the thin silky hair on Felise's narrow head. 'I think the smoke came in from outside. Somebody must have a fire in their garden.'

Felise wanted to climb onto the toilet to look. They'd stood there, Felise's thin hot arm around Lauren's neck, her breath warm against her cheek. Lauren had watched her niece's wide blue eyes move as her gaze roamed the neighbourhood. 'What can you see?' she'd said.

'The whole wide world.'

Lauren had hugged her close.

How could Thomas even contemplate hurting her?

How could he call her 'the kid', as if she was just *some kid*, and not the centre of the world?

She could almost feel the slight body in her arms again now as she stood at the lights, almost hear Felise's giggles over the noise of the traffic rushing along Parramatta Road.

The kid.

The light turned green and she strode across the street, sure of herself again.

★

Detective Ella Marconi turned to the next page in the print-out and rested her forehead in her hand. Across the room Detective Murray Shakespeare was fiddling with the aerial of an ancient radio he'd dug up from somewhere, and the staticky whine of its poor reception made Ella grit her teeth.

Murray swung the aerial in a wide arc. 'Stupid thing.'

'Do we really need music?'

'Sit in here all day reading these lists, drive any-one nuts.' There was a quick blat of sound and he stopped the aerial short, feeling for the spot on the airwaves.

Ella tried to focus on the page before her. Her eyes blurred and the numbers ran into each other. She felt surrounded, leaned in upon, by the stacks of print-outs looming on the desk beside her. Of all the things she'd imagined she'd get to do in the Homicide Squad, searching for three specific phone numbers in a list of thousands had been strangely missing.

'—*Eagers think he's doing?*' a voice shouted from the radio and Murray fumbled for the volume. '*Zero tolerance is what's needed in this country, not the namby-pamby softly-softly approach. Next thing, Eagers and his cronies in State parliament will be offering to hold the hands of the criminals, offering them counselling to help them deal with the traumatic experiences they had as dealers.*'

'We might need something to listen to but that's not it,' Ella said. 'The Family Man's rantings are more than I can stand.'

But Murray held the aerial perfectly still.

'*This drug amnesty will do nothing for our country's*

youth,' the voice barked. '*All it does is get rid of some higher dealers for long enough for the ambitious small-timers, the ones who've just been given immunity from prosecution, to move up the ladder and take their places.*'

'Turn it off,' Ella said.

Murray turned the volume down till the words became indistinct. 'He's got a point.'

'I think it's a good idea,' Ella said.

'You don't think he's right about the ambitious small-time dealer?'

'Better that we do something than nothing.'

'Not if it makes the situation worse,' Murray said.

'How can it be worse? Look what's happened in just the last few months with ice. If we can get information on some of the importers, find out how they're getting it into the country, there's not only some bad guys locked up but also some channels they can no longer use.'

Murray shook his head. 'We need to lock them all up, big or small. Freely giving people immunity like this is just wrong. It's like waving the big white flag: "Do what you want – we don't care."'

'As if getting the small guys off the street won't then allow even smaller ones to come up,' Ella said. 'At least this way we strike some bigger blows.'

Murray switched the radio off and sat down. Ella turned to the next page of numbers and bent closer to it, but still her concentration wandered. The bustling Homicide office was three floors down and they were stuck up here in a file room dusty with disuse. Their boss, Detective Sergeant Kirk Kuiper, had said he'd call if he needed them. She leaned over and picked up the phone, listened to the dial tone, and put the handset down. Murray watched, then sighed.

They took a break twenty minutes later. Murray stood staring out the window, his coffee steaming the glass. Ella got out her mobile and dialled Detective Dennis Orchard. They'd trained together at Newtown, centuries ago it felt like, then worked at Hunters Hill while dreaming of Homicide. Dennis got his transfer a few years ago, leaving her pissed off and certain that her application was being stonewalled by an evil cabal working with then-Assistant Commissioner Frank Shakespeare, who she'd once inadvertently told to get the fuck out of her crime scene. (Not that she'd ever admit to Murray the hold she believed his father had over her career.) But earlier in the year Dennis had brought her in to work the Phillips case with him, and it had finally felt like the first step in the right direction.

The bad thing was that it could also mean a quick slide backwards.

'No news?' she said when Dennis answered.

'They'll call you before they call me,' he said.

'Sometimes my reception's crap up here.'

'Oh sure,' he said, a smile in his voice. 'I'll send a carrier pigeon if they call me first and I can't reach you, okay?'

She put the phone away. Murray was looking at her. She shook her head.

She'd run through the incident in her mind a thousand times, a thousand times a thousand, seeing the kidnapper outlined against the background of sky and trees, gun aimed at Chris and Sophie Phillips who were curled up together on the grass. Ella remembered her sprint across the slope, her own gun out. Her voice shouting 'Drop it! Drop it!' and then the moment of knowing she had no choice, the kidnapper was about to shoot, and she'd held her breath and pulled the trigger. There was the noise, the recoil, and the sight of the kidnapper falling to the ground. And then she'd reached the couple, sobbing with their arms around each other, and the beautiful, perfect and safe little child between them.

She rubbed her forehead, shielding the dampness in her eyes in case Murray was looking.

She'd thought about that child, Lachlan Phillips, a lot, and talked about the case at length with Dennis, and read her copy of the statement she'd given to the Critical Incident Team detectives so often the pages were soft and creased. She always came up with the belief that she was one hundred per cent justified in the shooting, but still couldn't be sure the Team's verdict would go her way. Even with the broom of Strike Force Gold having swept more than a few officers out of the job, clearing sufficient space in the various squads for fresh blood – including her and Murray – to step into temporary secondments, she knew that a poor report from the Team would see her shipped straight back to the suburbs. Even an average report, combined with an average perform-ance during her secondment, could see her gone.

What she needed was a great case. Something open and shut – something with clearly defined good and bad guys, strong solid witnesses, textbook evidence and a good hearty sentence at the end. Something she could get stuck into, proving that she did have skills, that she knew how to work a case and was worthy of a permanent spot.

She stared at the phone.

TWO

Lauren caught the bus from the Coroner's Court through the city to The Rocks and walked up the top end of George Street to the ambulance station. The roller door was up and her work partner, Joe Vandermeer, stood on the footpath talking to a group of tourists. Laughter rose as she neared them. Joe posed, smiling, by the ambulance and two of the group took pictures. They thanked him in Scottish accents before wandering off.

Joe smiled at Lauren. 'Look at you. New boots, new belt, new tie.'

'Got to be spiffy on court day.' She yanked the tie off.

'How'd it go?'

'Fine,' she said. 'Got to change my shirt though.'

'Court always makes me sweaty too.' He followed her inside. 'They sent a guy over from Randwick but he went home sick about half an hour ago,' he said through the locker room door.

Lauren threw her grimy shirt into her locker and

pulled on a fresh crisp one. She did up the buttons, avoiding herself in the mirror. 'Were you busy?'

'Nah. Nothing interesting either.'

She pushed open the door. 'Good. I don't want you running round doing fun things without me.'

He grinned at her. 'I told Control that. I said he had to hold the good stuff for this afternoon.'

The phone rang. Joe lunged for it. 'Rocks, Joe.' He bent over a scrap of paper. 'Okay, yep, gotcha. Ta.' He put down the phone and gave Lauren a double thumbs up. 'Man's crying in Woolloomooloo.'

'What man?'

'Some man,' he said. 'I don't know. The neighbour called it in, said she can hear this guy through the wall, crying.'

'Call this good stuff?' Lauren grabbed her bag and the keys and followed Joe to the ambulance. 'They ever think to knock on the door, ask him if he's okay?'

'They call, we haul, that's all.' Joe got into the passenger side.

'It's crap.' Lauren slammed her door. 'Imagine this guy's face when we turn up. I vote that after we talk to him, we talk to this neighbour.'

She started the engine and drove out of the station. Joe hit the remote to close the roller door. Lauren turned on the lights and siren and pushed into the traffic on George Street.

'I don't know if it's that urgent,' Joe said.

'They call it, I floor it, that's all.'

'That doesn't rhyme,' Joe said. 'Are you okay?'

'Because I can't rhyme?' She punched the horn to

change the siren from wail to yelp as she approached a red light.

'You're all antsy.' He looked out at the traffic. 'Clear this side.'

Lauren accelerated through. 'Court.'

'I know what you mean,' he said. 'Whenever I'm up there in that box I feel like I'm the one in trouble. I feel I have to be so careful with my words, that the lawyers are waiting for me to make a mistake and then they'll get me.' His hands seized and mock-strangled his own throat.

'The families of the dead guy's victims were there,' Lauren said.

'Oh.' Joe dropped his hands. 'You're clear this side.'

Lauren had watched the faces of the people in the courtroom as she described how she'd found Blake's body. There was one woman, about the same age as Lauren, whose right eye twitched while Lauren told how she'd checked for a pulse, as if she couldn't imagine touching the man's flesh herself. Or maybe she could, and thought about more than just touching it. Maybe she imagined the satisfaction of bringing down the unrecovered blunt object, of feeling the skull crack and sink deeper with each wet blow.

The fact that so many of the victims had come to court more than twenty years after Blake had assaulted them was evidence of his effect on their lives. Thinking about that, and seeing that woman's twitch and the lined faces of the older people that were probably the victims' parents, had made her feel that Thomas had done something of a community service. She'd read somewhere that people like Blake could not be rehabilitated. Whether or not he deserved to die, children deserved protection. Nobody could argue with that.

'Bus,' Joe said.

'I can see it.'

She wondered, though, why Thomas had done it. He hadn't grown up here, couldn't have been a victim of Blake's.

'Clear this side,' Joe said.

Thomas and Kristi had been together almost a year, and Lauren had been glad when he disappeared soon after the car accident. He'd eventually written from Austria to say he'd been deported for overstaying his visa, how that meant he couldn't come out again, he was so sorry, but by then Kristi had been clean for a couple of months and able to recognise their relationship for the disaster it had been. She'd sat in the neonatal ward cradling Felise and shaking her head over the man who wanted nothing to do with his daughter. It was no surprise to Lauren. Kristi, when pregnant and out of her head, had been foggy to say the least, so hadn't noticed how Thomas always changed the subject when the topic of the baby came up, how he looked at her growing belly with distaste. Lauren, however, had seen, and remembered, and stewed.

'Next left,' Joe said. 'Number four ten, flat seven.'

She had to put it all behind her now, stop thinking about it. The case was over, if not entirely closed; the cops didn't give two hoots who'd done it, and they had enough work without spending more time looking; and Thomas had probably been back in Austria for months anyway. She'd protected her sister and that was all that mattered. After losing Brendan nine years ago, she knew that for the rest of her life she'd do whatever was necessary to keep Kristi safe from harm. Everything was fine. She and Kristi and Felise were free and clear.

She wriggled back in the seat a little, sat up straighter. 'Four ten?'

'Yep. There it is.' Joe pointed, and Lauren switched the lights and siren off and parked in a no standing zone.

They met at the ambulance's side door, pulling out equipment. 'Bets?' Lauren said.

'Break-up with his girlfriend.' Joe slung the Oxy-Viva over his shoulder.

Lauren twisted the portable radio into its clip on her belt. 'I'm going with the utter hopelessness of life.'

Joe laughed and started up the stairs. Lauren followed, the monitor and drug box stretching her arms from their sockets. 'Coffee at Gilly's says I'm right.'

Joe reached the third-floor landing and knocked on the door. Afternoon sunlight streamed in the landing window and made the delicate hairs on the back of his neck glow. Lauren, looking up at him and climbing the last few steps to where he stood ready to knock again, felt a rush of happiness.

'Hello?' The voice was muffled by the closed door.

'Ambulance,' Joe called. 'Is everything okay?'

'I'm stuck.'

'On the floor?'

There was no answer. Joe looked at Lauren. She pulled a face, the radar in the depths of her brain starting to ping. Joe leaned close to the door. 'You there?'

'It's my head.'

The voice sounded like the speaker had changed position in the flat. Lauren whispered, 'Let's go back down.'

But Joe was reaching for the door handle. 'He's confused. Probably fallen, got himself a head injury.' He raised his voice. 'Sir? Do you need some help?'

Lauren looked at the other doors on the landing. 'I'll get Control to ring the caller back, see if they know anything about him.' She put down the monitor and drug box and raised the portable radio. 'Thirty-four.'

'Thirty-four, go ahead,' Control answered.

Joe opened the door and in a flash a man lunged out and grabbed him. Lauren saw the blade of the knife, the wild red eyes and the stubbled chin, caught the smell of his unwashed body.

'Don't,' the man said, looking at her. She saw his decayed teeth when he spoke. *An ice addict.*

She moved slowly, raising her other hand to take the radio aerial between two fingers, showing him she wasn't going to transmit. Before releasing the body of the radio she slid her hand along it and flicked the volume to zero. Control would call her again in a minute or so and she didn't want the man to hear. If he made her say that everything was fine, forget she called, no help would come their way for an hour or more. If Control got no reply, they would realise something was up and send help.

Or she could throw it, she could throw it really hard and startle him.

Her eyes met Joe's and read the silent message there. Joe was ex-Navy, trained in who knew what. She would do what he said. She lowered the radio to the floor beside the equipment, the sweat on her fingers making the aerial slippery.

'Come here,' the man said.

She walked slowly, shooting a glance at the closed door of the next flat. Maybe somebody would look out of the peephole and see what was going on. Maybe the person who'd called them – people loved to watch paramedics doing stuff. Or maybe somebody would trip over all the gear left on the stairs and realise something was wrong.

The man backed into his flat, dragging Joe with him. The knife pressed into Joe's neck. Lauren could see where it obstructed his jugular, making the vein bulge above the blade. It made her own throat and neck sore to see it, a physical reminder of Thomas's attack in the alley. She was shaking.

'Now,' the man snapped.

Joe's eyes flicked madly from Lauren down the stairs, back to Lauren, back down the stairs. She shook her head slightly. They had a better chance if they stayed together. If she ran for it, who knew what the man might do to him?

She stepped inside the flat.

'Shut the door.'

She did as he said.

'Lock it.'

There was no way to pretend to lock the door and leave easy access for the police who would hopefully arrive soon. She turned the deadlock. At least the door itself felt flimsy.

The man adjusted his grip around Joe's neck. Joe's face was turning red and he made calming motions with his hands down by his sides. Lauren drew in a shaky breath.

'What's your name?' she said.

'That's privileged,' the man snapped. He wore blue football shorts and a faded Nirvana T-shirt. She could smell the rot on his breath.

'I'm Lauren and that's Joe.'

'Shut up.'

She glanced around the small room without turning her head. The floor was covered with cracked and dirty linoleum. The only furniture was a pair of blue plastic milk crates. Aluminium foil was taped over the glass of the windows, blocking the alien death rays or mind-reading impulses or whatever he was fixated on. All but one window were closed. Lauren could hear the traffic on the street below through the small gap at the bottom of the open one.

A tiny kitchen area opened off the far end of the room, empty takeaway containers covering the bench and spilling onto the floor. To her left was another doorway, leading to a bedroom and bathroom she guessed. The place stank of rotting food and blocked drains.

She met Joe's eyes again. The man's arm was high up under his chin and it was clear he couldn't speak.

Lauren swallowed. 'Did the voices tell you to do this?'

'Voices.' The man hauled Joe backwards across the room to the wall and pressed against it.

'I'm just wondering why you're doing this,' Lauren said. 'What you want us to do.'

The man's red eyes flicked about the room. 'Are you with them?'

'Joe and I are from the ambulance service,' Lauren said. 'We're here to help you.'

'How did you get the message? Did it come down from them?'

'Your neighbour rang us on the telephone.'

The man's eyes blazed. 'God will get you, you know.'

'Why don't you let Joe go?' Lauren said.

Somewhere outside a siren wailed. The man seemed to grow another ten centimetres at the sound. 'Devils!'

This was bad. You couldn't reason with a person who'd lost touch so completely with logic and reality.

Lauren wished Joe was free and they could talk about what to do. His face above the man's arm was turning purplish. He was blinking at Lauren. Some kind of code? Or just dry eyes?

The siren grew fainter and disappeared in the noise of the city.

'Please let Joe go,' she said again. 'Let him go, and we'll just walk out the door and leave you alone.'

The man clacked his teeth together and peered towards the window.

Lauren took half a step forward. 'If you need to

look out there, you can't do it while holding onto Joe.'

The man appeared to think about this. He took his arm from Joe's neck and Lauren saw the knife had cut the skin. Blood trickled down onto the collar of his crisp white shirt. The man stepped to one side, the point of the knife at Joe's chest. 'Take off your shirt. Let me see the wires.'

'There are no wires.' Joe's voice was croaky. He cleared his throat.

'Let me see!'

Joe started unbuttoning.

'You too,' the man said to Lauren. When she hesitated he faked a stab at Joe and she held up her hands then grasped her buttons.

'See?' Joe said. 'No wires.'

'Sit down. There. Back to back.'

In her bra and uniform trousers Lauren sat on the cracked lino. The man grabbed a wide roll of silver gaffer tape and bound their hands behind them, then wrapped the tape around both their bodies. His proximity made her skin crawl, and she smelled his acrid sweat. Her heart kicked harder in her chest and the tape pulled at her skin. Drops of nervous sweat ran down her sides and she wondered how much it would take to defeat the tape's stickiness.

The man went to the window and peered out.

Joe's back was warm and damp against Lauren's. 'You okay?' he whispered.

The man looked around. She pressed against Joe and didn't speak. When the man turned his back she whispered, 'What are we going to do?'

'You should've run away.'

She moved her shoulder blades against him in an emphatic *no*.

'Devils!' the man shouted out the window.

That should get some attention, Lauren thought.

'Devils, all of you!'

That's the way. You tell them!

She felt Joe's fingers slip inside the waistband of her trousers, then out again. She sat still. What was he doing? He tugged at something, then she felt her new belt begin to turn around her body. He was pulling it through the loops. She shifted her weight to help the buckle through each one, while watching the man ducking and weaving by the window. He looked like he was avoiding being shot. Aliens and their laser beams.

Joe stopped pulling on her belt. She felt it tighten for a second then go slack. He'd undone the buckle. His hands twisted and worked between their backs. He pressed the buckle into her hands and she grasped it, feeling pressure against it, realising he was trying to cut through the tape around his wrists with the buckle's tongue. She felt the turning of his forearms against hers, felt the skin becoming slicker with the sweat of his efforts.

The man pulled a milk crate to the window and hunched down onto it, staring outside. Lauren hoped he'd forgotten about them. Maybe they'd be free before he remembered.

She wondered what time it was, how long it'd been since she'd called Control. Surely they would have someone on their way to check on them by now, once they realised they couldn't raise her on the air. Surely this would not be the place of their deaths. But it was too easy to make a mental amalgam of the murder scenes she'd been to – the slumped bodies, the cut throats, the finger marks in the blood, proof of the final struggle.

Joe's back towered over hers, and when she leaned her head back it rested at the nape of his neck. She only did it for a second before realising it would interfere with his arm movements, but was aware even in that short period of time that they fitted together like they were moulded.

The man stood up. 'Devils!' he gasped, looking down at something in the street. The cops?

Lauren felt Joe work faster. The heat between their backs was intense. She could feel sweat beading on her face. She thought of the long blade of the man's knife. A patient had once described how it felt to be stabbed, how you felt a blow like a punch rather than the sharp pain of the knife going in and out.

The man was muttering, making thrusting movements with the knife. Lauren tried to swallow. Her mouth and throat were dry. The air was hot to breathe. She and Joe didn't deserve this. They only wanted to help. She wasn't a religious person, and she didn't believe in karma, but she wondered now if being stuck here with this psycho was what she got for letting Thomas go free then lying about it in court.

No. She wouldn't think that way. She *knew* life didn't work that way. How many good people had she seen hurt or killed just from being in the wrong place at the wrong time? What about drink-drivers (*like Kristi* – but she shied away from that thought) – how many had she seen stumbling out of wrecks without a scratch on them while the family coming the other way lay screaming in their mashed car? She needed no more proof than that to understand that they were here simply because they happened to be on duty and nearby when somebody happened to call. She shut her eyes. *They call, we fall. That's all.*

A siren sounded a short half-wail outside. Lauren pictured a cop making somebody move their damned car. How would this work? Cops kick the door down and stream on in? She strained for sounds of bodies massing in the stairwell, the soft shuffle of black boots and body armour, the smell of leather belts and gun oil and rescue.

The man's attention was caught by something across the street, higher than them. He crouched, then darted to the side, then slammed the foil-covered window shut. He pressed against the wall facing them, looking at the ceiling and muttering. Lauren hoped he'd spotted police across the street, spying from a window to see what was happening. She hoped they'd seen her and Joe strapped to each other on the floor, knew where in the room they were, how far away the man was, at that moment anyway.

Joe changed angle. His movements felt increasingly desperate. The corners of the buckle dug into Lauren's palms and she could feel the tension of the tape against it, as firm as ever. The tongue was cutting nothing.

The man seized the front of his own shirt and

slashed at it with the knife. 'Devils!' His skin underneath was fish-belly pale in the gloom. The air was growing hotter and harder to breathe. Lauren flexed her biceps, testing the tape on her arms, but her sweat had made no difference.

Joe stopped trying to cut. His fingers took the buckle from her hands, then he put his palms on her lower back, curving around her hips. His skin was warm, his fingers spread wide. She pressed her shoulders against him. He adjusted his hands, as if taking a better grip, then pushed her to the left. Instinct made her resist for an instant then she felt his body going that way too and she let herself fall with him.

They thudded onto their sides on the cracked lino floor.

The man said, 'What?', and a second later a crowd of police in navy jumpsuits crashed through the door. The man went down screaming under a storm of shields and bodies. Lauren let out the breath she didn't know she'd been holding. A police officer cut the tape binding her to Joe, then the tape around their wrists, asking, 'Are you okay? Are you hurt?', but Lauren couldn't answer, could only let her head rest on the floor, her eyes on the most beautiful forest of boots and trouser legs.

Two paramedics from Headquarters rushed in, kits swinging from their shoulders. Marcia Dunleavy's face was pale, her eyes wide as she helped Lauren sit up. 'Shit, mate, you okay?'

Lauren pulled at the tape still hanging from her arms, suddenly needing to get it off. 'Got any Hexol?'

Marcia rummaged through the drug box. 'Here.'

Lauren squirted the alcohol solution along the tape where it stuck to her skin but it did nothing to the adhesive.

'Let me do it.' Marcia pushed Lauren's hands away and started to peel the tape away. Lauren felt like a child being ministered to. She leaned back a little and found Joe's back with her own. The other paramedic, John Hawthorn, was wiping at Joe's neck with a dressing. Lauren felt Joe flinch.

'Sorry,' John said.

Lauren felt for Joe's hand and gripped it as the police hauled the handcuffed and still-screaming man to his feet. The knife lay on the floor by the wall. Officers marched the man past Lauren and she made sure to look him in the face, telling herself he wasn't scary any more. Joe's fingers curled around hers.

A police officer brought their shirts over. The white cotton was stained with dirt from the filthy lino. Lauren couldn't stand the thought of putting it on and dropped it back on the floor. Marcia Dunleavy put her hand on Lauren's arm. 'Sit tight and I'll get a blanket.'

Lauren sat with her arms folded across her chest. She was shivering now, cold even in the stuffy room. Police searched the flat. One dropped the knife in an evidence bag. Lauren could see blood on the blade. She drew in a long shaky breath.

'Okay?' Joe said. He was on his feet. A dressing was taped to his neck. He reached down a hand to her. She took it and stood, weak in the knees. He put an arm around her shoulders, and when Marcia came back with two white cotton blankets he helped her wrap one around Lauren, then draped the other over himself.

Marcia said, 'I've told the police we're taking you to St Vincent's for a check-up before you'll do statements.'

On the landing Lauren looked across to the neighbour's door. It was open and an old lady was peering out, her dark hooded eyes sharp on them. Lauren nodded, and the woman nodded back.

They walked downstairs as a group. Marcia and John carried their own gear plus the kits Joe and Lauren had taken up. It seemed so long ago to Lauren that they'd come up here, joking about the reason for the man's crying. She could hear voices on the ground floor and pulled the blanket close around her neck and torso. She was aware of the beat of her heart and the movement of air in and out of her lungs. She wanted to go home.

The day had turned cloudy in the time they'd been held, and the gloom of the apartment block's foyer gave Lauren an eerie feeling. She could see onlookers trying to peer through the grimy glass doors, and a TV crew frantically setting up. She felt Marcia gather up a handful of the blanket at her back. 'Ready?' she said.

Lauren nodded.

Outside the air was humid and full of noise. Marcia and John's ambulance, twenty-seven, was parked beside Lauren and Joe's. The hazard lights flashed just out of synch. As the group neared the vehicles the clouds parted and sunshine lit the world. Joe opened the side door of twenty-seven for Lauren and held out his hand. 'Your chariot.'

She took his hand and pulled him to her. He smelled of nervous sweat. The blankets slipped partly off and Lauren was aware of the skin of her chest against his.

'How did you know they were there?' she asked.

'Lucky guess.'

She looked up at him.

'I know safeties going off when I hear them,' he said. 'Even through a door.'

'Thank you.'

He kissed the top of her head.

Three ambulances and a supervisor's car were already at St Vincent's Hospital. The officers crowded around as Lauren and Joe climbed out of twenty-seven.

'You okay?'

'Joe, what happened to your neck?'

'Was he a loony?'

'Give them some space,' Marcia shouted, still inside the ambulance.

Joe held the back of Lauren's blanket as they moved towards the doors of the Emergency Department. She liked the feel of his hand so close to her back and let him steer her through the concerned paramedics.

The doors slid back and Joe's fiancée, Claire Bramley, rushed out. She threw her arms around both of them, her RN badge poking the side of Lauren's neck. Her grip was tight. 'I was so scared for you guys.'

Joe shifted her arm from his throat. Claire gasped at the dressing. 'What did that maniac do?'

'It's nothing,' Joe said. 'Doesn't even need stitches.'

Claire pulled the corner of the dressing free but Joe took her hand. 'It'll be healed well before the wedding. You won't look like you're marrying Frankenstein.'

'That's not what I'm worried about.' Claire looked him over, making him raise his arms in his blanket and turn around on the spot. She then turned to Lauren. 'You okay?'

'I am,' Lauren said. 'Thanks to Joe.'

He smiled. 'It was nothing.'

Lauren felt a lump rise in her throat, and Joe went blurry. She clutched the blanket tightly around her. *Don't cry, don't you dare cry!*

'Come on, pilgrim.' Joe nudged her. 'I'm dying for a coffee.'

She followed him through the Emergency Department doors, breathing deep, her throat aching. The doors slid shut behind them and they were alone in the corridor, Claire still outside.

'Lots of sugar, hey?' Joe said. 'Boost the levels.'

'Joe.' It came out squeaky. 'I want to say . . .' But she couldn't say anything.

'It's okay.' He put his arm around her.

She closed her eyes over her tears and rested her head on his shoulder.

'Come on,' he said after a moment. 'Coffee and a sweet biscuit. You'll feel like a million bucks.'

Lauren wiped her face with a corner of the

blanket as the doors slid open and Claire came in. She stopped short just inside. 'Weren't you going for coffee?'

'On our way right now,' Joe said, and Lauren let herself be steered down the corridor, feeling safe with his arm across her shoulders.

THREE

In the café next door to the police building in Parramatta, Ella watched Dennis Orchard tear a cinnamon roll to pieces and stuff the largest bit in his mouth. He saw her looking and held out the plate. She shook her head. 'Thanks anyway.'

He mumbled something unintelligible. He'd stopped smoking again, and looked like he'd put on weight over the last month. Well, she couldn't talk, and she didn't have giving up smoking to blame it on.

He swallowed. 'Find those phone numbers?'

'They weren't there.'

He smiled and took a sip of coffee.

'We've got a new list now,' she said. 'Twice as long.'

His mouth full again, he gave her a wink.

'I'm in a holding pattern and I think I know why.'

He raised his eyebrows.

'Unless that shooting report comes in clear they don't really want me.'

'Not true.' Crumbs fell out of his mouth.

'I also think it's going to come back bad.'

He twirled a finger beside his forehead.

'Why are they taking so long then?' She put her folded arms on the table. 'I knew this move was too good to be true. I'm going to be back in that little room at Hunters Hill before the week is over, I bet you.'

Dennis swallowed, grimacing as it went down. 'It's a committee thing. Plenty of red tape. They always take ages.'

'I have a bad feeling.'

'That's hunger.' He held out the plate again.

She pushed it aside. 'If only I could get a strong case before the report comes back. They wouldn't move me in the middle of an investigation, would they?'

'They're not going to move you at all.'

'This city needs more murders,' she said.

He barked laughter. 'A case will come along soon enough.'

Maybe, maybe not. 'How's yours going?'

He shrugged. 'Straightforward. Guy still denies killing his brother for his share of the inheritance, but it's more than a million dollars and he's in debt up to his ears. Blood traces on his shoes and clothes, witnesses saw him in the area, he's behaving very nervously. I reckon he'll confess by the end of the week.' He bit into the final piece of roll. 'How's your mum?'

'The actual hip replacement went fine but she picked up an infection.'

'So she'll have to stay in for longer? Bet that'll piss her off.'

Ella didn't want to talk about domestic stuff. 'What's the latest on Gold?'

'Looks like they've tracked Wilson down. He turned into a bit of a hermit in the wilds of Scotland, apparently.'

'Good,' Ella said.

Evidence found in the previous case she and Dennis had worked together, the Phillips kidnapping, had indicated that Officers Wilson and Battye were part of the bank robbery gang that Strike Force Gold was after. In the six months since, investigators had discovered that the entire gang was police. Grant Battye had suicided, gassing himself in his car, while Matt Wilson and two others, Caleb Peters and John Fenotti, had disappeared. Two more officers had turned witness for the police and confirmed that Peter Roth and Angus Arendson were part of the gang too, though both were now dead. Dennis had told her they'd given up information on all aspects of the group's operation, including details of offshore bank accounts where the money had gone.

'Wilson'd need to be a hermit,' Dennis went on, 'seeing as we froze all his money.'

'Living on moss and stream water,' Ella said.

'Delicious.' He dabbed crumbs from the plate with his forefinger.

Ella checked the screen of her mobile.

Dennis smiled. 'You'll be fine.'

'I need to know.'

'Or what? You'll explode?'

'Don't laugh,' she said. 'Maybe I will.'

Lauren's head was throbbing by the time she and Joe had found theatre smocks to wear, gone over the entire event numerous times with their area supervisor then with a couple of detectives, and filled out the necessary reams of workplace injury paperwork. She wanted nothing more than to go home.

They were given the rest of the shift off. The supervisor dropped them at the station. 'Sure you guys're okay?'

Lauren nodded as Joe unlocked the station door. The supervisor nodded back then drove away.

Their ambulance was in the plant room, parked crookedly by the wall. John and Marcia had brought it back. Lauren remembered how she'd felt when they'd left the station in it that morning, and realised she'd hardly thought about court since then. *No big surprise.*

'You want a lift home?' Joe said.

'That'd be good.'

She checked her watch as they got into his car. Her headache eased a little and she decided that today's events – both the court appearance and the hostage situation – were best locked away in her mind and never thought of again. Her attention would be better spent on the world ahead of her.

Joe lived in a small flat in Parramatta, so it was nothing for him to drop Lauren right at the door of her ramshackle rented terrace in Summer Hill. A train clattered past on the other side of the road as she climbed out then bent to look back in the open window. 'Thanks again.'

'You're on the way.'

'I'm not talking about the lift.'

He said, 'Next time I tell you to run away, you better do it.'

'And miss out on all that fun?'

He smiled at her. 'See you tomorrow night.'

She stood up and he drove off. She started towards her front door but paused to watch the car brake at the corner of the street then swing right. She saw Joe's head turn her way just before the car disappeared behind the wall of the railway bridge. She stood there a moment longer, then took in and released a deep breath.

She and Joe had worked together for almost two years and knew each other so well that they hardly needed to speak while on a case. Whichever one of them was treating the patients that day, the other knew what equipment they wanted and when to fetch it. They were great friends too; best friends, in her mind. She could talk about anything with him. She remembered a night when they'd been sent to stand by at a quieter north shore station and had taken the opportunity for a lie-down in the bunk room. She'd lain there in the dark, knowing he was in the bed just across from her, that she could reach out and touch him if she wanted. They'd told ghost stories like a couple of kids and when the job phone rang she'd hardly been able to speak for fits of giggles.

She was glad he'd been there today. His efforts to

try to cut them free had made her feel less of a victim. It was a childish wish, but she hoped they'd be able to stay working together forever.

Inside the house she checked her watch again then ran up the stairs. She almost tripped over Felise's one-eyed mostly bald toy gorilla and hoiked it with her toe into Kristi's room, then in her own room she stripped off her uniform and pulled on jeans and a T-shirt. She pushed her bare feet into runners then hurried back downstairs and out the front door.

The school bell rang when she was still a block away, and she moved faster. She only slowed once the group of mothers and younger children standing around the gate came into view.

Kristi was talking to another young mum. Beside her Felise clung to the fence, her red sneakers jammed into the weldmesh, her hands grasping the top of a metal post, her gaze fixed on the wide double doors leading into the school building. She wasn't starting school until next year but couldn't wait. Mondays were a high point in her life because they came to the hallowed buildings to collect their six-year-old neighbour, Max Saleeba. As a stream of children burst out of the school Felise stood up on her toes, neck straining, thin arms like sticks below the sleeves of her shirt. Kristi put her hand on the back of her daughter's neck and leaned down to speak to her, and Lauren's throat swelled. Times like this she imagined what it would be like to still have their brother Brendan around, how he'd have loved to play with Felise and would have watched with such pride as she grew.

She had done absolutely the right thing in court that morning.

As she reached them, the object of Felise's urgent staring came into view. With his real uniform and his school hat and lunchbox and backpack, Max represented everything grown-up and important to Felise. Unable to contain her excitement any longer she jumped down from the fence and ran to the gate. Kristi watched with a smile on her face, a smile that grew when she caught sight of Lauren.

'Let you off early, did they?' Kristi said.

'Something like that.'

Kristi came closer. 'Have you been crying?'

Lauren shrugged and smiled and looked away at Felise who had Max by the hand and was dragging him over. 'We can go now,' Felise announced. 'Hi, Aunty Lolly.'

'Hi, Flea.' Lauren smoothed Felise's thin hair back from her narrow forehead. The top of the scar that ran down her chest was visible in the open neck of the pink 'My Little Pony' shirt.

They turned for home. The bells on Kristi's embroidered slippers jingled and Lauren could smell the essential oil of whatever that she liked to dab on herself. It used to annoy her, but now it was the smell of home. Max and Felise walked in front, Felise with Max's pack on her back, asking, 'Who did you play with at playlunch?'

Kristi pulled a leaf from a shrub, crumpled and sniffed it, then passed it to Lauren. 'Seriously,' she said in a low voice, 'have you been crying?'

Lauren gave the leaf a token sniff then dropped it.

'It's just work.' She couldn't go into detail. The incident reminded her too much of Thomas's assault.

'Keeping emotion in is bad for your spleen,' Kristi said.

Lauren produced a smile. 'My spleen's tip-top.'

If somebody had told her five years ago that Kristi would be like this now, she'd have booked them into the nuthouse. But maybe some alcoholic drug-users were like smokers – there were none so rabidly against their old lifestyle as the reformed.

At their house Kristi unlocked the door and Max and Felise charged up the stairs. Max's mum, Tamsyn, worked five days a week, and his dad, Ziyad, worked in an office on Mondays and from home the rest of the week, so that day Max spent the after-school hours at Lauren and Kristi's. Lauren felt for him because he always wanted to run in their yard and swing from the tyre that hung in the ancient mulberry tree, but Felise and her will of steel forced him to play school in the big attic playroom first. From the living area on the first floor Lauren could hear her bossing Max around. 'You sit there and be the teacher, and I'll sit here and write in my book, then I give it to you and you mark it and give me a big gold star and tell me what a good girl I am.'

Lauren pressed the button on the answering machine. '*Hi, I'm calling for Kristi Yates,*' a man said. '*We'd like you to come round and give us a quote for a feature wall in our courtyard. Can you call me back on–*'

'Delete it.'

'It's a job,' Lauren said, trying to hear the rest of the message.

'He didn't even say please.'

'He might have at the end. I'll rewind it and see.'

'He sounds like a wanker,' Kristi said. 'Just delete it.'

Lauren ignored her, rewinding the tape and copying down the man's contact information.

'Told you he wouldn't say it.'

Lauren played the next three messages, all left by people with similar requests, and wrote down their details. Across the room Kristi scratched with scissors at the grout that had dried around her nails.

'This is money,' Lauren said.

'We're getting by.'

'Only just.'

'We're happy,' Kristi said. 'That's what matters.'

The sound of running feet echoed down from the attic. Felise shouted, 'No! You have to sit *there*!'

'I have more than enough work to go on with anyway,' Kristi said.

Lauren rubbed her forehead. The headache was coming back. 'I'm going to have a shower.'

'Oh, I forgot to tell you.' Kristi put down the scissors. 'There's no hot water.'

'Why?'

She shrugged. 'I'm not a plumber.'

'Did you call one?'

'I only remembered just then.'

Lauren stood very still.

'You want me to call one now?' Kristi said.

'Might be an idea,' Lauren said. 'Don't you think?'

★

The water heater was dead and needed replacing but the plumber couldn't do it that day, so in the evening Lauren and Kristi and Felise trooped gratefully into the Saleebas' house. Back at home later, Felise declared her intention of having a bath with Max every day for the rest of her life.

Lauren's headache persisted despite aspirin, and when turning the lights out before bed she paused in the kitchen and took down the bottle of bourbon they kept for emergencies.

'You going to tell me now?' Kristi stood in pyjamas in the doorway.

Kristi was a good listener and always made you feel better – made you feel so good, in fact, that once you started talking you didn't want to stop. Lauren doubted her ability to control herself tonight. All evening her memories of the incident with the ice addict had blended in her head with those of Thomas in the alley. She'd tried to highlight the differences in her mind: that had been night and this was day; there she'd been alone and here she'd had Joe. But it was at a deeper level that it was hurting her; the level where the feel of fear and adrenaline dumps were stored. Physical memory. Even standing there now, she could almost feel where Thomas's fist had been, up under her chin. She touched the skin there and shivered. 'Actually I think I'll just go to bed.' She pushed the dusty bottle to the back of the top shelf with her fingertips.

'Spleen,' Kristi said.

Lauren turned off the kitchen light and walked past her. 'Goodnight.'

She woke at four from a nightmare. She'd been at the car crash again, finding Kristi drunk, pregnant and sobbing behind the wheel of one car, the dying boy at the wheel of the other. With it came the stale taste of her old life: the silence of her cramped flat broken only by the dull clink of the bottle against the glass, the desolation of Jeffrey leaving her for his panto career in the UK, the inability to get out and meet new people like magazines and work colleagues and her GP said she should.

She got out of bed and went into Felise's room. The child was an active sleeper, and while Lauren stood there she rolled from her left side to her right, onto her stomach, then thrashed the covers off before curling up into a shivering ball. Lauren lifted the covers over her and tucked them down behind her back, then with one finger smoothed a lank ringlet behind her ear.

She turned to go and found Kristi in the doorway. She put out a hand and felt the sweat-soaked back of Lauren's pyjama shirt.

'Don't say it.' Lauren kissed her on the cheek as she passed. Kristi sighed.

Back in bed Lauren couldn't sleep. When she finally pulled the covers close behind her as she'd done for Felise, the contact reminded her of Joe's back against hers. With that in her mind, she settled.

'Not working today?' Aunt Adelina said.

'Afternoon shift.' Ella was perched on the seat of her mother's wheely-walker, the only place left by the time she'd arrived. The ward was stuffy, the air full of chatter in English, Vietnamese, Lebanese and Italian. Her mother, Netta, was sitting up in the bed, Ella on one side, her father, Franco, and Adelina in plastic chairs on the other. A child in a nappy and singlet made his way around the room from bed to bed, holding onto chairs as he went. A woman in a headscarf saw Ella watching him and they exchanged smiles.

Voices grew louder across the room. Her father tilted his head. 'You hear that, Netta?'

'Dad, don't eavesdrop.'

'How can you not, when they talk so loud?' Her mother shifted position gingerly in the bed. Her steel-grey hair lay tangled on the pillow. Her nightie was buttoned to the neck.

'The Italian just goes straight in.' Her father jabbed his index fingers at his ears. 'I can't help that.'

'You turn your head off,' Adelina said. 'That's what I do.'

'Easy for you.' Franco grinned. Adelina slapped him on the arm.

Ella wondered sometimes what it would be like to have a brother, who'd stir you up like that, who would still be joking with you at age seventy. Adelina had never married, and Ella's father was staying at her house in Sutherland while Netta was in hospital. Franco had wanted to stay home, but he'd grown frail in the last year, was on a wheely-walker of his own now, and couldn't cook more than Cup-a-Soup.

Adelina was looking at the bedside table. Next second she hopped to her feet, pulled a handkerchief out of her handbag and started wiping the surface. 'Don't they dust?'

'This is what I'm saying,' Netta said. 'It's no good for me here.'

Ella nodded at the intravenous line feeding her antibiotics. 'You can't get that anywhere else.'

'She wouldn't have got the infection if she was somewhere else.' Her aunt reached across to dust the nameboard fixed to the wall above the bed.

The Italian family were getting louder. Franco and Netta exchanged glances again. Ella sighed. The argument was about nothing more exciting than somebody's school report. Talks too much and could do better. *Show me a kid whose report doesn't say that.*

She turned her mobile on. No messages. She turned it off again. What was wrong with the people of this city that they were continually failing to murder one another? And what about the shooting report committee – did they want her to die of suspense?

'The doctor said I can start to walk tomorrow without that thing,' Netta said, nodding at the walker. 'I might be home by the end of the week.'

'I thought you had to go to rehab once you're out of this ward,' Adelina said.

'I can rehab at home.'

'Says who?' Ella said.

'It's just taking it easy,' Netta said. 'Some little exercises, and be careful. Nothing to it.'

'What if you get stuck in the bath?' Adelina said. 'Franco's too weak to help you.'

'Hey,' Franco said.

'I can go to Ella's.'

'No, you can't,' Ella said. 'I'm not home enough.'

'I can't eat the food here.'

Adelina laughed. 'You think you'll get better there?'

'I can teach her,' Netta said. 'It'll be fun.'

'It's not that I can't cook, it's just that I don't like to,' Ella said.

'Maybe you could take some holiday time,' Adelina said.

Take leave now, when she'd just got her foot in the door? When a big case could come along at any second? No way in the world. Ella felt in her bag for her phone and switched it on again. 'I thought the doctor said at least a week in rehab.'

'Maybe after that then,' Adelina said.

They were all looking at her. Ella knew it would be a package deal – her dad would come too, as they hated being apart, and Adelina didn't like to make the drive up from Sutherland more than a couple of times a week.

'My house isn't really suited–' she began.

'You can come home, stay with us,' Netta said.

'Just like old times,' Franco said.

I have a home. The room was getting smaller and more stuffy. *Ring, phone, ring!*

Her mother grasped her arm. Her palm was cool. Ella looked down at the IV taped in the back of her hand, the sun-spotted skin, the tendons visible across her knuckles. An old lady's hand. When had this happened?

'It's okay if you don't want to,' Netta said.

Ella remembered coming home from school to

find her mother in the kitchen, fitting a knife deftly into the joints of a chicken, those hands smelling of onion, and how she'd duck away from their touch.

'Maybe you could just ask if you can take time?' Franco said. 'See what they say?'

'Can't hurt,' Adelina put in.

Ella heard the meal trolley coming and got to her feet. 'Lunch is here. Time for us to go.'

Her mother made a face.

'They shouldn't end visiting hours until after lunch,' Adelina said. 'Why can't we stay while you eat?'

'They don't want you to see how bad the food is,' Netta said darkly. She still had hold of Ella's arm. 'Will you at least ask about getting time off?'

This was another reason she wished she had a brother. Or sister. Anyone would do. Share the focus. The limelight. 'I'll ask.'

Netta pulled her down for an embrace. 'Thank you.' Up close she smelled of hospital soap and talc. Her hair was knotty and needed brushing, and her lips were soft on Ella's cheek. 'Come tomorrow?'

'Or I'll ring,' Ella said. 'It depends on work.'

Franco was waiting behind her to hug his wife. Ella stood near the Italian family, listening to their goodbyes, then walked from the ward with her father and aunt.

They said goodbye at the lift. With Franco's disabled tag Adelina could park in the hospital grounds. 'Have a safe drive,' Ella said.

Franco let go of his walker long enough to hug her tight. 'Ciao, carina. Stai bene.'

'Si, papa, e tu. Ciao.'

Outside, the day was warming up. She walked through the streets to her car, feeling guilty about not wanting to stay with her parents. It wasn't that she didn't love them, it was just the timing. Here was her shot at Homicide – maybe her one and only shot – and she needed to be free to spend twenty-four hours a day there if necessary.

Assuming, of course, that something better than checking phone lists came along.

FOUR

Lauren lay on her stomach, head to head with the dead man in the twilight, peering into his wide-open mouth. They were in a shallow culvert by one of the railway lines just out of Central station. She'd worked her elbows into gaps between the rocks but the rest of her felt every sharp corner.

The man looked to be in his fifties, though it was hard to tell for sure with the severe lacerations to his cheeks and forehead. There were more cuts on his scalp. His nose was smashed and caked with blood, and the inside of his mouth and throat were the pale no-longer-pink you saw in the freshly dead. Lauren lifted the tongue with the laryngoscope blade, searching with the light for the white flash of the vocal cords and the dark space between them.

Joe squatted beside her over the drug box, lifting his collar off the dressing on his neck. The younger half of a crew from Paddington did cardiac compressions, grimacing as he adjusted his knees on the rocks, while the older squinted in the late evening light for a vein on the man's arms. The air smelled of hot dust and oil and the metal workings of the train which sat ticking on the tracks nearby. Two uniformed police talked anxiously beside it, the dusty knees of their trousers proof of their initial frantic CPR efforts.

Lauren saw the cords. She took the ET tube from Joe and slid it down the pharynx and into the dark space, inflated the cuff to hold the tube in place, connected the resus bag and started squeezing to blow air into the man's lungs. Joe stuck the earpieces of his stethoscope into place and held the diaphragm on the man's left and right chest then over his stomach, making sure the air was going into the lungs and not the gut. He nodded. Lauren handed him the bag and slid the white fabric tape under the man's neck then looped and tied it around the tube.

Joe squeezed the resus bag hard and fast. The Paddo para said, 'I'm in,' over the man's arm, and Lauren started setting up vials of adrenaline for him to inject through the cannula into the vein.

A senior cop came stumbling and swearing along the rocks beside the line. He peered at the dead man then up at the younger officers. 'What's the story?'

'We pulled him over for running a light in Redfern,' the first officer said. 'He seemed really nervous when we talked to him, and then when we were checking his licence he bolted. We chased him to Redfern station and he jumped onto the train. We followed and almost had him, but then he went out the door between two carriages and tried to climb up on top. Then he fell.'

'What'd Radio give you?'

'His name's Adrian Nolan, no warrants, no record. He was driving a rental car.'

The man hadn't gone under the train's wheels, but Lauren thought he'd landed on his face and scrambled his brain. Not much anyone could do in those circumstances, but because the police had made an attempt to resuscitate him, and especially because there'd be an investigation into their actions, it was best to carry on with the effort and let the doctors do the white-sheet thing.

The older cop touched her shoulder. 'How's he look?'

'We'll keep working on him and run him up to St Vinnie's, but they'll probably pronounce him the moment we arrive,' Lauren said.

The cop nodded. The young one looked like he was going to cry.

St Vincent's Hospital's ambulance bay was busy. The young Paddo paramedic edged the ambulance along the side and Lauren, looking out the side window as she did compressions, winced at the scrape of the fibreglass body on the wall.

The back door was reefed open and a couple of paramedics from other vehicles pulled the stretcher out. Lauren clambered out then Joe jumped down, catching his foot on the stretcher wheel and stumbling into Lauren. She caught him around the waist then helped him up. 'You okay?'

'I hit the tube with my arm.' He started to pull his stethoscope from around his neck as the doors to the Emergency Department slid open and a doctor looked out.

'This the arrest?' he said.

'Just be a second,' Lauren said.

The doctor huffed and looked at his watch.

Lauren rolled her eyes at Joe. 'Let's just get in there.'

'I bumped it pretty hard.'

'Guy's dead,' she said. 'The tube being a little out of place isn't going to make any difference.'

They wheeled the stretcher towards the doors, which slid back to let them in. Lauren looked up at the security camera overhead and smiled her thanks, knowing that somebody at the nurses' desk had seen them coming and hit the door button.

They took the stretcher into the bright light of the ED's resuscitation room, the police officer who'd ridden in the front of the ambulance close on their heels. Lauren held the patient's head in her gloved hands, steadying the tube between her fingers as Joe and the ED staff untucked the sheet from the stretcher. She counted aloud to three and the team lifted the body on the sheet across to the hospital bed.

The doctor checked the patient's pupils and frowned. 'What's the story?'

Lauren ran through it quickly. 'He's been in asystole the whole time,' she finished up. 'No response to CPR, adrenaline, sodium bicarb and lignocaine.'

The doctor listened for heart sounds with his stethoscope. 'How long's it been now?'

Lauren looked at her watch. 'Forty minutes.'

'Okay, I'm calling it,' the doctor said. The tall male

nurse who was doing cardiac compressions lifted his hands from the man's bare chest and stepped back from the bed. The female nurse who'd been squeezing the resus bag disconnected it from the ET tube. 'Time of death is twenty-ten.'

The doors swung open and Joe's fiancée, Claire Bramley, walked in.

'No more staff needed here,' the doctor said, eyes on his paperwork.

Claire glanced around without answering. Lauren smiled at her but she didn't seem to see. Lauren heard her hiss something at Joe, and saw Joe look up, surprised, from packing away the monitor leads.

What was her problem?

Lauren stripped the sheets from the stretcher then lifted the Oxy-Viva on top. She put her hand out to Joe for the monitor but he was deep in muttered conversation with Claire.

Lauren wheeled the stretcher out to the ambulance and left it. Joe's job as driver for the shift was to clean and restock the equipment. Hers as treating officer was to do the case sheet. She'd finish her own work first, then she'd start on his if Claire was still haranguing him inside. But he came out in a couple of minutes, looking distracted. Lauren didn't ask, just sat writing in the passenger seat, the stereo on, while in the back he was quiet, changing the cylinder in the Oxy-Viva and restocking the drug box.

Lauren had almost finished the case sheet and Joe was making up the stretcher with a clean sheet when the ED doors slid open.

Claire came to stand in the open passenger door. 'Who tubed him?'

'I did,' Lauren said.

'You checked it?'

She restrained the urge to say, *what am I, an idiot*? 'Of course.'

'Didn't notice it was in the right main bronchus?'

'That would've happened just as we got here,' Joe said behind Claire. 'I bumped him and didn't have time to check it.'

But Claire hadn't taken her eyes off Lauren. 'It was your tube,' she said.

'It was.' Lauren kept her voice even.

'You put it in, so it was yours to look after.'

'Oh, come on, Claire,' Joe said, 'it doesn't work like that. We're a team.'

Claire stared at Lauren a moment longer then turned and went back inside.

'She didn't mean that,' Joe said. 'She knows as well as anyone he was dead. The tube being in the bronchus might make a difference to someone who actually had a chance, but this guy was a goner. You said so yourself.'

Lauren tore the case sheet off the pad. 'I can't afford a complaint.'

'She's not going to complain.'

'Has she still got that friend in State Headquarters?'

'She's not going to complain,' Joe said. 'Trust me.'

'Coming on top of the bus accident the other

month, this could get me reviewed,' she said. 'They can send me for retraining. They can move me from The Rocks.'

'Stop spouting crap,' Joe said. 'I'll go and talk with her, okay?' He walked back through the sliding doors.

Lauren pressed the folder hard against her chin. The thought of being moved away from The Rocks, away from Joe, made her chest hurt. She slammed the folder down once, hard, on the dash, making her ears ring with the sound.

The resus room was empty except for the covered corpse. Lauren left the hospital copy of the case sheet on the top of his medical file and went back out.

Joe and Claire were nowhere to be seen in the corridors or at the nurses' desk, and she went back to the ambulance and got in. She put the stereo on, but it annoyed her now, so she sat and worried in silence instead.

Joe reappeared after ten minutes and climbed behind the wheel. He started the engine but didn't pull out of the bay.

Lauren breathed in his aftershave mixed with railway dust and sweat. 'She's going to complain, isn't she?'

'I don't know what she's going to do.' Joe sighed. 'I'll talk to her again tomorrow.'

Lauren knew she should call Control to say they were clear. 'Let's drive.'

But Joe didn't move. He held the steering wheel

in the small circles made by his thumbs and index fingers. 'It's my fault.'

'I stopped you checking the tube,' Lauren said.

'It's not really about that,' he said. 'Claire found me cutting out the picture from the newspaper this morning. The picture of us.'

Heat rose in Lauren's throat. The colour shot of the two of them standing with their arms wrapped around each other between the ambulances had been on the front page of that day's paper. Kristi had read the accompanying article and said, 'No wonder you were upset. Why didn't you tell me?' Lauren hadn't been able to explain. Felise had wanted to stick the picture on the fridge but Kristi told her to take it to the attic, much to Lauren's relief. It would've been strange to see that embrace every time she went to get the milk. It made her think of a couple in love – not that she was in love, of course. Survivor's glee was the term she'd come up with. Sitting tied up, back to back, no shirts on, while the crazy ranted and raved and waved the knife about – who, she wanted to know, *wouldn't* come to rely on Joe's wide warm back as the safest and most precious thing in the world? Who wouldn't feel a bond afterwards?

'Car Thirty-four,' Control called. 'Thirty-four, I need you for a stabbing.'

Joe drove out of the hospital grounds as Lauren grabbed the mike and tried to clear her mind. 'Thirty-four's complete at St Vincent's.'

'Thanks, Thirty-four. I have a man stabbed on New South Head Road in Edgecliff, outside the shopping centre. Bystander CPR in progress. Police are on their way.'

Joe hit the siren and beacons and put his foot down. Lauren hung the mike up and braced a hand against the dash while she was there. People said she flogged the truck around but Joe was much worse. He was just lucky he'd never pranged one or been snapped speeding like she had.

'What did Claire say?' she asked.

'She wanted to know why I wanted to keep it.' His eyes were glued to the road. 'Reckon this will be genuine or false?'

'False,' Lauren said. 'What'd you say to her?'

'CPR's in progress.'

'By a bystander. That's no guarantee he's in arrest,' she said. 'What did you tell Claire?'

He made a face. 'I tried to explain that it was just such a weird and intense time,' he said. 'It's a good picture, our faces are mostly turned away from the camera, we're kind of two anonymous paramedics.' He made the same face again, adding lamely, 'It makes me think of . . . just . . . people looking after each other.'

'Me too,' she said. 'Exactly.' The streetlights flashed by. The beacons twirled red and blue across the fronts of houses. She pulled on gloves. 'What'd she say to that?'

He swung around a corner. 'She didn't seem convinced. Even after I said that if it was her in the paper she'd be cutting the picture out too.'

'Thirty-four for an ETA?' Control said.

'Two to three,' Lauren said into the mike.

'Still going for false?' Joe said.

'Drunk asleep on the footpath. He'll be moaning every time they press on his chest. We'll have to transport him for fractured ribs.'

'I don't know.' A cat dashed across the roadway and Joe lifted his foot from the accelerator for an instant. 'There's something in my water telling me otherwise.'

'You and your water.'

He glanced over at her. 'Standard wager?'

'Gilly's *and* an Egg McMuffin.'

'You're on.'

He turned onto New South Head Road and flipped the siren off.

'There.' Lauren pointed to a group of people on the footpath as one ran out to the road and waved.

There was nowhere to park. Joe stopped in the left lane of traffic, leaving the beacons going and switching on the hazard lights for good measure. Lauren jumped out and reached into the back of the ambulance for the Oxy-Viva and first aid kit.

'Quick!' someone shouted.

'Told you it'd be genuine,' Joe said, grabbing the monitor and drug box.

'Yelling means nothing,' she said over her shoulder as she moved towards the group. They didn't step aside as she drew near and she had to say 'Excuse me, excuse me' and butt the back of someone's leg with the first aid kit to get in.

The man lay on his side, his arms stretched out in front of him. His shirt was soaked with blood, the yellow *Quiksmart Couriers* emblem on the pocket drawing up the liquid. In the glow from the nearby shop windows Lauren saw the deathly pale colour of his face and knew Joe was right.

She knelt and put her hand on the man's shoulder. 'How're you going, mate?' He opened his eyes and looked at her. She pulled his shirt free from his trousers to find an inch-wide stab wound in his left chest, in the area of his heart. One bloodstained hand reached for her and she took it, squeezed it. 'What's your name?'

'James Kennedy,' he gasped.

She needed both her hands so she moved his hand to her knee. She could feel his fear and desperation in the grasp of his fingers on her trousers. 'Do you know what happened? Can you take a deep breath?' She grabbed a thick dressing from the first aid kit, pressed it over his chest wound and taped it down.

'Can't breathe . . . much.' Blood bubbled on his lips.

'Are you hurt anywhere else?'

Joe reached around her, putting an oxygen mask on Kennedy's face, attaching the monitoring electrodes. 'Back-up or load and go?' he said in Lauren's ear.

Kennedy's skin was slick with sweat. He'd lost a lot of blood externally and who knew how much internally. Lauren calculated the time of a run on lights and siren back to St Vincent's against the time it'd take another crew to arrive. 'Let's load and go.'

Joe ran off for the stretcher. Lauren could feel the press of watching people behind her as she strapped a tourniquet around Kennedy's bicep and searched his arm for veins. There wasn't much light. She glanced at his face. He was breathing heavily, his eyes wide open and fixed on hers. She checked the oxygen flowmeter. It was as high as it could go. 'How're you feeling, James?'

He shook his head wordlessly.

Joe barrelled through the crowd with the stretcher and pulled the release handles to drop it to half-height. He slapped the carry sheet out on the footpath next to Kennedy and they gently rolled him onto it, then with help mustered from the onlookers they lifted the sheet onto the stretcher.

Once inside the ambulance Lauren jammed her stethoscope into her ears and listened to Kennedy's chest. Breath sounds were down on the left side. She felt her way over the goose-pimpled, pale flesh of his chest and back and found no telltale crackling indicating air under the skin. She checked the position of his larynx. Pneumothorax, probable haemothorax, but not tensioning. Not at this stage.

'Am I dying?' he gasped.

'Not if I can help it.'

She felt Kennedy's eyes follow her every move as she took a quick blood pressure, ran off a strip from the cardiac monitor, and checked his oxygen saturation. She propped his arm against her thigh and searched the cold flesh again for veins. His fingers trembled against her elbow.

'I know I am,' he said.

'You think I'm going to sit here and let that happen?'

In the bright light she found a small vein on the back of his right forearm and as Joe accelerated away from the scene she slid the cannula under Kennedy's skin. She connected up a bag of Hartmann's and started squeezing the pump chamber, getting the fluid in as fast as she could. She could hear Joe asking Control to tell St Vincent's they were on their way. She looked into Kennedy's eyes. 'Do you know what happened?'

'I was walking.' He coughed. 'A man bumped into me. I felt this.' He waved a hand towards his chest. 'A burning pain, not too bad. Then warm, from the blood. Somebody tried to give me mouth-to-mouth while I was lying there.'

'You were just walking and a man stabbed you for no reason?'

Kennedy closed his eyes. 'I need you to tell my wife something.'

'You'll be able to tell her yourself at the hospital.'

He shook his head and coughed. A fine spray of blood appeared on the inside of the oxygen mask. Lauren saw his heart rate increasing on the monitor screen. She squeezed the pump chamber with one hand and smoothed the other over the cold skin of his free arm, feeling for any hint of a vein. He grasped her hand in his. 'I need you to tell her,' he puffed. 'I need you to write it down.'

At the look in his eyes she nodded. An empty dressing packet lay on the stretcher and she rested it on her knee, pulling her pen from her pocket. 'Go.'

She was ready to write *I love you*, but instead he

said, 'When we have run our passion's heat, Love hither makes his best retreat.'

Lauren scribbled the words. 'When we have run our . . . ?'

'Passion's heat, Love hither makes his best retreat,' he finished. He was starting to gasp for air.

Lauren stared at his throat, checking the location of his trachea. A tension pneumothorax would push it to one side as the pressure in his chest built up. It looked central, but the way he was breathing didn't make her happy. She dropped the paper and pen and reached for her stethoscope.

It was hard to hear his breath sounds when he was grunting and moaning and Joe still had the siren fired up. Lauren pressed the earpieces deeper into her head and shut her eyes to concentrate. She thought the breath sounds were still present on the left side, but only just. She took a quick BP and found it down to seventy systolic. She caught Joe's eye in the rear-vision mirror and twirled a finger above her head.

Kennedy watched her through half-open eyes. 'What's that mean?'

'Just asking him to turn the aircon on,' Lauren lied. She felt the lurch as Joe accelerated harder.

Kennedy started to cry. 'I don't want to die.'

Lauren smoothed her hand across his forehead. Her bloody glove left a red smear on his cold skin. She could see out the windscreen that they were only minutes from St Vincent's and she hoped they'd reach it before he arrested. She exchanged the almost-empty fluid bag for a full one and went for the pump chamber again. Kennedy's eyes closed and he sighed.

Thinking it was his last breath, she shot a glance at the monitor at the same time as she grabbed for his neck to feel his carotid pulse.

The rhythm on the monitor continued, and his pulse still fluttered under her fingers. Kennedy opened his eyes. 'See. You think I'm a goner too.'

She took his hand and held it. 'We'll be at the hospital any minute. You just have to hang in there.'

He looked up at the ambulance roof. 'Write something else for me?'

'You love her, I know.'

He shook his head, a feeble movement. 'It's for the police. I know who stabbed me.'

Lauren grabbed the paper and pen in her free hand.

Kennedy's hand squeezed her fingers. 'His name is Thomas Werner.'

Lauren felt like she'd been stabbed too. She stared at Kennedy in horror.

'Write it,' he gasped.

'You're sure it was him?'

'Thomas Werner,' he said, his voice getting louder. 'Thomas Werner stabbed me!'

Lauren saw Joe look up at them in the mirror. 'Thomas Werner, I got it.'

'I saw his face. Right there, against me, in the street. I know him.' Tears ran from Kennedy's eyes. 'God help me, I know him.'

Lauren scribbled on the paper. It was bloodstained from her gloves. She was shaking and blinking back tears. *Thomas Werner, oh Jesus.*

'How do you know him?' she said.

Kennedy wept. 'I'm not a good man.'

She scrawled this down too. 'What do you mean?'

'The things I did,' he said. He closed his eyes. He yawned, a sign of his falling blood pressure. She squeezed the pump chamber desperately, and saw through the windscreen the brightly lit *Emergency* sign.

'Almost there, James.'

He didn't answer.

'James!' She grabbed his shoulder and shook him. He murmured once. On the monitor his heart rate was up to a hundred and ninety. She shook him again and shouted his name. She felt the ambulance jolt over the kerb into the bay outside Emergency. She palpated his external jugular, thinking about the time it'd take to have a go for a line there, whether the benefit of getting it outweighed the delay before going into Emergency. It didn't, and as soon as Joe pulled up she was disconnecting the monitor leads, ripping off the BP cuff and kicking open the back door.

Inside the resus room they lifted Kennedy onto the hospital bed and Lauren gave her handover to the doctor who scrawled notes and yelled instructions to his staff as she spoke.

'Last obs were pulse one-ninety, beep seventy,' Lauren concluded.

'Hurry with that tube!' The doctor turned back to her. 'Got an ID?'

'Here.' A nurse held up the wallet she'd pulled from Kennedy's pants' pocket. The doctor rushed off and the nurse said to Lauren, 'You want to copy down his details?'

Lauren looked about for Joe. She needed to know how much he'd heard. 'I'll be back for them in a moment.' She hurried from the resus room. Joe had looked in the mirror when Kennedy was shouting about Thomas, but that didn't mean he'd heard the exact words. The siren was loud in the cabin, and his mind would have been on the road, not on the back of the truck.

Joe wasn't in the corridors or the staffroom. Lauren picked up her pace. The crumpled dressing packet was in her pocket. Nobody else had seen it. If he hadn't heard what Kennedy said, what was she going to do?

She was practically running as she went through the doors to the ambulance bay. 'Joe?'

'Here.' He was standing with a police officer. 'That was some job.'

'You think he'll die?' the police officer asked.

'Possibly,' Lauren said.

'More like probably,' Joe put in.

'But you wrote down what he said?' the officer asked.

Lauren's heart shrivelled. 'What?'

'The stuff he was saying, about Thomas Werner stabbing him,' Joe said. 'You looked like you were writing it down.'

It felt like Thomas had his hands at her throat again. She tried to swallow, and reached into her pocket for the dressing packet.

The officer took it carefully and read what she'd written. 'This is great.'

Lauren felt faint.

FIVE

Ella glanced across at the speedo and was surprised to see they were actually doing sixty.

'The man's not going anywhere,' Murray said.

'Except maybe . . .' She pointed skywards.

'If he's that close to the edge they're not going to let us near him anyway.'

Bloody Murray, so full of reason. Ella sat forward in her seat and willed the cars in front of them to move out of their way. She didn't believe in God but she wasn't above praying now and then, just on the off-chance it might do some good. *Please keep this guy alive long enough to talk to us.*

They'd been talking in the office car park after their evening shift when Ella's phone rang. DS Kirk Kuiper had said there was a stabbing victim at St Vincent's, one likely to become a homicide if the reports were accurate, and would they mind popping on over? One of Eagers's super-duper new crime-fighting initiatives was to get Homicide detectives on the job as soon as possible, the theory being that the quicker their knowledge and experience were brought to bear on the case, the more likely a speedy result. As crime was one of the major platforms of the next year's election, Ella knew it was an exercise in political grandstanding more than anything – it sounded impressive for the Police Minister to say Homicide was on the case – but she didn't care. She'd leapt into Murray's car as it was closest. The previous case they'd worked, the Lachlan Phillips abduction, Murray had been the Commissioner's liaison so had only ever tagged along, not driven. *Next time we go somewhere important, I drive.*

'I bet he doesn't die.' Murray crawled around a corner. 'It'll just be an assault and the local Ds will take it over.'

Ella was so conflicted. It was wrong to hope that he would die, but he'd apparently identified his attacker to the paramedics. What juicier open-and-shut could there be?

When they finally arrived in St Vincent's Emergency Department they found a uniformed officer leaning over a computer chatting to a nurse. When he saw them he straightened up and held out a man's wallet. 'This is the victim.'

Ella opened it and pulled out a driver's licence. 'James William Kennedy. He's fifty-one.' The dark-haired man stared out at her with a half-smile.

'I asked Radio for his info,' the officer said. 'He's got a neg driving causing death from three years back – ran a red and killed a woman in her family car. Kid and husband were injured. Nothing else. Got a motorbike in his name, rego LM 326. That address on the licence is still current. And the paramedic gave me this.' He held out a crumpled piece of paper in an evidence bag. 'The blood's all dry.'

Ella took it from him. It was an empty dressing packet and on the back, between the printed brand name and size specifications and the smears of blood, were scribbled the words: *When we have run our passion's heat, Love hither makes his best retreat. I know who stabbed me. Thomas Werner. Thomas Werner stabbed me. I saw his face. Right there, against me, in the street. I know him. God help me, I know him. I'm not a good man. The things I did.*

Ella felt a shiver run up her spine.

'VKG gave me various Thomas Werners around the state but none with any record that leaps out.'

'Is that the paramedic?' Murray said.

Ella looked where he pointed, at a woman in the paramedic uniform of white shirt and navy trousers writing in a folder at the nurses' desk.

'That's her. Name's Lauren Yates.'

The paramedic turned in response to hearing her name, and got up and crossed towards them. The front of her shirt was spotted with blood and smeared with dirt and her short dark hair hung lank and sweaty over her forehead. She looked nervous. 'Hi.'

Ella smiled. 'Detective Ella Marconi, Detective Murray Shakespeare.'

'Lauren Yates.' They shook hands. Lauren's palm was sweaty.

'You're certain this is what he said?'

'Word for word.'

'Did he say how he knew this Werner?'

'When I asked, he said that about not being a good man,' Lauren said. 'I asked what that meant and that's when he said "the things I did".'

'He didn't explain any further?'

Lauren shook her head.

'How was he? Will he make it?'

The paramedic pulled a face. 'He'd have to be lucky.'

'Did he know how bad it was, do you think?'

Lauren nodded. 'He kept saying he was dying.'

'Did you agree with him?'

'I kind of jollied him along a bit, saying not while you're in my care, stuff like that,' Lauren said. 'I don't like to say, yeah, mate, you're cactus. But then once I thought he'd stopped breathing, and I grabbed him, and he opened his eyes and said, "See, you know I'm dying too".' She stopped.

Ella nodded. If Kennedy lived, at least long enough to talk, she'd ask how he and Werner knew each other, why he thought Werner attacked him. They needed this to build the case. But even if he died, she had in her hand a dying declaration, and before her stood a witness savvy enough to write down word for word what the dying man had said. Ella looked Lauren up and down. She held herself confidently. Something of the nervous look remained but Ella put it down to the circumstances.

She looked at the paper again. 'What's this other bit?'

'He asked me to say that to his wife.'

'It's poetry,' Murray said. 'It's from "The Garden", by Andrew Marvell.'

'Never heard of him,' Ella said.

'It's about a changing love, and especially about passion. "When we have run our passion's heat, Love hither makes his best retreat. The gods that mortal beauty chase, Still in a tree did end their race –"'

'Yes, okay,' Ella said. 'Thanks very much.'

'Excuse me.' The uniformed officer was behind them. 'Word just came down that Kennedy died.'

Lauren let out a little sound. Ella saw that she'd gone pale and was blinking back tears. 'You okay?'

Lauren looked at the floor.

Murray said, 'I guess it's tough sometimes, when they go.'

The paramedic's emotion made Ella feel bad over the excitement bubbling inside her, but only for a moment. This was her job, and the puzzle lay before her just waiting to be put together. She clutched the dying declaration tightly behind her back. She imagined tracking this Werner down, the solid brief of evidence she'd deliver to the DPP, the eventual conviction. The temporary secondment to Homicide would surely become a permanent posting.

Lauren would be fine in a moment. When you saw death all the time, you adjusted to another one PDQ.

She handed Lauren her card. 'We'll need to take a proper statement from you tomorrow. What time do you finish?'

'Eight in the morning,' Lauren said, taking a deep breath. 'If I don't get overtime.'

'You'll be right to make it to our office in Parramatta then?'

'I guess so.'

'Great.' Ella held up the dressing packet. 'Thanks so much for this.'

'Yes, thanks,' Murray put in. 'It's gold.'

Lauren went back to her paperwork. Ella watched her go, thinking that she as a witness together with the dying declaration weren't gold. They were way more valuable than that.

'Ella,' Murray was saying.

'Huh?'

'We've got a lot to do.'

She followed him to the door, then glanced back at Lauren at the desk. 'How good is she going to be on the stand?'

Murray said, 'Got to catch the guy first.'

Lauren finished the case sheet by writing that Kennedy had given her information about his assailant, which she'd passed on to police. She signed the form and left the hospital copy on the nurses' desk. It would work its way through the system to meet up somewhere with Kennedy's file, which she guessed was on its way with him to the hospital morgue.

Outside in the ambulance bay Joe was resting his folded arms on the truck's bonnet, talking with a couple of paras from Headquarters. Lauren knew the detectives had spoken briefly to him too. She stayed at the rear of the vehicle, leaning against the back door. She wished she'd had a moment in the resus room to hold Kennedy's hand one more time, to silently say goodbye and promise to give his wife his message. No doubt the police would do so when they went to tell her the bad news, but she thought she would too. If she was in Mrs Kennedy's shoes, she knew she'd want to speak to whoever talked to her husband last.

Oh, who was she kidding? She sank down onto the step. The real reason she had to see Mrs Kennedy was that Kennedy's death was her fault. If she hadn't been fooled by Thomas's playing dead and let him tackle her and get away so quickly, maybe the cops would've seen him. He'd be locked up somewhere nasty, and Kennedy would be alive, not cooling in a drawer in the hospital morgue. She owed Kennedy something now. Facing his widow was the least she could do.

And look where she herself stood. Tomorrow she had to give a formal statement, so before then she had to decide whether to confess that she knew a Thomas Werner right up front, or tell them later, or just keep her mouth shut and hope the police never found her out. She squeezed her eyes shut, trying to think it through. Thomas's name wasn't on Felise's birth certificate, Kristi having left that part of the form blank as part of her put-the-past-well-behind strategy. Lauren wondered about that terrible bed-sit they'd rented, whose name the lease had been in, whether the police could link Thomas and Kristi that way. She was certain Thomas had never been arrested while he'd been here, so he shouldn't appear in their records. What else could there be? She didn't know.

She felt bad about hiding what she knew from the police. The services worked together, helped each other, had done so forever, and keeping her mouth shut ate away at the foundations of those relationships. But what choice did she have?

Besides, there was surely more than one Thomas Werner in the world. Lauren tried to imagine an Australian one, washing blood out of his clothes in some suburban Sydney laundry right that moment. One who hadn't threatened her, who didn't know her and wouldn't know how to find where she lived.

She was such an idiot.

She fought tears, tilting her head back when they threatened to spill over, while above her the moths burned themselves on the floodlights.

When Ella and Murray pulled up in Edgecliff Road, crime scene officers were examining the location, taking photos of the bloodstained concrete, digging into rubbish bins and climbing into drains. Four witnesses stood on the footpath some distance away, kept silent and apart by a uniformed officer. Ella wasn't expecting a whole lot from them. Someone falls over in the street, the first thing you look at is them on the ground, not the person walking casually away.

'I'll take the men, you take the women?' Murray said, already heading for his chosen victims.

Ella took the two women to stand by the well-lit shop windows so she could see their faces. She didn't expect much, but you never could tell. While it meant something that these people had hung around to tell the uniformed officers what they'd seen, Ella often found witnesses' enthusiasm lessened as time went by and they considered the ramifications of what they were doing. A man who'd so cold-bloodedly stabbed another in the street was not one they wanted as an enemy, and sometimes they started 'forgetting'. But at the same time, ordinary people weren't good liars. You could tell it in their faces, and a little gentle pushing often brought out that last bit of detail.

She chose to start with the older woman, and asked the younger one, a sad-looking woman in her fifties with a brown beehive hairdo, to stay where she was while they walked a few steps further.

She smiled at the woman, guessing she was in her seventies, noting the glasses, the tweed suit, the grey hair in the tight bun. 'Thank you for waiting, ma'am. I'm Detective Ella Marconi.'

'I have fish here.' The woman raised a green enviro shopping bag. 'Out of the fridge too long, it's no good.'

'I'll make this as quick as I can.' Ella opened her notebook. 'What did you see here tonight?'

'I'd been at my friend's place, and stopped in at the shops for a piece of fish for tomorrow's dinner on my way home. Back on the street here I was walking along, slowly, you know, when I heard a strange noise.'

'A noise like . . . ?'

'Like when one person walks into another, and that one has the wind knocked out of him. An "oof" noise.'

'Right,' Ella said.

'I turned to see the man fall to his knees then onto his hands. Someone almost trod on him, he went down so fast,' the woman said. 'People kept going past him, can you believe it?'

'I can.'

'I asked him if he was okay, and he muttered something I didn't catch. Then somebody else said there was blood, and for someone to ring an ambulance.'

Ella said, 'So did you see who walked into him?'

The old lady shook her head. 'I only saw him fall. He was behind me. I turned when I heard the strange noise.'

'You didn't notice anybody hurrying away?'

'There were a lot of people around,' she said. 'Everyone's always in a hurry.'

Just as I thought. Ella clicked her pen away and got out her card. 'Thank you for your time. We may be in touch again, but in the meantime please call me if you think of anything else.'

The woman took it. 'How is the man?'

'I'm afraid he passed away.'

A frown creased the old lady's forehead. 'This city.'

When Ella approached the beehive witness, she found her blinking back tears and plucking at a fray on her handbag strap.

'It was awful.'

'Take your time,' Ella said.

The woman took a deep breath, and pointed along the street. 'I was coming along here, in a bit of a hurry because I wanted to get home. Then suddenly there was this bit of a bustle in front of me.' She squinted at the footpath as if remembering. 'There were two men together, just for a second, as if they'd collided with one another, then one moved on and a split second later the other fell to the ground.'

'What did you do then?'

'As I got closer I could see the man on the ground was grabbing at himself, at his chest. I thought maybe he was having a heart attack, from being knocked over, you know. But then I saw the blood, and I got out my phone and called an ambulance.' She pointed to one of Murray's witnesses. 'That man there started CPR.' She lifted her chin. 'I made him stop.'

Ella wrote quickly. 'What did the other man look like?'

'He was white, in his thirties or so I'd guess.'

'Hair colour? Clothing?'

The woman hesitated. 'Dark hair, I think. Brown more than black. Clothes, I couldn't really say. Long sleeves, I think. Maybe jeans.'

Ella asked the woman to wait for a moment, and went to speak to Murray. 'I've got a description.' She read out what the woman had said.

Murray looked at his own notebook. 'Matches with what I've got. White male, blue jumper, short dark hair.'

Ella went back to the beehive woman. She took down her details, explained that they'd be in touch to get a formal statement later, thanked her, and let her go just as Detective Sergeant Kirk Kuiper strode along the footpath.

Ella and Murray met him near the taped-off area around the bloodstain. He frowned at it as Ella summarised what they had so far, his face haggard in the lighting from the shop windows. She gave him the dressing packet, and its protective plastic bag crackled in his hands as he studied it.

'Okay.' He gave her the packet back. 'Go do the notification, see what the family has to say. Try to get the formal statements tonight. We'll get started on the canvass here. Give me a call later, let me know where you're up to.'

'Will do.'

Ella and Murray got into the car. 'Damn,' Murray said.

Ella looked up to see one of his male witnesses standing in front of the car, waving at them. 'Reckon he's remembered something?'

Murray shook his head. 'He's nuts. I'll get rid of him.'

Alone in the car, Ella smoothed out the plastic and the dressing packet.

Thomas Werner.

I'm not a good man.

She wondered what the wife's response would be. Well, no, not that, she knew what her response would be. But what light would her response shed on Werner's reason for stabbing Kennedy? Would she be able to tell them how Kennedy and Werner knew each other? Would she explain why Kennedy had said he wasn't a good man? Perhaps the killing was related to the car crash he'd caused, the victim's family taking revenge. Mrs Kennedy should be able to tell them if she and her husband had been threatened lately.

A truck rushed past, the slipstream buffeting the car. Ella watched the tail-lights blur down New South Head Road, and shivered with anticipation.

SIX

The Kennedys lived in a top-floor apartment in an ageing block in Bondi. Ella looked around at the dark and quiet street, at the clogged traffic on Campbell Parade at the end, while they waited for Mrs Kennedy to answer the buzzer.

'Bet they've got some view,' Murray said. 'Some money too.'

Ella could smell the ocean. 'More likely they bought years ago when it was cheap.'

'Sitting on a goldmine then.'

The speaker clicked. 'Hello?'

'Mrs Deborah Kennedy? I'm Detective Ella Marconi, with Detective Murray Shakespeare. May we have a moment, please?'

There was silence.

'You're not in uniform.'

'Detectives don't wear them.' Ella showed her badge to the new-looking security camera overhead.

'What station are you from?'

Ella didn't want to say Homicide. 'We're based in

Parramatta. Would you like a phone number to call to check us out?'

'Wait a moment, please.' The speaker clicked off.

Murray said in a low voice, 'I had a man once look up the phone book to ring the station, he was so sure we were impostors who would've given him a fake number.'

'I guess if she's doing that she'll soon find out we're Homicide,' Ella said. 'Makes you wonder what she's afraid of though.'

After a few moments the door buzzed. Ella pushed it open and they entered the foyer.

The lift was slow and tired. As it stuttered to a stop Murray said, 'You do it.'

She eyed him. 'You owe me.'

The doors slid open. A woman stood on the landing, her face anxious. She was in her late forties with short ash blonde hair, the build of a runner, and skin that saw too much sun. She wore a navy track-suit. Her hands were deep in the pockets of the top, arms pressed close to her sides as if for protection. Ella understood. There were no *good* reasons why police came to your door late at night.

She held out her badge wallet. 'I'm Detective Ella Marconi and this is Detective Murray Shakespeare. May we come in?'

Deborah Kennedy peered at Ella's ID card then up at her face. She did the same to Murray, then held open the door to the apartment.

Ella felt the woman's eyes on her as she walked by. The living room's deep beige carpet, oversized plush lounge chairs and velvet curtains drawn against the night made the place feel soundproofed and silent. Ella was aware of the dressing packet in its bag in her pocket, heard it crackle as she walked. On the sideboard a silver filigree butterfly sat amongst family photos. Ella mentally matched the pictures of the man, his rounded features, his dark grey hair and friendly brown eyes, with his licence photo. Smiling alongside him in the frames were Mrs Kennedy and a blonde teenaged girl.

Ella turned to face Mrs Kennedy, who closed the door gently and came into the centre of the room. She gestured vaguely for them to sit but Ella always stood when delivering bad news. Anything else felt too casual.

'Mrs Kennedy, I'm very sorry to have to tell you that your husband James was assaulted tonight.' She let that sink in for a moment.

Deborah Kennedy stared. Ella took one step towards her. 'He was rushed to hospital but unfortunately could not be saved.'

Mrs Kennedy put her hands over her face.

'I'm very sorry,' Ella said again.

The woman started to sob. Her arms shook. Ella placed a gentle hand on her shoulder. Across the room on a coffee table was a box of tissues and she motioned with her eyes for Murray to get it.

When Deborah Kennedy looked up he proffered the box but she paid no attention, instead grasping Ella's hand. Her nails dug in. Ella held back a wince.

'How did it happen?' Tears flooded down her face. She looked suddenly about seventy. 'Who did it?'

'Could we all sit down?'

They sat side by side on a lounge. Murray took a single chair at an angle. Ella's fingers were hot in the double-handed grip Deborah Kennedy now had on her; the grip that clenched tight every few seconds as if in time to waves of pain, but she wasn't going to pull away. She curled her fingers around the woman's trembling ones and looked into her eyes.

'The incident happened on New South Head Road in Edgecliff,' Ella said. 'Do you know why your husband would have been there?'

'Near the shops?'

Ella nodded.

'There's a bakery there which does a special rye bread that he likes. They always keep a loaf for him. He picks it up on his way home from work.'

'Where does he work, Mrs Kennedy?'

'He's a courier for Quiksmart. He drops the van at the depot in Leichhardt at six and rides his motorbike home.' She closed her eyes. 'Tonight it was getting so late, though, and he didn't answer his phone. I knew something must have happened.'

'He was definitely on his bike?'

'Yes, it's quicker than the car.'

'And he always finished at six?'

'They don't like giving overtime. He's usually home by seven.' She shook her head, eyes still closed. 'How did it happen?'

'He was attacked with a knife,' Ella said softly. Stabbed sounded so violent. 'He was very brave. He was able to talk to the paramedics and tell them what happened.'

Deborah Kennedy looked at her. 'He was talking?'

Ella nodded. 'He also gave them a message for you. The paramedic wrote it down.'

'He . . . Do you have it? Can I see it?'

'Could you first tell me, please, if you know of anybody who might want to hurt your husband?'

'I can't think of anyone. We live a very quiet life.' She gulped. 'Lived.'

'There had been no recent problems with the family of the woman who died in the car accident three years ago?'

'The Harveys,' she said. 'No, nothing. We didn't even know what Alan Harvey was saying back then until the people from the TV show came around and told us. They wanted to know what we felt, but we just closed the door.' She grimaced. 'We felt awful, of course we felt awful over it. But those shows.' She let go of Ella's fingers and held out her trembling hand. 'Please. I want to see what he said.'

Ella hesitated. 'There's blood on the piece of paper.'

'Please.'

Ella took the bagged dressing packet from her pocket. Mrs Kennedy received it like a devout worshipper receiving a communion wafer. Ella met Murray's gaze over her bent head, grateful to Lauren. What she'd done was not only going to seal their case against Werner but meant a lot to this woman.

She let a few moments go by, then said, 'Do the lines of poetry have some special meaning for the two of you?'

Deborah Kennedy stared at her, but she had the feeling the woman wasn't seeing her at all, instead looking through her to whatever meaning the poem had.

'James used to read poetry to me when we were courting,' she said suddenly.

Ella pointed to the declaration. 'Do you have any idea what he meant here, when he said he wasn't a good man?'

Deborah Kennedy focused on the packet again. She frowned and shook her head. 'That makes no sense. He *was* a good man.'

'Just a couple more things,' Ella said. 'Had you ever heard James mention that name, Thomas Werner?'

'No.'

'You're sure?'

'I'd remember,' she said. 'Our nephew's named Thomas. I always notice it when I hear it.' She looked at the packet again. 'I have no idea who he's talking about here.'

'You and James have a daughter, is that right?'

'Tess. She's at uni, Sydney Uni.'

'Does she live here with you?'

'No. She shares a little flat with a friend in Newtown.' Her face crumpled. 'How am I going to tell her?'

Ella touched her arm gently. 'When was the last time you saw and spoke to your husband?'

'When he left for work this morning, just after eight.' She pressed the heels of her hands to her eyes.

Ella took back the bagged dressing packet, then grasped her hand again. It was wet with tears. 'Mrs

Kennedy, we need someone to identify James's body to us. It doesn't necessarily have to be you, if you don't feel up to it. We can contact one of his friends, or another relative.'

But Deborah Kennedy was shaking her head. 'I'll do it. I want to see him.' She drew in a deep quivering breath. 'Where is he?'

'At St Vincent's Hospital.'

'So what . . . how does . . .'

'He will be moved to Glebe Morgue in the morning, for a post-mortem examination to be done. Once you choose a funeral director, they'll get in touch with the morgue staff and arrange everything from there.'

Deborah Kennedy looked down at her hands. Ella imagined her wondering how it could be that this morning she was a happily married woman and now she had to decide on a funeral company for her husband.

'Would you like to call anybody before we go?'

She'd ended up on the phone more than once, breaking the news, when the caller had started crying too much to talk. She'd been asked to go around and tell them in person too. She was prepared for anything.

'I need to tell Tess.' Mrs Kennedy's eyes welled again. 'She'll want to see him too.'

'We can pick her up on the way.'

Tess Kennedy lived in a flat in a small block in a dark and narrow street in Newtown. Ella and Murray waited in the car for Deborah to bring her daughter down. Murray opened the door a crack to see the time on the dashboard clock.

'They're grieving,' Ella said.

'We're missing the action.' Murray pulled the door to. 'Why don't you go up and prompt them along?'

'She didn't want me to go up before, so I'm hardly going to be more welcome now.'

A man walked along the footpath, looking in at them as he passed. Ella stared back at him, then tilted the side mirror to watch his progress along the street.

Murray shifted impatiently in his seat. 'They'll probably have it solved by the time we get back.'

'Calm down,' Ella said.

'You want it just as bad.'

Worse, probably.

'Here they come.' Ella got out and opened the back door for the weeping women. Tess was gangly, coltish, looking more like a thirteen year old than a university student. She wore jeans and a brown Bali T-shirt, her blonde hair tied back in a messy ponytail, sandals on her feet. Her eyes were red. She helped her mother into the car.

'I'm sorry about your father,' Ella said. The girl thanked her in a low voice and got in.

They drove in silence to St Vincent's where Murray parked in the 'police only' bay. They asked for directions from an ED nurse, who called a wardsman to take them down to the morgue.

He asked them to wait a moment in the corridor while he went in.

The Kennedys stood close to each other, fingers intertwined. Tess gripped her mother's forearm with her other hand.

'When we go in,' Ella said, 'we need you, Mrs Kennedy, if you still feel up to it, to confirm that the body is that of your husband, James.' She looked at Tess and the way her knuckles blanched on her mother's arm. 'Would you like to come in as well, or stay here?'

'I'm coming in,' she whispered.

The door opened and the wardsman cleared his throat. They walked in single file, Murray pulling the door shut behind them. In the centre of the small white room stood a stainless steel trolley, and on top lay a man. A sheet covered his body to his upper chest. His arms were outside the sheet and intravenous lines were taped to his forearms. His face was pale with a purplish tinge and his dark grey hair was smoothed back. His eyes were closed and a plastic tube was tied into his mouth with bloodstained cotton tape.

Deborah started to sob and she laid one shaking hand on his shoulder. Tess wrapped her arms around her mother and looked at Ella, tears pouring down her face. 'It is my father.'

'You want to pay your debt now?'

Lauren looked up from the street directory open on the case sheet folder on her lap. 'Huh?'

'The coffee you owe me for saying the stabbing wasn't going to be serious,' Joe said. 'Fancy it now?'

'Can we do it later?'

He shrugged and started the engine.

'And listen,' Lauren said. 'Before we clear, can we take a little drive?'

'Going to see your boyfriend?'

She pointed out the windscreen. 'Straight ahead.'

'Yes, ma'am.'

He drove, and she kept one finger in the relevant page in the directory and one eye on the road while scribbling out the case sheet for the job they'd just done. *Ninety-year-old female, lost balance and fell in the bedroom, no loss of consciousness. Suffered skin tears to right arm. Wound cleaned and dressed. All obs within normal range.*

'Left here,' she said.

Joe swung around the corner. 'So what's he look like?'

Pt refusing transport – will see GP in the a.m.

'I bet he's tall.'

Lauren signed the case sheet and closed the folder. 'Right at the lights.'

'He's tall, isn't he?'

Joe was great to work with, there was nobody better, but by god she wished he'd shut up now. She stared out the windscreen, her hands flat on the open directory. Her stomach was pure knots. 'Right again.'

This was the street. She watched the numbers and saw Kennedy's building. 'Stop for a sec.'

Joe pulled over.

Lauren leaned close to the window and looked up. All the flats were dark. She wondered which one was Kennedy's, and whether his widow was up there pacing the rooms or sobbing on the floor or . . . what?

Taking sips alternately from a glass of scotch and a bottle of tranquillisers?

She couldn't imagine now ever being able to face her.

Joe touched her back and she started forward, hitting her chin on the glass.

'Jesus, sorry.'

''S okay.' She sat back, rubbing her chin.

He turned on the cabin light. 'Let me see.'

She wouldn't look at him.

'Loz.'

'I'm okay.'

'This is that stabbed guy's place.' He put his hand on her shoulder. 'You know we did all the right things.'

The right thing would be to call that detective and tell her everything. Confess how she knew Thomas, how he'd attacked and threatened her in the alley, how he as much as told her he'd killed Stewart Blake. That if she'd had half a brain and kept away from him back then, or had been able to delay him longer, or even told the cops and had them start a search the instant they arrived, Kennedy would still be alive.

Maybe she should tell Joe first. A kind of practice run. Get used to the way the words came out, how it felt to admit to lying and perjury and whatever else it was. She looked over at him. He smiled at her. She opened her mouth, but nothing came out.

He undid his seatbelt, leaned over and wrapped his arms around her. 'It's tough when they hold your hand.'

Her face was hot with shame at what she'd done, and she pressed it into his shoulder, breathing in the smell of his aftershave and sweat. 'I did something bad.'

He went to move back but she tightened her grip. If he wasn't looking at her, she might be able to say it.

'Bad like what?' She could hear the smile in his voice. 'You lied about the bet? You're not going to buy me coffee after all?' He tried to pull away again. Again she held him close. They stayed like that, silent, for a moment. 'Lauren.'

She pressed her face harder against him. She couldn't do it. The words wouldn't come out. And now she thought, what good would it do anyway? They already knew Thomas killed Kennedy. If they caught him for that he'd go away for a long time, and really, what difference would it make to know that he'd killed Blake too? Besides, how could they prove it now, so long after the fact? Her testimony couldn't be worth much after she'd lied so often and for so long. Then the case for Kennedy would be in jeopardy too: the defence would have a field day with anything she said, especially about Thomas. It would come down to her word against his, and meanwhile she'd probably get the sack, and who would then hire a perjurer? She and Kristi wouldn't be able to keep up the rent and they'd lose the house, Felise wouldn't get to go to big school next year with Max . . . their life as they knew it would be gone. Lauren swallowed back bile. It was wrong, she knew it was completely wrong, but she was going to keep this to herself.

'That's right,' she croaked. 'I'm not going to buy your damn coffee.'

Deborah Kennedy said she was up to doing the statement tonight, if that was what they wanted. They took her to Paddington Station and used a quiet room there to type it out. Down the corridor a meeting room was being prepared for the initial case briefing. From tomorrow it would be worked out of the Homicide office at Parramatta, but for now it was better to be close to the scene.

Tess sat close to her mother, holding her hand, saying nothing. Ella offered them coffee, tea, water, biscuits, more than once, but they shook their heads.

When it was over Ella and Murray drove them back to the flat in Bondi, and walked them to the door. 'Would you like us to come up?' Ella said. 'Stay with you for a while?'

'We're okay,' Tess said. 'Thanks anyway.'

Ella gave them her card. 'Ring any time, for anything. Somebody will be around tomorrow to talk with you further.'

Deborah Kennedy's hand trembled as she tried to fit the key into the lock. She was crying silently.

'We'll catch him, Mrs Kennedy,' Ella couldn't help but say.

The Kennedys let themselves in and closed the door.

'What'd you say that for?' Murray said once they were back in the car. 'What if we don't?'

*

The briefing was well underway when they got back to Paddington. They squeezed into the rear of the room while Detective Sergeant Kirk Kuiper scribbled information on a whiteboard at the front.

'A woman putting rubbish in her bin in Ocean Avenue saw a man walking, in her words, "extremely quickly" down the footpath.' Detective Marion Pilsiger was in her twenties, with gelled bleached blonde hair and round blue eyes. 'She said when he saw her he slowed, but she's sure once he was out of view she heard him speed up again. She's described him as young, medium build, dark hair and clothing. She said it was too dark to see anything else.'

'The timing fits too,' Detective Jason Lambert said. He was all elbows in his short-sleeved cotton shirt, his thin pale hair scraped sideways on his scalp. 'The calls for an ambulance started at eight-forty-five. She saw the man at about ten-to-nine. I walked in the way she described from the scene to her house and it took roughly five minutes.'

'Good,' said Kuiper, writing up the numbers.

'I have an elderly man in Albert Street who saw somebody get into a car parked in front of his house soon after that,' said Detective Graeme Strong. His voice was deep, roughened by the cigars he smoked. 'He was looking out his window for his daughter who comes by after she finishes a TAFE class at eight-thirty.'

'He get the numberplate?'

'Too frail to go outside,' Strong said. 'He said it was a dark sedan, maybe blue or green, possibly Holden or Ford. He didn't know how long it'd been parked there, but after about ten minutes more a man hurried along the footpath, got in and drove off. Pretty smartly, the old guy said. He couldn't give us any better description than a man of average height, average build, possibly with dark hair. None of the neighbours saw the man or noticed the car. We called the daughter up but she hadn't seen it or anything else unusual when she got there about five minutes later.'

'No weapon found anywhere? Blood away from the scene?'

People shook their heads.

'We'll extend that search tonight and tomorrow,' Kuiper said. 'Marconi, Shakespeare?'

'James Kennedy worked as a courier for Quiksmart Couriers in Leichhardt,' Ella said. 'According to his wife, he usually finished work at six then went to a bakery in the shops on New South Head Road. They apparently kept a certain loaf aside for him every day.'

'There was no loaf found on the scene?' Kuiper looked around. 'Check with the bakery people in the morning then, see if he'd made it there yet. If so, was he alone.'

'Kennedy was on his motorbike, and would usually be home by seven, even with that detour,' Ella went on. 'Mrs Kennedy said she tried to call him but he didn't answer. She suspected then that something was wrong.'

Kuiper nodded. 'There's a mobile in the list of his effects and clothing. We're getting onto his service provider to check all recent calls.'

'We'll need to confirm with Quiksmart that he did indeed leave at six,' Murray said. 'But assuming for now that he did, that leaves a sizeable period of time unaccounted for.'

'We'll need to locate that motorbike too.'

'Maybe the killer stole it,' Strong said. 'Did Kennedy still have the keys?'

'Keys are there with his belongings.' Kuiper's pen ran out and he grabbed up another one. 'Anything with the neg driving?'

Ella said, 'Mrs Kennedy says there's been nothing.'

'Check the husband out later anyway,' Kuiper said. 'Okay, tasks for tonight. Continue that canvass of the scene and all the streets around there. We want that weapon. Keep an eye out for CCTV on private properties – we might just get a glimpse of our man that way. We need to find that motorbike, and then track Kennedy's progress from there to the shops.

'Questions? Okay then, people, clock's ticking. Let's get out there.'

SEVEN

The bright morning sunlight hurt Lauren's eyes. She shoved her sunglasses on as she followed Joe out of the station to his car.

'We should ring them, tell them we're too tired, we can't do the statements today,' she said. 'Tell them we have to go home and sleep because we have to work again tonight.'

'They need them.' Joe started the car and pulled out.

'For what?' Lauren said. 'It's not like they'll help them catch the guy.'

'They might.'

'The detectives already know what we know, they took down the pertinent details last night,' Lauren said. 'This is just paperwork.'

'It won't take long.'

'Yeah, right.' She folded her arms and glared out the window at the heavy traffic coming the other way. Reflected sunlight flashed from bumpers and windshields, and she hated all the cars and all the people inside them. Night shifts generally left her feeling like crap, but last night she hadn't been able to rest even when they did get back to the station for a short time. When she'd tried to drink coffee she thought she could smell blood on her hands, and repeated washings didn't help that or the occasional stickiness she felt on her palms. She hadn't been able to decide whether to tell the detectives she knew a Thomas Werner, and her head hurt from worrying.

'I'll even buy you breakfast afterwards,' Joe was saying.

Lauren raised the sunglasses to rub her eyes. 'I'm not hungry.' Outside, a truck blasted its airhorn at someone, making her want to scream.

Ella said, 'They're late.'

'They don't finish till eight,' Murray said. 'Then it's, what, forty minutes' drive out?'

'Less than that. They're coming against the traffic.'

'Maybe they got overtime.'

'And didn't have time to call us?' She was restless, wanting to get going on the next task, wanting to be out there, talking to people, digging for facts. She was tired but buzzed. She wanted more action than typing.

Movement at the door caught her eye. The paramedics stood there looking in, and she elbowed Murray. 'I'll take the woman.'

Murray took the man across to a far corner of the room while Ella led the woman back to Murray's chair. 'Lauren, right?'

The woman nodded. She looked tired but tense, as if she was exhausted and running on caffeine alone.

'Can I get you anything?' Ella said. 'Tea, coffee?'

'I'm fine.'

Ella had the computer ready to go. 'You've done statements before?'

Lauren nodded.

'Let's get started then. Name, address, age and occupation?'

Lauren kept her hands clenched between her knees under the desk. Every time she said Thomas's name she felt herself tense up further. She watched Ella for signs that she picked up more in Lauren's voice or behaviour than she should, but the detective typed on merrily, pausing to nod every so often when Lauren talked, rephrasing some things she said into the statement-speak Lauren had seen before. There was no room in statements for emotions, and though she knew she never could tell anyone – perhaps *because* she knew she never could tell anyone – Lauren found herself wishing she could open up to the detective about how she felt knowing that Kennedy's death was down to her.

'And then what?' Ella said.

'I completed my handover to the hospital staff and they took over Mr Kennedy's care.'

Ella typed the words then hit the full stop. 'Beautiful.'

Lauren looked across the room. Joe and the male

detective were laughing about something. They'd probably been long finished, as Joe hadn't heard as much as she had. If Joe had heard nothing, would they be there now?

'Just read this over then sign at the bottom of each page.' Ella handed her the printed pages of her statement. 'Then you can go.'

Lauren skimmed it and signed and gave the pages back. 'So,' she said. *Tell her you might know him, tell her! You think it will be easier later?* But she couldn't make the words come out.

'Yes?'

'Have you caught the guy yet?'

'I wish,' the detective said.

Lauren gestured at the computer. 'Was he on your system there already?'

'We've found a number of people with that name actually.'

'All from, um, Sydney?'

'Or elsewhere in the state,' the detective said.

Lauren thought of Kristi. 'Are you going to release his name to the media?'

'We have no plans to.' Ella studied Lauren for a moment. 'I know why you're asking.'

Lauren felt a jolt of adrenaline.

'I saw last night that this one affected you a bit, so I understand you want to know what's happening, how quickly we'll get the guy.'

Lauren nodded and got to her feet. 'Soon, I hope.'

'We hope so too,' Ella said.

In the lift Lauren stood silently beside Joe who

jabbed at the button with his thumb. 'You'd think it'd be faster in a newish building like this.'

She felt weak with fear and guilt.

At home, she was inside before Joe had driven off. She ached with fatigue and tension, and the sound of Felise banging about in the attic made her grit her teeth. In the kitchen she took down their collection of medicines. She didn't like to take sedatives to help her sleep because of the fog they left in their wake, but today she felt she had little choice. She had another night shift that night; lying in bed awake all day would do her no good at all. She weighed the box of tablets in her hand and wished her brain had a switch she could flick to 'off'.

'See what we made you?' Kristi came into the room and yanked open the fridge door. 'It's on the table.'

It was a small mosaic featuring something that looked like a purplish ear against a sky blue background. Next to it was the plumber's bill for the new water heater. Lauren took a closer look and winced. The landlord wasn't going to be happy.

'It's our new teapot stand.' Kristi shoved a large bottle of water and three apples into her work knapsack.

'A mosaic of an ear?'

'A spleen.'

Lauren popped out a tablet and swallowed it dry. 'Great.'

Kristi spooned tabouli into a small container. 'How was your night?'

'Crap.'

'Ordinary night shift crap, or more?'

'More.' Lauren slumped into a chair. 'I went to a stabbing. The man died.'

'Oh my god.' Kristi dropped the spoon. 'How did it happen?'

'Somebody just walked up to him on the street and stabbed him. He was still conscious when we got there, and we got him in the ambulance and I was filling him up with fluids, and then he gave me a message for his wife.'

Kristi sat down next to her and smoothed her calloused palm over Lauren's forehead. 'Are you okay?'

The action reminded Lauren of how she'd done exactly the same thing to Kennedy, and she looked away from the touch. 'He knew he was dying,' she said. 'He told me who stabbed him. I had to give a statement to the police about what he said.'

Kristi's eyes were round. 'That's amazing.'

'Not quite the word I'd use.'

'No, but listen,' Kristi said. 'You saw a man die, you wrote down his last words including the identity of his killer. I know you think you've built up this layer around your heart, this tough stringy layer like beef jerky, and that you need this to cope with your work, but really, Lauren, this is something else. Apart from the fact that it comes so soon after the ice addict attack, this was you and this man at the final moments of his life, him standing on the precipice of the great unknown and you the only one holding his hand, looking into his eyes, simultaneously trying to hold him back and to ease his passing if that was how it was to be, to take down his last message for the world, words which will both comfort his family and help the police avenge his death, and Jesus, you know what? What you've done allows him to point his hand from the grave, identifying his killer, ensuring that justice with a capital J is done.'

'I wanted so badly to save him.'

'I know you did.'

'You don't understand. I needed to save him. I had to,' Lauren said. 'But I didn't.'

'You can't save everyone,' Kristi said. 'The universe has its plan.'

'That's bullshit,' Lauren said. 'This man should still be alive.'

'Violence is a terrible thing.'

'You don't get it.'

Kristi stroked her hair. 'Then help me get it.'

'I can't.'

'I've looked death in the face too, remember,' Kristi said. 'When I was in that car accident–'

Lauren squeezed her eyes closed. 'That's not the same thing and you know it.'

'I'm just trying to demonstrate that we have shared experiences, common ground on which to talk. I know where you're coming from.'

'You haven't the slightest idea,' Lauren said.

Kristi stared at her for a moment. 'I'm not encouraging you to talk for my benefit, you know.'

'I know,' Lauren said. 'You're doing it for my spleen.' She turned away from the hurt in her sister's eyes, sorry she'd ever mentioned the stabbing. 'Look, I just want to go to bed.'

'Then go.' Kristi got up, slammed the lid on the tabouli container and shoved it into her knapsack, then yelled up the stairs, 'Are you ready?'

'I want to stay home!' Felise shouted back.

'We've been over this already,' Kristi said, 'and if you're not down here with your things, ready to go, by the time I count to three, you won't be allowed to play with Max for the rest of the week.'

There was an exasperated sigh and a blonde ropey-haired naked plastic doll flew down the stairs.

'You remember what happens to toys that get thrown?' Kristi grabbed it and flung it into the bin.

'I didn't like her anyway!' Felise stamped down the stairs, the old bowls bag full of pencils, paper, dolls and books that she took to Kristi's jobs thumping down each step behind her. She stopped on the last one to shout, 'And I hate you, Mummy!'

'Like I haven't heard that before.' Kristi turned her back. 'Say goodbye to Aunty Lolly.'

Felise came over and pecked Lauren on the cheek, her pinched little face red with anger. Lauren got in a brief hug before Felise stormed away and down the stairs to the ground floor. Kristi followed without a backward glance, and Lauren stayed at the table, listening for the turning of the lock and the starting of Kristi's car, before pushing herself to her feet and heading tiredly for the shower.

Her skin red and tingling, her heart sore, Lauren fell into bed with the tablet kicking in. She pulled the covers up in a daze, praying she would be able to disappear into sleep, away from her thoughts.

★

At 10am Kuiper asked if they wanted to go home but both Ella and Murray said no. With fresh coats of deodorant they headed for James Kennedy's workplace.

The Quiksmart courier depot was in a busy street just off Parramatta Road in Leichhardt. Inside the front office, a woman in her fifties sat behind a high counter. Her eyes were red and she typed with her head bent over the computer keyboard. Through a glass-panelled door behind her Ella could see five people with phone headsets at computers. They were all talking and typing.

Murray showed the woman his badge. 'We're here to see Daniel Peres.'

She dabbed at her eyes with a damp-looking tissue. 'I'll call him.' She lifted the phone and spoke into it in a low voice. A couple of people in the closed room behind her looked their way. Ella stared back at them. She had no doubt they knew who she and Murray were. Two suits turn up at your workplace the morning after one of your colleagues is killed, it doesn't take much brain power to figure it out. Both the watchers turned back to their screens but one also angled his chair a little as if to hide his face. Ella narrowed her eyes.

The woman stood up and opened a door at the side of the office. Stairs led upwards. 'Mr Peres is waiting for you.'

Daniel Peres's office was walled with glass and overlooked the activity in the huge warehouse area below. His desk stood near the opposite wall. As they entered the room he lumbered from behind it, his hand out in front like it was leading him. 'How do you do,' he said. 'Daniel Peres.'

Murray did the name thing for them both.

Peres indicated chairs. They sat, and Ella crossed her legs and placed her palm on the arm of the chair, hoping the fabric would absorb Peres's sweat from her skin.

'Have you caught the offender yet?' Peres said.

'These things can take considerable time,' Murray said.

Peres nodded. 'So how can I help?'

'How long had James Kennedy worked here?' Ella said.

Peres touched the computer mouse. 'I was just looking it up. Seven years he'd been here, three of that working under my predecessor.' He smiled nervously. 'He was a good employee. Hardly took a sick day the whole time I'd known him.'

'How did he get on with the other staff?' Murray asked.

'Fine, fine, no problems at all.'

'Kennedy was a driver, correct?' Ella said.

A bit of bobble-headed nodding.

'Can you run us through a typical shift?'

Peres checked the screen. 'James worked eight-hour shifts, starting at nine in the morning, with one hour off for lunch, then finishing at six. He'd come in, get his run sheet, go out. We have a number of regular customers we move goods for, but also during the day when new customers call up with a request that goes out on the radio to one of the guys and so they might get that on top of the usual runs.'

Murray wrote in his notebook. 'You have records of everywhere each vehicle goes?'

'Yes, delivery dockets, mileage sheets, all that.'

'Did Kennedy always drive the same vehicle?'

'Yes. Well, I mean, he always drove a van, not a truck. But the van itself varied.'

'And how did he get on with the customers? Were there ever any suggestions of conflict?'

Peres shook his head. 'Like I said, he was a good employee. Did as he was asked, never caused any bother.'

'Did he ever finish later than six?'

'We try to avoid overtime,' Peres said. 'We have a few evening drivers and we give the late jobs to them.'

'Were you here when he finished on Tuesday?'

'No, I'm usually gone by five-thirty.'

'So how can you be sure what time he left?'

Peres pointed to the computer. 'All employees log out with their PIN code when they leave, plus there's the security guard who lets them out the door.'

'Can the PIN log be falsified?' Murray said. 'If another employee knows your code, he could put it in for you, couldn't he?'

'I suppose so,' Peres said. 'It's against the rules though. The guard would notice too.'

'Is he here now?'

Peres shook his head. 'He doesn't start till later.'

'Okay, we'll need his address then, please,' Ella said. 'We'll also need a print-out of your log there, and a copy of Kennedy's personnel file. We'd also like to talk to some of your staff.'

'Is that necessary? We're very busy, and—'

'It's necessary,' Murray said. 'Also, what about the crash Kennedy had three years ago? Had the survivors ever come around or been in touch?'

'The woman's family?' Peres said. 'Not that I heard of.'

'There'd been no threats made, nothing like that?'

'I'm certain that the staff would have let me know if anything like that was going on. But I can ask about, just to be sure, if you like.'

'What did Kennedy do while his licence was suspended?'

Peres gestured at the window overlooking the warehouse floor. 'Storeman duties, offsider on a truck if it was required, that sort of thing.'

'You didn't have any qualms about putting him back on the road afterwards?'

'It was an accident,' Peres said. 'If the court was happy that he drive again, so was I.'

They followed him downstairs. He had a brief muttered conversation with the woman from the counter, who then went back to the computer. A moment later a printer started to click and whirr. Ella stood where she could see into the back room again. The nervous-seeming young man had gone. She went around the desk and started to open the door.

'It might be better,' Peres said, hurrying over, 'if you want to talk to those people, if I ask them out one by one. Rather than disturbing them all at once.'

Ella put her head inside the room but couldn't

see the young man. 'The person from that chair.' She pointed at the empty space. 'Where's he gone?'

Peres looked into the room then checked his watch. 'I don't know.' He looked around at the front-desk woman. 'Did you see Benson leave?'

She shook her head. 'I just went to the bathroom. He must have gone then.'

Peres frowned and leaned into the room past Ella. 'Tina?'

A tired-looking woman in her mid-forties glanced up from her keyboard.

'Where did Benson go?'

'He said he was sick and was going home.'

Peres sighed, a sound of exasperation, and turned to Ella. 'They're supposed to come see me first.'

She shot a glance at Murray. 'We'll need his address too.'

EIGHT

The nervous young man was named Benson Drysdale, and he lived in Lidcombe, according to his employment records. Ella parked along from his building and got out of the car, eyeing the dingy flats with rows of washing hung on the balconies. Murray came around the front of the car and they walked in silence to the red-brick block.

At Drysdale's third-floor flat Ella listened, then knocked on the door. There was no sound from inside but she had the feeling she was being watched. She stared at the peephole, looking for a change in the light.

'Not home.' Murray turned away.

Ella kept staring. She knocked again. Still nothing. Murray started down the stairs and, after a long moment, Ella slid her card under the door and reluctantly followed.

Outside Murray said, 'Maybe he really was sick.'

'Then he should be home and answering the door.'

'Perhaps he's at the doctor's.'

Ella strode to the car. There was a reason Drysdale hadn't wanted to have any contact with them. If he was so skittish as to feel he had to flee his workplace while they were there, he wasn't likely to withstand a bit of shrewd questioning. Once they found him.

She rang Kuiper again. 'Drysdale's still MIA.'

'Okay,' he said. 'Hoskins checked with the bakery folks, who say Kennedy never got there last night. They all say he was a decent guy and they can't believe somebody would want to kill him. And Strong's just spoken to Quiksmart's security guard, who confirms what the sign-off print-out shows: Kennedy did indeed leave at six last night. Guard seems solid. He's ex-job. Said Kennedy seemed distracted, in a bit of a rush, when he left.'

Ella wondered what that could mean.

'Anyway, next up is the PM for you two,' Kuiper said. 'Start driving now, you'll get to Glebe right in time for the kick-off.'

The pathologist straightened Kennedy's head on the stainless-steel table while Ella confirmed for him that the body was indeed that of James William Kennedy, identified to her by his daughter last night. Murray stood beside her, his arms folded.

'No weapon found?' the pathologist said.

'Not so far.' Ella could hear a squeaky wheel somewhere, indicating the progress of some body-laden trolley along the corridor outside.

Julie Connolly from Forensic Services stood on a

box to get above the table with her camera. Kennedy was naked, having been stripped at the hospital before all efforts to save him failed and he was declared dead. The pathologist held a ruler against the dark-edged wound on Kennedy's left chest and Julie fired off some shots, then the pathologist leaned closer with a magnifying glass.

'There are sharp edges at both ends of the wound, indicating that a knife with a double-sided blade is most likely your weapon,' he said. 'There's also a slight contusion around the wound, suggestive of the impact of the hilt against the skin.'

Murray unfolded his arms and wrote a few dot-points in his notebook. Julie got snap-happy again, getting some close-ups, then the pathologist probed the wound and measured the depth. Finally he took up a scalpel. 'I'll excise the wound and preserve it. We'll be able to compare then, when you find a weapon.'

He lifted the piece of flesh from Kennedy's chest with tweezers and dropped it into a jar of formalin.

Ella heard the wheel again and looked towards the door. She could see the end of a stationary trolley and the bare feet of a young woman. As they'd walked in past her, Ella had seen her painted toenails, how her naked thighs bulged against the clear plastic she lay wrapped in, the colourful tattoos on her belly and shoulders.

The pathologist cut through Kennedy's ribs with something that looked like tinsnips only much more expensive. Kennedy's head moved a little with each closing of the blades. Ella thought again about what he'd said to the paramedic. It was a heroic effort really. He would've known that the information would be passed to the police, and Ella felt fortunate to be the one to receive it. They were part of a team now, she and Kennedy, and as the pathologist drained dark blood from the open chest cavity, measuring the liquid as he went, she silently vowed to hold up her end of the deal. He'd given them the key piece of information, that little nugget they often searched so hard for, and from here on in it was a puzzle to be fitted together. Track Thomas Werner down; work out why he did it and precisely how; find proof that he was there or at least in the vicinity; build that case so solidly that a conviction was only a matter of time.

'Fifteen hundred ml,' the pathologist said.

'Is that a lot?' Murray asked.

The pathologist nodded. 'Considering you said he was conscious and talking at the scene.' He pushed his gloved hands into the chest. 'Ah. Here's the wound in the pulmonary artery. Half a centimetre across. He was lucky he wasn't dead within a couple of minutes.' He moved aside a little, letting Julie put the camera close.

Lucky wasn't quite the word Ella would use.

Out in the corridor the trolley squeaked again.

Back at Parramatta, the detectives gathered in the Homicide office meeting room at four that afternoon. Kuiper was late. The room grew stuffy and smelled of coffee breath. Ella's back and legs ached, and her eyes were sore and dry from being awake for so long. She sat with her arms folded and one foot tapping the leg of the desk. Beside her Murray licked his thumb with a small wet noise each time he turned a page of the newspaper.

Finally she said, 'Could you stop that?'

He looked up. 'Stop what?' His lower lip and thumb were tinged black with newsprint.

'Forget it,' she said, looking away.

Her tiredness was dragging her spirits down as well. It was early days, she knew – *very* early days – but she couldn't help feeling that what had seemed like a pot of gold landing in her lap when they'd gone to the hospital was turning tarnished. She was meant to have had Werner nabbed and behind bars by now, with Kuiper calling her in for a meeting with him and Detective Inspector Bill Radtke, Homicide head honcho, to tell her she was in the squad to stay. Being on temporary secondment was like standing on the edge of a cliff. You never knew when the earth would give way and send you plummeting back into the Valley of the Shadow of the Boring Suburban Station.

She realised she was making a face and stopped herself just as Kuiper rushed in.

'Sorry, folks,' he said. 'Let's get started.'

Ella opened her notebook and scribbled details as other detectives spoke about what they'd found. The five Thomas Werners listed in the police and RTA computers and phone directories had been checked out and cleared. The electoral roll check had turned up one more living in the Sydney area, but he was seventy-nine and could hardly walk. Next step was to check interstate.

'Kennedy's motorbike was found, parked and undamaged, on the roadside next to Steyne Park, down by Double Bay,' Detective Graeme Strong said. 'It doesn't make much sense that he'd have parked there then trudged all the way up to New South Head Road for his bread. We know he left work in Leichhardt at 6pm and was stabbed near the bakery at eight forty-five. Much of the intervening time was daylight, even if it was fading, and so there's a good chance that people in the houses or out enjoying the evening in the park would have seen him arrive.'

Kuiper nodded. 'We'll start a canvass, see when he got there, what he did, if he was with anyone. Kanowski?'

Detective Rebecca Kanowski, assigned to victimology on the case, sat forward. 'I've spent a lot of time with Mrs Kennedy today. We talked about the accident with the Harveys but she's adamant they never received any threatening calls or anything like that. We discussed Kennedy's dying declaration, which she says is mostly poetry from their courting days and so a message of love, but she still says she has no idea who Thomas Werner is or who would have any reason to attack her husband.'

'You searched all his stuff, got the bank records and so on?'

Rebecca made a face. 'I'm taking it slowly for the moment. She's very edgy. I suggested we call a doctor for some sedatives, and even took a moment to talk to the daughter and ask about any psychiatric history. She says it's just the grief, that her mother needs some time and then she'll give us everything we want.'

'She knows it could help solve the case?'

'She knows,' Rebecca said. 'But like I said, she's very . . .' She moved her hand from side to side. 'I don't want to push her when she's so fragile.'

'We need that information.'

Rebecca nodded. 'I'm going back later.'

Kuiper looked around at them all. 'I talked with Commissioner Eagers earlier, about this case and also about Steven Spiers.'

Someone groaned. 'The Family Man.'

'You've no doubt all heard his latest,' Kuiper said. 'It was bound to happen when he lives just streets from the crime scene. Despite his suggestions to the contrary, the murder rate is not going up at ten per cent per year, and Kennedy is – as far as we know at the moment – not a victim of out-of-control street crime. We've got plenty of avenues to investigate, so let's get on with the case and ignore all the hot air.'

Ella fought back a yawn.

'Okay,' Kuiper said. 'I know some of you have been on shift for hours, and some are fresh. Before we start dividing up the evening's tasks, let me ask of those who started yesterday – hands up who wants to go home?'

Ella hurt her shoulder shooting her hand into the air.

When Kristi and Felise came home, Lauren was in the bath, trying to soak away her headache and the sedative fog before getting ready for night shift. Kristi knocked on the bathroom door and stuck her head around the edge. Lauren pulled the washer from her face. 'Hi.'

'You okay?'

Lauren nodded and smiled. 'You?'

Kristi smiled back, then closed the door gently.

Lauren sank deeper into the water, wishing she really was okay. The knots in her shoulders were tight and hard. *Kennedy at the precipice.* She shut her eyes and felt the heat of the water join with the boil of her insides.

The phone rang. She heard Felise answer in her clear high voice then there was a tap at the door. Felise came in with the cordless phone in her hand. 'It's for you.'

'Who is it?'

Felise put the phone to her ear. 'Who is it, please?' She listened, then said to Lauren, 'He's your friend.'

Probably Joe. Lauren got out of the bath and wrapped a towel around herself then took the phone. 'You'd better not be ringing to say you're taking a sickie tonight.'

'Was that who I think it was?' the accented male voice said.

Thomas.

'She sounds lovely. I should get to know her.'

Lauren sank down onto the side of the bath. Felise was jumping at the sink, trying to see her face in the mirror, then Kristi bustled in and stuck her hand in the bathwater.

'You finished?' she said.

Lauren managed to nod. How did he know where they lived?

'No point wasting it.' Kristi turned to Felise. 'Into the tub with you, missy.'

Felise grumbled but started to unbutton her dress.

'What's she doing now?' Thomas said.

'Nothing.' Lauren turned away as if he could see down the phone into the room. When her legs felt stronger she'd get up and walk out. She should hang up right now, but she was paralysed.

'I really should get to know her,' Thomas said again.

'Oh, you think so.' The hair bristled on the back of Lauren's neck.

Kristi looked at her.

'I do,' Thomas said. 'And I will, if you don't do exactly what I say.'

Kristi mouthed, *You okay?*

Lauren covered the mouthpiece with a sweaty palm. 'It's just work.'

Thomas said, 'You'd better call the detectives on that case and tell them you were wrong.'

'I don't know if that will fit,' she said. Kristi glanced over again, and she added, 'With my roster, I mean.'

'You've got twenty-four hours.'

'But–'

'That's a pretty old house you live in,' Thomas said. 'You have to be careful with old houses like that.'

She sat frozen.

'Bad things can happen.'

Don't listen to this – hang up, hang up! But she couldn't move.

'Imagine coming home after nightshift; first you smell the smoke, then you see the fire engines, then the police turn as you approach, their faces sombre, and you know without being told that–'

Lauren pressed the 'end' button on the handset. Kristi was on her knees by the tub, soaping Felise's narrow back. Lauren pushed the back off the phone and yanked out the battery.

'What are they ringing you for?' Kristi slapped the washer into the water. 'Your time off is just that. They should leave you alone.'

'Ow,' Felise said. 'You're pulling my hair.'

'Sorry, honey.' With one wet hand Kristi looped Felise's straggling blonde hair up onto her head, and with the other she pressed the washer onto the back of her neck. 'There. How's that?'

Felise giggled. Lauren squeezed her hands and the dead phone between her knees.

Thomas knows.

Lauren got dressed in a daze.

Thomas knows!

But how could he know?

She buttoned her uniform shirt, then glanced in the mirror as she attached her epaulettes. She looked haunted. She *felt* haunted.

How the hell could he know?

She sat on her bed, hands clenching the mattress, and tried to work out what to do. It was Kristi's deepest fear that Thomas would one day turn up and want to be part of Felise's life, so the mere mention that he was in the country would send her into a frenzy. To then say that he'd been in touch, that he'd made threats, was unimaginable. But to leave her here, innocent, unknowing – was that inviting disaster?

She checked the clock. It was after five, and she'd have to leave soon to get to work by six. She had to go, there was no way around that. She needed to talk to Joe. She'd spill her guts about everything – well, maybe not everything, maybe she'd keep Blake to herself. But just being able to talk the rest over with him would make it clearer in her head. Joe had a wondrous knack of listening and helping you talk things through that showed you the way.

Kristi and Felise would be okay. Thomas had given her twenty-four hours, after all. He wouldn't do anything to them tonight, would he?

She shivered, suddenly sick.

Why on earth would you believe him?

Sal Rios couldn't believe what he'd just heard.

Thomas leaned back in the passenger seat as if they were out for a Sunday drive, as if he hadn't just threatened to burn down a house with his daughter in it.

'Here,' Thomas said.

Sal glanced in the rear-view mirror, trying to see against the glare of the late afternoon sun. 'There're still cars coming.'

'There'll always be cars coming. Just pull over.'

'It's too shallow.' On the other side of the road the waters of Botany Bay glittered beyond a narrow strip of beach. 'Some kid'll find it, hand it in.'

'Drive to a cliff then.'

'Nice evening like this, people are out walking. We'll be seen.' And what could be more obvious, raise more suspicion, than a man throwing a mobile phone off a cliff into the sea?

'Fuck 'em,' Thomas said.

That had been his attitude all along – towards the couple who'd stopped their kissing to watch him climb the path from the water near Vaucluse and dump his scuba gear in the boot before getting in the car; towards the people he'd made scatter with his stare when they went to empty the flat; and just now on the phone towards Kristi's sister. Sal felt sick. He couldn't understand how Thomas could do it, and how he wasn't seeing the risk all these things were creating.

But he knew he couldn't really claim to be surprised after what happened with Blake. He'd only wanted to teach Blake a lesson, secure in the knowledge that he wouldn't tell the cops because his reason for going into the alley would count as a breach of his probation. But Thomas had gone nuts, and then those other two had walked in, busy with each other, and though he doubted they'd ever tell the cops what they'd seen, their fleeing had brought the paramedic. Kristi's sister. What kind of bad luck was that?

'Here,' Thomas said again.

'Let me take care of it,' Sal said. 'Please. I'll pull it to bits then smash them and scatter them in dumpsters.'

'You don't trust me, huh?'

'No, no, it's not that.' Sal hated his new nervousness. He tensed his lats against the seat. 'You've got enough to do, that's all.'

Thomas shrugged and tossed the phone into Sal's lap. 'Better do it properly.'

You're one to talk.

When Sal heard that Kennedy had lived long enough to tell the paramedic that Thomas had stabbed him, he knew his fears about everything collapsing around him were coming true. The only way to be safe was for Thomas to get out of the country. But would he do that? No.

Sal seriously doubted that the cops would pay attention to the paramedic, even if she did exactly what Thomas said. *This could go on forever.*

His blood chilled at the sound of a siren. It'd be just his luck to get pulled over now, only a couple of minutes away from the factory, with everything there in the boot. But a fire engine rushed past, going the other way, and Sal turned into the industrial area with no drama.

Most of the businesses were closed. He drove slowly, looking for the sign. *Preston's Plastics.* There it was, opposite a panelbeater's, along from a welder's. The door was open. Sal eased the car up onto the concrete forecourt.

'What's this guy's name again?' Thomas said.

'Colin Preston. His sons Gary and Grant work here too.'

Sal looked around but couldn't see anyone watching. Preston was a friend of his late Uncle Paulo, and Sal had never met him. This had been arranged by Julio. *Julio wouldn't let me walk into a trap.* But Julio was dying, and who knew what connections might be loose in his head?

An older man appeared in the doorway, startling him. Preston, he guessed.

'I'll pull up the roller door so you can bring the car in,' Preston said.

Sal nodded. Good idea. Even if nobody was watching, it couldn't be a good idea to lug the components of a drug lab out of the boot and into the factory one by one.

On the train Lauren sat at the end of the carriage, next to the guard's compartment, hugging herself in the plain jacket she wore over her uniform. A man in a grey suit shook out a newspaper in the seat opposite her, and trains going the other way rushed past the window behind him, but all she saw was Kennedy's pale face.

Thomas had done it. He'd killed Kennedy.

Thomas had killed Kennedy because he was free to do so, because she hadn't turned him in for Blake. And now Thomas had threatened her, had told her to tell Ella and the other detective that she'd been wrong. It was an impossible task for so many reasons. For one, she'd written Kennedy's words down, she'd made a statement and agreed that it was correct and signed her name to the thing. For another, Joe had heard Kennedy cry out Thomas's name too, and then given his own statement about the fact. To try to put the detectives off now would simply stick her in the situation of having them wonder just what was going on and look at her more closely.

But what choice did she have? She felt sick at

what Thomas had said. His own ex, his own child! She thought of the old house, the light from the bare bulb shining off Felise's hair as she told stories to a circle of dolls and bears in the attic. Above the roofline the sky would be turning dark. The pigeons would be roosting in the top of the blocked-off chimney, and Kristi would be dancing in the kitchen to the radio, hits of the eighties, up to her elbows in mashed potato. The ground floor would be quiet and dim. The windows weren't barred. Lauren shivered. It would be easy to get in. Easy as pie.

And how did he know? How could he possibly know that Kennedy had told her his name, and that she'd told the police? Nobody knew about that except her and Joe and the police themselves. Which meant . . . what? He knew people inside the police?

Maybe he hadn't been bullshitting about his contacts in the alley that night with Blake.

NINE

Ella lay back with a sigh. She'd thrown one of her mother's frozen, single-serve, somebody-has-to-feed-poor-Ella vegetable lasagne dinners into the microwave to defrost while she'd showered, switched it to cook while she'd made her bed with clean sheets (was there anything as lovely as a fresh bed when you were exhausted?), then shovelled the meal down while sitting propped up against the pillow.

Now she pulled the covers up to her chin, the fumes from the Dencorub she'd put on her shoulder filling the air. The sun's last glow still lit the sky. She watched the shadows of next door's palms move on the ceiling through half-closed eyes. The ache was easing in her back and legs. It was so wonderful to lie down . . .

She was drifting off when the phone rang.

She couldn't not answer it: what if there'd been a break-through?

'Hello?'

'Ella, carina, how are you?'

'Hi, Dad.' She took the phone back to bed. 'Is everything okay?'

'I just spoke to your mother,' he said. 'She said she hadn't seen you, but she thought you were going to visit.'

'I said it depended on work.'

'She's worried,' Franco said. 'Do you think you can ring her?'

'I've been up all night and all day.'

'Five minutes, that's all she wants.'

It wouldn't be five minutes if her mother got going. 'Okay.'

'Thank you. Ciao, bella.'

She had to get out of bed again to find the phone book and look up the hospital switch number. They put her through to her mother's room.

'Hi, Mum.'

'Ella! Are you okay?'

'Actually I'm exhausted,' she said, the phone between the pillow and her ear. 'I've been up since yesterday morning.'

'They shouldn't work you so hard.'

'It was my choice to stay, it's a big case,' Ella said, her eyes closed. 'How's your infection?'

'Fine, good, all gone.'

Sure.

'Did you ask about holidays?'

'I can't, Mum, with this case.'

'They don't need everybody on it, do they?'

Ella yawned hugely. She could feel sleep creeping up on her again. 'I'm really sorry but I have to go.'

'Well, if you have to.'

'I'm sorry, Mum. I'll talk to you tomorrow.'

She dropped the phone onto the floor and snuggled deeper under the covers. *At last, a big case, I have my big ca . . .*

Joe had the truck running when Lauren rushed up minutes before six. She jumped in and slammed the door and Joe accelerated out of the station.

'We're backing up day shift at a burns case in Darlo. Everyone else is tied up.' He roared down George Street. 'Night's going to be shit if the start's any indication.'

Lauren tried to clear her mind. She wouldn't be able to talk to Joe until the job was over. 'Is it a bad one?'

Joe nodded. 'Attempted suicide.' He braked hard as a pedestrian ran across the street in front of them. 'Guy tipped petrol on himself and lit it. He's in an eighth-floor penthouse and the lift's fucked.'

Lauren took in a deep breath. The case would take an hour, at least. Then they might have to come back to the station and shower and change. Bad burns left crews smelling like cooked meat, and not in a good way.

So we won't get to talk for a while. Put it to the back of your mind, try not to stew.

As if that was even remotely possible.

'Got gloves?' she said.

Joe nodded.

Lauren got a pair for herself and yanked them on as Joe turned into the street. It was clogged with traffic, cars squeezing past a fire truck and police cars and an ambulance. Joe pulled up behind them.

Lauren grabbed the radio. 'Thirty-four's on location.'

'Thanks, Thirty-four,' Control replied.

The radio crackled. 'Thirty-eight to Control, permission to speak direct with Thirty-four?'

'Thirty-eight, go ahead.'

'Thirty-eight to Thirty-four, set up the stretcher in the foyer, then bring up the carry sheet, clean sheets and a blanket, thanks.'

'Thirty-four copy,' Lauren said.

'Jacob sounds happy,' Joe said.

'His first big burns.'

Lauren took the rolled bundle of plastic carry sheet and linen that Joe handed out of the truck. He jumped down and pulled the stretcher out, and people watched from the footpaths as he manoeuvred it up the kerb and into the building's foyer. A middle-aged man in ironed jeans and a white buttoned-up shirt dropped his mail on the floor and grabbed at the end, trying to help.

'You're right, mate,' Joe said. 'Where are the stairs we'll be coming down?'

'There.' The man pointed across the tiled floor at a heavy grey door. Joe lowered the stretcher to half-height and positioned it so they could come down the stairs and out of the doorway with the patient feet-first on the carry sheet, and put him straight onto the mattress.

'Mate, have you got a minute?' Joe said to the man. 'There's an important job I need you to do. Stay here and guard this, and don't let anybody move it in any way, okay?'

The man nodded seriously.

'Thanks, buddy,' Joe said, following Lauren to the grey door. 'Appreciate it.'

The stairwell echoed with their footsteps. The air was cool and smelled of paint and concrete. They were both puffing by the time they reached the eighth floor. Lauren heaved the door open to inhale a lungful of burnt meat stink. She pulled a face at Joe.

The door to the penthouse was propped open by a chair. Inside, the lounge room had once been white and gold. Smoke now stained the ceiling and walls, the carpet was charred, and the twin white leather lounges were half-burnt. Everything was soaked through from the sprinkler system. In the middle of the floor paramedics Jacob Milne and Renee Webb and two firefighters struggled to control a thrashing charred man.

'Et me ii!' he screamed.

'Mate, just relax, would ya?' Jacob said. 'Let me give you a bit of morphine and you'll feel much better.'

'Jut et me ii!'

Lauren caught hold of the man's flailing right arm. The heat that remained in his flesh from the fire came straight through her gloves. It was like holding something fresh out of the oven but alive. She could feel the pressure in the swollen tissues. His skin was charred, white in places, and he was naked except for a singed leather belt and a leather shoe on his left foot. All his clothes and hair had been burnt off. His eyelids were gone, the outer edges of his ears burnt away, his lips shrunken and blackened. He stank of burnt meat and petrol.

His right foot was bare and undamaged, the shoe and sock remnant tossed aside. A tourniquet was still clipped around his ankle and an open cannula packet lay nearby.

'I almost had the line and he just started fighting,' Jacob panted.

'Ripped the oxygen mask off too,' Renee said.

'Let's get the line first,' Lauren said. 'He might settle down with some morph on board.'

Joe changed position to help hold the man's leg still while Jacob tightened the tourniquet and palpated a vein on the top of his foot.

'Do we know his name?' Lauren said.

Renee shook her head. 'He wouldn't say.'

'I'm in,' Jacob said. 'Going for five of morph.'

In less than a minute Lauren felt the man relax. Burns that went so deep that the skin was charred black or white killed nerves, so he was only feeling pain from the shallower burns in the areas around his ankles, and probably in his airway too, she thought. But the trauma of the event, plus whatever mental state he'd been in to do this in the first place, would be causing him deep distress. Morphine helped with that too.

She leaned over him. 'What's your name?'

He turned his head to look at her. It was eerie, seeing his eyes between their burnt-off lids. 'Anfony.' The damage to his mouth and lips made his words indistinct.

She smiled at him. 'We're going to help you feel better, okay, Anthony?'

'Wi ii iii?'

'I'm sorry, say that again?'

'Wi. I. Tie?'

'Will you die?'

He nodded.

Lauren didn't know what to say, where to look. Nobody survived burns like this for more than a few hours.

'At okay,' he said. 'Ont oo ii.'

Lauren squeezed the side of his foot, the only place where he would feel her touch. 'I'm Lauren, this is Jacob and Renee and Joe. We're going to do a couple of things then take you to hospital.' She reached for the oxygen mask hissing on the carpet. 'I need to put this on your face, okay? Just tilt your head forward, that's the way.' She slipped the elastic down over his burnt scalp and fitted the mask gently to his face. 'There we go.'

Renee unfolded the carry sheet then took the linen into the bathroom to wet it thoroughly with clean water. Joe set up a bag of Hartmann's to run into Anthony's right foot, and Jacob cannulated his left foot for further fluid.

Lauren said, 'Anthony, how old are you?'

'Orty un.'

'Forty-one?'

'Ess.'

'You tried to kill yourself, is that right?'

'Ess,' he said. 'Etrol.'

'With petrol, yes, I can smell it. Can you tell me why you did it?'

He let out a high-pitched keening. 'I ite.'

'I'm sorry?'

'I. Ife.'

'Your wife?'

He nodded. 'Ee ied. Anter.'

'Cancer?' Lauren said.

He nodded again.

'She died of cancer.'

He made the same high-pitched sound. He was crying, she realised. He had no tear ducts, his airways were damaged, and this was how his crying sounded. He reached towards her with one burnt claw of a hand and she took it gently. Maybe his skin couldn't feel the contact, but he needed it anyway.

'I ife.'

The doctor at St Vincent's knew him. 'He was in last week with a tablet overdose,' she said to Lauren outside the resus room. 'We pumped his stomach and made him an appointment next week with a social worker, the earliest one we could get. His wife died in here three months ago of an inoperable cerebral tumour. Lovely young woman, only diagnosed four months before that. I was on duty when she came in with severe headaches.' She shook her head. 'CT scan, here's your death sentence.'

Lauren nodded. She didn't need to ask what would happen to him now; she knew he'd be stabilised, given more fluid and morphine, and his family notified. Then he'd be put in a single room somewhere, his morphine kept up so he was comfortable, and let die.

'So sad,' the doctor said. Her beeper went. 'Excuse me.'

Lauren headed for the bathroom, locked herself inside a cubicle, and sat on the closed toilet with her elbows on her knees and her face in her hands. She stank, and every breath she took reminded her of Thomas's threat.

First you smell the smoke, then you see the fire engines, then the police turn as you approach, their faces sombre, and you know without being told . . .

She'd already lost one sibling.

She would do exactly what Thomas said.

It was a long night, made longer by the effort it took to keep the secret from Joe. Lauren felt it as a pressure building up in her chest, wanting to force its way from her mouth. But she only had to inhale to remember the price Thomas had threatened – even after long showers, hair-washing and a clean uniform, she could still smell the burnt man on her, and on Joe. Patients commented on it, asked about it, and Lauren lied, saying they'd been to a factory fire and it was the plastics that smelled strange, because you couldn't say they were inhaling microscopic particles of charred human flesh.

At 8am Joe drove her home. 'Got big plans for the day?' he said.

'Not much,' she lied. 'You?'

'Sleep this morning, of course. Then this afternoon me and Claire'll probably do something.'

She nodded. 'Still doing that overtime day tomorrow?'

'Try and keep me away.' He rubbed his fingers together. 'You are too, right?'

'Shit, yeah.'

'Good.' He pulled up outside her house. 'Wouldn't be the same working with someone else.'

She again felt the urge to tell him, but then he looked past her and waved. Lauren turned to see Felise at the front door, waving back. *Protect them.*

'I'll see you tomorrow,' she said.

'Betcha.'

Kristi wrinkled her nose when Lauren came up the stairs. 'Now there's a smell.'

'Don't even ask.' Lauren tilted her head surreptitiously at Felise.

'Oh. Okay.' Kristi continued packing her knapsack.

'Where are you working today?' Lauren asked.

'That flashy place in Point Piper.'

'How far along are they with the building?' she said. 'I mean, the doors are on, you have to buzz to get in, that sort of thing?'

'Hardly. Place is crawling with tradesmen. They just prop the doors open.'

Crawling with people. That was good. Safe.

'Why?'

Lauren shrugged. 'Just curious.'

Kristi came over to hug her goodbye then stopped.

'We'll just wave today,' Lauren said.

'You ready?' Kristi called to Felise. 'Got your bag?'

'Coming.'

Lauren saw them into the car and away. She glanced up and down the street but spotted no lurking man, nobody slumped low in a car. Inside she locked the door and went up for another shower, trying to plan what she'd say to the detectives and how she'd say it.

Please make them accept it.

TEN

'I've got a good feeling about today,' Ella said. 'I think we're going to catch him.'

'Benson Drysdale?'

'And maybe Thomas Werner.'

Murray braked for a red. 'I'll settle for Drysdale.'

That was where they were headed now. Ella wound her window down and rested her arm on the sill in the sunshine. It was amazing what a good sleep could do. She felt bright, cheerful, energetic; she felt she could work sixty hours straight. She felt like chasing somebody – as long as they caught him in the end, of course.

Her mobile rang.

'You'd better get back here,' Kuiper said. 'Your paramedic's turned up and wants to speak to you.'

'About what?' Ella gestured for Murray to turn around.

'She won't say.'

Ella didn't like his tone, and at the office, when Kuiper met them in the hallway, she liked his expression even less.

'Whatever it is, she's nervous.' Kuiper knocked on the door to a small meeting room and opened it for Ella to go in, then closed it behind her.

Lauren stood on the far side of the wide table. She looked pale and had dark circles under her eyes. She wore a blue T-shirt with *000 Club* printed on the chest, and stuck her hands deep into the pockets of her jeans.

'I'm sorry if I smell,' she said. 'I've come pretty much straight from work.'

It was an odour Ella recognised from jobs she'd done over the years. Burnt person, overlaid with deodorant and perfume. 'It's okay. That one's particularly hard to shift.'

Lauren nodded.

'Have a seat,' Ella said. 'Can I get you something to drink? Are you hungry? There's a café downstairs, I hear they do a blinder of a cinnamon roll.'

'I'm okay.' Lauren dug her hands further into her pockets. Her arms were pressed tight to her sides. 'I need to talk to you about something.'

'Shoot.'

'It's about my statement. I'm not sure that it's right.'

Ella blinked. 'I'm sorry?'

'I think I was wrong in what I said in my statement.'

'Which part?' *Don't say it, oh god don't say it!*

'What Kennedy said.' Lauren glanced at Ella then looked away.

When Ella was able to breathe again she said, 'You signed those pages. You declared they were all true and correct.'

'I know,' Lauren said. 'It's just that the more I think about it, the less sure I am of what I heard. What Kennedy actually said.'

'You wrote it down.'

'He was kind of mumbling.'

'Your partner heard it too.'

Lauren made a face.

'Have you talked to him?' Ella said. 'Is he still sure of what he heard?'

Lauren hesitated. 'As far as I know.'

'Well then,' Ella said. 'You were sitting next to the man, your partner was in the front of the vehicle, is that right? So how come he can be certain while you're apparently not?'

'He had the siren on and that would have affected what he heard. Just because he feels certain doesn't mean he's right,' Lauren said. 'People do make mistakes.'

Ella tried to keep calm. 'I don't understand why you feel so differently all of a sudden.'

Lauren looked at the floor. 'I know somebody by that name. And I think that may have affected what I heard. Made me think I heard that name when really it might have been something different.'

'You know a man named Thomas Werner?'

Lauren looked around the room as if hoping for escape. 'He used to go out with my sister. He's a deadbeat.'

'Where does he live?'

'That's the thing,' Lauren said. 'I'm positive it can't be him because he's from overseas.'

'What country?'

'Austria,' Lauren said. 'I also wondered if Joe had

heard me mention him, years ago when he was with my sister, and kept that name in his subconscious, and when he heard Kennedy yelling something that *sounded* like that, he just filled in the gap, same as I did.'

'Why didn't you bring this up before?'

'I thought it didn't matter.' Lauren scraped her teeth over her lip. 'I thought it couldn't be him, he's overseas, so why even trouble you with it?'

Ella's head was spinning. She struggled to pull herself together and focus on what she needed to do. 'It's unlikely that it would be him, but I'd like to take some details anyway.' She fetched an A4 pad from a cupboard at the end of the room, and got out a pen. 'How and when did you first meet this Austrian Thomas Werner?'

'When he started going out with my sister, Kristi, about five and a half years ago.' Lauren sat down and put her folded arms on the table. 'My sister used to be a different person. She had a drink and drug problem, and she hung with a group of people who spent most of their time partying. She met Thomas through these people. They kind of lived together for a while.'

'Here, in Sydney?'

Lauren nodded.

'Then what?'

'They broke up and Thomas went back to Austria, about four years ago, or a bit longer ago than that I guess, just before Felise was born.'

'Felise being?'

'Their child. My niece.'

'Does he keep in touch? Does he visit?'

Lauren shook her head. 'He has nothing to do with our lives now. He's never tried to contact us. He's never even seen Felise, and we don't want him to.'

Ella wrote quickly. 'Where does your sister live?'

'We share a place in Summer Hill.'

'Is she home today? I'll need to talk to her.'

'Why?'

'To check if she knows whether this Werner's in the country, whether he's been in touch.'

'He hasn't.'

'I still need to talk to her.'

'She's working today.'

'Does she have a mobile?'

'No,' Lauren said quickly.

'What time does she get home in the afternoon? I'll drop round.'

'About five would probably be okay.'

Ella made a note.

'So,' Lauren said, 'about my statement.'

Ella looked up.

'It's withdrawn now? Do I have to sign anything?'

'You can't withdraw it,' Ella said. 'It's done. You can't.'

Lauren sat perfectly still for a moment. 'So there's nothing I can do.'

'It's a legal document,' Ella said. 'Look, I'll keep your concerns in mind, and talk to my boss and your sister, and we'll check out this Werner. You know how it is – a big investigation like this, we have to chase down even the thinnest leads, just to be sure.'

'Okay,' Lauren said weakly.

'We've already found more than five Thomas Werners in New South Wales alone. Just because you know one doesn't mean it's not the same name that Kennedy said.'

'I guess so.'

Ella slid a card from her purse. 'Any more worries or problems, give me a call, okay? My mobile's on there. Day or night, it doesn't matter.'

'Thanks.'

Lauren got to her feet and Ella held the door open for her, then walked her down the corridor.

'I'll see you this afternoon, about five?'

Lauren nodded and got in the lift.

'Cheers,' Ella said, smiling in at her, and not failing to catch the way that Lauren's very forced grimace of a smile dropped from her face before she was fully gone from view behind the closing doors.

Kuiper's office door was shut and she could hear him talking to somebody. She went to her desk and booted up her computer. She opened the Central Name Index, looked in her files for Lauren's date of birth, and typed it and her name into the database.

The screen showed that the paramedic had no criminal record, but had been a victim in an assault and hostage situation by a violent and psychotic drug-user just last week, a witness in a homicide earlier in the year, and a witness in a couple of assault cases in the last five years, all related to her job. Ella typed in the case number of the homicide to bring up the full description of the event. The investigating officers had written that Lauren was first to come across the scene, had been alerted to the fact that something was wrong by two men running onto the road in front of her ambulance in which she was alone. She'd stopped, but both men ran away, one jumping into a car down the road, but she couldn't see the numberplate. She'd then gone to look in the alley and found one Stewart Blake deceased on the ground. She'd called it in to ambulance Control and waited there until police arrived.

Ella sat back in her chair. It didn't give her much detail. It didn't explain why Lauren had looked in the alley, although two men tearing away from a location would surely make anybody wonder what they'd been up to.

The case had gone to Coroner's Court recently and Lauren had more than likely testified there. Ella scrolled back to the top of the page to see the investigating detective's name. Lance Fredriks had been in Homicide but now worked out of the Sydney Police Centre in Surry Hills. She dialled the number of the Centre's switch.

Fredriks remembered Lauren well. 'She was great,' he said. 'A perfect witness. I guess being a paramedic helps you be cool and calm, and she was exactly that. She described what she'd seen, described the guys who ran out of the alley, how she then found the body there.'

'How about when she was on the stand?'

'Wonderful,' he said. 'I wish they were all so stable.'

Stable. Huh. 'So those guys were the culprits, do you reckon?'

'We never found them,' Fredriks said. 'She didn't get much of a look at them, couldn't see the rego of the car, but it sounded like they were a male prostitute and his customer who'd just stumbled across the body. There were no other witnesses. Coroner said it was homicide by an unknown person. But you know about him, about Blake, don't you? He was a real pervert. Child molester. He just escalated until he killed that little girl near Eastwood, twenty or so years ago. Lucky they nabbed him then, put an end to things.'

Ella remembered the ruckus in the papers when he was released. 'So is anything else happening with the case?'

'Technically it's open, but realistically – well, there's always something else to do.'

Ella thanked him and hung up. So Lauren was all cool and collected then, but wanting to back out of her statement now. Was she thinking ahead to the time when she'd be on the stand again but this time retelling Kennedy's words while Thomas Werner was sitting there? Ella had dealt with a lot of witnesses over the years and they weren't usually so nervous until right before the court date. Here they were now, without anyone in custody, and Lauren was acting like somebody was skulking about her house at night with a big knife, threatening to cut her head off if she didn't withdraw her statement.

Ella turned back to the computer and entered Kristi's name in the database. The screen showed her that Kristi had once been convicted of negligent driving occasioning death and driving with alcohol and cannabis in her blood. She looked up the case details and read that Kristi's car had collided with an oncoming car four and a half years ago, resulting in the death of the nineteen-year-old male driver, who tests had later found to be also over the limit. Kristi, heavily pregnant, had suffered only minor injuries. She'd had the child and been through rehab by the time her case came before the courts, and because of that, her remorse and her newborn's heart condition, she was given a suspended sentence, a fifteen-hundred-dollar fine and lost her licence for two years.

Ella heard Kuiper's door open. She hurried to catch him in the hall. 'Can we talk?'

Once they were sitting down he said, 'It's not good, is it?'

'She asked to withdraw her statement,' Ella said. 'She said she's no longer sure about what Kennedy told her. Specifically the name.' She explained about the Thomas Werner that Lauren knew.

Kuiper jotted notes as she talked.

'I'm just not sure what's really going on, though,' Ella said. 'When she did her statement she was clear about what Kennedy said. She'd written it down, for god's sake. I don't understand why she's reconsidering now.'

'How did you leave it?'

'I said she couldn't withdraw her statement – she'd signed that it was true and it's a legal document. I'm going to meet her sister this afternoon at five – they share a house. I'll see what she has to say, if she knows anything, and also talk to Lauren again then, feel her out a bit more.'

'Maybe she's just a bit scared,' Kuiper said. 'Apprehensive about going to court some day.'

It didn't jell with what Ella knew of the paramedic from the Blake case, but he could be right. 'I gave her my contact details, said if she was concerned she could ring me any time.'

'Good,' Kuiper said. 'Now, you and Shakespeare are going to look for that Benson Drysdale again, right? After that, slip on over to Coogee and check out Alan Harvey. His wife died in the car accident with Kennedy.'

Ella took the file he held out.

'Meanwhile I'll get onto Immigration and so on, put out a feeler about this Austrian,' Kuiper said. 'Just in case.'

Joe's flat was ten minutes from the Homicide office. Lauren walked there in a daze. The door to the small block was propped open with half a brick, and she climbed the two flights of pebblecrete stairs, pulling herself up on the railing, and came to his door. Her knock echoed in the stairwell.

The peephole went dark. 'Lauren?' He opened the door, yanking on a T-shirt, his hair wet. 'What's wrong?'

So much was wrong she didn't know where to start. She shook her head.

'Hey, it's okay. Come on in.' He locked the door behind her and followed her into the living room. 'Is it about the burnt guy?'

She rubbed her hands over her face. If he went

with her to the detectives, if both of them said they weren't certain what Kennedy had said, maybe they had a chance.

'The other night,' she said. 'James Kennedy. I wondered if I was wrong.'

'About what?'

'Maybe Kennedy wasn't saying Thomas Werner at all.'

Joe shook his head.

'I mean it,' she said. 'Maybe he was saying . . . I don't know . . .' She couldn't think of anything that rhymed with Thomas. 'Some other name.'

'It was definitely Thomas Werner.'

'But how can we be sure? The siren was on,' she said. 'The situation was bad. Those times your blood thumps in your ears and you're thinking about everything to do, and what if this and what if that. And you were concentrating on getting us to the hospital quick and safe.'

'Not me,' Joe said. 'I heard him yell out "Thomas Werner stabbed me". I'll get up in court and say so, a million times over.'

There went that idea. Lauren felt sick.

'Are you . . . you're shaking,' he said. 'What's the matter?'

'Do you remember me telling you about a guy Kristi was living with, a few years ago? Felise's dad? He went back overseas before Felise was born. Do you remember me ever telling you his name?'

'I don't think you ever said. Why?'

'It's Thomas Werner.'

'You're kidding me.'

She took a deep breath. 'I've been thinking about it since, and today I told the detective that I knew somebody by that name and so it was possible that I'd been confused about the name Kennedy told me.'

'No. That was what he said.'

'But like I said, the siren was on,' she said. 'You were looking at the road. And maybe I had told you Thomas's name and it was in your subconscious, and whatever Kennedy said we both came up with the same interpretation.'

'The right interpretation,' he said. 'I'm sorry, but that's what he shouted. But it doesn't matter anyway – I mean, there must be more than one person with that name. It's not going to be him. You just said yourself he went back to Austria years ago.'

'It's him,' Lauren said. 'He's threatened me.'

Joe went still. 'Threatened how?'

'Yesterday he rang me up and said I had twenty-four hours to withdraw my statement or he would do something bad.'

'How the hell could he know about it?'

'He must know somebody in the police,' Lauren said. 'Nobody else knew about what was going on.'

Joe paused. 'What exactly did he say?'

She didn't want to repeat the words. 'It involved fire and the house when people other than me were in it.'

Joe was silent. A muscle worked furiously in his cheek. 'What are the police doing?'

'I didn't tell them,' Lauren said. 'Thomas told me to withdraw my statement and I thought it was best to do exactly what he said. When the detective said

I couldn't withdraw it, all I could think was to come here and talk to you. That you would know what to do.'

'You have to tell them,' he said. 'They can protect you and Kristi and Felise.'

'But if there's a leak in there, maybe they can't,' Lauren said.

'But if they can find that leak, it could lead them straight to him. You telling them what's going on could be the best lead in the case so far.'

There was the sound of a key in the lock and the door opened. Claire walked in and stopped dead. 'I thought we were going out,' she said to Joe.

'I'm running a bit late.'

She looked at Lauren. 'Didn't expect to see you here.'

Lauren knew she should explain, come up with a reason why she was there, but all she could think of was Thomas's threat and the question of what she was going to do.

'We were talking about the burns case from last night,' Joe said. 'She's a bit upset about it.'

'You drove all the way here for that?' Claire said.

'Actually I caught the train,' Lauren said.

'That's even crazier.'

'Don't say crazy,' Joe said. 'Jobs like that can really get in your head.'

'I have looked after a few myself.'

'Yeah, but by the time you get them they're all doped up and cooperative – we've stabilised and treated them,' Joe said. 'You haven't wrestled with them on the burnt carpet of their home or–'

'I was just going anyway.' Lauren got to her feet. 'Joe, thanks for the talk.'

'I'll walk you down,' he said.

Claire eyed her as she went past.

In the stairwell Lauren said, 'I'm sorry about that.'

'It's fine,' he said. 'Listen. You should go straight back to the police now. They need to know.'

They walked outside and stood on the pavers under the big oak tree that shaded the entrance. Lauren could see Claire on the balcony upstairs, making no pretence about watching them.

'I hope she's not angry at you all day.'

'Don't change the subject,' he said. 'Is it my imagination or are you reluctant to tell them?'

She knew she should, but at the same time she could see that path leading to the discovery somehow of her lies about Blake. Her perjury. The night before, when Joe was having his second shower at the station, she'd sneaked a look at the policies folder. Conviction of a serious offence could get her sacked.

'I don't want to cross him,' she said. 'If whoever's the leak hears about it, who knows what he'd do.'

Claire threw a twig at the back of Joe's head. 'We'll be late.'

'Just a minute,' he said.

'Anyway,' Lauren said, 'the detective's coming round to see Kristi this evening. I'll tell her then. Nobody else will be around, so there's no risk of it getting back to Thomas straightaway.'

'Promise?'

'Promise.'

He hugged her.

Lauren heard Claire mutter something and slam the balcony door. 'Are you going to tell her what we really talked about?'

'I'd classify it need-to-know, and she doesn't.'

'She'll be suspicious.'

'She'll be fine.' He let her go. 'Do you want a lift to the station?'

'I'm okay, thanks.' She glanced up. The balcony was empty. 'I'll see you tomorrow.'

'Keep safe, hey?'

On the train Lauren sat on the top deck and stared out the window. She still wasn't sure that she'd tell Ella when she saw her that afternoon. She kept thinking there was some way to do what Thomas had said, though at the same time she knew it was dangerous to trust that he would keep his word.

She just wanted him gone. Back in Austria, away from all of them. There was so much danger while he was here – not only of physical harm, but because he knew what had really happened with Blake. While it was ridiculous to think he would admit to his part simply in order to prove that she'd lied, what if the police somehow managed to put the case together? Thomas's defence could weaken both prosecution cases, Blake and Kennedy, just by telling what she'd done.

The other thing was whether Thomas might try to lay any claim to Felise. She knew Kristi would panic about this more than anything else; in her mind, the threat of injury would seem remote beside the threat of a custody battle. She had to tell her though. This morning.

The train slowed going through Clyde. East of the station three workmen poked at a fire in the waste ground by the lines. Lauren stared at the flames and the dead black grass and thought of the man's charred skin from the night before. While Kristi's greatest concern might be custody, hers was something else.

The train went on but the flames stayed in her mind.

ELEVEN

Ella slid lower in her seat as the late-morning sun slanted in the windows and filled the car with light and warmth. They'd been there twenty minutes, talking quietly about Lauren and the Thomas Werner she knew. She felt increasingly conspicuous, sure that anyone wandering past and seeing the two of them sitting in the car would recognise them for what they were.

'We should get out,' she said. 'Walk the street a little.'

'March up and down in front of his block?'

'Go for a walk, I said.'

'And Drysdale'd turn up the moment we're out of sight at the end,' Murray said.

They'd sent a uniformed officer up to knock at his door. There'd been no answer. When the officer came down and got in his car, ignoring them as he'd been asked, Ella stared at Drysdale's balcony till her eyes watered. If he was home, he'd be out taking a peek, surely. But there'd been nothing.

'Maybe he's done a runner. Gone interstate or somewhere.'

Murray's gaze was fixed on the rear-view mirror. 'Is this him?'

Ella shifted to look in the wing mirror. 'That's him.'

Benson Drysdale approached like a frightened cat. Ella saw his eyes dart about, examining each car parked on the street before he came alongside. It was only a matter of time before he spotted them and fled.

'Ready?' she said.

Murray eased his hand onto the door handle.

Drysdale came closer. He carried a plastic shopping bag. Ella could make out the shape of a carton of milk.

'Any second,' she breathed.

Drysdale reached the rear of the car, looked in and began to scramble into a turn. Ella shoved her door open and was running down the footpath behind him before he'd made ten metres. He dropped the bag and she leapt over it. She could hear Murray's feet slapping behind her. Drysdale stumbled and she reached out and grasped the back of his shirt and yanked him to a halt.

'Silly boy,' she said. 'Why are you running?'

Murray came up beside them, Drysdale's plastic bag in his hand. Drysdale put his hand out for it but Murray held it out of reach. 'Don't panic, nothing's broken.'

'Just groceries?' Ella said.

'And a bit of light reading material.' Murray fished out a porn magazine.

Drysdale jutted out his chin. 'That's private.'

Her grip firm on his arm, Ella turned him around and pushed him towards his building. 'So is your flat, but we're still going in there.'

His apartment was small and dank. A table in the centre of the living room held a huge computer. Drysdale stuck his hands in his pockets and faced Ella. 'So what's the problem?'

'Why did you take off from work on Wednesday?'

'I was sick.'

'Oh, really.' She folded her arms. 'We checked in with your boss, Daniel Peres. He said you haven't been back, you haven't rung in or anything. He said he might have to fire you.'

He shrugged. 'Crappy job anyway.'

Murray came back in from the other rooms. 'Repair a few computers, do you?'

'It's a hobby,' Drysdale said.

Ella said, 'How well did you know James Kennedy?'

'He was a driver at Quiksmart.'

'How well did you know him?' she said again.

'We'd chat,' he said. 'That was it.'

'You're not much of a liar,' Ella said.

Murray pushed a chair against the backs of Drysdale's legs. 'Sit.'

'This is a homicide investigation,' Ella said. 'You know what that means?'

'That a guy died.'

'It means that we don't stop digging for information until we know everything,' she said. 'How we deal with people is determined by how hard they make our job. If you were up to something dodgy with Kennedy or someone else at Quiksmart, and that's why you ran away and why you're lying now, we need to know. Tell us now and we'll help you if we can.'

Drysdale looked at his hands, clenched in his lap.

'Or,' she went on, 'you can make us work harder, and waste time, and in the end we'll find out anyway, and then we won't be inclined to help you one little bit.'

He sighed. 'I sell stuff on eBay. Computers that I repair or do up, you know.'

'And?'

'And James would deliver them around Sydney for me, for a cash-in-hand delivery fee from the buyer, like at a discount rate, and we'd split the money.'

'He did this on his rounds, you mean? Slipped extra stuff into the load?'

'Yes.'

'What else?'

'Nothing else.' Drysdale shook his head. 'That's it.'

Ella looked at Murray, who laid his hand on Drysdale's shoulder. 'You ran away from us for that?'

'I didn't want Peres to find out.' He looked up at Ella. 'Did he really say he'd sack me?'

Ella stepped closer. 'Did you ever hear Kennedy mention the name Thomas Werner?'

Drysdale sat up straight. 'You think Thomas killed him?'

'You know someone by that name?'

Drysdale nodded. 'Yeah, he was with James one day when he was working. They came round here – I took a sickie but I had some stuff for him to pick up and deliver, you know – and when I saw the van pull up I took the stuff down there to give to him. James came round to open the sliding door and put the stuff in, and this guy was in the passenger seat. I said something like, hi, I'm Benson. He said his name. He had an accent and I said, oh, are you German, guten tag, my mum's family comes from Germany and I know the accent, you know? And he says, kinda smirky, as if I should know the difference, no, I'm from Austria. But then Kennedy's getting toey, it's obvious he wants to go, so I step back and off they shoot.'

Ella's heart hammered in her chest. 'You met an Austrian Thomas Werner with James Kennedy.'

'He definitely said that was his name?' Murray asked.

'Thomas Werner, yep.'

'What'd he look like?'

'Short brown hair,' Drysdale said. 'Average-size guy, I guess. It's hard to say when they're sitting in a van and you only see the top half.'

'Eye colour?' Ella said. 'Anything distinctive about what you could see?'

'Eyes, I'm not sure. There wasn't really anything distinctive about him. Just his accent. And he seemed really arrogant.'

'Did he say if he was living here, or a tourist?' Murray said.

'He didn't say,' Drysdale said. 'You really think it was him who killed James? Oh, man.'

'When did you meet him?' Ella asked.

'Maybe six months ago,' Drysdale said. 'I can probably narrow it down.' He switched on the computer. 'I think I know what I gave them to deliver, so I'll just look that up and then I'll be able to tell you the exact day.' He turned his chair around as the screen came to life.

Ella tilted her head for Murray to follow her into the tiny kitchen.

'We need to call Kuiper,' Murray said.

'We need to get down to Immigration,' she said.

'Here you go,' Drysdale called. 'Computer hard drive and a monitor, to two different addresses on the twenty-seventh of May.'

Murray wrote down the information.

'Did you and Kennedy ever discuss Werner afterwards?' Ella said.

'Just once, in a roundabout way,' Drysdale said. 'This was a couple of days later. James was in the warehouse and I went to see him. He was moving some stuff from a truck into his van, and I asked him how it went, could Werner be trusted. Before he could answer somebody else came past and he shut up quick. Afterwards he put his finger to his mouth, you know, like a shh signal, then slipped me my half of the delivery money. I guess I figured that meant the guy was cool and it didn't need to be discussed.'

'Did Kennedy seem worried, or scared?'

'Nup. He was just the same as ever.'

'Was anyone else in the company involved in this kind of thing, this surreptitious delivering?'

'Not with me.'

'With anyone else?'

He pinched his lip. 'James once said something that made me think other people were doing it too, but I don't know who, or what they were moving.'

'What'd he say?'

'I'd said to him that I hoped we didn't get caught, 'cos we'd be in the shit with Peres, and he said something about more than just us being in the shit.'

Interesting.

Ella said, 'We'll need you to go to our office and make a formal statement about this. Here's the address.' She gave him her card.

He screwed up his face. 'Do you have to tell Peres what I was doing?'

'We won't tell him directly,' Ella said, 'but it might come out at some point.'

Drysdale's face fell.

Ella dialled Kuiper on her mobile before they were out of the building and told him what they'd learned.

'Head on over to Immigration,' Kuiper said. 'I called them earlier, but I'll get onto them again now and let them know you're coming.'

She ended the call. 'I'll drive,' she said to Murray.

Kristi's current mosaic job was in a new building on a narrow street on a west-facing slope in Point Piper. Lauren squeezed between a plumber's van and a plasterer's ute parked on the footpath. The glass doors to the foyer were still covered in plastic, the left side propped open with a wedge of two-by-four. Lauren went inside and pressed the lift button. Three radios played different rock stations in apartments nearby, accompanied by the pounding of hammers and the buzz of an electric saw. Lauren shook her hands out by her sides, trying to settle herself down, trying to think of what to say. It wasn't every day you had to tell your sister that her ex was a murderer.

The lift travelled smoothly then opened onto a glass-walled foyer. The harbour views were stunning even through the protective plastic but Lauren didn't pause to look. There were only two apartments on each floor, and the door to 16A stood open. She could hear Felise singing inside, hitting the high notes in a space that sounded like a bathroom. The place smelled of fresh paint.

'Kristi?'

'In here.'

Lauren's shoes squeaked on the polished wood floor of the apartment. Felise ran out to meet her. 'Did you see the sea?' she said.

'I did.'

She took the girl's small warm hand and let her lead her to the bathroom where Kristi was on her knees by a feature wall opposite an empty spa.

'What's up?' Kristi said, gluing a piece of green tile into place.

Lauren briefly squeezed Felise's hand – *give me strength* – then let it go. 'Felise, sweetie, could you take your sketchbook into the other room and draw me a picture of the biggest boat you can see?'

'But I'm doing school.' She pointed to the shower cubicle. Dolls and bears sat around the walls and in the centre was a spread of pencils and a notepad covered in scribble.

'Just for five minutes, please,' Lauren said.

'No.' Felise folded her arms.

'I'm sick of arguing with her this morning,' Kristi said. 'Let her stay.'

'I need to talk to you.'

'So talk.'

Felise sang the rollcall. 'Big Bear and Blue Bear and Little Alice and Benjamin.'

'I can't, like this,' Lauren said. 'Come into the other room.'

'I'm on a deadline.' Kristi selected another piece of tile from an assortment on the floor. 'While she's singing, she's not listening. So just tell me.'

'Freddie Frog and Jumpy Jim,' Felise went on.

Lauren lowered her voice. 'It's about Thomas.'

Kristi was on her feet. 'He wants Felise.'

'No. Listen.' Lauren made her sit beside her on the side of the spa. 'You know the man I told you about the other day, the one I looked after, who told me about what happened to him? Specifically? Remember?'

'I think I know what you're talking about,' Kristi said.

Felise had turned around and was watching them.

Lauren lowered her voice even further. 'He told me that Thomas did it.'

Kristi stared at her. 'What?'

'I want to know the secret,' Felise said.

Lauren dropped her voice to a whisper. 'Thomas stabbed that man.'

162

Felise grabbed Kristi's knees. 'Tell me too!'

'Killed him?' Kristi said faintly. The piece of tile fell from her hand and broke on the floor.

'Yes.'

Felise jumped up and down. 'Tell me the secret!'

Lauren pulled her into a hug. 'Just a minute, Flea.'

'How do you know it's *him*?' Kristi said.

Felise struggled in Lauren's grip. 'It's not fair!'

'He rang me,' Lauren said. 'He told me to withdraw my statement or else.'

'Or else what?'

Lauren said, 'Don't even ask.'

'I want to know the SECRET!' Felise kicked Kristi's leg, and Kristi grabbed her by the arm.

'Do you want a smack?' Kristi's face was pale and her eyes blazed. 'Do you?'

Lauren knew it was a fury born from fear. Felise wrenched her arm free and kicked Kristi's mobile across the floor.

'I swear, Felise, if you've broken that.'

'I don't care!' Felise stamped into the other room and threw herself sobbing on the floor.

Kristi was shaking, tears in her eyes. Lauren squeezed her arm. 'I went to the detective this morning and said I wanted to withdraw my statement because I'd made a mistake. I said I knew somebody by that name and so probably misheard what the victim said, and thought he said this name when he'd really said something else. She said it was a legal document, I couldn't take it back. And they're going to look into him, and they want to talk to you tonight. They want to know if he's been in touch.'

'You didn't tell them that he called?'

'I've only told you and Joe,' she said. 'Joe said I should tell them. I don't know what to do.'

Kristi stared out the plastic-covered window. 'What was his name again?'

'James Kennedy.'

Kristi mouthed the name to herself. 'Did he tell you why?'

'He said he was a bad man, but that was all.'

'The police don't know?'

'Not that I've heard.'

Kristi nodded. 'I think we have to tell them. You said she's coming over tonight? We should tell her then.' She hugged her. 'We've already lost Brendan. I don't want anything to happen to you.'

Lauren smelled her sister's shampoo, felt the warm skin of her cheek. 'Okay.'

'Why won't you tell me the secret?' Felise demanded from the doorway, her face red and streaked with tears.

'We're just talking, honey.' Kristi held out her hand. 'There are no secrets, I promise.'

Maybe just one, Lauren thought, about a dead man and an alley.

Immigration occupied the majority of a tall building in the CBD. Ella and Murray showed their badges to a stern woman at the desk who sent them to the fifteenth floor. There the lift doors opened to a chubby man with a broad smile. 'Ah, detectives. We got your subpoena just now, and the files you need are being retrieved. Perhaps you'd like to wait here.' He showed them an empty office cubicle.

'Great,' Murray said. 'Thanks.'

The man left and they sat down. 'Feels too easy,' Ella said.

'If they want to help us, I'm not arguing.'

'Here you go.' A young woman held out a manila file. Ella took it and thanked her. She put it on the desk and opened the cover, palms sweaty all of a sudden, heart loud in her ears.

They went through the immigration cards and paperwork in quick order, then stared at each other in shock.

'He's not even in the country,' Murray said. 'How can that be?'

Ella grabbed her phone and dialled.

'How'd you go?' Kuiper said. 'Where is he?'

'Still in Austria, as far as we know.'

'What?'

'Last recorded entry was five and a half years ago, departure almost a year later.'

'You're kidding me.'

'I wish,' Ella said. 'It also puts a question mark over Benson Drysdale's head. Was he lying when he said he'd seen Werner six months ago, or is there another Thomas Werner from Austria getting about, or what?'

'Good question,' Kuiper said. 'Look, I've already lined the airport people up to help find him on the tapes as he came through Immigration, so head on over there and we can at least see what the bastard looks like. We'll have to decide later whether to burn

Drysdale as a witness and show him the picture, confirm it's one and the same man.'

'Okay,' she said.

'Anything in the file about what he did when he was here before? Whether he was working, and if so where?'

She thumbed through the file. 'According to his incoming passenger card he was staying at an address in Crows Nest. There are no details of whose place it was, anything like that. He gave a mobile number as his contact while he was here – got a pen?'

'Go,' Kuiper said.

Ella recited the numbers. 'Also, it says he was here on a holiday, so he wasn't supposed to work, and it gives his emergency contact back home as a Mrs Gretel Werner in Vienna.'

'Wife or mother, I wonder,' Kuiper said. 'Thanks. I'll get onto all that. You find that photo then call in again.'

Murray had his head in his hands. 'Where're we off to now?'

'Airport. Find his picture on the tapes.'

'Even if we find it, what then? If he's here on a false passport, he's going to be just about impossible to pin down. He might even have left already. How can we prove he did it if we can't prove he was here?'

'Calm down,' Ella said, though the same thoughts – and more – were rushing through her own head.

So much for cementing my spot in the squad.

★

A surly man escorted Ella and Murray through the bowels of the airport to a small room with a TV and digital player. He slapped a remote on the table and pointed at the buttons. 'Play, stop, pause, fast forward, rewind.' He turned on his heel and went out, yanking the door shut behind him.

Murray sat down in one of the plastic chairs. 'Happy chap.'

Ella stayed on her feet and started the five-year-old recording. The date and time marker in the bottom corner ran forward through the minutes. 'What time do we want?'

Murray opened his notebook. 'Immigration stamped him through at 8.50am.'

Ella fast forwarded. The view was from a camera above the head of an immigration officer. At one edge of the screen she could see the number eight on the desk. 'He did come through booth eight, right?'

Murray nodded.

The minutes whirred by on the counter. People rushed up to the desk, handed over passports and immigration cards, talked at high speed as the immigration officer's head bobbed about and their passport was stamped, then they were through. Ella pressed the button to 'play' once they got close.

When the figures clicked over to eight fifty, a man stepped up to the counter. Ella's back prickled. He had short brown hair, a round face and brown eyes.

'So this is him?' Murray said.

'Keeps his face angled down.'

'Sort of.'

'He does.'

The man in the picture looked at the officer, not up at the camera, and said something in apparent answer to a question. He nodded once. His face was bland, blank. Ella tried to picture him stabbing James Kennedy, his face twisted in – what? Rage, greed, hate? They had yet to learn the reason.

The officer stamped his passport and gave it back to him, and he took it and walked away.

'And that's that.' Murray slapped his notebook down on the table. 'So now we get all the footage since, and sit for hours watching, looking for some-body who looks like him?'

Ella pressed 'rewind', searching for the clearest image of his face. 'Maybe they have software that can match him up.'

Murray made a sceptical noise.

She inspected a single frame. 'This one, do you reckon?'

The man's face was centred in the screen, his eyes attentive on the officer, his mouth closed.

'Looks good.' Murray wrote down the frame number and exact time. 'Now to ask Mr Happy for the print-out.'

'This one you do,' Ella said. 'I'll update Kuiper.'

TWELVE

Lauren lay in bed, exhausted. The sedative she'd taken was pushing her under but her mind was fighting hard. Each time she drifted off, images of the burnt man would fill her head and she'd lurch awake with a deep intake of breath.

She tucked herself up into a ball on her side, pulling her T-shirt down at the back, unwrinkling the boxer shorts under her hip. Across the room the top of the dresser was filled with framed photos and her unfocused gaze travelled over them. Her and Kristi and Brendan, the Christmas that they all got new bikes. Hers was a glittering red ten-speed, Kristi's a banana-seated purple speedster with a flowered basket, while Brendan still had training wheels on his gold mini-BMX and hated not being able to go as fast as them.

Her eyes closed. Her body relaxed. Then the burnt man looked at her from his burnt eyes, clutched her with his burnt hand, and she was awake again.

She sat up and rested her folded arms on her

knees. She felt bad enough before, sick with fear and worry. Fading in and out of consciousness like this was making it worse. She knew it wasn't really because of the burnt man, who she'd helped as much as she could, but because of Thomas. The burnt man was a . . . what was the term? She was so tired she couldn't think straight. A symbol. That was it. He was a symbol of Thomas's threat. Every time she saw him she knew she was really seeing Kristi, or Felise. Or herself.

She pressed her chin into the crook of her arm. Maybe she should take another sleeper, really knock herself out. She'd be a zombie that evening but at least she'd get an hour or two's rest.

She got out of bed and padded barefoot to the kitchen. The house was warm and sunlit, and she could hear cars driving past on the street outside and the hoot of a train horn up at the station. She poured a cup of water from the heavy glass jug they kept in the fridge then heard a noise behind her.

By the time she turned Thomas was on her. She caught a glimpse of a blade in his left hand slashing down towards her in an arc. She flung up her right arm and the glass jug struck his forearm, the impact jarring her hand so that she almost lost her grip. Icy water splashed over them both. His momentum slammed her into the cupboards and for a second his shoulder was against her face, his T-shirt reeking of chemicals and smothering her. Then she felt him move and knew he was swinging the knife in again. She screamed 'Fire!' and brought the jug up sharply to the side of his head. The jug handle was wet and slippery and she fought to keep her grip as he forced her back against the cupboards again, the blow jolting her back. 'Fire! Fire!'

Thomas grunted and pushed her hard against the benchtop. She was hyper-aware of his left arm, aware of the movement of his shoulder, knew he'd be trying to bring the knife in from behind for a clear shot at her lungs, her heart, but the microwave at her back blocked his thrust. She worked her right arm around behind him and brought the jug up to the back of his head, but it struck only a glancing blow then hit her own face. Thomas tried to push her sideways, clear of the microwave, but his feet slipped on the wet floor.

'Lauren?' There was pounding on the front door downstairs. 'Lauren!'

Ziyad from next door.

'Fire!' she screamed. She swung the jug up again and this time felt the thud through Thomas's body. He faltered and she hit him again. She heard the knife clatter to the floor and felt the warm spatter of blood on her forearm behind his back.

Thomas staggered. She hurled herself at him and swung the jug at his face but he fended her off with his forearm. She slipped on the water and fell, hitting her head on the leg of a chair.

'Lauren!' There was heavy thudding at the door.

Thomas scrambled to the front window. Lauren struggled to get to her feet as he shoved the window up and climbed out. She clung to the back of the chair and heaved the jug at him as he clambered out the window but it smashed against the sill as he disappeared onto the awning.

'Lauren! For god's sake let me in!' Downstairs, Ziyad was going hoarse.

Thomas would go from the awning down the tree, there was no other way off. Ziyad was a big guy. Thomas was injured and had no knife. Lauren stumbled down the stairs and scrabbled at the lock.

'Watch out at the tree!'

'Are you okay?' Ziyad said through the door. 'The fire brigade's coming.'

The lock wouldn't turn. Her fingers slipped off it. 'The tree!'

'What?'

The lock slid open. Ziyad burst in and knocked Lauren onto the floor. 'Shit, sorry. Are you okay? Where's the fire?'

'The man.' Lauren pointed a shaky hand to the open doorway. The sunlight was blinding in contrast to the gloom of the ground floor.

'What man?' He carried a small fire extinguisher with a dented bottom rim. 'Are you all right? There's blood on you.'

'In the tree. Getting away.'

Ziyad went and looked. 'There's nobody out there.' A siren wailed in the distance. 'Where's the fire?'

'In the tree! The man!' She felt sick and weak.

'There's nobody there,' he said. He started up the stairs.

'There's no fire.' Lauren lay back, exhausted. 'Call the police.'

He pulled his mobile from his pocket. 'I'll get the ambulance for you too.'

'It's not my blood.' She held up her arm, turning it to show there were no cuts.

'What about that?' He pointed to her side.

She looked down to see a spreading stain on her T-shirt. She rolled onto her side and pulled it up awkwardly, starting to feel pain now across her back. 'How bad is it?'

Ziyad turned white.

'Sit down,' Lauren said. Ziyad swayed on his feet. 'Sit.' His legs gave way and he folded onto the floor. 'Roll onto your side,' she said. 'Don't look if it makes you feel worse. Lie there with your face near the door for the air.'

He groaned. 'Your back.'

'Don't think about it,' she said weakly. 'Give me your phone.'

He held it out behind him with a shaking hand.

'Big deep breaths and you'll be okay.' Lauren rested a shaking hand on his calf while dialling Kristi's mobile with the other. The sirens were close, and she could hear the roar of the fire truck's engine.

'You have to come home,' she said when Kristi answered. 'You have to come right now.'

Ella opened the file on Alan Harvey then closed it again. 'If we showed that still from the tape to Drysdale, we'd know for sure whether Werner was here six months ago.'

'Harvey's an equally valid lead.'

'No, he's not,' she said. 'Harvey's just something that has to be looked into.'

Murray took a corner nice and slowly. 'You're so impatient.'

I'll ignore that. Ella opened the file again and started to flip through it. 'Look at all this stuff.'

Murray glanced over.

'We've got Alan Harvey's record – one disorderly conduct and resist arrest back in seventy-nine. We've got the PM report on Karen Harvey and the hospital reports on their injured son. We've got the full report of the prang including copies of photos; we've got witness statements by every man and his dog; we've even got a copy of the insurance documents listing the contents of Kennedy's van and what was damaged.' Ella ran her finger down the list. 'Says here Kennedy was carting supplies to a florist – one box of ornamental glass vases shattered, two boxes of something called oasis undamaged, two rolls of plastic wrap and one each of purple and pink paper undamaged; to a toy distributor – two boxes of snow domes undamaged, one of small plastic dolls and one of children's assorted costumes ditto; and to a medical centre – a box of dressing kits, boxes of needles and syringes of various sizes, boxes of urine sample jars–'

'Nice.'

'–all undamaged. No computers or parts thereof.'

'Not listed, anyway.' Murray slowed, looking at the houses. 'What number is it?'

'Thirty.'

The house was small and neat, the white-painted woodwork a pleasant contrast with the red brick. Murray parked a few spaces along and Ella straightened the pages and closed the file before getting out.

The sun was hot but in the shade of the Harveys' verandah the air was cooler. Ella knocked on the door and waited.

There was the sound of locks sliding back then the door opened. The man who looked out appeared older than his forty-seven years. 'Yes?'

'Mr Alan Harvey?'

'Yes.'

'I'm Detective Ella Marconi, this is Detective Murray Shakespeare. Could we come in, please?'

'May I ask why?'

'James Kennedy is dead,' she said.

'And that's got to do with me how?'

'It would be better if we could talk inside.'

He paused for a moment then shrugged.

The cane sofa in the living room creaked when Ella and Murray sat down. Alan Harvey took a single chair opposite but looked past them at the dark television. Ella glanced over to see the family photos lined up on top of it. The woman with her arms around the two young boys had a brilliant smile.

'You know who Kennedy is?' she said, just to be clear.

'Of course.'

'You don't seem surprised to hear that he's dead,' Murray said.

'Man drove like a maniac,' Harvey said. 'It was only a matter of time.'

Ella said, 'It wasn't a car accident. He was attacked on the street.'

'Oh.' Again that look at the photos.

'How does that make you feel?' Murray said.

'Did he have a family?'

Ella nodded.

'Then it's tragic, no matter how I might person-ally have felt about the man.'

There was a noise behind them. Ella looked around to see a boy of about twelve standing in the doorway. His head was partly shaved and a line of staples was visible down the left side of his scalp.

'Evan, go back to bed, please,' Alan Harvey said.

'But I'm hungry.'

'Go,' Harvey said. 'I'll bring you some Milo and biscuits in a minute.'

The boy turned and walked away. Ella waited a moment but Harvey didn't speak. 'Mr Harvey,' she said, 'where were you on Tuesday night, between eight thirty and nine?'

'I was here.'

'Can anybody vouch for that?'

'My sons were here too, asleep in bed.'

'Nobody else?'

He pointed at the doorway. 'That's my son Evan. He suffered a head injury in the crash that Kennedy caused. He's got a shunt in his brain now, and every so often it gets blocked and he needs more surgery. Tuesday was his first day out of hospital. He's more prone to fits in the few days after the procedures, and the fits can be fatal, so there is no way in the world I would have left him and my other, younger, son alone in the house.'

Murray moved forward on the sofa. 'But you understand why we're here.'

'Anyone in my shoes would've made the same comments.'

'They were threats.'

'The man was a professional driver,' Harvey said. 'He should be better at it than the rest of us. He should be held to a higher standard. The man drives through a red light because he's looking at a street directory and he kills my wife and ruins my son's life and he gets a fine and a licence suspension. Put yourself in my position.'

Ella cleared her throat. 'Do you know a man named Thomas Werner?'

'No, I don't.'

'Dad.' The boy was back in the doorway.

Harvey stood up. 'I'm coming, Ev. We're finished here.'

Outside in the hot car Murray put the key in the ignition but didn't start it. 'What do you reckon?'

'He hated him but I don't think he had anything to do with it,' Ella said.

'Coulda hired Werner as a hitman.'

'Coulda left the kids alone and snuck out, or coulda got a babysitter too.' Ella wound down her window. 'And he'll probably raise a glass tonight, but I still don't think he was involved.'

Murray started the car. 'Might take some of the anger away at last.'

Ella's phone rang. Kuiper said, 'Are you finished with Harvey?'

'Just done now,' she said. 'He says he was at home on Tuesday with his kid who'd just had an operation. You want us to check that with the hospital?'

'No. Get on over to your paramedic's house.'

Ella's scalp tightened at his tone. 'What happened?'

'Somebody broke in and attacked her.'

Murray had to park well down the block from Lauren's house because of the police vehicles lined up along the kerb. Ella was out of the car before he'd yanked the handbrake on. She hurried up the footpath with her pulse going hard in her throat.

A uniformed officer stood guard near the step. The door was dotted with semi-circular dents, some with fragments of red paint embedded in the timber. Ella flashed her badge at the officer. 'They're all okay?'

He nodded. 'They're next door. Detectives are upstairs.'

Ella stepped carefully inside the door, avoiding the bloodstains on the floor. A woman appeared at the top of the stairs. 'Ella? Come on up.'

Sascha Ninkovic had worked at Newtown with Ella, way back when. Now she was with the Summer Hill detectives. Ella made her way up the stairs and paused at the top. Sascha stood with another detective on one side of the room, making notes. A Crime Scene officer was taking photographs and another one was crouched by the window. Ella looked around the room, taking in the open fridge, the open window, the shards of glass, the blood on the floor and the kitchen bench and the windowsill.

'You're certain she's okay?' she asked.

'Shit, yeah,' Sascha said. 'Says she doesn't even need hospital. Got her para mates to patch her up.'

Ella was embarrassed to feel tears of relief welling up.

Murray peered over her shoulder. 'Jesus, what happened?'

'He came in through a window at the back of downstairs there,' Sascha said. 'Pried it out of its frame and climbed on through. The occupant—'

'Lauren,' Ella said.

'Yeah, Lauren, she came into the kitchen to get a drink and was attacked from behind. She had a glass jug in her hand and kept belting him as he was trying to stab her. They were right up close to the bench there next to the fridge. You can see the marks of the knife blade on the side of the microwave.'

Ella looked at the shiny scratches in the paint and the knife on the floor. It was a single-sided blade, so not the one used to stab James Kennedy.

'Meanwhile she's screaming out "Fire!" at the top of her lungs.'

'Why fire?' Murray said.

'It gets attention quicker,' Ella said. 'Scream help, people are nervy, they worry about getting involved in something dangerous. Scream fire and people think it's safe. Plus, fires are interesting. They come running.'

'As her neighbour did,' Sascha said. 'He tried to belt the door down with a fire extinguisher. Eventually Lauren hurt her attacker bad enough that he dropped the knife and ran.' She pointed to the window. 'Went out there, across the awning, down the tree, timing it by happy accident that Lauren's neighbour was by then inside the front door and didn't see him. We've got a blood trail from his head wound heading up the street though, to a spot where we believe he had a car parked. We have people canvassing for witnesses.'

Ella said, 'She say who it was?'

Sascha nodded. 'Your boy Thomas Werner. She's got more stuff to tell you too.'

'What stuff?' Murray said.

'She wouldn't say.'

THIRTEEN

Ella and Murray went next door. The woman who answered their knock was in her mid-twenties and had long black hair tied up in a knot and held in place with a silver pin. She held out a slim and trembling hand and introduced herself as Tamsyn Saleeba. 'It was my husband, Ziyad, who heard Lauren screaming.'

'He really helped her,' Ella said.

'It's still so hard to believe it's happened. I don't think it's sunk in for any of us,' Tamsyn said.

'They're all here now?' Ella said.

'Ziyad's keeping the kids entertained in the back-yard. Lauren and Kristi are in the living room.' She led them to the doorway. 'Can I get you something? Tea? Coffee?'

'We're fine, thanks.'

Ella went into the living room to find Lauren perched bolt upright on the edge of the lounge, her gaze fixed on the opposite wall. Kristi sat beside her, folding and refolding a damp-looking tissue. She looked up at them but Lauren didn't.

'Lauren,' Ella said gently. 'How are you?'

Lauren blinked and focused on her. 'Good,' she said. 'Okay.'

Ella sat down in an armchair at right angles to their lounge while Murray dragged a chair over from the dining suite that occupied one end of the room. Directly opposite Ella, French doors looked out onto a backyard where a checked tea-towel flag flew above a ramshackle cubbyhouse. A tall man with dark hair sat precariously on a tiny plastic chair, along with a stocky brown-haired boy in a school uniform and a little blonde girl. The girl sipped from a toy teacup and the boy poured nothing from a toy teapot into the cup the man held between his thumb and fore-finger. Tamsyn Saleeba crossed the lawn to stroke the children's heads.

'I'm sorry that this happened,' Ella said. 'Do you feel up to talking about it again?'

Lauren nodded. 'We need to catch him.'

'Him being . . .'

'Thomas Werner.'

Murray produced the photo they'd got at the air-port. 'Is this him?'

Both Lauren and Kristi looked and nodded.

Ella clenched her fists. 'Can you first run over what happened today?'

Lauren told her the story that Sascha had already outlined, adding in the detail about how the jug glanced off Werner's head and hit her own, causing the bruise and swelling that Ella could see on her right forehead, and how she hit her head on the chair. 'If I hadn't slipped, maybe my aim would've been better when I threw the jug. Maybe I would've been able to stop him.'

Kristi shook her head.

'What other injuries did you sustain?' Ella said.

Lauren lifted her hair to show them the swelling on her temple from the chair, then stood and turned and lifted her shirt. A dressing ran at an angle over her lumbar and right hip area, held in place by a wide bandage that wrapped around her torso. 'It's not even deep enough to stitch. I was very lucky.'

Kristi huddled over her knees. Ella felt shaky herself. She looked out at the yard. The little girl glanced in at them now and then, distracted from the tea party.

'I need to tell you something else.' Lauren sat down. 'Thomas rang me yesterday and threatened to burn our house down if I didn't withdraw my statement about what Kennedy said.'

Ella and Murray exchanged glances. The details of Kennedy's dying words had not been released to the media.

'Who had you spoken to about the case?' Murray said.

'Only Joe, who was there,' Lauren said. 'And you, and the uniformed officer at the hospital. I told Kristi today.'

Ella looked at Kristi.

'Who'm I going to tell?' Kristi snapped.

'We have to ask.'

Kristi put her head down again. 'I haven't spoken to anyone about any of it.'

'What's Joe like?' Ella said.

'He wouldn't tell a soul,' Lauren said.

They had to consider a leak then. Maybe in the department, or somebody in the hospital perhaps. Ella understood why Lauren had been hesitant to tell her: a threat was a threat, and if Werner had learned that much, who knew what else he could find out.

'There's more,' Lauren said. 'Six months or so ago, I found a body in an alley.'

'The Blake case,' Ella said.

Lauren nodded. 'That was Thomas too. He was still there. He attacked me and threatened to get me if I told that I'd seen him. I knew who the victim was; I thought the best thing was to do what he said. So I told the officers I saw nothing.'

Ella's head was spinning. Thomas Werner was a double-murderer . . . Even more reason to get him. But now Lauren's status as a witness was compromised.

'Do you realise what you're admitting?' she said.

'I felt that you needed to know everything,' Lauren said.

'We do,' Murray put in.

'When we get to court, this is going to come out,' Ella said. 'The defence will try to say you're lying about everything because you lied about that. Also, the Blake case will be reopened, they'll interview you again, you could be charged with perjury.'

Lauren took a deep breath then winced, a hand at her back. 'I understand.'

Ella looked down at her notebook. What she didn't say was that the risk to Lauren was probably greater than they could have imagined. She was the key witness who could put Werner away for two murders. He'd already made one attempt on her life, just a day after making the initial threat. What would he do next?

'Kristi, I need to ask you some questions too. Are you okay for that?'

The woman nodded curtly.

'You lived with Thomas Werner, is that correct?'

'About five years ago, yes,' she said. 'We had a flat in the Cross. We were there for about nine or ten months.'

'How did you meet?'

'At a club in the city, the Marble Bar. I was in with a group of—'

'Drug-users,' Lauren said.

'Well, yes,' Kristi said. 'I'm clean now, have been since the car accident. I don't even drink. I'm a professional mosaic artisan and it's important to keep my head clear.'

'When did you last see Thomas Werner?'

'Just before the car accident,' Kristi said. 'Just over four years ago. I was pregnant with Felise. After the accident I was kept in hospital until she was born, and then she needed heart surgery. He never showed up. Lauren went round to the flat but he'd gone. Then we got a letter from him in Austria saying that he'd been deported for overstaying his visa and he was sorry but he could never come back.'

There'd been nothing about deportation in Werner's Immigration file.

'We didn't believe that but we didn't care,' Lauren said. 'We wanted nothing to do with him.'

'And there's been no contact since? Not even a phone call?'

Kristi shook her head. 'Until he called Lauren yesterday.'

'Did you know he was back in Australia? Had any of your friends seen or heard from him?'

'I don't have any contact with anybody from those days,' Kristi said. 'It was a complete clean break.'

'We'll need their contact details,' Ella said.

'I threw out my address book from back then, but I'll give you what I can remember.' Kristi looked out the window to where Felise was laughing on the swing. 'Alice Leslie and Reynaldo Gamboa were probably the core of our group. He was this small, intense, shaven-headed South American. Alice was red-haired and towered over him. They lived in a share-house on South Dowling Street, I can't remember the number but it was a big purple place, on the Paddington side.'

Ella scribbled notes. 'Go on.'

'Chrystal Fowler – that's spelled with an "h" – and Amos Lucas and Bekka Van Sprang – two words – had a flat in Darlinghurst, in Liverpool Street. Awful scuzzy place. Though ours was no better.' She shrugged. 'That's it.'

'And you haven't seen any of these people for more than four years?'

'Chrystal sent me a card in hospital when Felise was born, but that was all,' she said. 'I didn't try to contact them because of the clean break thing, you know.'

Ella nodded. 'We need to go and talk to our boss

186

about all of this, but I'll come back afterwards and let you know what will happen. First steps will be to put surveillance in place, along with a tap on your phone in case Werner rings again.'

'So if he comes around again, you'll catch him?' Kristi said.

'We'll be waiting.' Ella smiled at her but Kristi didn't smile back. 'Crime scene will be in your house for an hour yet, maybe two, then you can go back in.'

'But we're not going to stay there tonight, are we?' Kristi said to Lauren.

Ella said, 'I understand your fears, but it's best if you can keep to your normal routine as much as possible. This includes being at home, travelling your usual route to work, that sort of thing.'

'So you're using us as bait,' Kristi said.

Lauren said, 'They need to catch him.'

'Like I said, I'll be back later to go over the details with you,' Ella said. 'In the meantime, there will be officers next door, and you can call me with any questions or worries. Anything at all.'

She gave Lauren another of her cards. She wanted to say something about how well Lauren did to fight Werner off, but it felt a silly comment to make when the woman had been fighting for her life. *Congratulations, you survive!* No.

'Are you okay for now?' she said. 'Is there anything else you want to discuss?'

Lauren shook her head. Kristi was at the French windows, looking out at the children who were wrestling Ziyad to the ground.

'We'll see you soon then.'

Outside, in the car, Ella found she was shaking. The case was turning into a monster. Two murders plus an attempted, a leak somewhere, and a foreigner in the country on a fake passport. Talk about something to get your teeth into. But caught in the middle of it all was Lauren, who'd already almost paid with her life.

Murray started the car and Ella clipped in her seatbelt. She looked up at the old house as they drove away. Surveillance was good, phone taps were useful for court, but a determined man could find a way to get what he wanted.

Lauren sat in the doorway of the cubbyhouse, holding a wrapped icepack to her head. She had to keep her back straight or the wound stung. She leaned her shoulder sideways against the frame and watched Felise and Max pretending to be puppies and gambolling on the grass.

Kristi and Tamsyn were in the kitchen. Through the open doorway she could see them talking. Kristi was crying. Tamsyn smoothed Kristi's hair back and folded her into a hug.

Lauren looked at her feet. Her first thought after it happened had been to call Kristi, but when she'd arrived Lauren hadn't been able to handle her distress. She'd found herself keeping Kristi at arm's length, as if to bring her close was to be dragged down into a whirlpool of panic. Kristi was hurt, and scared, anyone could see that, but Lauren felt like she was struggling for every breath, every heartbeat. That took all the energy she had and more. She was drained.

Ziyad was on the bottom step, beside her feet. 'Sure you don't want a beer?'

'Thanks, no.'

He rested his elbows on his knees and picked at the edge of the label on his bottle. The late-afternoon sun shone across their roofs, making the chimneys cast black shadows on the red tiles. The pigeons preened themselves on the ridge capping. The crime scene people were still in her living room, and she felt a swelling bubble of something – grief? pain? fear? – push up inside her chest.

She tried to put her head down on her folded arms but the wound pulled at her back.

'Hi.'

She looked up. Joe stepped down from the back door, a smile on his face and worry in his eyes. 'Kristi called me, told me you'd been up to mischief.'

'You know me.' She met him with a hug, frightened a little by the strength of her emotions towards him. She made herself let go and step back.

'Those cops are leaving.' He pointed a thumb at their house. 'I thought I might borrow a mop and bucket and see what I could do.'

'I'll help,' Ziyad said.

'And keel over again?' Lauren said. 'No way. I'll go.'

Joe shook his head. 'You should stay here, continue your life of luxury in the doorway of your mansion.'

'It's nothing I haven't seen before.'

'Ah, but it is.' Joe touched the bruise on her temple with a gentle thumb. 'You're unbelievable, you are. I leave you alone for a few hours and look what happens.' The tremble in his voice made her heart ache.

'We'll do it together.' She looped her arm through his.

Kristi was in the bathroom when they went through the house. Lauren was glad not to see her.

Next door they found the last of the crime scene officers packing up his gear. 'There are a couple of commercial companies who can clean up for you,' he said.

'We're right, thanks,' Joe said.

The officer shook both their hands. 'All the best.'

Lauren closed the front door then led Joe upstairs. He went into the kitchen and looked around. Lauren saw the water, the blood, the glass, and for the first time the scrapes on the microwave. She tried to blink back her tears.

Joe came close. 'If you die, I'll be very annoyed.'

She tried to laugh. He wrapped his arms around her and she buried her face in his shirt and let the bubble of grief and fear and pain explode into sobs.

The HR girl wheeled a clean whiteboard into the meeting room. 'Thanks, Trace,' Kuiper said, pulling it to the centre and writing LAUREN YATES across the top.

'So you all heard what Marconi just said,' Kuiper

said, looking around at the detectives. 'First things first: we no longer discuss the case with anyone outside this room. Anybody who asks you questions, who seems particularly interested, I want you to let me know. Finding the mole could be our best link to finding Werner himself. I'll be talking with DI Radtke after this, but I don't doubt there will be outside detectives brought in to assess the situation also.'

Ella knew this was standard procedure in such circumstances.

Kuiper went on. 'Lauren Yates was certain that it was Thomas Werner who phoned her yesterday and attacked her today, and Benson Drysdale stated he met a man with the same name in James Kennedy's company six months ago. However, Immigration shows the last recorded entry of Werner's passport was just over five years ago, with an exit date of a year later. We've sent a request to Interpol for information on his record and to ascertain his whereabouts. Meantime, however, we'll have surveillance on the Yates house and a tap on their landline, and we're getting the records of calls in and out to see if we can track down where he called from. Lauren is to be followed to work, and followed home at the end of each shift. While she's at work she's to remain in the company of at least one other person. She'll be given a tracker device also. Marconi, I want you to explain all that to her, and keep in regular contact throughout each day. Make sure she knows she's not alone, that she can get help whenever she needs it.'

Ella nodded.

'Now, the case is still proceeding along other

avenues. I believe we've got some info from around Steyne Park, Strong?'

Detective Graeme Strong cleared his throat. 'The canvass of the area near where Kennedy's motorbike was found turned up a witness who says she saw him park his bike then walk into the park and sit on a bench, at about twenty to seven Tuesday night. She didn't see him leave though. Latest news, however, is that I just took a call from a wheelchair-bound resident in a house on Ocean Avenue, who arrived home from hospital today to find our card under her door. She spends most of her time watching the people coming and going in the park, and believes she's seen Kennedy's motorbike there often over the last couple of months, and that she's seen Kennedy meeting a woman in the park.'

A murmur went round the room. Ella jotted a sentence in her notebook and embellished it with a love heart around a question mark. The most common reason for murder was love or lust or whatever you wanted to call it, and the jealousy or anger that resulted when it was thwarted. She wondered how it fitted with Thomas Werner.

'Furthermore, she believes this woman to be a local. She's seen her in the park often, with a small brown dog of indeterminate breed. The description she gave of the woman is as follows.' Strong paused and people bent over their notebooks. 'Tall, at least as tall as Kennedy, who we know to be a metre seventy-five. Skinny. Cropped dark hair so short it's almost a crewcut. Usually wears long shorts and shirts with no sleeves.'

'How does she know it's Kennedy?'

'She described him and the bike and his work uniform as well,' Strong said.

'She should be put on the payroll,' someone said.

'She told me she's very active in Neighbourhood Watch,' Strong said with a grin. 'Unfortunately she was in hospital last Tuesday, so we don't know if Kennedy was meeting the mystery woman then too.'

'Any pattern to his earlier visits, was she aware?'

'She said it was usually a weekday evening, but on all different days.'

Kuiper turned from the whiteboard. 'Kanowski, how's Deborah Kennedy coming along?'

'She's worse, if anything,' Detective Rebecca Kanowski said. 'Her daughter Tess took her to a doctor for sedatives. When I talk to her she's in a fog, and nothing gets through. Her daughter can't tell me anything about their financial and legal matters either.'

'We need that info.'

She nodded. 'I talked to the doctor this afternoon and he said that by tomorrow he expects her to have stabilised and be able to talk to me.'

Kuiper tapped his watch.

'I know,' she said.

'Okay, tasks,' Kuiper said. 'Pilsiger, get onto the hospitals, medical centres, doctors – find out about any men coming in with head wounds that could match the one Werner suffered. Lambert and Hoskins, check out the list of friends that Kristi Yates described. Marconi and Shakespeare, tonight you go talk to Lauren again, then in the morning check out the Crows Nest address Werner listed on his incoming passenger card. The mobile number he wrote down as his contact belongs to a Jules Cartwright of that address. Computer says she's still there.

'Hopefully by tomorrow we'll also have some info from the canvass the local Ds are doing of the street where the blood trail from Lauren's house ended. Fingers crossed for a witness who saw Werner get into a car and then wrote down the plate. The rest of you continue on with the tasks you've already got, and we'll meet here again tomorrow.'

FOURTEEN

Kristi stood in the dark, looking out the front window. 'I can't see them.'

'You're not meant to,' Lauren said. 'That's the whole point.'

'I would've thought the point was to make it obvious that they're there so he won't try it again.'

'They want to catch him.'

'By dangling you on a hook.' Kristi snorted. 'What's the good of having somebody watch the house and follow you to work, when you then spend the day out and about in a big white truck, vulnerable to everything?'

'Out and about is the key,' Lauren said. 'How can he corner us when we're mobile like that? What's he going to do – stalk me in public? Kill me in the middle of the CBD?'

'Yeah, like nobody ever dies on the street.'

'Joe's with me, and I've got this tracking device to carry, plus I ring them and they ring me all through the day.'

'Joe's a target too,' Kristi said. 'We shouldn't stay here.'

'With them outside and Joe staying over I think we're okay.'

'I don't just mean tonight. The next few weeks or however long it takes them to find him,' Kristi said. 'We should go to Mum and Dad's.'

'Dad's only just home from the clinic. Having us there would be too much too soon.'

'We'll stay in a motel in the town then,' she said.

'Thomas knows they live in Glen Innes,' Lauren said. 'It'd be the first place he'd look.'

Kristi turned to the window again. 'We're sitting ducks.'

'It's going to be okay.'

'But what if it isn't?' Kristi pressed her hands to her eyes. 'I keep thinking about Brendan.'

Lauren thought about him a lot too. He'd been living in Narrabeen with his girlfriend, but they'd broken up and he'd moved back to their childhood home in Strathfield for a while. As prone to depression as their father, he'd shifted his stuff into the garage and kept the doors closed and the music loud on his headphones. All through a week of all four of them – Lauren, Kristi, their mother and father – trying to talk to him, he refused to see any of them. And then one day it was too quiet in there, and their father had forced the door while their mother had tried to hold back tears of worry, and they found that it was too late. Lauren remembered laughing with some other paramedics in the driveway of Royal Prince Alfred Hospital, and seeing their area boss approach, looking sombre, and that moment when he touched her arm, and his words sinking in.

'I can't lose you too,' Kristi said.

'You're not going to.'

'Then don't go to work. Stay home, stay where the police can watch over us. We'll have them come inside. He won't try anything if they're in the house.'

'If I'd stood up six months ago and told the truth we wouldn't be in this position now,' Lauren said gently. 'I deserve to take some risk.'

'No, you don't. You made a mistake, that's all. You don't deserve anything, and even if you did, what happened today was enough.'

She was rambling. Lauren tried to keep her voice reasonable. 'They'll probably find the leak and get him that way. He'll be locked up before we know it and everything will go back to normal.'

'Why didn't you tell me about Blake, about Thomas being in the alley?'

'Don't feel left out. I didn't tell anyone.'

'Don't joke.' Kristi sat on the windowsill. 'Felise asked me who Thomas was. She must've overheard us. I told her he was nobody.'

'Good.'

'We'll have to deal with it one day.'

'But not today.'

Down the hall, Joe growled and chased Felise. She screeched in mock fear, then his mobile rang. 'Hang on a second, Flea,' he said.

'Chase me!'

Lauren went into the hall to catch her. 'Give Joe a minute.'

'No, I'm not at home,' Joe said into his phone. He mouthed *Claire* at Lauren. 'I'm at Lauren's.'

Felise struggled in her grasp. 'I want Joe to chase me!'

'Just a second,' Lauren said.

'Somebody broke in this afternoon,' Joe said. 'I came to help clean up and we had dinner and then they asked me to stay the night. It's scary after – Yes, her sister and niece are here too. I'm sleeping in her niece's room.'

Felise flailed and kicked.

Joe said, 'No, I'll go straight to work. I've got a spare uniform at the station.' He listened. 'Okay. Love you too. Bye.'

Lauren let Felise go. 'Is she okay?'

'She's at work.' He put the phone in his pocket as Felise grabbed him around the legs. 'She wanted to meet for breakfast.'

'You don't have to stay.'

'I'm staying, then I'm driving us both to work,' Joe said, picking Felise up. 'That's that.'

'You're so bossy.'

'Hey, somebody needs to keep you in check.'

'Yes, but are you qualified?'

He smiled at her over Felise's head. 'Like you wouldn't believe.'

She felt her heart swell.

Ella got home at eight that night to find a letter bearing the official police crest in her letterbox.

She hurried into her house, locked the door and

pressed her back against it. She'd forgotten about the shooting report since the case began, but this was it, she was sure. The envelope felt flimsy – nothing long then. Probably just one page. She fitted her thumbnail into the corner of the flap then paused, imagining what it would feel like to read the decision she so desperately wanted.

It wasn't merely the fact that her wait would be over. Though she was certain she'd done the right thing – what was she going to do, stand there and watch the kidnapper shoot a defenceless victim? – doubt still niggled. It was because of the seriousness of her actions, she thought. If she'd hit somebody with OC spray, or knocked them off their feet in a struggle, or even broken their arm during an arrest, that was one thing. Here, she'd actually taken somebody's life. To see the service acknowledge that she'd done precisely what was necessary would remove that doubt from her mind, lift that weight from her shoulders.

If they said otherwise, however, if they found that she wasn't justified in the shooting, then she had not only disciplinary problems to face but could see herself bowed down by guilt forever.

The envelope was going soft from the sweat on her palms. *I can always appeal.* In the meantime though, she'd be out of Homicide. Taken off her big case.

She gritted her teeth and tore the flap open.

Officer Marconi, it began. *Re: the investigation into Case 40762.*

Ella held her breath.

Due to a backlog of cases and a temporary staffing shortage, a decision on your case has been delayed for approximately twelve weeks.

We apologise for any inconvenience.

Ella stared across the room. *They apologise!* Here she'd been, standing on the brink for what felt like forever, looking forward to a resolution, and now she was going to have to wait three more months?

She read the letter again, then picked up the phone.

Dennis Orchard answered on the first ring. 'I've been expecting your call.'

'I can't believe this,' Ella said.

'Don't sound so worried.'

'But what's it mean?'

'All it means is what it says.' There was a rustle of paper as he handled his own letter. 'There's a backlog, a staff problem, they're busy.'

'How come they didn't let us know before now?'

'There's no deadline on these things,' he said.

'Well, I reckon there's more to this than meets the eye,' she said. 'Maybe they've got some new evidence, something new to nail me with.'

'They interviewed everybody who was there,' Dennis said. 'It's not like they've found a new witness or some CCTV's suddenly turned up.'

Ella crumpled the letter into a ball.

'It's nothing,' Dennis went on. 'They're busy. You have to forget about it. Think about your case instead.'

That was a point. With the verdict delayed, there

was no reason to move her. She could concentrate on Werner. The delay simply made a strong performance even more necessary.

'How's it going? You catch him yet?'

'The trail's hotting up.' Her call waiting beeped. 'I'd better get that.'

'Could be a development,' he said. 'Talk to you tomorrow.'

It was her mother. 'Hello, sweetie, how are you?'

'Busy with work, you know.'

'We thought you must be when you didn't come for visiting today,' Netta said. 'I'm well too. Back to normal. I could run down the halls if they let me.'

'Mum, don't even think about it.'

'Did you ask about your leave?'

'I can't, Mum, I'm sorry. The case just got bigger and there's no way I can get time off.'

'Bigger how? Why?'

'I can't talk about it,' Ella said. 'I'm sorry.'

'I understand.' Netta sighed. 'Will you visit tomorrow?'

'I'll try, okay?'

Later, in bed, she couldn't sleep. She thought of Lauren in that big house, the downstairs window barricaded up now, the smell of disinfectant strong in the kitchen where they'd cleaned up the blood. Usually it was best to limit the number of people who knew about their surveillance plans, but she'd asked Lauren's work colleague Joe to sit in while she ran through it. He was just as involved, after all, plus he'd be the one she'd be staying close to when avoiding being alone at work.

Lauren's sister hadn't been happy. This was the problem with such operations. You didn't have the staff or the money to stick two officers either side of the person until the bad guy was caught. Life had to go on. You sized up the risk; and in this case, there was a strong chance that Werner would turn up injured somewhere, or that he would figure out – or know already, if the mole knew – that surveillance was in place and decide it was too dicey to try another attack. Ella was torn. Another phone call, traced by the tap, or another assault on the house could be their best chance for grabbing him. But she'd seen the look in Lauren's eyes and knew the woman couldn't take much more, regardless of the front she was putting up.

The next morning Joe pulled up outside The Rocks station. 'And there they go.'

The brown unmarked sedan went past slowly, the officer in the passenger seat giving them a nod. Lauren raised a hand in reply. The car drove along George Street, under the bridge and out of sight.

The station doors were down, night shift still out somewhere. Lauren saw Joe looking in all directions as she got stiffly out of the car, one hand at her back.

'You should've called in sick,' he said.

'And let you roam the streets on your own? Anyway, I'd go nuts cooped up at home.'

He walked behind her to the door, tested it first, then let her in. He locked the door then made her wait while he searched the station.

'You'd better relax or you'll have a stroke,' she said.

'Didn't we decide I'm the boss?'

'Ha.' She called Kristi's mobile. 'We're here.'

'No sign?' Felise squealed in the background, and Lauren could hear Ziyad chasing her.

'Not a thing,' she said. 'Ziyad's not going to get much work done with you in his house.'

'She'll settle down soon,' Kristi said. 'Keep safe. Ring me later.'

The station phone rang and Joe answered. Lauren went to her locker as Joe took the message. The bruises on her head throbbed when she bent for her work bag.

Joe hung up. 'Vaucluse, a diver, query code four.'

They went for the keys at the same time.

'I thought you might prefer a break,' he said. 'You've got a lot on your mind.'

'It's my turn.'

'I might be a specially trained Navy stunt driver, for all you know.'

'We're not going to end up in a car chase through the CBD.' She wiggled her fingers at the keys. 'Give.'

In the ambulance she turned on the lights and siren and roared out of the station. She belted through the streets of The Rocks, then doglegged east until she hit William Street. Joe was looking in fifty directions at once, including his side mirror.

She said, 'Where in Vaucluse?'

'Off Steel Point.'

'*Off?*'

'Still in the water, apparently.'

'They're just letting him bob about in there?'

'Caller thought things looked suspicious. He actually asked for the cops, said the guy is dead as, but they thought it best to send us anyway.'

Lauren screeched around a corner.

Joe braced against the door and glanced at the speedo. 'Guy won't get any deader before we arrive.'

'Guy's not dead till I say he is.'

Joe checked his mirror and didn't reply.

Most of the traffic was coming against them, which made for some hairy on-the-wrong-side-of-the-road moments as Lauren overtook buses and slow trucks, but was otherwise a relatively easy drive. Joe got out the street directory and guided her into Vaucluse, along a narrow twisting street to a park. Beyond it the green water lay heavy in the harbour. Joe switched the siren off.

Lauren turned into the driveway into the park and found two metal poles in settings in the concrete blocking their way. She could see padlocks at their base. 'We got keys for those?'

Joe shook his head.

The police obviously didn't either. A marked car was parked on the beachfront path beyond the poles and Lauren could see the tyre marks on the grass where the officer had driven. She followed, working the ambulance up the kerb then down again, then flipped off the lights and stepped on the brake.

A uniformed constable came over and she put the window down. 'Where is he?'

The officer gestured at the lapping water.

'Still?'

'We're waiting for divers and crime scene.'

'We need him out,' she said. 'We might be able to save him.'

'Not according to that guy.' The officer pointed at a skinny man in a worn blue wetsuit who stood on the concrete path facing the sea, his arms folded across his chest and snorkel gear lying by his feet.

'You mean you haven't even seen him?'

The cop shrugged. 'He's like three metres down.'

'Fair enough,' Joe said. 'We'll go talk to this guy.'

The cop went back to his car and Lauren stuck close to Joe as they crossed the grass. Out in the open she felt hyper-sensitive to every noise, every movement that she caught from the corner of her eye. *He can't have followed you here, he couldn't have known you'd come here. He doesn't have a scanner, and anyway you never said your location on the air.*

'Hi,' Joe said to the wetsuited man. 'You found the body?'

The man's straggly hair flapped wetly when he nodded. 'You here to transport it to the morgue?'

'We don't transport bodies,' Lauren said.

'Only on rare occasions,' Joe put in. 'No, the police called us here just in case.'

'Dude's a total goner,' the man said. 'Caught on a rock by a rope, regulator's out of his mouth, he's just rolling back and forth with the sea. Pretty peaceful.'

'I'm sure he was delighted,' Lauren said.

Joe nudged her. 'Thanks,' he said to the man. 'You want a blanket or anything if you're waiting around for the other cops?'

'Nah, I'm right in this.' He patted his wetsuited thighs.

Joe prodded Lauren ahead of him back to the ambulance. 'Relax,' he said. 'Sit in there, lock the doors, listen to some music. I'll deal with all this.'

Lauren's neck was sore from turning her head all the time. She got in the truck and squeezed the wheel hard. 'I thought I was doing good.'

'You are,' he said. 'Shit, most people would be hiding under their bed. You're doing marvellous.'

He shut the door gently and she knocked the button down with her elbow. He winked at her through the glass then walked away. She rested her folded arms on the bottom curve of the wheel while he spoke to the uniformed officer, then to the next batch of cops who turned up, three jumping down from a rescue truck and a couple in civilian clothes getting out of unmarked sedans. Joe obviously knew one of these men, going over to him with a huge grin, shaking hands and talking animatedly. He glanced back at the ambulance often.

Lauren checked the mirrors, touched the tracking device buttoned securely in her shirt pocket, and tried to relax. Sunlight glinted off the water. Most of the beach was contained inside a shark net and a group of elderly women in swimmers stood in the shallows, talking and watching the police with interest.

Joe came over. She unlocked the doors. He climbed into the ambulance's passenger seat, pulled the door shut and locked it, and picked up the microphone. 'Thirty-four to Control.'

'Thirty-four, go ahead.'

'Police are requesting we stay on location until the code four has been retrieved.'

'Thirty-four, thank you. Call me when you're clear on that.'

'Copy.'

Joe racked the mike and looked at her. She stared out the windscreen at the police. 'You know that guy, huh.'

'Simon Bradshaw,' he said. 'We were in the Navy together, years ago. He just transferred from Penrith to the detectives in here.' He chuckled. 'Small world.'

Three police pulled on blue wetsuits and checked their dive gear on the shore. A ferry cut through the green water leaving a churning trail of foam. Passengers crowded along the side. Clouds moved across the sun and over on Middle Head it looked like rain.

The police divers waded into the water. They signalled to each other then went under. Lauren stared at the lines of bubbles.

'What's the guy doing diving here anyway?' She struck at her tears with the back of her hand. 'Alone, and with no flag?'

'It'll be okay,' Joe said.

She shook her head, knowing things would never be okay again.

FIFTEEN

In Crows Nest, Murray found a park in a street off Willoughby Road and they walked back around to the tall sand-coloured block of units. 'Unit twelve,' Ella said, and Murray pressed the buzzer.

They waited. The traffic on the street behind them was loud. Ella went for the buzzer again, a long press. This time the intercom came to life.

'What!' The woman's voice was hoarse.

'Police,' Ella said.

'What?'

'Detectives. We'd like to speak to you for a moment.'

There was a pause. 'I'm coming down.'

They got their badges out. Ella tried to push Lauren from her mind. *She'll be fine.*

The door beside them opened and a woman looked out. She was in her mid-twenties with long curly red hair falling to the shoulders of a tightly cinched dressing gown. 'Yes, you did wake me,' she said.

Ella put her badge in front of the woman's face. 'Are you Jules Cartwright?'

'Yes. Why?'

'You were living here five and a half years ago, is that correct?'

'Yes. Again, why?'

'We're investigating a homicide,' Ella said. 'And we'd like to talk to you inside.'

The woman made a face.

'Or you can come with us to the station, if that's more convenient.'

The woman shoved the door fully open. 'Come on then.'

Her flat was spacious, and dark until she pulled back the living room drapes. 'You may as well sit down.'

'Thanks very much,' Ella said.

Murray got out his notebook. 'Is Jules short for Julia?'

'If it was I would've said so,' Jules said, then apparently hearing the bluntness of her tone added more gently, 'wouldn't I?'

Ella frowned at her. 'Our investigation has turned up an incoming passenger card from five and a half years ago with your address on it. The person we want to speak to wrote that he was staying here.'

She screwed up her face. 'It's too early to think back that far.'

'Try,' Ella said. 'Or do you let so many foreigners put your address down as their next port of call that it's hard to separate them out?'

'Hey,' Jules snapped, then stopped. 'Thomas.'

Ella's heart jumped. 'Who?'

'Thomas Werner.'

'Nationality?'

'Austrian.'

'How old?'

'Early thirties by now I guess.'

'Do you have a photo of him?' Ella said.

'Sorry.'

'Can you describe him?'

'Um, about a metre seventy-five, average build, brown hair, brown eyes. Wore jeans all the time. Good tan, or he did have back then anyway. Loud laugh.'

'Can you confirm that this is him?' Murray handed her the photo taken from the airport tape.

'That's him all right.'

'How and where did you meet?' Ella said.

'We met on holiday in Spain the year before, partied together, and I said – as you do – if you're ever in Australia, come and stay. Everybody says that, but nobody ever expects to be taken up on it! Especially with no prior contact.' She shook her head. 'He turned up here expecting to move in.'

'What did you do?'

'I was stunned. He was going on like we had a boyfriend/girlfriend thing happening. I told him I was already seeing someone. I mean, it wasn't like anything serious had happened in Spain.'

'How did he respond to that?'

'Actually he wasn't too shattered. He kind of *acted* disappointed, but I got the feeling that he would've taken it if it was on offer, as well as being convenient to have somewhere to stay, but seeing as it wasn't, oh well.' Jules rolled her eyes. 'I mean, he brought a girl home within the week.'

'So you let him stay?'

'Well, we *had* had fun in Spain,' she said. 'I said he could bunk on the lounge there for a few days until he got sorted out. He was here for just over a week, I think.'

Ella looked down at the lounge she was sitting on.

'Do you know where he went?' Murray said.

'Nope.'

'Do you know of any other friends he had, any possible places he could've gone? Any place he mentioned?'

'I never met anyone. A guy did ring a few times, but he never said his name and Thomas never talked about him or anybody else. We didn't spend all that much time together. I work most nights and he was going out and so we slept a lot of the day.' She crossed her legs. 'Oh, I remember in Spain I heard him talking to some other Aussies about the Barrier Reef, what it was like to visit and dive on and so on. But he never talked to me about it when he was here.'

'What about friends in Spain? Did he introduce you to anyone?'

'Can't remember,' she said. 'Bit of a blur, most of it.'

'Did you see him or spend time with him later, after he left here?'

'Once,' she said. 'I was out with friends at this nightclub, what's it called – Rosie's, I think, in the city. I saw him having an argument with this other guy.'

'When was this?'

She thought for a moment. 'I guess two, maybe three years ago.'

'You're certain of that? You've seen him more recently than four years ago?'

'Absolutely. No more than three years.'

'What happened?'

'There was a bit of push and shove, then the bouncers kind of moved in and yanked the other guy away.'

'They didn't yank Thomas too?'

She shook her head. 'I kinda wondered if he knew the bouncers, actually. Usually they rip it into everybody, but they seemed friendly towards him.'

'Any idea what the argument was about?'

She hesitated. 'Can we go off the record for a second?'

'Certainly,' Ella lied.

'I met Thomas in Spain because he was selling Es. Ecstasy, you know. So when I saw this going on in the club I figured that he was probably doing the same here, and the argument had to do with that.'

'Did you ever see any evidence he was selling here?' Murray said.

'Like did he leave them lying around the lounge room, or did I buy any? No.'

Sure, Ella thought.

Jules moved forward on her chair. 'Can I ask, is Thomas the one who's dead or the one who did it?'

'His name's come up in our investigation, that's all we can tell you,' Murray said.

Ella asked, 'Would you be surprised either way?'

'Not particularly,' she said. 'He's a nice guy, don't get me wrong.'

'But?' Ella said.

'But he could be so . . . superficial. Like nothing really touched him. Like I said, when I told him I was seeing somebody and he couldn't stay for long, I swear he was only pretending to be disappointed. As if he thought that would get him something.' She twirled a ringlet of hair around her finger. 'It's not hard to imagine him getting into trouble with the drug thing, selling Es on somebody else's turf and not caring, not trying to fix the situation, and then finally getting himself knocked off.' She looked from one to the other. 'I'm right, aren't I? He's the victim.'

Ella stood up. 'Thanks for your time.'

'Here they come.'

Lauren looked up to see the divers emerge from the water. Beyond them the police boat nosed into the chop that was building in the wind. One of the divers carried a big underwater camera, which he handed now to someone else. Another gestured at a waiting rescue officer, who unfolded a white body bag on top of a big green tarp on the sloping beach. People had gathered along the path to watch, and the elderly women in their swimmers, now with their towels wrapped around them, edged closer along the sand.

The divers carried the body out of the sea to the bag and laid it carefully down. The dead man slumped to the side, the tank on his back keeping him on the slant. He wore a black wetsuit with red panels and trim. A dripping brown rope was tangled around the valve on the tank. Someone looped his regulator back over his shoulder and the plainclothes detectives huddled over him.

'We'd better go see,' Lauren said.

'I can go alone.'

She shook her head and got out of the ambulance. She walked across the path and down onto the beach, Joe close behind, the sand squeaking under their boots.

The dead man was Asian, and young. Drops of seawater clung to his short black hair and eyebrows. His skin was pale purple. She could see where fish had started to nibble on his lips and swollen tongue. He smelled like cold meat.

'Found this too.' One of the divers held a dive knife by its yellow and purple bungee cord. The blade was bright stainless steel, solid with a raking point and a row of deep serrations near the hilt. 'About three metres from him, still well within the reach allowed by the rope.'

An empty knife sheath was strapped around the dead man's right calf. His steamer wetsuit covered all but his face and hands. He wore wetsuit booties on his feet.

'Maybe he panicked when he got caught, couldn't think straight.' The man who'd reported the body was behind them. A uniformed officer came around to move him away.

'PM'll show us more.' Joe's detective mate stood up. 'Could you guys transport?'

'Sorry?' Lauren said.

'The doctor's coming to confirm him deceased but there's a backlog with the contractor's vans. They can't get here for an hour at least. We'll be done in about fifteen, and we're starting to attract a lot of attention.' He nodded at the growing crowd. 'We just need him shipped to the morgue, that's all.'

'We'll check with Control,' Joe said. Lauren went with him back to the ambulance. 'This is all right, hey? Nice easy job. Patient we don't have to talk to.'

'You know what those body bags are like,' she said. 'He'll leak everywhere.'

'So I'll mop it out.'

'It'll smell.'

'We've got air freshener.' He leaned into the cabin and picked up the radio microphone. 'Thirty-four.'

'Thirty-four, go ahead.'

'Thanks, we've been asked by police to transport from this location.'

There was a pause. Lauren crossed her fingers.

'Thirty-four, that'll be fine. Advise when you're departing.'

'Thirty-four copy.' Joe hung up the mike and looked at Lauren. 'You'd rather be doing a proper job?'

She headed back towards the police. She didn't want a dead guy in her truck today, and she didn't want to go to the morgue. It was just too close.

The doctor had arrived. He chatted to the police while he laid a clipboard on the grass and pulled on gloves. He drew back the dead man's eyelids and looked into his eyes. He put the back of his wrist against his cheek. He took a stethoscope from around his neck, inserted the earpieces, and pressed the diaphragm briefly to the wetsuited chest. He took the earpieces out and let the scope dangle as he pulled a pen from the clipboard, signed the certificate of life extinct, and handed it to Bradshaw. 'Cheers,' he said.

Fifteen minutes later Lauren and Joe pushed the loaded stretcher into the ambulance. The scuba gear was still on the body and it made a strange and lumpy shape in the body bag.

Lauren stood in the doorway looking at the silent shape. 'Do you ever feel that sometimes the world is just all death and bad stuff?'

Joe put his arm across her shoulders. 'You want me to drive?'

'I'm fine.'

They got into the front and she started the engine.

Joe said, 'When's your next block of leave?'

'Not till March.'

'Maybe you should see if you can get some earlier. Swap with somebody.'

'I don't need a holiday, and I can't afford to go anywhere anyway.'

She put the ambulance into gear and moved slowly over the grass. A council ranger had turned up and unlocked the poles from the driveway, and the crowd of gawkers shuffled apart to let the ambulance through. Lauren stared straight ahead, feeling their eyes on her, not meeting their gazes.

Joe picked up the microphone and said, 'Thirty-four is code five.'

'Copy that, Thirty-four.'

Lauren glanced in the rear-view mirror at the strapped-down body bag. 'They find any ID on him?'

'Nope.'

'Looked pretty young.'

'About twenty, they think,' Joe said.

Lauren pulled out onto the street. 'So what will they do?'

'Simon said they'll check the car parks for a car that could be his, see if they can find anybody who saw him going in, if anybody had seen him before. Check missing persons reports.'

Lauren thought of the family wondering where their brother and son was, why he hadn't called or come home. She hit a bump and looked into the mirror again. The dead man didn't move.

At the morgue they were buzzed in by a staff member. Lauren took a deep breath of air before pushing through the heavy doors. The smell of death wasn't strong, but even the faintest whiff could cling to clothing for the rest of the day. She wheeled the stretcher along the tiled corridor, wondering if her burnt man was here yet.

I could've been here too. Easily. Lying on a steel trolley, waiting to be cut up, having photos taken of my stab wounds, my skin washed with cold water and gloved hands.

But she wasn't. She reached up and touched the tracker in her pocket. She was alive and they were going to get the bastard.

She had to believe it or go mad.

★

Sal Rios tried to make himself walk slower. Tough guys didn't hurry. He shoved his hands in his pockets and dipped his head as if to a beat that only he could hear. But he could feel his breath coming faster, and as he looked from side to side at the bustling Botany industrial estate from behind his dark glasses he felt even more watched than usual.

His back prickling, he crossed the concrete fore-court, passing through the shade cast by the sign saying *Preston's Plastics*. The doors of the small fac-tory stood open and he was glad to step inside, out of view of the street, and exchange a nod with Colin Preston and one of his sons, Gary or Grant, he hadn't worked out which was which. He walked through the processing area, the stink of plastic making his nose burn and his eyes water, and knocked on the solid steel door to the storeroom.

After a moment there was one tap in reply.

'It's me,' he said into the crack.

Bolts slid back and the door swung open. Tho-mas wore a paper mask over his nose and mouth but the annoyance in his eyes was clear. 'What?'

Sal sniffed. It didn't smell too strong. The exhaust fan whirred on the wall. 'We need to talk.'

Thomas muttered something but let him in, locking the door behind him.

'They've put surveillance on her.'

'That's no surprise.' Thomas turned back to the bench.

Sal could see the caked blood in the hair on the back of his head. He and Julio had cleaned it up as best they could last night, Thomas stone-cold silent under their hands. He put his hands back in his pockets and dipped his head again a couple of times, being cool, but couldn't keep it up. Sweat ran down his ribs and his chest was tight, making it hard enough to breathe without the stink from the ice that bubbled on the burners on the trestle table behind him.

'So what are we going to do?' he said.

Thomas said nothing. Sal wanted to sit down and talk it all through, what they could and should do, whether it was still worth their risk to carry on. *No, it isn't.* He folded his arms and held onto his biceps, tensing them up, trying to feel stronger.

'Thomas?'

Thomas, bent over some glass contraption, shot him a look that made the skin tighten on his face. Sal turned away and walked the length of the room, looking at the containers of chemicals on the floor, bumping one with the toe of his shoe to see how full it was.

'Don't touch that.'

To Sal's shame he felt tears start to build. The fuck he would cry. He pinched at his biceps and tightened his throat and glared at the peeling grey paint on the walls. This was happening more often lately and it pissed him off. So what if his family was going to shit, brother dying, sister with all her dramas? So what if Blake came to see him when he slept, if he heard that crunch of breaking bone, that groan, those dying gasps over and over again? If those other dead guys appeared there too, just standing there and staring at him? Tough guys went straight through all that and let it roll right off them like none of it mattered.

He tensed his lats, feeling them push against his shirt, and straightened his back. He thought of the money, of how Tracy salivated at jewellers' windows, how she would once again smile and press up hard against him when he told her to choose whatever she liked. She had this thing about diamonds. He sometimes thought that if she was so desperate for bling she could get herself a better-paying job, but then of course there would go their . . . what was the word? *Conduit*. So he kept his mouth shut.

He thought of the stuff he would get for himself. That big home gym system, first off. The way things were at home there was no room to set it up now, but that would change when Nona found her feet and moved back out. He liked to think of him and Julio working out together. This new herbal crap Julio was on, you never knew with that stuff. It was in the magazines all the time. *I was dying until I started taking this stuff and now I'm running marathons!* You just never knew. Things would get better, he told himself. If we get through *this*.

Thomas straightened, frowning. 'This shit's not working.'

'Doesn't it take a couple of days?'

'I know how long it takes, and I know if it's working, and I know this isn't,' Thomas snapped. 'It's too cold and damp in here. Go and buy some fan heaters.'

Sal felt for his wallet. 'With cash? I don't–'

'Just fuckin' buy them.'

Sal wanted to say that they should chuck the half-made ice, just cut their losses now, before they got caught and locked up. His Uncle Paulo had been in jail and had told him about what happened in there. His mouth dried up at the thought of it. But Thomas would never give in; the money meant too much to him.

'How much longer till we're done?'

'It'd be a lot quicker if I had fan heaters and didn't get interrupted.'

Sal let himself out of the room and heard the bolts slide home behind him. Grant or Gary was looking at him over some plastic thing he was cutting, and Sal tried to give him the eye but had to drop his gaze. These guys were another problem. Thomas said they were getting money for nothing, so why would they tell anybody about it? But Sal didn't trust that, nor the years-old friendship between his late Uncle Paulo and Colin Preston that Julio said promised them safety. He wished for the old days, not even a year ago, before Paulo died and Julio got diagnosed and it was them running the show, with Thomas doing his own shit overseas, and Sal as Julio's sidekick, just along for the ride.

He hesitated by the main door, blinking against the bright sun outside, looking for police slumped low in parked cars and loitering in doorways behind newspapers. Times like this, when he felt really scared, he wished for the years before any of it had started, and his mum was still alive.

SIXTEEN

Ella and Murray were almost all the way in the
city, heading for Rosie's, the club where Jules
Cartwright had last seen Thomas Werner, when Ella's
phone rang.

'Got something else for you,' Kuiper said. 'A
woman's just called in to say she knows Kennedy and
she feels she should talk to someone.'

Ella made a face. 'What's that mean?'

'I don't know, but her address is right near
Steyne Park, and I could hear a dog barking in the
background.'

The lift was silent and smooth, and the landing was
bright with afternoon sunlight. The door of number
eleven was identified by filigreed silver numerals. Ella
took hold of the silver knocker in the shape of a bird
pecking at the wood, and the noise was answered by
furious yapping from inside. There was the sound of a
woman's voice, the tone of the barking changed, then

the door opened. A tall red-eyed woman in her fifties held the yapping dog in one hand against her chest.

'Good afternoon.' Ella showed her badge. 'Detectives Marconi and Shakespeare. Are you Helen Flinders?'

'Yes.' She opened the door wide. 'Please come in.'

Flinders was about a metre eighty in her bare tanned feet. Her brown hair was cut short and shot through with grey. She wore khaki cut-off shorts and a pink collared shirt, and around her neck hung a tiny silver butterfly on a black silk cord. Ella felt short, stubby and downright inelegant beside her.

The living room was bright and sunny, with green lounges facing the windows that overlooked the sparkling water and a large work desk occupying one wall. Ella saw an array of delicate tools, twists of silver wire, and five silver butterflies in a line, each one slightly different from its neighbours but also similar to them and to the one Ella had seen on the Kennedys' sideboard. She saw Murray was looking too.

'My little home business,' Helen Flinders said. 'Please, sit down. Can I get you a drink? Tea? Coffee? Water?'

'We're fine, thank you.'

Ella sat on the edge of one of the lounges and Helen sat opposite her. She kept the dog on her lap. He sniffed the air and watched Murray, who'd stayed on his feet.

Ella said, 'You called in to say that you knew James Kennedy and you wanted to talk to somebody, is that correct, Mrs Flinders – it is Mrs?'

She nodded. 'My husband died three years ago.' She tapped her chest. 'Bad heart.'

Ella nodded. 'What did you want to talk about?'

Helen Flinders smoothed the hair between the dog's ears. 'I've been away this week and I came home last night. This morning I got my mail from my neighbour, started to read the local paper, and there it was. It said he was attacked on the street – stabbed. Is that right?'

'I'm afraid so,' Ella said. 'How did you know him?'

'We were friends.' She wiped away her tears with slender fingers. 'Who would do such a thing?'

'We're trying to figure that out,' Ella said. 'Which is why you need to tell us everything you know about him.'

Helen Flinders pinched her lips together as a flush crept up her throat.

'What was the nature of your relationship?' Murray said.

'At first we were just friends,' she said. 'He delivered some silver and other things to me here once, I guess that was about eight months ago.'

'In his job as a courier?' Ella said.

'Yes. He was such a nice man, he admired the numbers I'd made for the door and we started talking. I offered him a coffee but he didn't have time. I said perhaps another day? And he came back a few days later.' She ran her tongue over her lower lip. 'I never intended it to be anything. Mostly we would just talk. I walk Pepper in the evenings and we would often meet in the park there and chat.'

'But things developed?'

'It can be so hard, losing your partner. It's not having somebody to talk to about all the minuscule details of your day, but also just being able to touch a person, and be touched . . . I remember when James first took me in his arms.' She stared out the window at the harbour. 'I hadn't been held like that since Bob died. It wasn't a sexual thing, not then, but there was something about being hugged by a man who was not my son-in-law.' She looked at Ella. 'Am I making any sense?'

Ella nodded. 'When did it become sexual?'

'A month or so later.'

'Did he tell you he was married?'

'No,' Helen said. 'I thought he probably was. He bought one of my butterflies and that's usually a thing a man buys as a gift for a woman. But we never talked about it, or about the future or what we would do, or anything like that. We just lived in the moment.'

Ella could hear the scratching of Murray's pen. 'Did you always meet here?'

'Here and in the park. Never anywhere else. It suited us both that way, I suppose.'

'How often did he come by?'

'Usually once or twice a week, less often once a fortnight,' she said. 'He would either drop by on his route during the day, or come to the park in the evening on his bike.'

'And when did you last see him?'

'On Tuesday evening, in the park. I guess it was the day he died,' she said. 'We hadn't arranged to meet. I was flying to Brisbane later that night for business, and took Pepper for a last-minute stroll. I was surprised to see James there. He was talking to a man, and he glanced up and saw me but gave no sign of recognising me, so I thought, obviously he doesn't want me to acknowledge him, and I walked right on by.'

Ella felt her blood surge. 'What time was this?'

'A little after seven. Five past, something like that.'

'Can you describe the man?'

'He was a little shorter than James, balding, with dark hair going grey,' she said. 'They both looked very serious.'

'James didn't seem bothered, upset? Frightened of this man?'

She shook her head. 'I got the feeling they knew each other. They were standing at the sandstone wall there, their backs against it. They were standing fairly close, talking in low voices.'

'Had you ever seen the man before?'

'No.'

'Can you recall what he was wearing?'

'I didn't take much notice,' she said. 'I think he was in dark trousers, and a light-coloured short-sleeved shirt. That's about all I can say.'

'Did James ever give you the impression that he knew other people who lived around here?'

'Never.' Helen Flinders blinked back tears and bent to kiss the dog.

'Just a few more questions,' Ella said. 'Did James ever mention being in any kind of trouble?'

'No.'

'Did you ever hear him say the name Thomas Werner?'

She shook her head. 'Is that who you think did it?'

'His name's come up as part of the investigation, that's all,' Ella said. 'Did James ever seem worried or bothered by anything?'

'He was a very even-tempered man who didn't let things bother him, as far as I saw,' she said. 'Although there was one time, the second-last time we met, I think, when he took a call on his mobile and didn't seem too happy about it.'

Ella sat forward. 'What was it about?'

'He didn't say. We were in the park, and he turned away from me a little when he answered. I initially thought it may have been his wife.'

'Could you hear any of the conversation?'

'I could tell they were arguing. James was saying, "No, no. I told you I don't want to do that any more. None of us want to."' She shrugged. 'I walked away to give him privacy.'

'What did he say about it afterwards?'

'Nothing,' she said. 'I thought, he'll tell me if he wants to, and if he doesn't want to then it's none of my business.'

'But you thought it was his wife?'

'I didn't know who it was, but that was my first thought, yes.'

'What day was that, can you recall?'

She thought for a moment. 'The last time I met him, to speak to, I mean, was Thursday the eleventh, and the phone call was the week before that, on the Wednesday.'

'The fourth,' Murray said, looking at a calendar on the wall over the desk.

'That would be it.'

'What time, roughly?'

'In the evening,' she said. 'Perhaps six thirty, quarter to seven.'

Ella nodded. Oh, this was good. They had the records for Kennedy's mobile, so this caller he'd argued with shouldn't be too hard to track down. She wondered if the wheelchair-bound watcher had seen this other man too, maybe getting into or out of a car. Oh, it was all coming together nicely.

'Where did you stay in Brisbane?' Murray said.

'With my daughter,' she said. 'I can give you her contact information so you can confirm I was really up there, if you want, and Stan O'Connor from next door can tell you he looked after Pepper and collected my mail for the couple of days. Although I would appreciate the nature of my relationship with James being kept quiet.'

'We understand, Mrs Flinders,' Ella said pulling out her mobile to call Kuiper. 'Thanks for getting in touch.'

'You don't smell of morgue, I promise,' Joe said as Lauren backed the ambulance into the station.

'You wouldn't know.' Lauren turned the engine off. 'It's on you too.'

She went inside to her locker and sprayed

deodorant all over herself.

Back in the muster room, Joe screwed up his face. '*Now* you smell.'

Her mobile rang. Ella said, 'Things good?'

'No problems here,' Lauren said.

'You're carrying the tracker?'

'Absolutely.' Lauren touched her pocket. 'Have there been any phone calls to the house?'

'Nothing so far. Hopefully he's crawled back into his hole,' Ella said. 'I'll check in again later.'

Lauren clipped her phone back on her belt. Joe was sitting on the bench, swinging his legs. 'How's your back?' he said. 'Lifting the stretcher was no bother?'

'It's pretty good,' she said. 'Why?'

'Follow me.'

He went into the lounge room and pushed the recliners and the TV cabinet back against the walls.

'You're going to vacuum?' Lauren said. 'You want me to watch?'

'Ahem,' he said. 'When I was a wee lad in the Navy I learned a bit about self-defence techniques. One thing they told us is that a person can be lucky once, but is rarely lucky twice.'

'That's a heartening thought.'

'Forewarned is forearmed, et cetera,' he said. 'The main thing is, do you feel up to it?'

She shrugged, trying to keep her breathing slow. 'Teach away.'

'The most common type of attack is from behind, because people like to try to get the advantage of surprise. The most common reaction is panic.'

'I can understand that.'

'There are things you can do, however, if you can keep your head. As you obviously managed to do yesterday.'

'Hm.'

'Stand here,' he said. 'Turn around. You're sure you're okay with this?'

She nodded.

'Let me know if you want to stop.' He slid his arm across her neck and chest. 'Still fine?'

'I'm getting annoyed by the questions.' She was starting to sweat. *Stay calm, it's Joe. Focus on that. Joe is holding you. You are completely safe.*

'Okay,' he said, his breath warm against her ear. 'Think for a moment of the position of your body and of mine.'

She closed her eyes. His chest was pressed so close against her back she could feel his heartbeat. His arm was hard up against her neck, his hand grasping her shoulder.

'If you panic in this situation, he wins,' Joe said softly. 'He pulls up against your carotids and next thing you're out to it. But you don't have the upper body strength to fight him off directly, especially if he's much bigger than you.'

'Okay,' she whispered.

'Instead, think about the position of your feet. You know his are there somewhere too. You can stomp your heel onto the top of his foot and, unless he's in steel-caps, he's going to be feeling somethin' nasty.'

She raised her right foot and brought it down

gently, searching with her heel for his foot, pressing into it briefly, imagining slamming it down.

'Then you use your body weight against him,' Joe said. 'Try this. Shift your weight a little lower and move your hips to the left, and at the same time swing your right elbow back into his stomach as hard as you can.'

She tried it, finding a certain rhythm in moving sideways and bringing her elbow down and back.

'That's it,' Joe said. 'You get that momentum going and it puts your whole body behind your elbow, so it's not just a weak little poke.'

She did it again, fitting her elbow into his side. 'I kinda like this.'

'Then, when he's folded that way a little in response, you twist around and rake his face, especially his eyes, with your nails, as hard as you can.'

He leaned over sideways a little, and she turned and put her hands to his face. He smiled at her through her fingers. 'Nicely done.'

'One slight problem,' she said. 'What if he has a knife?'

'That gets tricky. You have to accept that you'll probably get hurt, and defend yourself with whatever's at hand. Or your hands themselves.'

She grimaced.

'It's better to have cut hands than to be dead,' he said. 'You need to get facing him as soon as you can – you need to see what he's doing. Use whatever's in reach as a weapon. Throw stuff. Scream and shout. But you know that already.'

Lauren's heart pounded.

'If he's taking big swings, try for the old kick to the groin,' he said. 'Are you sure you're okay? This makes me feel funny and I wasn't even there.'

'Do you know, I'd wanted to move that microwave. Kristi wouldn't let me because it hides a rust pattern on the side of the fridge which she thinks is in the shape of a ghost.'

'Jesus, Lauren.'

She was dizzy. 'It's so strange. We see people all the time who are alive or dead because of coincidence. But now that it's happened to me, I can't believe it.' She laughed, a hollow sound. 'Although that's what they all say, don't they! "I can't believe this has happened."'

Joe pulled her into a tight embrace. 'Don't talk about it any more.'

She felt the warmth of his skin, caught a hint of the morgue on him still, but underneath that was the clean smell of soap and shaving foam. She pressed her head against his chest. She wanted to reach up and touch the smooth skin of his cheek. She wanted to slide her hands around the back of his neck and pull his face down to hers.

She wanted to kiss him.

He said, 'I don't think we should do any more of that.'

She could almost feel his lips on hers. *Close your eyes, reach up, do it!*

'Not today anyway.' His voice was a low rumble in his chest.

Do it!

'It's too soon. And we don't want to hurt your

back.' He still held her but she felt him relax his grip. 'Here, sit down. Have a break. I'll get you a drink of water.'

She sank into the chair and listened to him turn on the tap in the station's tiny kitchen. The pain from her wound pressing against the seat was nothing compared to the pain in her heart. She had almost kissed him, and she only regretted that she hadn't. Because who knew what he would do? Maybe he would kiss her back! Even as she imagined this, she knew it was silly. Joe was a caring man who was good at looking after people who'd been through traumatic experiences, and that's all he was doing now. Besides, he was engaged. People didn't get engaged and then start kissing their co-workers. If they loved their co-workers, they didn't get engaged. Simple – and devastating – as that.

'Here you go.' He sat on the edge of the other recliner and watched her drink. 'Are you really sure you're okay to be at work?'

Movement behind him startled her and Joe whirled around as Claire stepped into the room. 'Jesus,' he said.

'Not quite.' She looked around. 'What've you two been up to?'

There was no way in the world they could tell her. Even forgetting about her jealousy, the detectives had asked that they tell nobody what was going on. Saying that Joe was teaching her self-defence would only set off a whole string of questions that Lauren knew she couldn't answer.

'There's talk of us getting a new lounge,' she said.

'We were seeing how much room we'd have, if it'd fit in okay.'

Claire eyed them.

'What do you think, we've been dancing?' Joe said with a laugh.

Claire looked at the carpet. The pile was scuffed up from their boots, but that could have been just as easily caused by dragging the lounges, Lauren thought. *And she can't read your mind, she doesn't know you almost kissed him. Just relax.*

'How was your night?' Joe said.

'Can I talk to you outside?'

Joe followed her out to the plant room. Feeling sick, Lauren took her glass to the kitchen and poured the rest of the water down the sink. She could hear the tones of their voices but the traffic rumbling on the bridge overhead drowned out their words.

After a couple of minutes the sensor in the doorway buzzed. Lauren guessed that was Claire crossing the beam as she stormed out of the station, and realised she'd never heard it buzz when she came in.

Joe came into the kitchen looking thoughtful. Lauren finished drying her glass and put it away. 'She okay?'

'She wants to move the wedding.'

'To when?'

'March.'

'But I thought you were planning for the summer honeymoon, the beach, all that, in December next year,' Lauren said.

'Now she's talking Tasmania in autumn.'

'Bit of a change.'

'I told her my holidays are locked in, but she wants me to try to swap.'

Lauren's holidays were in March. *Please don't ask me . . .*

'She's seen the holiday roster, she knows that's when yours are, but I said you're going away,' Joe said. 'Anyway, March is too soon. You know how much stuff we have to organise?'

'Nope. Never got married.'

'There's no way we can get it done in time.'

They were silent for a moment.

'You know, I never heard the buzzer go when she came in,' Lauren said.

Joe frowned. 'Maybe it's on the blink. We should keep the door shut, anyway. Safer.'

The buzzer had never been on the blink before. Lauren wondered whether a suspicious fiancée might stoop to crawling under the thigh-high sensor beam in the hope of catching certain parties out. She was offended by the thought, but knew she had no right to be. After all, Claire nearly *had* caught them.

'Has she said anything more about that train job complaint?'

'Nah. I reckon she's over that.'

Lauren wasn't so sure. 'If she puts that in, it could be the last straw.'

'How do you mean?'

'I looked up the policies folder the other night,' she said. 'If I get charged with perjury for the Blake thing, the service can sack me. I figure the only reason they might not is because of my good clinical record. If she complains about the tube, there goes that.'

Joe shook his head. 'She hasn't said a word about it. I'd say she's completely forgotten. She probably forgot it by the end of that shift.'

But she might remember it if she gets jealous enough, Lauren thought, and starts casting about for some tool of revenge.

SEVENTEEN

Murray took a hand off the wheel to fiddle with the stereo and soon the booming voice of the Family Man filled the car.

Ella raised her voice over the noise. 'What is it about him that you like so much?'

'He's interesting.'

'*Murder rates are up, assaults are up, gun crime is up – where are we living, the States? Tough action is what we need, but what does the government give us?*'

'He gives me a headache,' Ella said.

'*They give us fudged statistics, they give us long-term forecasts and planned outcomes and target scenarios. Take the drug amnesty. They say it's too early to know how it's working, that no figures are available yet. I say, take a look at the stats on violent crime. Has anything dropped?*'

Ella said, 'You like him because he's anti-amnesty too.'

'What?'

She turned the volume down and said it again.

'You wait,' Murray said. 'After the next election it'll be scrapped.'

She snorted. 'Everything gets scrapped after every election.'

'And what do you think they'll find in the wash-up?'

'Perhaps that it would've worked if people got behind it, if people gave it time.'

Murray shook his head. 'It's like the Broken Windows thing in the States.'

'This isn't another poetry thing, is it?'

'In the eighties in New York, they found that by fixing up the little things that bother people in a community, like graffiti and broken windows and public disorder, it changed the atmosphere so much that all their violent crime dropped way down. It's the same thing here: to say that we accept and forgive the small-time dealer is to create an atmosphere in which criminals feel it's okay to do anything.'

'But we're not accepting and forgiving,' Ella said. 'We punish them less, sure, but they have to give us names and information in return. They pay their debt to society that way.'

'It still creates that atmosphere though, and the atmosphere is the problem.'

'But surely letting the small guy stay free on the streets with us chasing our tails behind him is the equivalent to leaving the windows broken? With the amnesty, at least we're starting to patch them up.'

He mumbled something.

'I missed that,' she said pointedly.

'My dad said you'd take that stance.'

'Did he.' Good ol' Frank Shakespeare. She doubted he'd have much to say about her that was complimentary. So she hadn't recognised him at that crime scene all those years ago, thought he was a nosy civilian and said he could fuck off or be arrested. Would he never get over it?

'He said people who are pro-amnesty are goal-orientated–'

'Nothing wrong with that.'

'–and overly so,' Murray went on. 'Such people believe that the end result justifies the means, but in police work so much depends on sound means.'

'Do you guys talk about me across the dinner table often?'

'The means are the ways by which we as police establish and maintain our relationship with the community. This has to be a constant, so people know where they stand. If we start changing the rules, if we let some people off for doing wrong, nobody knows what's going on. Us included.'

Ella cranked the stereo back up.

'I've seen these things first-hand! My home country of Canada is following the United States just as your fine country is doing, and I'm here to tell you the time to turn back is now!'

The afternoon was cooling by the time she stamped along the footpath behind Murray to Rosie's, the club where Jules Cartwright said she'd seen Thomas two or three years ago. There were so many odds stacked against anybody who was there then still being there now *and* remembering Thomas. She wanted to go take their information from Helen back to the office and find out what had shown up on Kennedy's mobile records, but Kuiper had said for them to come past here first.

'Stupid long shot,' she muttered at Murray's back.

He ignored her.

The front of the club was tinted glass and steel. A skinny man stood in the late-afternoon sun wiping fingerprints from the glass doors.

'Excuse me,' Murray said.

'We're not open yet.' The man turned and saw their badges. 'Oh.'

'We need to speak to your boss.'

'Boss isn't in.'

'Who's in charge at the moment then?' Ella said.

'Martin, assistant manager.'

'Then we'll speak to him.'

The man gave a final cursory wipe to the glass then pulled the door open.

They followed him inside to a roomy bar area where the air smelled of carpet cleaner and spilled alcohol and Ella could feel the deep bass beat of the techno music in her chest. A lone man behind the bar rattled about in a glass-fronted fridge. A short corridor on one side led to three closed doors. The man knocked on one and waited. When a voice said, 'Yes?' the man turned the knob and went in. 'Pleece to talk to you.'

Ella caught a muttered *fuuuck* and she stepped in behind the skinny man. 'Detectives Marconi and Shakespeare, Homicide.'

The man behind the desk was jowly and sallow-skinned, in his early forties Ella guessed. He wore a black T-shirt and a silver signet ring and kept his veined hands curled together on a closed red binder.

'How can I help you, officers?'

'Your name is?'

'Martin Everly.'

From the corner of her eye Ella saw Murray write this down. 'How long have you worked here?' she asked.

'Bit over two years.'

'What about your superior? How long's he been here?'

'Less than that,' he said.

'And the owner?'

'It's owned by a company. They own a few clubs, have done for years. Ten, fifteen years I think.'

'We'll need some information on this company.'

'I don't have much here.' He opened the desk drawer to his left and shuffled through some papers, finally producing a sheet of paper with a black and red letterhead. 'You can contact them through there.'

Ella took the page. It gave the address and phone numbers of a company called Clubs Inc. She handed it to Murray then looked back at Martin Everly. 'Do you know a man named Thomas Werner?'

'Never heard of him.'

Murray got out the photo from the airport tape. 'Seen this man before?'

Everly studied it briefly then handed it back. 'Nope.'

'Mind if we speak to your staff before we go?'

'There's hardly any here. We don't open till later.'

'We'll need their home contact details then.'

'Certainly.'

He pulled a ring binder from a desk drawer and took three pages out, fed them into a fax and gave them copies. Ella ran her eye down the list. No names jumped out at her, but they'd take it back to the office and run the names through the system.

They were almost back at the car when Murray's phone rang. Ella took the keys dangling from his hand and ensconced herself in the driver's seat. He got in putting his phone away, looking distracted. 'Deborah Kennedy's disappeared.'

'What?'

'We're to help search the flat.'

Ella was already pulling away from the kerb. 'Circumstances?'

'Kuiper didn't say.' Murray tugged his seatbelt tight.

'I mean, do they think she's kidnapped or dead?'

'He really didn't say.'

She saw his foot working the floor, looking for the non-existent brake, and smiled to herself, and went a little faster.

Ella felt strange walking into the Kennedys' flat again. It looked bigger now, though that might've been because Mrs Kennedy wasn't there to fill it with her grief.

Detective Rebecca Kanowski talked to Kuiper in the middle of the lounge room. 'If it wasn't for the neighbour who heard me pounding on the door, and had a key, I would never have gotten in.' She was sweating. 'I thought they'd suicided.'

Ella peered into the other rooms. The double bed was neatly made, the wardrobe doors closed, the bathroom looked and smelled clean, with a towel hanging neatly over the rail. Nothing was upturned or dishevelled. Even in the lounge room everything looked normal; the TV remote was on the coffee table, the flowers that Ella guessed had been delivered after Kennedy's death were ranged along the side-board. The silver butterfly was still there.

'That neighbour didn't see them go,' Rebecca continued. 'We found a spare key to their garage and checked it but their car's gone.'

Kuiper nodded. 'Marconi, Shakespeare, canvass the other neighbours in this block and the ones either side and across the street. See if anybody saw them go, or if there was anyone with them.'

Ella and Murray divided the work up. Nobody that Ella spoke to, either in the Kennedys' block of flats or elsewhere, had seen or heard anything out of the ordinary. She returned to the flat to find Murray already back. Rebecca and Detectives Matt Lyons and Prue Hoskins sat on the lounge going through piles of papers. Kuiper stood listening to Murray.

'In their car, and definitely just Mrs Kennedy and her daughter,' Murray finished.

'So they've done a runner,' Kuiper said.

'Got it.' Rebecca held up a bank statement. 'It's in both Mr and Mrs Kennedy's names.'

Kuiper looked it over. 'Let's get down to the bank

before they close, see what she's been trying to hide from us.'

'I wasn't certain that she was,' Rebecca said.

'We'll know soon enough.' Kuiper turned to Ella and gave her a sheet of paper with *Simply Sydney Funerals* in fancy script across the top. It was a receipt for money paid. 'Hop on over to these blokes, find out when the funeral's on. The morgue only released the body yesterday, so with any luck Mrs Kennedy's still in town.'

A call to a collapse in the Cross turned out to be a heroin overdose. Lauren gave the unconscious woman a shot of naloxone, and after she woke up she abused them roundly then took off through the crowds up Darlinghurst Road. 'Yeah, you're welcome!' Lauren shouted after her.

'Hey,' Joe said. 'People are watching.'

Lauren threw the gear into the truck. Wherever paramedics went, whatever they did, people watched. It made her feel vulnerable, a target, especially in a crowd like that where who knew who could be working his way through to get close to them. She got in the cabin and slammed the door. 'Can we go?'

They were passing the museum when Control called. 'Thirty-four, I have a man behaving strangely in the traffic on Market Street. Cross street is given variously as Pitt or Castlereagh. Police on way also.'

'Thirty-four copy, on the case.'

Joe flicked on the lights and sirens. 'Fake or genuine?'

'Genuine.' Lauren pulled on a pair of gloves and got out a pair for Joe, reaching over to tuck them under his thigh. 'Drug problem.'

'That's not fair,' Joe said. 'Drug problem covers a million things.'

She managed a grin. 'You have to be fast round here, mate.'

They turned right onto Elizabeth Street then left onto Market where the traffic was hardly moving at all. Joe pushed along bit by bit, waving at cars to inch over so he could manoeuvre the ambulance through to where a man yelled and flailed his arms in the middle lane.

Lauren picked up the mike. 'Thirty-four is on scene, no sign of police yet. I'd say we're going to need them too.'

'I'll call them again,' Control said.

Joe said, 'Ah, shit.'

Half out the door, Lauren said, 'What?'

'It's the same fucking guy.'

Lauren looked again and her heart sank.

Joe came around to her side of the ambulance. 'He's even wearing the same bloody clothes.'

The football shorts were low on the man's hips, and the slash in his Nirvana T-shirt flapped in the breeze.

'How's he out on the streets?'

'Psych wards must be full,' Joe said. 'Worse one comes in, out he goes.'

Lauren yanked the mike from its hook. 'Thirty-four.'

'Go ahead.'

'This is the same patient who assaulted both officers five days ago while armed. Require police as soon as possible, please.'

'Copy, Thirty-four,' Control said. 'Stay clear if you can.'

The man pounded on the bonnet of a car with his fists. Lauren could see drivers elbowing down the lock buttons on their doors.

'We have to do something,' Joe said. He was close by her, standing inside the open door. She could rest her arm on his shoulder if she wanted. 'At least this time we know what he's like.'

The man clambered onto the bonnet then roof of a car and jumped up and down. Lauren could feel people looking at them, and she slid reluctantly down from her seat. She could hear a siren, somewhere far far away. Perhaps they could distract him long enough to stop him. She walked beside Joe. The cut on her back hurt. It was hot on the street with the exhausts of all the cars going, and she could smell the stink of the man's body odour even over that. 'We never found out his name.'

Joe snapped the wrists of his gloves. 'Fuck him.'

The man scrambled forward onto the next car and dropped to his hands and knees, trying to grab the screaming woman inside through the half-open sunroof. Unable to reach her, he started pounding his head into the metal.

'Feet first,' Joe said.

Lauren nodded.

The man's feet were bare, toes braced against the top of the rear window, soles cracked and bleeding.

'Go!'

Lauren rushed to the driver's side of the car while Joe ran to the back passenger door. She grabbed one ankle, Joe snagged the other, and they yanked hard, pulling the man down off the roof and onto the rear window and boot. He writhed like a snake, turning to lash at them with his fists. Lauren held on tight with both hands and dodged his swings. The man snarled, his forehead bruised and starting to bleed from where he'd been hitting it on the car.

They dragged him further down, onto the road-way this time, Lauren feeling the thunk of his landing through her grip on his leg.

Joe let go of the man's leg and leapt onto his back. Lauren threw herself onto the man's skinny buttocks and thighs, pressing her head against Joe's side to avoid the man's thrashing legs. He screamed and swore, heaving under them, and she fought to pin his legs to the ground with her hands and knees. She felt the cut on her back split open.

'Shit's trying to bite me,' Joe grunted.

Lauren tried to ignore the pain in her back and press down harder. Where were the coppers? She couldn't hear any sirens now over the ruckus the man was making. *You fucking bastard, just stop it!*

A body landed on the man's legs next to Lauren and she looked around to see a nuggety young man in dirty Stubbies and workboots give her a grin while trying to grab hold of the man's kicking feet.

'Thanks,' she panted. 'Careful of the blood.'

'Lie still!' Joe shouted. But the man kept fight-ing. He got his arms loose of Joe's grip and flailed.

Lauren looked around just as Joe ducked away, and copped the back of his head against her mouth. Her eyes watered at the pain and she felt her lip start to swell. She hated the man, hated his behaviour and all the trouble he caused them, now and in his flat, and slammed her knee hard into the back of his thigh. The action had no effect on his struggles. She did it again. She wanted to hurt him. She hated him. She hated everybody.

'Okay,' she heard somebody say, and saw a swarm of blue uniforms around them. Two took the place of the nuggety man, restraining the screaming man's legs, then two got ready to replace her. 'Ready, and go.' Somebody hauled her up and out of the way and the burly officers dived in. Two more grabbed hold of his arms and cuffed him, then they carried him screaming to the waiting paddy wagon.

The struggle had been brief but Lauren was trembling and damp with sweat. She leaned against the car and took a deep and shaky breath. Her lip throbbed. Her back stung. The knees of her navy trousers were grimy with the man's sweat. The back of her wrist looked clean; she touched it to her lip but saw no blood. She twisted gingerly to see her shirt, but no blood was coming through the dressing and onto the fabric.

She looked inside the car. The woman was bent over the wheel, shoulders heaving. A police officer was crouched inside the open door, his hand on her shoulder.

Joe came to lean on the car with her. 'Talk about strong.' His eyes widened at her lip. 'When'd he do that?'

'That was you, not him.' Lauren started back to the ambulance. The paddy wagon rocked on its tyres as the man threw himself against the walls.

'With these lily-white knuckles?' Joe said.

'With your rock-hard head.' She got in the ambulance and tried to shut the door but he stood in the way.

'Really? Did I?'

'It's fine,' she said.

'I'm so sorry, Loz, I didn't realise.'

'It's nothing,' she said. 'It doesn't even hurt.'

'You lie.'

She flapped a hand at him. 'Will you shut up and get in?'

Once he'd started the ambulance she called up Control. 'Patient is in police custody and we are clear.'

'Thanks, Thirty-four, you can return to station,' Control said.

'Thirty-four copy, thank you.'

But Joe headed the other way. Lauren looked at him. 'Where we off to?'

'You've suffered an injury in the workplace. You need to get it checked and have a record made in case of any future problems. And how's your back?'

'Hey, I'll fill out the worker's comp forms at the station but I do not want to see a doctor about a fat lip.'

'Nevertheless.' He kept driving.

She rolled her eyes, holding back a grin. 'Some people can be so bossy.'

EIGHTEEN

The funeral home was on Anzac Parade in Kensington. A woman in a pale blue suit looked up from the desk. 'May I help you?'

Ella showed her badge, then handed the woman the receipt.

'Ah yes. Mr Kennedy. Tragic situation.'

'When's the funeral?'

The woman checked her computer screen. 'It's not actually booked.'

'Why's that?'

'Mrs Kennedy requested it be delayed,' the woman said. 'Apparently there are relatives overseas who aren't yet certain when they can come.'

Murray frowned. 'How do the bodies stand up to that?'

'No problem whatsoever,' the woman said. 'Cold storage, embalming. We could keep you decent for months.'

Ella said, 'Did you deal with Mrs Kennedy yourself?'

'Yes.'

'How did she seem?'

'Grief-stricken,' she said. 'Like I said, it was tragic.'

'Where did she say these relatives lived?'

The woman thought for a moment. 'She wasn't specific, actually. I didn't care to delve. I am an ear only.'

'How did she pay?'

'Credit card,' the woman said. 'It says that on the receipt. Most people don't pay until after the funeral but she was keen to do so upfront.'

Ella wondered if Mrs Kennedy was ensuring good cold storage of her husband's remains until such time as she returned.

'Is Mrs Kennedy all right?'

Ella got out her card. 'Could you let me know if she contacts you, please?'

The woman read it. 'Should I be worried for her?'

'Please call if she gets in touch,' Ella said. 'Thanks for your time.'

In the car, Murray clicked in his seatbelt. 'Mrs K's turning out to be quite the little planner.'

'We'll have to check about that overseas family.' Ella started the car and pulled out.

'I reckon it was her,' Murray said. 'I reckon she found out about Helen Flinders and flipped out. Even if she didn't physically stab him, I reckon she was behind it.'

'You extrapolate all that from her disappearance?'

'And because she delayed the funeral and put off giving us the bank details.'

'Maybe she's frightened,' Ella said. 'She saw that note, remember, she knows James said Thomas Werner.'

'Who she said she'd never heard of.'

Ella stopped at a red. 'Maybe she lied.'

At St Vincent's, Joe rang Control and told them where they were and what they were doing. Over Lauren's protests he had the triage nurse log her into the system and made her stand still while the nurse peered at her lip. 'She's got a cut on her back too,' he said.

'It's old,' Lauren said. 'It's fine.'

'You want the doctor to check it anyway?'

'No,' Lauren said.

'Yes,' Joe said. 'Yes, she does.'

'We'll slip you in between patients, get a doctor to have a quick squiz and then it's done,' the nurse said. 'Meantime, bung an icepack on your lip there, if you want.'

'I'll get it,' Joe said, and hurried off.

Lauren leaned against the wall. Her lip throbbed but she wasn't going to admit to it. A fat lip was nothing compared to her back anyway. Tomorrow the swelling would be all gone and the lip as good as new.

'No icepacks.' Joe was back, holding a plastic cup. 'I could only get these.'

Lauren looked in to see two ice cubes sliding about in the bottom. 'It doesn't matter.'

'Yes, it does.' Joe pinched a tissue from the box on the nurses' desk and folded it over between his fingers, grasped a single cube and laid it gently against Lauren's lip. He looked into her eyes. 'I'm sorry I headbutted you.'

'You didn't mean it,' she mumbled around the cube.

He kept looking at her. His left hand rested on her shoulder, still holding the cup.

She became brutally aware of their surroundings: the triage nurse casting a curious glance their way, the fluorescent light overhead, a doctor somewhere explaining the mechanisms of a stroke in loud slow words. She could smell Joe's sweat, and the stink of the crazy man on them. Her hands prickled as her lip went numb. The cold contrasted with the flush that rushed over her.

'Joe.'

'I can't hold it on straight if you talk.'

The ice was melting and the water ran down his wrist, dripping onto her shirt, working its way through to her skin. He blinked slowly. His eyes had flecks of yellow in their deep brown irises. She looked away.

'Joe.'

'No talking.'

She looked back at him. He gave her half a smile and that was it, she couldn't help it, she leaned forward past the ice cube and pressed her lips against his. They were as soft as she'd imagined, and she tasted lip balm and coffee, and then she saw the surprise in his eyes and pulled back. *Oh god* . . .

'Sorry,' she whispered.

He glanced sideways at the desk.

The nurse. She was sitting behind the computer, out of sight. She couldn't have seen it – if she was sitting exactly like that when it happened. Lauren hoped she wasn't a friend of Claire's.

'I'm sorry,' she said again.

Joe smiled at her. 'See, I knew it was more than just a fat lip. You've got a head injury. You're concussed. You've obviously lost your marbles in a big, big way.'

Just the opposite.

The mood in the late-afternoon meeting was solemn. The doors were locked. Mobile phones were left outside. Ella had seen a couple of detectives, strangers to her, walking about the floor. Nobody introduced them. She guessed they were the investigators into the leak.

'Here's where we stand,' Kuiper said. 'There's been no threatening phone call to Lauren's house or mobile, no sign of trouble in the vicinity, and no approach made to her while she's been at work. We have to consider the possibility that the leak found out about our strategies and warned Werner off.'

It was more than a possibility, Ella thought. It was damn near a certainty.

'He might leave it a week or so, hoping we'll relax, then try again. Or he might try an attack in some other manner. We need to be vigilant. And remember, watch every word that you say until we find the mole.

'I contacted the detectives who worked on the

Blake homicide and let them know what we've learned,' he went on. 'Fredriks said he'll get in touch with the coroner's office on Monday about reopening the case, and probably then begin by reinterviewing Lauren. Perjury charges seem likely.'

Ella had expected as much, seeing as Lauren admitted her actions. It was in the conviction and possible sentencing that her circumstances would be taken into consideration. Either way, it would affect her standing as a witness when they finally got Werner to court for Kennedy. She felt bad for Lauren, bad for the case. She'd so loved that feeling she'd had at the start, the thought of the dying declaration and what it meant, the pure and simple *justice* of it all that Kennedy could testify through Lauren against his killer. Now the defence would be slagging the paramedic off at every turn.

'Moving on.' Kuiper looked at Detective Rebecca Kanowski. 'Where are we with Deborah Kennedy?'

'No word on her location yet,' Rebecca said. 'There's a state-wide alert on her car, and traces have been put on her credit card and bank accounts. We gained access to said accounts and found some interesting details.' She passed around photocopied pages. 'Over the three days since Kennedy was killed, the two accounts held in their joint names, one a savings and the other a cheque account, were all but emptied.'

Ella took a copy of the records and handed the rest on.

'As you can see, the total amount withdrawn was some two hundred thousand dollars,' Rebecca said.

'Further checking revealed a history of periodic cash deposits over the past three years, ranging between eight and fifteen thousand dollars, usually every couple of months. The total amount of these deposits is roughly one hundred thousand dollars.'

Ella doubted Kennedy had made that from delivering computers for Benson Drysdale.

'It's not much compared with some of the amounts we see, admittedly,' Rebecca said. 'But we've also found that the entire amount of his weekly pay was put into the account and then not touched, and this leads us to believe the Kennedys were living on cash they kept back out of those deposit amounts.'

'Did Mrs Kennedy work?' Murray asked.

'Not as far as we know,' Rebecca said. 'We're trying to find out more about these deposits now. A search of the flat failed to locate any evidence of the Kennedys using an accountant, but we're waiting on tax records to come back.'

Kuiper was up at the whiteboard again. Space was getting short. 'Marconi?'

Ella opened her notebook and smoothed down the page. 'Mrs Kennedy asked for the funeral to be held off indefinitely, saying that family from overseas couldn't yet come out.'

'We haven't found evidence that there is any family overseas,' Kuiper said to the group.

Ella said, 'She paid in advance – not the usual method according to the funeral staff, but they were happy to accommodate her wishes. They're going to contact us if she gets in touch with them.' She flipped over a page in her notebook. 'Also, we spoke to a

Helen Flinders who lives near Steyne Park and who says she's been having an affair with James Kennedy.' She summarised the history of their relationship. 'She said she saw Kennedy in the park on Tuesday night, just after seven, talking to a man who she described as a little shorter than Kennedy, balding, with dark hair going grey, dressed in dark trousers and a light-coloured short-sleeved shirt. She said they looked like they knew each other, and both looked very serious, though Kennedy didn't seem frightened or anxious. She's certain that Kennedy saw her, but when he gave no sign of knowing her she assumed the man was somebody from the other part of his life and she walked straight past.'

People jotted notes as she spoke.

'Flinders also told us that Kennedy took a call on his mobile back on Wednesday the fourth at six thirty, quarter to seven in the evening. She said Kennedy was saying–' Ella checked her notes, '–"No, no, I told you I don't want to do that any more. None of us want to". Afterwards, Flinders didn't ask what it was about, and Kennedy didn't tell her.'

Pilsiger said, 'We've checked his mobile phone records and the number that called him then is a local landline. Strongy's onto that one for us.'

Graeme Strong nodded.

'The other thing we found on those records,' Pilsiger said, 'is that though Deborah Kennedy claimed she'd called her husband on Tuesday evening, because he was supposedly unexpectedly late home, there were no calls to him from their flat or elsewhere in that time period at all.'

Murray nudged Ella, and she raised her eyebrows at him.

'If we knew where she was, we could ask her,' Kuiper said.

Ella saw Kanowski look at the table.

Kuiper picked up a sheaf of pages and started handing them out. 'Interpol got back to us today. Werner was arrested two years ago while driving a car erratically through a rural area outside Vienna and being found to be drunk and to have two hundred grams of cocaine hidden in the boot. He was sentenced to a year in jail and served ten months before being released on probation. A drug conviction like that would bring him to the attention of the authorities here if he applied for a visa or attempted entry on his own passport, so this adds strength to our belief that he's here under a false name.

'Now here's the good bit,' he said. 'Austrian police found the time to nip around to his address and see what's what. His information lists him as living with his parents, but lo and behold, he wasn't there. His parents swore black and blue that while he was here in Oz five years ago, he's not here now. Instead, he's currently said to be on a boat in the Mediterranean somewhere, been gone about a month, they're not sure precisely where, and they don't have contact details, not even a mobile.'

Murray leaned forward in his seat. 'Where does his passport put him?'

'These modern times, the European Union lets its citizens shoot about crossing borders whenever and wherever they please, with no need to show passports,' Kuiper said.

'That's convenient,' Strong said.

'Very,' Kuiper said. 'As is the credit card statement Werner's parents gave to the police showing that his card had been used a few times in the past three weeks in various Mediterranean ports.'

'That's simple enough,' Ella said. 'Give your card to your mate, tell him to load up on the fuel and groceries, and you're set.'

'What kind of record do the parents themselves have?' Strong said.

'Nothing too significant.' Kuiper smiled. 'Receiving stolen goods, social security fraud, dealing marijuana.'

'Hooray for genetic determination,' Murray said.

Detectives laughed.

Kuiper said, 'We've made the request to Interpol that Werner's exact whereabouts in the Mediterranean be determined, but that of course involves police from a number of different countries, and if he is constantly on the move he could be very hard to track down.'

'Particularly if he's really here,' Ella said.

Lauren sat in the back of the ambulance next to the drowsing old man with the blocked catheter and watched Joe in the mirror. He looked into it often, but not at her.

The case sheet folder was open on her lap but she'd filled in very little of the page. She coloured in another little box then glanced up at Joe again. This time he was looking at her.

'You okay?'

She nodded. 'You?'

'Fine 'n' dandy.'

She bent to the case sheet. Fine and dandy – what did that mean? He might be happy that she'd kissed him, or he might be over it already. Put it out of his mind. Forgotten.

She wanted to say something, but what did you say? She'd put it out there, she'd shown how she felt, now she had to leave things up to him.

The old man opened his eyes and looked around. 'Need to go to the toilet.'

'I know,' she said. 'The tube's blocked. We'll be at the hospital soon.'

'Need to go now.' He waited for her to respond, but his dementia had taken away his ability to understand her explanation.

'Okay.' She patted his hand.

If Joe wanted to say something he would. If not, then he wouldn't. It wasn't her place to do or say any more; she'd overstepped the line already.

They stopped at a red light. The old man dozed off with his mouth open. Lauren watched the early evening traffic out the side window. Control sent a car to a child fallen from a scooter, and Lauren looked to the front, about to say something about the case, only to find Joe watching her. He looked away quickly. She closed her mouth and turned to the side once more, but sneaked a look back moments later. Joe was touching his lips, running his fingertips over them, staring out the windscreen.

She smiled to herself. Perhaps things were fine 'n' dandy indeed.

Sal sat on the edge of the bed. Tracy leaned against the windowsill, her arms folded. 'I can't handle that noise,' she said.

The bedroom doors were closed but the guitar chords came through as though the walls were made of paper.

'She's just learning,' Sal said.

'Does she have to do it now?'

The guitar stopped for a moment then started again, a different chord this time. Sal pictured Lizzie concentrating on her fingering. She was thirteen, his sister's oldest daughter, and she thought he was stupid, but she was funny and brave and he liked her.

Tracy shifted her weight and sighed.

'Come and sit down, cookie.' He patted the bed. He wanted to feel Tracy's arms around him, to press his face to her neck. He wanted to stop thinking.

'Forget it.'

'The noise won't go on forever.'

'Your house smells funny,' she said.

'I can open the window.'

She rolled her eyes. Sal shifted his gaze past her out the window, to the tops of the trees in Mrs Seccombe's place next door. It wasn't just the smell or the noise, he knew. He had changed and she didn't like it. He'd made damn sure she hadn't ever seen him cry, but still he sensed she saw how weak he felt. He should stand up and tell her that if she was going to insult his house and his family like that she could just fuck off. There must be other ways to get the information they needed, ways that didn't involve being put down like this.

'You got that necklace yet?' she said.

'No.'

She sighed.

'I don't control the money, okay?' *Wrong thing to say.* 'We have to wait until the shit's processed before we can sell it, all right? You think that's done overnight?'

She muttered something about Thomas.

'What?'

She shrugged.

Sal stood up, anger giving him strength and making his throat tight. 'What'd you say?'

She stared straight at him. 'I said, maybe I should go directly to Thomas.'

'This is my family's deal. My uncle set it up, my brother and me run it. Thomas is just our helper, okay? You do *not* go directly to him for anything.'

'Yeah, but your uncle's dead, isn't he, and your brother's on his way, and it seems to me you don't do much running of anything any more.'

'Thomas knows how to cook it, that's why—'

'Whatever.' She flipped her hair over her shoulder and looked at her watch, a Cartier bought by Sal. 'I gotta go.'

'Thanks so much for stopping by.'

She flounced past him to the door and down the stairs. He listened as her footsteps stopped. There was a low murmur of voices. Was Thomas back? And now Tracy was talking to him?

He stepped softly to the top of the stairs. He was sure it was Thomas. He strained his ears but couldn't pick up any words. Then the front door opened and closed, and Thomas appeared at the foot of the stairs before he could move away.

'Everything okay?' Thomas said.

'Yep, sure, why wouldn't it be?'

Outside, Tracy's yellow Corolla started up and drove away. Thomas smiled and walked from view.

Sal went back into his room and sat on the bed. The chords, which had stopped when Tracy stamped out, started again. He put his face in his hands.

Julio's laboured breathing preceded him into the room. 'You okay?' He leaned against the wall. 'Not gettin' any love?'

Sal sat up straight and squared his shoulders. 'Silly bitch is playing up is all.'

Julio's beanie dwarfed his bony skull. His wrists were like twigs. The bedsocks he wore all the time sagged around his ankles.

Sal looked away. 'She was talking to Thomas.'

'So?'

'She's my contact,' Sal said. 'All info's supposed to go through me.'

'Somebody sounds jealous.' Julio looked like a dead man when he grinned, all teeth and skull.

Sal rubbed his eyes to block the sight. 'It's not that.' *She's gone right off me anyway, for everything except money.* 'How can we control what's going on if she's talking to Thomas behind our backs?'

'You always think there's some conspiracy, somebody's out to do somebody else over.'

'This is our thing,' Sal said. 'We should talk to Thomas together and tell him to leave. Just cut our losses and get out while we can.'

Julio shook his head. 'Thomas won't go.'

'He might if you talk to him.'

'He won't,' Julio said. 'That's money he's cooking. He won't just throw that down the drain and leave.'

'The cops put a tap on that paramedic's phone, they have people watching her house,' Sal said. 'They want him bad, and they'll keep coming till they get him.'

'All he needs is a few days now that he's got those heaters.'

'The cops could pull up any time.'

Julio went to the window and made a big show of peering out. 'Where? Where?'

'It's not funny.'

'Relax, bro. Think about the money. Nothing bad's going to happen.'

Easy to say when it isn't you who'll be going to jail. Furious at himself for even thinking that, Sal swiped his hand over his forehead. Julio wasn't going to be somewhere better. He wished his brother would sit beside him, maybe even put his arm over his shoulders. He glanced up but Julio was looking out the window at next door.

'When we get that money I'm going to buy the world's biggest satellite dish and plasma and show that bitch Seccombe who's got the best and loudest TV.'

Julio's room overlooked Mrs Seccombe's bed-room. 'She's deaf,' Sal said.

'Yeah, well, maybe, but she flips through those channels just to show how many she's got.'

Once he got stuck on the topic of Mrs Seccombe he was away. Sal changed the subject. 'Will you at least think about talking to Thomas?'

'It's you and him, bro,' Julio said. 'I told you that when I got sick. Christ, you wanted it that way.'

But that was back when things were good, when Uncle Paulo was still overseeing things and they'd all thought Julio would beat the big C.

Sal folded his arms and squeezed his biceps hard. *I'm alone.*

NINETEEN

It was just after eight thirty Saturday morning when Ella sat at her desk and called Lauren. 'How's everything? Peaceful night?'

'Quiet as,' Lauren said.

'You're working today, is that right? With Joe?'

'Yep,' she said. 'I've got my tracker, and the mobile's fully charged.'

'Good,' Ella said. 'I'll check in again later.'

The second she put the phone down, it rang. 'Homicide, Marconi.'

'You're sounding very serious this morning.'

She recognised the voice immediately. Wayne Rhodes. He'd worked at Lane Cove when she was at Hunters Hill and they'd often run into each other on jobs. 'Wayne, hi, how's it going?'

'Can't complain, you know how it is,' he said.

'Yeah – if you do you get the sack.'

They laughed. Murray came in with two coffees and put one on her desk, looking at her questioningly. She flapped a hand. 'So where are you working now?'

'Surry Hills,' Wayne said. 'And I'm not just ringing for a chitchat, as nice as that would be. I've got a case with a little intersection to yours. It's probably nothing, but I saw your name on the case info in the system and thought I'd just run things by you, see if it rings any bells on your end. Do you have a pen? Are you in your comfy chair?'

'I'm very rarely out of it.' Ella moved her coffee and grabbed a pen. 'Shoot.'

'Okay,' Wayne said. 'This is about a man who fell from a train and died. He'd been in his car, run a red light, officers were right behind him and pulled him over. He hands up his licence and when they're back at their car checking it, he jumps out and runs. They chase him to Redfern station and onto a train. They almost have him when he decides to try for the roof, and down he goes.'

Ella made a face. 'Under?'

'No, thank goodness. The officers are traumatised enough. Dude fell on his scone, had a heartie, officers did CPR till the ambos got there, and they took him to hospital but he was dead.'

'When did this happen? Name's not Thomas Werner, by any chance?'

'Tuesday evening, seven-thirty,' Wayne said. 'Name's Adrian Nolan.'

'My current case died Tuesday as well.'

'Bad day to be out and about, obviously,' Wayne said. 'Now listen, because here's where it gets interesting. Guy's driving a rental car, had it for three days, booked it for a month. Yet he had a perfectly good car at home.'

'Wow, that is mysterious.'

'But wait, there's more,' he said. 'He owned a warehouse, and he used Quiksmart for his deliveries. Most often, it was your guy who did the work.'

'Wouldn't couriers have particular routes they run? Regular customers they deliver for?'

'Are you shooting me down in flames here?' She could hear he was smiling. 'Are you crapping all over my theory?'

'So far I haven't heard a theory. Only a lot of coincidences.'

'I prefer to call them concurrent facts,' Wayne said. 'Here's another one then. See if you can guess the name of one of the paramedics who picked the dude up off the lines.'

'Lauren Yates was there?'

'The one and only.'

Ella couldn't see how any significance could be attached to that. 'You know how many paramedics are on duty in the city on a Tuesday night?'

'How many?'

'I have no idea,' she said. 'But there are probably, what, six stations in the city itself? That's probably only fifteen or twenty staff. Chances aren't bad that the same crew would go to both our deadies.'

'I love how you bite over coincidences.'

'I'm hanging up now,' she said.

Wayne laughed. 'I'm going to see Nolan's widow later. She left a message last night, said she's got something terribly important to talk to me about.'

'Is she thingy about how he died?'

'Well, grief-stricken, but okay otherwise. She

doesn't seem to blame the boys. She's grateful they worked on him,' Wayne said. 'I'll talk to you later.'

She put the phone down.

'Who was that?' Murray said.

'Wayne Rhodes.'

'Sounded like he's got something for us.'

'Not really,' she said. 'Or not yet anyway.'

Wayne was tall and well-built, and looked like the rugby captain he'd once been. He was quick with a joke but was serious, calm and empathetic with victims, and they loved him for it. Ella knew that whatever Mrs Nolan was worried about, she would soon be unloading everything to him.

Murray put down his cup. 'There's our man.'

Ella turned to see Detective Graeme Strong walk into the room carrying his coffee and newspaper.

'Give him a second to sit down,' Ella said, but Murray was already on his way.

'Did you get that record from your mate in the phone company?' he said.

'As a matter of fact I did.' Strong put his coffee down and reached into his pocket for his notebook. 'Rang me last night. Let's see . . . ah. Yes. He said the call came from a phone inside a club called Rosie's, on Aylett Street in the Cross.'

'That's fantastic,' Ella said.

Murray frowned. 'Could be tricky to tie it to any one person.'

'We haven't seen it yet,' she said. 'Maybe it's in a restricted area. Maybe there's CCTV on it. Who's got the job of looking into that company that runs it, what's it called, Clubs Inc?'

'Lambert.'

Across the room, weedy Detective Jason Lambert was talking to the HR chick as she put a stack of paperwork on Pilsiger's desk. Ella watched Jason smile and wink and oh-so-casually smooth back his thin hair, and wondered if the young woman was mentally rolling her eyes. Some detectives thought they were hot shit just because of the job they did, but if Jason could imagine an admin person being impressed then he was dumber than Ella had thought.

'Hey, Lamby,' she called, holding back a smile as the HR chick, obviously seeing her chance to get away, hurried from the room. 'How'd you go with that search on Clubs Inc and Rosie's nightclub?'

'Just basic stuff so far.' He went to his desk and took a page from a manila file. 'These are the company directors. I ran their names but none have records.'

Ella read down the list. No names jumped out at her. 'Oh well. Thanks.'

Her coffee was going cold. She pushed the cup out of her way. 'So what do you reckon, we go around to Rosie's and see what we can see?' she said to Murray.

'Better to leave it till this evening,' Murray said. 'Saturday night, should be lots of staff there to talk to. At the moment they're probably all asleep after working last night.'

'I guess,' she said. 'Where's that list of staff that Everly printed out? We run them through the computer, we might find a little something to hold over their heads when we do get there.'

★

Joe called clear at Prince Henry Hospital.

'Great timing, Thirty-four,' Control said. 'I've got an explosion and fire in a small factory in Saxby Street, Mascot. Police and fire on way also.'

Lauren flicked the beacons on, then added the siren as she left the hospital grounds. Joe opened the directory and ran his finger down the street index.

'Real or fake?' he said.

'A fake explosion?'

'Could be a firecracker,' he said. 'Next left.'

'And the fire was the match that lit it?'

'You never know.'

Lauren concentrated on the road, but she felt awkward, prickly even. Joe was his usual cheery self this morning. It was as if she'd never kissed him. As if he hadn't touched his lips in that way that made her shiver if she thought about it too long.

She'd relived it over and over last night, lying in bed, listening to Kristi get up and check the locks. Maybe Joe had put it down to stress, thought she'd done it because of emotional strain.

She braked hard behind a dithering driver. 'Come on, idiot.' She swung onto the wrong side of the road and shot him a look as she went past.

Maybe Joe didn't know how she felt at all.

But how could he not?

'Right here,' Joe said. 'Then second on the left.'

She turned into the street and saw the fire truck at the far end.

'Thirty-four's on scene,' Joe said into the mike.

A cop waved them down as they drew near. Lauren braked and lowered her window. 'Have to stand clear for a bit,' he said, his voice raised over the sound of the fire truck's engine. 'It's a meth lab, so we have to clear everything.'

'Any patients?' Joe said.

The cop shook his head. 'Got one shitbag out of it. He was in another room when it blew up so missed out on the burns. He's in cuffs at the moment but uninjured. Do you mind standing by for a while?'

'Not a problem.'

The cop hurried off and Joe picked up the mike. 'Thirty-four, we've been requested to stand by at this location until the scene is cleared.'

'Copy that, Thirty-four, I have you standing by.'

Lauren drove onto the concrete forecourt of a closed panelbeater's workshop. She turned the engine off and Joe put his window down and hung his arm out, fingers tapping the metal skin of the door. The morning was warm. Further along the street people stood about at the front of the few small factories and businesses that were open, shading their eyes to see. Police herded others out of the places that were too close, and they gathered in groups on the roadway, arms folded or hands in pockets, talking and watching. A photographer turned up and began firing off shots.

Joe leaned back in his seat and yawned. Lauren stayed forward over the wheel, arms folded on the top and chin resting on her wrists. She felt drained by everything that was going on. Her back hurt more today than it had yesterday, even after the ED doctor had cleaned and redressed it. She should ring Kristi, make sure she was okay.

'Last night Claire and I went to check out this wedding venue she found on the web.'

Lauren stared across the street at the locked roller door of an auto electrician's shop. Joe didn't often talk about the wedding, but when he did she felt sick. Today, though, it was better than talking about Thomas. 'How'd it look?'

He shrugged. 'Okay.'

'That good?'

'Have you seen the money these places want?' Joe pulled his left ankle up onto his right knee. 'It's only one day, but you could spend your entire house deposit on it easily.'

'Even a Sydney house deposit?'

'Easily,' he said again. 'I suggested we go with a barbecue at her parents' place, like we did for the engagement party. I liked that; it was nice and simple, people could just sit about and talk.'

'What'd she say?'

'Said I wasn't romantic. I said I couldn't see anything romantic about spending thousands and thousands of dollars when what really mattered was having your friends and family with you for the occasion, and you could do that anywhere, and save the money for a house.'

'So what will you do?'

'Look at more places, I'll argue the budget down, she'll argue it back up a bit, and we'll finally come to some kind of agreement.'

'You've got a whole year anyway.'

He shifted in his seat. 'She was asking this place last night if they have vacancies in March.'

'Even after you said you couldn't move your leave?'

'She said we can do it on my days off, have a couple of days away, then have the proper honeymoon later.'

'She just came out with that last night?'

Joe nodded. 'Out of the blue.'

She must know about the kiss. 'She hasn't asked about—'

'About what?'

'Well, I'm still worried about that train job.'

'I told you, she's forgotten all about it.'

Lauren hoped so.

A cop came over to them. 'Deadshit's decided he's injured now.'

Lauren started the ambulance and rolled across the asphalt behind him then parked where he indicated. Joe grabbed the Oxy-Viva and followed the cop towards the small factory. The windows were blown out, the walls above them were stained with smoke, and the drone of the fire truck's engine drilled into Lauren's head. The air stank of chemicals. She stepped over a fat hose that leaked water on the concrete and the cop pointed to a man lying face down in handcuffs, police in black jumpsuits standing around him.

'What's up?' Joe said to the patient, who turned his head to look up at him with difficulty. Lauren saw angry eyes, a cropped dark beard, and the glint of a row of studs in his ear.

'Get these fucking cuffs off so I can breathe and I might fucking tell you.'

'If you can talk like that you're breathing fine,' Joe said. 'Are you injured?'

'Yes, these assholes hurt my back, and I'm suing them for it, and I'll sue you too if you don't give me morphine.'

The wind picked up and the chemical smell got stronger. It was like a mix of cat urine and nail polish remover. Lauren shivered. She'd smelled it before. Recently.

She went closer to the factory and tried to see in. A cop stood outside writing on a clipboard. Lauren said, 'What's that smell?'

The cop gestured with his pen into the building. 'They've been cooking ice. Meth. Stinks, doesn't it?'

'Does it always smell like this?'

'Pretty much,' he said. 'It's why they hide the labs in industrial areas, or on big properties with nobody around. Places where the smell won't be so noticed.'

'Is that how they get found? When somebody notices it?'

'Sometimes it's that,' he said. 'Some get found when they blow up, like this one. We've also cleaned up a few lately because of that amnesty. The little guy dobs in a bigger guy and in return he gets looked after. We'll try to use it to flip this idiot too, on the next one up the line, but I don't like our chances.'

The ice cook was yelling again about how he was going to sue everybody. 'I'll take your fucking houses and you'll all be out on the street!'

The cop said, 'I'd take you in for a sticky-beak but they haven't cleared it as safe yet. These things are a full-on health hazard.'

Lauren stared at the blackened sopping floor. Thomas had smelled like this. She could close her eyes and recreate the entire scene in a heartbeat – his shirt in her face, the stink that filled her nostrils, the movement of his knife arm, the terror that threatened to take her voice and her strength when she needed them most. Yes, he'd smelled exactly like this.

'Are you okay? You've gone a bit green,' the cop said.

'Huh?'

'The fumes can do that sometimes. You'd better get out of here.'

'I will.' She pulled her phone off her belt as she walked to the ambulance, and hit the button to call Ella.

Ella put the phone down and hurried down the hall to Kuiper's office. He was on the phone and he gestured for her to sit. 'Right,' he said. 'Okay.' He jotted notes. 'Yes, let me know. Thanks.'

As soon as he hung up, Ella said, 'Lauren just rang me. She's at a meth lab explosion, and she swears that Thomas had exactly the same smell on him on Thursday.'

'She's certain?'

Ella nodded. 'If he's cooking meth, that could be why he's still here, and why he hasn't left the country despite knowing that we're onto him.'

Kuiper drew a line across the page and started new notes below it. 'We'll need to get people checking out local chemical suppliers, storage houses, places like that test tube factory in Ultimo, and look on chemists' databases for large purchases of pseudoephedrine.' He looked up. 'Lauren's fine, otherwise? No sign of our man?'

'Not a thing,' Ella said. 'She sounds pretty good, considering.'

'Good. What else is happening?'

'The call made to Kennedy's mobile when he was with Helen Flinders came from inside Rosie's nightclub. We're going there late this afternoon.'

Kuiper nodded and looked at the notes he'd made while on the phone. 'Deborah Kennedy's been spotted out near Griffith. A local officer saw her car this morning when it ran a stop sign. A male was driving, and there were two women in the car also. He checked the numberplate, found our alert and started a pursuit. Unfortunately he's new to the area and lost the vehicle on the back roads.'

'Does she have family out there?'

'Not that we know of,' Kuiper said. 'Kanowski's been in touch with her parents, who live in a retirement village in Drummoyne, and the only relatives they've told us about are in Melbourne. The Griffith boys are going to start a search of the area, see what they can turn up. Could be hard though. Huge region.'

Ella nodded. She wondered briefly about mentioning Wayne Rhodes's call, but there wasn't really much to say. Better to wait and see what else he found.

Kuiper said, 'If you and Murray are going to be

working this evening, do you want to take some downtime now?'

'I'd appreciate it,' she said. 'I'll let him know.'

He nodded. 'Meeting's at four.'

'See you then.'

Netta looked up as Ella entered the ward and let her mouth fall open in mock surprise.

'I know, I know.' Ella kissed her mother's cheek then sat down by her bed. 'It's this case. I start early and I finish late.'

'You should've been here before,' Netta said. 'I could've shown you my walking.'

'I saw the doctor outside. He said you're doing very well. You only have another week to go.'

'Less than that,' she said.

'They have to make sure the infection's gone and that you'll be safe at home with Dad.'

'Of course I'll be safe.'

'They need to be sure,' Ella said. 'How is Dad? And Adelina?'

'Dad's got his cough back.' Netta smoothed the blanket over the side of the bed.

'See, you don't want him getting sick and having to come into hospital because of the strain of looking after you.'

'I'm losing weight in here.' Netta raised her arm and plucked at the loose skin. 'I'm fading right away. If I was at home I could cook even just a few things, and I could get some decent sleep. Between you you could do it.'

'I'm sorry, but I have this case.'

'Should work always come before family?'

'If it was me that was killed, wouldn't you want someone like me on my case?'

Netta slapped her hand. 'Don't even say that.'

The nurse came in to see one of the other patients in the room. Netta leaned over to Ella and nodded at the patient. 'She's why I don't sleep. She snores all night. At home it's so quiet you can hear the plants grow.'

Ella forced a smile. She'd wanted to visit; she'd felt guilty about not getting there sooner, and had even looked forward to sitting and chatting. But now she felt cooped up and irritated. The case tugged at her mind. She should call Lauren again, for starters, let her know she'd passed on the ice info and it was a good lead for them. She could ask her also about Nolan, what she remembered of that job and whether anything odd had been going on. She had no idea what that might constitute, but if you didn't ask everyone everything you might miss something. And she could go and see Kristi, see how she was doing. Ask her what she knew about Rosie's, if Thomas had ever been there when they were together. Who he'd known.

Movement brought her back to reality. Her mother reached for the call buzzer. '–you'll be able to see how well I can go.'

'What?'

'I'm just saying I'll show you how well I can walk.'

'No, no.' Ella grabbed the buzzer. 'I believe you.'

'I want to show you.'

'Mum, really, it's fine. I have to get going anyway.'

Netta looked at the clock on the wall. 'But you have a whole hour yet.'

'I'm sorry,' Ella said. 'I have to get back to work.' She bent and hugged her mother, feeling the bones of her shoulders, the way Netta patted her back – pat pat rub – the same way she'd done all her life.

'Do you think if you get a chance you could go past the house and make sure the plants are okay?' Netta said in her ear. 'Lily next door is watching them but I think sometimes she forgets.'

'I'll try,' Ella said. 'I'll see.'

'And try and visit again? Or call? Ella, carina?'

'Si, mama, I will. Ciao.'

Once in the car she felt guilty. She couldn't spare another twenty minutes? Even ten?

She should go back.

She gripped the wheel and stared out the dirty windscreen for a moment, feeling torn, then reached for her seatbelt.

Mum would be fine. She had work to do.

TWENTY

Ella took Stacey Street up to the Hume Highway then turned into Chullora. She wouldn't stop, she thought, she'd just drive past her parents' house, then she could say things looked fine. Lily took care of plants like they were her children, so it was hard to imagine that anything would die before Netta got home. Lily was more likely to have propagated a whole new garden's worth of life for her.

She slowed as she neared the house. Lily was sitting on an empty fertiliser bag on the nature strip, her red legionnaire's cap pulled low over her face, a man's blue business shirt buttoned over her sundress. She was digging up bindii with a silver dinner fork. Ella looked past her at the house, seeing the greenhouse down the side, the roses along the low front wall, the fern trees by the verandah. Lily was looking at the car now, and Ella waved though Lily wouldn't see her behind the tinted windows. Never mind. She'd at least been past, and things looked fine. Netta would be happy. Well, not happy. Ella drove on and thought about her mother's usual cheerful demeanour. The unhappiness she gave off now was a clear sign of pain and fear and distress at being where she was. Ella turned back onto the Hume Highway, heading for Summer Hill, and wondered if there was some way to bring her home earlier. Both her mum and dad would be thrilled, she knew, but it was hard to commit herself when she never knew what might crop up with the case and when she might work late or even overnight. That'd be no good if Netta was sitting in the bathroom waiting to be showered. Might Adelina come and stay? If Adelina was there as well, Ella would be less restricted, and it might just work.

Well, she would think about it, but not say anything yet.

Traffic was stop-start all the way to Summer Hill, and then she had to wait for a break between oncoming cars to turn into Lauren's street. Sitting there, she glanced down towards Lauren's house and was startled to see an ambulance parked at the front. *Oh Jesus, what now?* She should've called to check if things were okay. She fumbled for her mobile in her bag, one eye on the traffic, then saw a gap and shot around the corner.

The ambulance was parked right outside the house but there were no people in sight and the front door was closed. Ella hurried across the footpath, her stomach tense over what she might find. A knock brought the sound of a window opening overhead. Ella squinted up into the sun.

'Hi.' It was Kristi's voice. 'I'll come right down.'

When she opened the door, Ella said, 'You had me worried for a moment.'

'Oh, because of the truck? Lauren and Joe were in the area so they dropped in.'

This was handy. Ella followed her upstairs. When she walked into the living room Lauren got up from the lounge. 'Hi.'

Squeals came from the attic. 'Joe, wait!' Felise shouted.

'Just thought I'd check in,' Ella said. 'Make sure all is quiet, and let you know that we're right onto that meth lead you gave us.'

Kristi perched on a corner of the kitchen table. 'I'd believe it of him.'

'That smell's pretty distinctive,' Ella said. 'I also wanted to check a couple of other things. Lauren, do you remember going to a man fallen from a train the same night that Kennedy died?'

She nodded. 'We worked on him but he died. Why?'

'There could be a link between him and Kennedy.'

'You're kidding. What kind of link?'

'We're not sure yet,' Ella said. 'There're lots of aspects to investigate, but I wanted to ask whether you noticed anything strange at that scene. I know I'm clutching at straws here but every little piece of information can help.'

Lauren looked thoughtful. 'The train was away from the station, so there was nobody around watching. The police were there, pretty anxious and upset. The patient's injuries matched the story that they told us, that he'd fallen from the train while it was moving. He'd landed headfirst. Joe was there too, and two other paramedics. We just worked on him by the train, then took him up to St Vincent's where they pronounced him.'

'Okay,' Ella said. 'Do either of you know of a club in the Cross called Rosie's?'

'I've been there on jobs a couple of times,' Lauren said. 'The usual nightclub calls: drug overdoses, collapse unconscious from alcohol.'

Kristi said, 'I've never heard of it.'

'You never went there in your time with Thomas?'

Kristi shook her head.

'Isn't it a fairly new place?' Lauren said. 'One of the cases I did was during their big opening-night party, and I'm sure that was since we've lived here.'

'So I would've been out of that life by then,' Kristi said.

Ella made a note.

'Are you any closer to finding him?' Kristi said.

'It's hard to say,' Ella said. 'We have all these little bits of information and we're slowly putting them together, but it's difficult to know exactly what we're looking at.'

A radio crackled. 'Thirty-four, are you still in the Summer Hill area?'

Lauren lifted the portable to her mouth. 'Thirty-four, affirmative.'

'Thanks, Thirty-four, got a transfer for you, from Western Suburbs into RPA.'

'Copy, on way.' Lauren stood up and hooked the radio on her belt. 'Joe?'

He came downstairs with Felise over his shoulder. 'Job?'

Lauren nodded.

'Just drop this in the bin on the way out, will I?'

Felise squealed and locked her arms around his neck.

Ella said to Lauren under the noise, 'Got your tracker?'

She touched her shirt pocket. 'It's never off me.'

'And there's been nothing suspicious at all.'

Lauren shook her head. 'I guess he found out about the surveillance and phone taps and he's lying low.'

Ella hoped so. In her experience, however, somebody like Thomas was not so easily stopped, particularly if he wasn't planning to leave until he had finished cooking up his drugs. It was likely that he would still try to take action, to get at these witnesses, or to slow the case down in some way.

The question was, what would he do?

It was rest period in RPA's main medical ward and the corridor was sunlit and quiet when Joe and Lauren delivered their patient from Western Suburbs Hospital. He was a fifty-seven-year-old man with a metabolic disorder and renal failure. Joe eased him across to the hospital bed while Lauren gave her handover to the nurse in low tones. They said goodbye to the patient then wheeled the stretcher back to the lift.

On the ground floor they headed for the

ambulance bay, then Joe stopped just inside the doors. 'Wait here.' He stepped out to look in all directions, even squatting to peer under the ambulance.

Lauren said, 'He couldn't possibly know where we are.'

'Never underestimate the enemy.' He unlocked the ambulance and they loaded the empty stretcher in.

'Yeah, but that's—'

'You were lucky once.' Joe pulled the back door closed, leaving the rest unspoken.

You might not be so lucky again.

Lauren knew he was right. It just struck her as silly to think Thomas might come after her in broad daylight, with Joe right there, hospital security only a scream away, and any number of possible witnesses walking past on the street. She touched the tracker in her pocket and got into the ambulance cabin.

'Thirty-four, you on the air?' Control called.

Lauren grabbed the mike from the dash. 'Thirty-four's clear at RPA.'

'Thanks, Thirty-four, got a crane collapse at a building site in Castlereagh Street, no number given but it's near Goulburn Street. Reports of three people injured, at least one possibly code four. I have another crew on way plus rescue. Will try to get a better location for you.'

'I know the place.' Joe started the ambulance.

Lauren said into the mike, 'Thirty-four's on way. We know where it is.'

'Copy, thank you.'

Signs in Missenden Road asked drivers to keep

noise to a minimum. Joe drove as fast as quiet would allow, beacons on and siren off until he hit Parramatta Road where he braked and reached for the siren at the same time.

'One coming,' Lauren said over the wail. 'Okay, he's stopped. You're clear.'

The tyres screeched as Joe accelerated onto the main road. 'Bloody big cranes at this place.'

'Must've rolled, do you think?'

'Or the boom's broken somehow.' He hit the horn to change the siren to yelp. A meandering truck finally pulled to the left and he shot past. 'Come down and landed on people.'

'Real or fake?' Lauren pulled on gloves.

'Thirty-four,' Control said. 'Just an update, no need to reply. Police on scene state one code nine and unconscious, one with severe limb injuries and two walking wounded.'

'No need to guess now,' Joe said, driving faster.

The site was a deep hole beside Castlereagh. An anxious-looking man in a hard hat waved them into a gateway, pedestrians stopping to let them through, and Joe negotiated the ramp down into the scene. Lauren shivered at the sight of the crane. The end of its boom lay in the mud and the middle sagged like limp spaghetti from the upright section. An ambulance was parked near the end of the boom. Lauren spotted one officer clambering on the metal structure, the other crouched beside a person in the mud four metres away. Workers in dirty hard hats stood around two men sitting on the ground nearby. Some were crying.

Joe drove off the ramp and onto the muddy ground. Lauren felt the wheels slip then grip as he made his way across to the first ambulance. Before he'd properly stopped she was out and yanking gear from the back, looking over her shoulder at the scene.

A man was trapped in the structure of the boom, lying face down at an angle on a metal walkway, his head over the side, one hand dangling free. Paramedic Danny Sutton was trying to assess him through the frame that pinned him down.

Closer to them, paramedic Bryan Forbes held a thick dressing to a pale and moaning man's left thigh. He nodded to her. 'If you can take over here, I'll go help Danny.'

Lauren carried the Oxy-Viva and first aid kit over and put them down in the mud.

'Big open fracture,' Bryan went on. 'He was thrown from the thing as it came down. Fell about five metres, landed on the leg.'

'No LOC?'

Bryan shook his head. 'Awake the whole time. Ready?'

Lauren took over holding the dressing. As Bryan got up he leaned close to her ear. 'The guy who's trapped is this guy's little brother.'

Lauren looked down at her patient. His skin was pale, cold and sweaty, and his brown hair was plastered to his scalp. The blood from his leg wound had soaked into the mud around them and seeped into the dressing under her gloved fingers. She could feel its warmth. He wore shorts and a work shirt, all covered with mud. He grimaced, grasping the top of his thigh above the wound, his eyes fixed on the boom where his brother lay. Lauren felt for him. 'What's your name?'

'Charlie Addison.' He tried to raise himself up. 'How's my brother?'

'The other paramedics are looking after him,' she said. 'Where's your pain, apart from your leg? Can you take a deep breath?'

Joe brought the monitor and drug box over then opened the first aid kit.

'Can't breathe too deep, my back hurts.' Charlie lay back in the mud. 'Dizzy too.'

Lauren eased the pressure off the dressing and she and Joe had a quick peek. The flesh was torn open by the jagged broken end of the femur. The bleeding had all but stopped now. The exposed muscle and fatty tissue were coated with dirt, and the protruding end of the bone glistened whitely through the blood.

'Okay, Charlie, just lie still for me there,' Lauren said. 'I'm Lauren and this is Joe. He's going to do a couple of things to your leg while you and me have a talk and check some things out, okay?'

Joe opened some vials of normal saline and squirted the liquid into the wound, washing away the worst of the dirt.

'What's happening with my brother?'

'They're looking after him. They're great paramedics, those two. He's in excellent hands.' Lauren wrapped a blood pressure cuff around his arm. 'What's his name?'

'Mitchell.' He tried to see again.

'Charlie, you have to lie still, please.' Lauren looked at Joe, who was folding a large moistened dressing carefully around the broken bone end. 'Ninety on fifty. Pulse one-twenty.'

'Will he be okay?' Charlie tried to peer around her.

A couple of the workers forced angle grinders into the metal of the boom. One simply squatted in the mud and held Mitchell's limp hand. Out on the streets cars droned by, and a news helicopter hovered overhead.

'Charlie,' she said gently, slipping an oxygen mask over his face. 'If that was you in there, and he was here, would you want him to take care of himself?'

He focused on her face. Tears made clean lines towards his ears. 'I got him this job.'

Lauren wanted to say that it would be okay, but Bryan was worming his way under the crushed boom with a resus bag in his hands trying desperately to fit the mask to Mitchell's face.

'What if he dies?' Charlie's voice was thick.

'Charlie,' she said. 'Look at me. We need to take care of you, okay? Once we know you're stable we might be able to send Joe here over to help them work on Mitchell.'

It was a lie. Charlie needed surgery and far from splitting up they'd be getting him off to hospital as soon as they could.

'Good pulse.' Joe had eased off Charlie's left boot and pressed his gloved fingers to the pale skin.

Lauren shone a penlight torch into Charlie's eyes.

The pupils were equal and reacting. 'Okay, Charlie, I'm going to put a little needle in your arm and give you some medication for pain and some fluids to replace the blood you've lost.'

'I hate needles,' he said, his eyes on his brother.

'So does everyone, but it'll help you feel better. And I promise that before we go anywhere I'll get an update on Mitchell for you, okay?'

Soon the IV was in and the fluids running. Lauren injected five milligrams of morphine into the IV line then reached up to turn the flow faster. Joe was standing, holding the fluid bag and gazing over her. She turned to see where he was staring. The gateway was crowded with onlookers, as were the gaps in the hoarding. She looked back at Joe. 'What is it?'

'Never underestimate.'

'Even though we're down here?'

He didn't answer. She squeezed Charlie's arm. 'How are you feeling now?'

He blinked slowly. 'Mitchell?'

She looked across at the crane. The squatting workman was crying, holding Mitchell's hand to his face. Fire officers attacked the framework with cutting equipment. The helicopter came lower. Bryan glanced across at her, on his back under the boom, and their eyes met. 'He's hanging in there, Charlie. He's a tough one.' The words were sour. She knew it was only a matter of time before Mitchell arrested, and how could you do CPR on somebody who was pinned face down on a metal walkway?

They log-rolled Charlie onto a spine board and lifted him onto their stretcher. The wheels bogged down in the mud so they carried the stretcher to the ambulance and eased it in. Lauren climbed in after it and arranged pillows around Charlie's leg so it would be supported on the trip to hospital.

'How's Mitch?' he said.

'Joe's just gone to find out.' She injected another five of morph.

Joe came back and leaned into the ambulance to squeeze Charlie's right foot. 'He's holding on, but he's pretty crook, mate.' Out of Charlie's view he shook his head at Lauren and held up two fingers. Code two – cardiac arrest. Then four fingers. Code four. Dead.

As Charlie grew dazed under the effect of the drug, Lauren buckled herself in, trying to keep her mind on what she needed to do. Make a quick radio report to Control for the hospital, check obs again, start the case sheet. But all she could think about was the moment when Charlie would find out he'd lost his brother. She knew what that felt like, and she grasped his hand as the emotion flooded back. She kept her head turned away from him and blinked hard.

Joe looked at her in the mirror as he started the ambulance up the ramp. 'Want me to make the report?'

She nodded, not trusting herself to speak.

He called up Control and asked for a code three to St Vincent's. 'Male, late twenties, open fracture left femur with severe tissue damage, distal pulses present. Also lower back pain, no tingling or loss of sensation. No LOC. Last obs–' He looked at Lauren.

She took a deep breath. 'Pulse one-ten, beep one hundred on sixty.'

Joe relayed the information. 'ETA about five.'

'Copy, Thirty-four,' Control said. 'Any information on the code nine?'

'Uh, I believe they'll be calling you shortly,' Joe said. He rehooked the mike and Lauren saw him turn the radio volume down low. If the other crew called up to say Mitch was dead, Charlie wasn't going to hear it.

At the top of the ramp the workman was holding pedestrians and traffic back, and Joe turned onto the street and flicked the beacons and siren on.

When he pulled into the ambulance bay at St Vincent's four minutes later, Lauren took a final set of obs, turned off the IV line and laid the fluid bag on the bed, disconnected the monitor and tucked the case sheet folder under Charlie's pillow.

'How are you feeling?' she asked him.

'I'm worried about Mitch.'

'I'll see what I can find out for you.'

He put out his hand. 'Thanks for everything.'

She stripped off her glove. The calluses on his palm were hard against her fingers. 'You're very welcome, Charlie.'

Inside the ED, Joe positioned the stretcher beside the hospital bed and, with the help of two wardsmen, they carefully lifted Charlie across. Claire Bramley appeared, her uniform covered by a plastic apron, and grabbed for the case sheet folder. Lauren was quicker and tucked it under her arm.

'Sheet's not done yet,' she said. 'How about I just tell you what you need to know?'

Claire huffed and put her hands on her hips.

'Charlie's twenty-eight and was working on a crane boom–'

'Am I meant to know what that is?'

'The long arm part.' Lauren squeezed the folder. 'The boom collapsed and as it fell he was thrown to the ground. Fall was approximately five metres and he landed–'

'No arterial bleed?' Claire peeled back the bandage and dressing on his thigh without waiting for an answer.

If there was, you'd be getting a faceful.

'I thought you said the damage was severe,' Claire said.

'Initial obs were–'

'Look at the dirt in here!' Claire said to Charlie. 'She did a bad job of cleaning that, didn't she? What else did she stuff up?'

She slapped the dressing back down. Charlie flinched and Lauren felt her blood rise.

'One good thing,' Claire went on, 'at least you didn't need a tube.'

Lauren saw red. 'Claire–'

Claire ignored her and looked at Charlie. 'You got off pretty lucky, I'd say. Unlike your mate.'

'What?'

'The other feller, the one who died.' Claire yanked the blood pressure cuff down from the wall and hoisted Charlie's arm so she could wrap it around his bicep, oblivious to both the tears in Charlie's eyes and the pure fury in Lauren's.

Lauren grabbed her arm and pulled her into the drug storeroom. 'What the *fuck* are you doing?'

'That's assault.'

'It was his brother who died.'

'You could've told me.'

'When, exactly? And why should you need to be told? At the very least it was one of his colleagues.' Lauren clenched her fists. 'Don't you have any heart at all?'

'I've got enough for Joe.' Claire held up her gloved left hand. Her engagement ring stuck out against the latex. 'It's me he's marrying, you know.'

'I'm talking about a patient's welfare,' Lauren snapped. 'We were holding back about Charlie's brother until his family could be here with him.'

'It's me he'll come home to every night—'

'So he could have some support around him — are you listening to me? Are you registering *anything* I'm saying?'

'Hey.' Joe stood in the doorway, stern-faced. 'Everyone out there can hear.'

Lauren stamped out of the storeroom. Another nurse was with Charlie now, talking to him and handing him tissues. So angry she could hardly see straight, Lauren stormed out to the ambulance bay.

Joe came out behind her.

'I cannot believe her.' Lauren slammed the case sheet folder down on the bonnet. 'She told Charlie about his brother, just dropped it into the conversation like it was nothing, then didn't even have the heart or the sense to realise what she'd done. Even when I hauled her into the storeroom she—'

'You shouldn't have left him,' Joe said.

'You don't get it,' Lauren said. 'She slagged off

our cleaning of his wound as well, just to have a go at me, right there in front of him. She even brought up that bloody tube again.'

'You still shouldn't have left him.'

'But she was going on and on,' Lauren said, slower now.

'You took her away and left Charlie completely alone right at the moment when he needed somebody most.'

Lauren's mouth went dry.

'What if he'd gone flat? What if he wanted to talk? Who was there looking after him? I came in and found him crying, no bedrails up, no monitor on, nobody with him. That's pretty shitful patient care if you ask me.'

Lauren flushed with shame. 'What am I supposed to do? Just take everything she dishes out? Let her bag our treatment in front of him without pulling her up?'

'If you want to be professional, yes,' he said. 'You walk away.'

Lauren couldn't believe what she was hearing. 'It's irresponsible for me not to finish my handover.'

'She had enough to start treatment. That's all that matters and you know it.'

Lauren burned with anger and humiliation. 'I can't believe you're taking her side.'

His eyes were sad. 'Lauren, you need to grow up a bit.'

He walked back to the Emergency Department doors. Her vision blurred with tears. She climbed into the side door of the ambulance, pulled it shut behind her with a bang, and sobbed in privacy.

TWENTY-ONE

The afternoon meeting was short, and Ella and Murray got to Rosie's earlier than they'd intended. The place looked locked up tight. Murray tugged at the doors then knocked.

Ella cupped her hands around her eyes against the dark glass. 'I'm sure there's movement in there.'

Murray knocked again. Ella squinted into the gloom. Had somebody just hurried out of sight?

She took out her mobile. 'You got that number from Kennedy's records?'

Murray held out his open notebook. Turning her back to the club, Ella dialled. She could just hear the faint ring from inside. Finally it was picked up.

'Rosie's is closed.' The voice was gruff.

'This is Detective Ella Marconi.' With her free hand she got out her badge and pressed it against the glass.

The man sighed. 'Just a sec.'

Ella put her phone away as the man came to the doors and unlocked them. He looked out and she showed her badge again. 'You are?'

'Paul Davids, the manager.' His head was shaved and he wore a tight black T-shirt and black jeans. The edge of a barbed wire tattoo was just visible below his right sleeve.

'That phone I just rang,' Ella said. 'Where is it?'

Davids pointed inside. 'On the bar.'

Ella stepped past him. Murray followed. The music was off, the club silent except for the hum of the fridges behind the bar. Davids flicked the overhead lights on and the club was revealed as nothing more than a dank-smelling, low-ceilinged room.

Ella went to the bar and saw a phone sitting on the staff side. She looked up and around for CCTV cameras. Nothing but black-painted ceiling. 'Who has access to this phone?'

Davids shrugged. 'Mostly staff, but customers sometimes ask to use it too.'

'You have no restrictions on that sort of thing?'

'I want to keep people happy,' he said. 'If that means absorbing a forty-cent call, well, fine.'

'Are you open every night of the week?'

He nodded.

'From what time?'

'Seven-thirty we unlock the doors, but not many people are here then. It gets busy from about ten.'

'A call was made from this phone on Wednesday the fourth, at around six-thirty, quarter-to-seven in the evening. Any idea who made it?'

'None whatsoever.'

'But you just said that you don't open until

seven-thirty,' Ella said. 'So the call could only have been made by one of your staff, correct?'

'Not necessarily,' Davids said. 'Staff sometimes bring their friends in early, and the DJs are here setting up at that time and they might have roadies.'

Ella said, 'We'll need a list of everyone who was here at that time on that night.'

'How can I be expected to remember that?'

'Is it really so hard?' Murray said. 'You put down everyone you're sure of, and then you add all the people who only might've been here. And we'll ask each of them who they recall being present that night, and at some point, after we've made numerous visits here, we'll find who made the call.'

Davids frowned. 'You want this list now?'

'If you're not too busy serving customers,' Ella said.

Davids went behind the bar and took an A4 pad out of a cupboard. When he finished writing he tore the page off and handed it over. Ella read down the list of seven names and their designations. 'Didn't you say you were the manager?'

'That's right.'

'You've got here that Sal Rios is manager/supervisor. What does that mean?'

Davids capped his pen and laid it on the bar. 'He's the son of one of the owners. That's his official title, though he only comes in now and again, and even then he doesn't really do anything but get himself and his girlfriend drinks.'

Of the other people on the page, two were listed as bar staff, one was a DJ, one the DJ's roadie, one was security and the last one was Davids himself.

'So did you make any calls on that phone that night?' Ella said.

'Nope.'

'Did you see who did?'

'Nope.'

'Where would you have been at about that time? Here at the bar?'

'Back in the office, most likely.'

'You said you didn't mind customers using the phone,' Ella said. 'Did your staff have to get your permission first?'

'They're supposed to, but obviously if I'm out the back I can't see them.'

'Obviously.' Ella folded the page. 'We'll be in touch.'

It was strange, Lauren thought, sitting at her kitchen table in the evening gloom, that with everything that was going on, she couldn't stop thinking about Joe.

Or maybe it wasn't so strange. Maybe it was a kind of self-defence for the mind. Think about Joe, his eyes, his smile, his lips, and you didn't think about how maybe you were only breathing today because of the location of a microwave.

She looked at it. Even in the dim light from the hallway she could see the shine of the fresh cuts was gone.

Kristi stood at the window. Felise was in bed down the hall. Lauren had finished work late and come home to a roast chicken dinner under foil in the oven. She balled up the foil in her hand, her plate now empty at her elbow. The dry chicken felt like it was caught halfway down.

'They're there?' she said, just to say something.

Kristi nodded, her eyes on the street.

The house stayed silent.

Lauren put her head in her hand. The arguments with Claire and then Joe weighed heavily on her mind. She and Joe had hardly spoken for the rest of the shift, besides what was necessary to get their cases done. 'Would you like the stretcher now?' he'd say. 'Yes, please, officer,' she'd reply, hoping for half a smile, for some response at least, but he'd only turn and walk out to the ambulance. One patient had even said, 'Are you just new working together?'

She'd wanted to come home to a busy house full of light and noise, and forget about both the argument and poor Charlie, her last sight of him sobbing in the arms of his parents, but Felise had a cold and had been put to bed early, and Kristi was angry and close-mouthed about something.

Lauren said, 'Did you paint the microwave?'

'Felise asked what the marks were from.'

She squeezed the ball of foil tight. 'Is that why you're mad?'

'Who says I'm mad?'

'Spleen,' Lauren said, with a smile so Kristi would know she wasn't being mean, but then she realised it was too dark for her to see it.

Kristi grunted and looked back to the window.

'Why do you have to watch them?'

'It's the only thing that makes me feel safe.'

'But he'd be an idiot to try again,' Lauren said.

'He's got more to gain than to lose.'

Lauren put her plate in the sink. She touched the side of the microwave. The paint was dry but lumpy. She smelled bleach, and looked at the aged linoleum under her feet. 'We already cleaned this.'

'Not right down into all the little cracks and splits, you didn't.'

'Is that why you're angry? Because you had to clean again?'

'Lower your voice, you'll wake Felise.'

Lauren shoved her hands deep into her pockets and frowned at the floor. She wondered about life; why on those exact nights that you needed something to lift you up, a bit of fun family time, a few laughs, you collided head-on with somebody else's bad day, the both of you needing something from the other that neither was capable of recognising or giving.

'And no, that's not why I'm angry,' Kristi said. 'It's because you never told me you were going to be late.'

'It's the bloody job.'

'Yeah, but you had time to ring the surveillance people so they'd know when to meet you and follow you home, didn't you?' Kristi came away from the window. 'Meanwhile, I'm watching the clock and wondering if I'm going to see that detective get out of her car alone and come up to the door looking all grim with her bad news.' Her voice wavered. 'If I'm going to have to say goodbye to you the way we said it to Brendan . . .'

'Nothing's going to happen to me.'

'How can you say that? I saw you on the news, at that crane job. They said a man died. He went to work this morning thinking he would live forever too.'

'What do you want me to say?' Lauren said. 'What can I do about any of this?'

'Take time off, stay home until he's caught.'

'I can't.'

'Why not?'

'Because—' *Because while you might only feel safe watching the police outside on the street, the only time I feel safe is with Joe.* 'I just can't.'

Kristi stormed away.

The evening was cooling, and a fresh breeze brought the smell of the river up the hill as Ella parked in the driveway of her half-house. Murray had been keen to knock off, so she'd agreed to check the Rosie's names out in the morning and they'd gone their separate ways. Now she unlocked the letterbox and peered in to find only a folded note on which her half-house neighbour Denzil had scrawled, *Big job in Melbourne, back next week*.

She walked up the path alongside the house, scrunching the note in her hand. The lawn was getting long with the warm weather, the paspalum brushing against her legs. She'd have to get somebody to mow it before her dad found out. Last time he'd almost killed himself trying to lift his mower into the boot of the car. She could just imagine her mum hurrying to help and getting entangled, and both of them ending up on the ground with fractured hips.

She unlocked her front door and went inside, careful to deadlock and chain the door behind her. She loved her house, small and bloody expensive though it may be. She felt . . . well, she felt at home. She dropped her bag and kicked her shoes off and fell into her big blue armchair. She turned sideways to dangle her legs over the arm. From there she could stare out the window at next door's palm trees and the sky turning pink behind them.

It was funny the way a case unfolded. Clues came in from all over the place – like today's information that Deborah Kennedy had fled from police out at Griffith, and the fact that the call to Kennedy's phone had been made from inside Rosie's – but you couldn't tell what you had until it was over and you looked back at the detail that broke the case open. And things could change so drastically at any moment. She could go into the office tomorrow and find that Deborah Kennedy had turned herself in and confessed to paying Thomas Werner to kill James because of his affair with Helen Flinders. Or she and Murray could knock on the door of one of the names on the Rosie's list and run into the man himself.

She loved this work, and the deeper she got into the case, the more it hurt to think of being sent back to the suburbs. Back to stolen cars, petty assaults and break-and-enters. Ugh. She did her best work here, where it really mattered that they caught the guy. Surely the bosses could see that, and would change her status to permanent sooner rather than later?

Oh well. No point sitting there stewing. Ella rubbed her face with both hands and got up to see about dinner. There was more of her mother's vegetable lasagne in the freezer but she couldn't deny a sudden craving for pizza. Oh, a mushroom special from the gourmet place up on Vicky Road at Gladesville! Her mouth watered and she knew it was all over; once you hit that point, you weren't firing up the stove and making something yourself.

In the kitchen she reached for the flyer on the fridge but it was gone. The apple magnet was there, as were the rates notice and the phone bill and the photo of Lachlan Phillips on his first birthday, all under their respective fruit-shaped magnets, but no pizza-shop flyer. It wasn't on the floor either, nor had it somehow fallen and slipped under the fridge. She got up and brushed off her knees and tried to think.

Had she stepped off the scales one morning recently and decided enough mushroom pizzas were enough, out of sight was out of mind, and so it was time that flyer went into the rarely opened cupboard of recipe books? She shuffled through the books and torn-out magazine pages that Netta sent her, but the flyer wasn't there.

Had she thrown it out?

No, she wouldn't have done that, not even on the worst-scale day. Mushroom pizzas were an important part of life, it was a recognised fact. Or if it wasn't, she thought, it should be.

No use fussing. She looked up the shop in the phone book and rang in her order. Twenty minutes, they said.

In the bathroom she stepped into the shower. The water was hot and lovely. She reached for the shampoo but found an empty space. She blinked through the water at the rack on the wall. Razor dangling from the bottom, facial scrub, conditioner, fancy bath gel stuff she never used and should get around to throwing out, but no shampoo. She looked on the floor, at the top of the vanity, at the windowsill. She was sure she hadn't finished the bottle and tossed it. She was certain it was new just last week.

She felt ridiculous standing there in the water with her hands on her hips. So maybe she was confused, she thought. Life had been hectic, you can't remember every little thing you did. Get the spare and get on with it. Pizza will be here soon!

She got out of the shower and looked in the vanity cupboard, but there was no spare. Back under the water, knowing the clock was ticking and there was no way she'd miss the delivery, she shoved her fingers through her hair. Not too bad, but what could she do anyway? She could run a bit of conditioner through, perhaps. Or could you wash with soap? She remembered the dolls she had when she was little, how their hair went ropey after a good scrubbing. *Yeah, but that's plastic, idiot.*

Stuff it. It wasn't so bad. Just think of those mushrooms.

Once towelled off she went into her bedroom and pulled on jeans and a T-shirt. There was a hard lump in the pocket of the jeans. She felt it on the outside, then slid her fingers in gingerly.

A stone. A white pebble, from somebody's

decorative garden perhaps, but with two black dots drawn on it.

Eyes.

She held it on the palm of her hand.

Face to face.

'Oh, grow up,' she said aloud, wanting suddenly to chase away the silence in the house. 'What are you thinking? Somebody sneaked in and left this here?'

It's looking at me.

She squeezed her hand into a fist around the stone.

'You think somebody left this here and took your pizza leaflet and your shampoo? Are you nuts?'

She stamped into the kitchen and kicked the lid off the plastic bin in the corner. It was empty, a fresh liner in there from that morning.

She went to the front door. It was getting dark. She hit the switch for the security lights. She checked the peephole then opened the front door, went out and locked it behind her, testing it twice before she stepped away.

She held the stone tightly in one fist, the keys jutting through her fingers in the other. The wind was picking up and it touched the back of her neck. She could hear a TV in the neighbour's house, smell the roast somebody was cooking. She turned the corner to the backyard with the hair prickling on her arms, but there were only the two bins, the empty garden beds and the long and straggling grass.

With the tip of one key she flipped back the bin lids. Denzil wrapped his rubbish in newspaper. His bin contained only a few small parcels. Hers was messier, some things inside plastic bags and some dropped in individually. She pulled the bin down so she could reach inside it, using the keys to shuffle items apart, looking for the striking red and green of the pizza flyer and the pale pink of the shampoo bottle. They should be on the top if she'd chucked them that morning, but they weren't. She ripped into the plastic bags, the air filling with the smell of the sardine tin from three days ago and the eggs she'd tossed when she'd noticed they were weeks out of date.

They weren't there.

She shoved the bin upright and slammed down the lid. The keys bit into her fingers, she was gripping them so hard. The rock was smooth and rounded and didn't bite at all.

Back in the house she locked the door, then did the rounds of the windows. Each one was secure, as was the back door which was deadlocked and chained. She stood on a chair and tugged at the padlocked bolt on the manhole in the ceiling.

'Nobody can get in,' she said aloud. She put the rock on the kitchen table and stood with her hands on her hips.

A knock at the door almost stopped her heart. *Pizza, that's all. Just relax!*

Through the peephole she saw a girl in her late teens holding a pizza box. She unlocked and opened the door.

'Hi.' The girl smiled at her. 'It's fifteen bucks.'

Relieved, touched in some way, Ella gave her a twenty. 'Don't worry about the change.'

'Thanks.'

The box was hot in Ella's hands but she was reluctant to let her go. 'Be careful.'

The girl looked at her. 'Sorry?'

'I'm just saying.' But Ella knew there was no point trying to explain. 'Good night,' she said instead.

'Yep.' The girl was already walking away.

Ella closed and locked the door again. She sat at the table to eat straight from the box. The pizza was hot and good and made her feel a little better. As she ate she stared at the rock, which stared back, until finally she moved it under the box lid.

Sal knew they were humouring him. Tough guys took no notice of such things, however. He pushed his dinner plate out of the way, cleared his throat and opened the notebook he'd bought specially for the occasion. He felt his father's eyes on him and looked up, but his father immediately shifted his gaze to Julio who sat picking fluff off his beanie, his bald and skeletal head shiny in the light.

'Can we bring this thing to order?' Sal said.

Thomas sucked food from between his teeth. He was slumped sideways in his chair, his arm over the back and his eyes fixed on the TV in the next room, though Nona had the sound so low it couldn't be heard at the table. Upstairs, Nona's kids, Lizzie and Mardi, were meant to be doing their homework, but Sal could hear them arguing.

He clicked his pen. 'Okay. We don't have an agenda, so I think it's best if we just take turns to bring up issues. Dad, you go first.'

His father licked his thumb and picked up a crumb from the tablecloth. 'Things are going pretty well.'

Sal frowned. He always had a lot to say when Paulo was alive and chairing. 'What about today's . . .' He couldn't think what to call it. 'Incident? Development?'

'It's nothing.'

'The police coming into the club and asking about a phone call is not nothing.'

'It's a phone that every man and his dogs have access to.' His dad stood up and started to collect the plates. 'They can't pin that onto any one person. So it's nothing.'

'Dad,' Sal said, but he didn't respond. He took the plates out to the kitchen and Sal heard the tap running.

'It's okay.' Julio pulled his beanie back on. 'He knows what he's talking about.'

'We should still discuss it. Develop some kind of contingency plan.' Sal had imagined that a big part of it would be making Thomas leave, but everything was going on as normal. Thomas was still sucking his teeth, even.

Julio elbowed Sal gently. 'Go on, bro. It can be your turn now.'

'Turns' made it sound like they were just playing games. 'It's done on seniority. That means you go next.'

'What do you want me to say?'

'Tell me about the money,' Sal said. 'Uncle Paulo taught you about how we move it, and now you can teach me.'

Julio shifted on his chair. 'It's not urgent.'

'No, but it's best if two of us know,' Sal said.

'Two of us do know,' Thomas said, his gaze still on the TV.

'Thomas,' Julio said.

Sal stared at Julio. 'You taught him but not me?'

'You're stressed.' Julio laid his bony arm across Sal's shoulders. 'We didn't want to bother you with that stuff when you've got so much on your mind.'

Sal's skin prickled under his brother's touch. 'We're family.'

'Still are,' Thomas said.

Sal lowered his voice. 'We're supposed to come first.'

In the kitchen their father dropped something and swore in Spanish.

Julio smiled at him. 'You're still my little bro, you know that.'

Thomas burped.

Sal rounded on him. 'What about you? You got anything to bloody say?'

'Sal.' In the lounge room, Nona raised her eyes to the ceiling, to upstairs where the girls were.

Thomas said, 'I'm taking care of things.'

'If you take one step near that paramedic, the cops'll bloody know, you know.'

'Who said it's her?'

'Who else? The bloke she works with, who heard what Kennedy said too?' Sal shook his head. 'She's the key.'

Thomas didn't answer.

Sal clicked his pen back in and slapped the

notebook closed. What was the point in having a meeting if nobody took it seriously? Tough guys valued their time too much to waste it in such a situation.

Upstairs in his room he left the lights off and sat on his bed. Lizzie and Mardi had stopped arguing and Lizzie was back at her guitar again. He thought of her frowning over the chords. She was so like Nona at that age, with her wide eyes, long honey-coloured hair and a kind of lanky elegance that she didn't know she had. It was no wonder that Nona freaked out when Blake was released from jail, right when Lizzie turned thirteen. When she'd first moved back home, after her marriage finally imploded, she used to stay up late talking to Sal, and one night over too much red had told him about Blake. Sal had listened in shocked silence. He'd been at the same school, two years ahead, and it hurt to think of his sister being assaulted and suffering in silence while he went merrily about his schoolboy life.

She hadn't blamed him, or Julio, two years older again, or their parents for not realising what was going on. But he'd still felt responsible – she was his little sister! – and for that, and some vague notions of payback and prevention, he'd found himself in that dark alley, hands sweaty on the axe-less axe handle, Thomas nudging him from behind while Blake sidled in, anticipating a meet with another paedophile bearing a gift. Thomas had set things up, and when it was obvious that Sal was frozen with doubt and fear, Thomas took the axe handle from him. Sal had cowered by the skip, hearing the blows, not realising that the spirit of Blake would follow him from the scene or that he'd just joined himself with Thomas forever.

And now the cops were looking into who made that phone call.

He felt the heat of tears, and gritted his teeth.

TWENTY-TWO

Ella was thankful to find the Sunday morning traffic light as she drove to the Homicide office. Her eyes were dry and sore from her crap sleep and now were blurry as well from the eye drops. 'Eye relief, my arse.'

For the first time in her adult life she'd left a light on overnight. She felt silly about this, but she felt even sillier for having shut the stone away in the microwave. This morning she'd opened the door and looked in at it, thinking she should nip down to the river on her way to work and hurl it in. But something in her whispered that it could be evidence, and anything with even the slightest whiff of evidence about it brought out her hoarding instincts. She didn't want to think about what it was evidence of, but she'd shut the door on it and left it there.

She sat up straighter in the seat and tried to concentrate on the case. This morning they'd divvy up the list of names Paul Davids had given them, then do a bit of door-knocking. The list of all the staff they'd got from Martin Everly hadn't produced any criminal record hits, but at least now they had a reason to talk to these ones, actual questions to ask. She checked her watch and moved into the right lane to overtake a slower car.

When she reached the building she found Murray pacing the car park. He jumped in the passenger seat. 'What's with your phone?'

She pulled it from her bag and checked the screen. 'Flat. Shit, I'd better call Lauren.'

'I just did, trying to find you. They're all fine.' He yanked on his seatbelt. 'You owe me for this.'

'Where are we going?'

He pointed cityward. 'You owe me so seriously. You owe me like you've never owed anyone before.'

A flicker of excitement built inside her. 'What's going on?'

'Detective Simon Bradshaw rang about a homicide he's doing,' Murray said. 'He's going to meet us on the scene. Kuiper wanted to send somebody else but I said you'd be here soon.' He gestured impatiently at the exit.

Ella accelerated. 'And?'

'They found a link to Quiksmart in Bradshaw's victim's place.'

The laneway outside the decrepit building in Chinatown where Bradshaw was meeting them was narrow and jammed with cars, vans and dumpsters. The air smelled of cooking from the restaurants that backed onto the lane, Sunday being peak yum cha day, and as Ella picked her way along the broken asphalt a young Chinese man emerged from a door and threw a bucketful of garbage into one of the dumpsters.

A green Ford sedan was parked in a no standing zone. Detective Simon Bradshaw climbed out of the driver's side as they neared it. Ella recognised him from the office, though she wasn't sure they'd ever actually spoken. He was tall, slim, in his mid-thirties with curly hair and a constant smile.

'Thanks for waiting,' Murray said.

'No probs.' Simon led them between parked vehicles and over a choked-up gutter. 'This started as a diver found dead in the water on Friday. Initially it appeared a possible accidental death, but the PM showed bruising consistent with a struggle. The scenario we're working on is that his scuba regulator was pulled from his mouth and he was held underwater until he drowned. He had no ID on him, and we couldn't find a car near the dive site, and nothing showed on missing persons or matched his fingerprints. So basically we had to sit and wait until somebody rang in to say their mate was missing. Somebody did, yesterday – his chemistry professor. Said this guy had an important experiment to complete, and when he didn't show the prof knew something was wrong.'

Ella followed Simon into a narrow doorway then up a dark stairwell. It stank of chemicals and sour food. The building looked like it might have been a warehouse at some stage, then was haphazardly divided into separate flats. The stairwell walls were unpainted gyprock, stained, graffitied and full of holes.

'This professor ID'd the body as Feng Xie, Chinese national, twenty-two years old. He was studying chemistry, and had been here almost two years. The professor was the guy's mentor or something, said he was a really intelligent guy, quiet, didn't have many friends. Serious, got on with his work, careful with his money, only recently started diving – went on a freebie trial trip with the uni dive club and loved it, apparently. Still had another student's borrowed gear.'

They reached the third-floor landing. Four closed doors waited silently.

'So the professor gets us Feng's address from student records,' Simon said. 'We come around here and as soon as we hit the stairs we can smell the chemicals. We retreat and get the equipment and everything that we need, Hazmat and that, come back, pop the lock and find one shitbox little flat with a panel from the bathroom to the meth lab out the back.'

'A meth lab,' Ella said.

'It was mostly cleaned up, but some of the stuff had been spilled – that's what we could smell – and the rest of the place had been done over, I guess clearing out anything incriminating. Hazmat then crime scene did their bits, and then during the search we found a box with half a Quiksmart courier's label. When we plugged that into the system, your case popped up. I ring. And here you are.' He put his hand on the doorknob. 'Shall we?'

The door opened into a small room. Ella saw more walls of unpainted gyprock, the plaster crumbling from old gouges in its surface. A camp bed lay upturned on the floor, a grimy brown sheet and worn army blanket hanging off it. There was no pillow. A couple of pairs of underpants lay in the corner along with a pair of black trousers and a grey shirt. The single window had no blind and the glass was cracked and held together with peeling brown tape. Above a small sink with a single tap hung a plywood cupboard with no door. Ella could see tins of baked beans and polystyrene cups of instant noodles, some on their side, some fallen to the floor. There was one chair, its back missing, and next to it on the floor lay four chemistry textbooks, pages torn and spines broken.

'Lab's through there.'

A doorway with no door led to the bathroom. It was about twice the size of the average toilet cubicle. The floor was bare wooden boards that moved under Ella's feet. There was no bath or shower, just a toilet and another small sink. The window was covered with black paint. Fingerprint dust covered the toilet and the sink edges.

Along the wall beside the toilet a panel had been cut out of the gyprock. Simon took a torch from his pocket and shone the light into the space. Ella saw the missing panel on the floor. Simon bent low to squeeze through, and Ella followed, her nostrils full of the stink of the drug.

Once through the opening she found she could stand up again. It was a long narrow space, and she guessed it ran along the side of the makeshift flats. Along the wall were a couple of benches made of rough planks laid over stacked milk crates. There was broken glass and a chemical stain on the floor. An industrial fan was lodged in a hole cut roughly in the sloping roof.

'What'd the neighbours say?'

'The way they scarpered when we got here, a lot are illegals or up to their own kind of no good. We've got a number in custody now, and are trying to get whatever info we can about Mr Feng and his regular visitors.' Simon waved at the benches. 'The action obviously took place there, and we figure he got rid of the waste by flushing it or chucking it in one of those dumpsters downstairs. All the other gear was taken, probably by whoever killed him.'

Ella looked around. 'So where's the Quiksmart thing?'

Simon shone the torch beam at a hole in the wall, down low under the sloping roof. 'It was cut in half and jammed across there. We figure they either missed it in the clean-up or it's not significant. Might've been there from before, even. Anyway, we have the logo and half a barcode, and it's getting fed into Quiksmart's system now.'

Ella thought of sweaty Daniel Peres and the pressure he'd feel from this.

'Of course, even if the victim did put it there, it still could mean nothing,' Simon said. 'He could've picked up the box out of a skip behind one of those restaurants down there, or got it from uni.'

Murray said, 'Have you found any witnesses to him going into the water?'

Simon shook his head. 'People are canvassing. We've contacted his parents in China, through

Interpol, and we know he's got no record. But talking to the professor, young Feng was quite the brain. He was destined for great things in the chemistry world, or so the prof reckons. Why he was wasting his nut cooking up ice, the professor has no idea.'

Back at the office they found everyone was out. A note was sticky-taped to Murray's computer monitor. 'Strongy left us three names from the Rosie's list.' He typed the men's names into the database and wrote down their addresses. 'Should we call Kuiper about Feng Xie?'

'It's all a bit vague so far,' Ella said. 'I reckon hold off till the meeting. We might have some clearer info by then.'

She sat at her desk and yawned. She had to focus on the tasks ahead, not on how tired she was or whether she was developing dementia. She would push the stone and all the rest of it to the back of her mind and get on with the case. This afternoon there'd be a meeting, and they'd hopefully know more about Feng, and find out the latest on Deborah Kennedy, and who knew what the detectives who were looking into the other names from the Rosie's list would've found out.

'Ready?' Murray said.

'Let's get coffee on the way.'

Dan Sommerson lived in a tiny flat under the flight path in Tempe. He opened the door to Murray's knock with a spatula in his hand. 'I already have a religion.'

Ella pulled out her badge. 'Dan Sommerson? We'd like to speak with you.'

He stepped back to let them in. Bacon and eggs sizzled on the stove. He pointed with the spatula towards the kitchen. 'Do you mind if I just . . . ?'

'Go ahead.'

He poked at the contents of the frypan then turned off the heat. 'Sorry.' He wore pilled navy tracksuit pants and a faded Newtown Jets T-shirt. His feet were bare. He tucked his hands into the rear waistband of the pants. 'What's happened?'

'You work as a roadie, is that right?'

'Actually I'm a food technology student. I do a bit of roadie work in the evenings.'

'We're trying to trace a phone call that was made from Rosie's club in the Cross on Wednesday the fourth. The manager told us that you were there that evening.'

Sommerson nodded. 'I was working for a DJ called Steve Fonti.'

'Did you use the phone behind the bar that night?'

'No.'

'Did you see anybody use it?'

He shook his head.

'How long were you there?'

'Only about twenty minutes,' he said. 'I would've been gone by probably half-seven, then back again about two to pack up.'

'How many people were there in the evening?'

'Not many.' He furrowed his brow. 'Me and Steve,

a couple of staff wandering about. I'm too busy to look around much.'

Ella said, 'Ever noticed any weird stuff going on at that club?'

'Like what?'

'You tell me.'

'Nothing apart from the usual,' he said. 'People off their faces, you know.'

'Ever see anyone selling drugs there?'

'I thought this was about a phone call?'

'It's about the club,' Murray said.

'I guess people are selling,' Sommerson said. 'I don't pay any attention. I just do my work and go. I'm doing honours this year, I don't have time to fart about.'

Ella showed him the photo of Thomas from the airport cameras. 'Recognise this man?'

'Nope.'

'Okay,' Ella said. 'Thanks for your time. Hope we didn't stuff up your breakfast.'

He smiled. 'Quick refry and it'll be fine.'

Back in the car, Ella opened the street directory to look up the next address. 'Seven Cowley Road, Maroubra. This is Sal Rios, the supposed manager slash supervisor.'

'Son of one of the owners, I remember,' Murray said. 'Maybe he'll know who made the call, seeing as the forty cents is coming out of his family's pocket.'

Lauren and Joe did a couple of minor cases on the trot – a woman with abdo pain, a man with the flu – then headed for the station. Joe sat in the passenger seat looking out the window. Lauren was sure he knew she was glancing at him from behind the wheel, though he gave no sign.

'Nice day,' she said.

'Mm.'

'Maybe wash the truck this morning if we get a chance.'

He didn't reply.

She reversed into the station, and he got out and went inside without a word. She turned the engine off and sat there for a moment, watching the tourists walk along the street and stare up at the bridge.

When she went into the muster room Joe was at the bench, a form in front of him. He covered it half-heartedly with his arm.

She smiled. 'You putting in a complaint on me?'

He smiled sheepishly back but said nothing, and she looked over his shoulder.

Transfer application.

'That's a joke, right?'

'It's Claire,' he said.

Lauren dropped into the chair next to him.

'It's not like I want to go.'

'Then don't.'

He put down the pen. 'We had this big argument last night.' He rubbed his eyes. 'She reckons you and me have something going on.'

Lauren choked out a snort.

'She says if I really do love her, I'll transfer west. She says the wedding can stay when we planned it originally, and nothing else changes; I'm just not working here.'

'With me,' Lauren said.

'She said it's a small price to pay for her peace of mind.'

The many things Lauren wanted to say welled up inside her, fought against each other to get out.

Joe said, 'It's probably just pre-wedding nerves.'

'But it's still months away.'

Joe looked down at the page. 'I love her.'

Lauren wanted so badly to say *But do you? Really?* She felt that this was one of those moments when you teetered on the edge of momentous change. Did she dare to put her hand on his arm and tell him exactly how she felt?

She started to reach out, but then he said, 'I love her, and she's right. Besides, marriage is about compromise, right?' and picked up the pen.

Lauren's hand fell. Black anger and jealousy rose up in her chest, and underneath it despair lay like a stinking swamp.

'Wh–' Her throat got tight and she had to cough and try again. 'When will you go?'

'It'll probably take a couple of weeks to come through.' He hesitated. 'But she wants me to take leave until then.'

'She doesn't trust us for even one more shift?'

'She gets these . . . premonitions. She said last night she thinks something bad's going to happen.'

Lauren made a scornful noise. 'Bad like what? A busy night shift? A flat tyre? Somebody's going to hurl all through the ambulance?'

'She was serious. She was crying.'

Oh, there's a surprise. 'She'll say anything to stop

you working with me.'

'I'm just telling you what she said.'

Lauren wanted to get up and storm away. 'Fine. So this is your last shift, is it? You're on leave from tomorrow?'

'No,' he said. 'I told her I'd compromise. I'm not taking leave, and I'm staying until this thing is over.'

'This thing . . .'

'With Werner.'

'Because of her premonition?'

'It just seems best,' he said. 'Don't you think?'

All choked up, Lauren didn't know where to look.

TWENTY-THREE

Cowley Road was long and they came into it at the wrong end. Ella yawned as she watched the numbers fall. 'Fifteen,' she said. 'Eleven. There.'

The Rioses' house was two storeys of blond brick. A concrete driveway led up to a double garage. There were shrubs in the front yard, a small area of trimmed lawn, and white curtains in the white-framed windows on the upper storey. There were a million houses just like it right across suburbia; hell, there were a hundred in Cowley Road alone.

The front door was behind a locked security screen. Ella pressed the doorbell and listened to it chime inside the house.

Footsteps approached, the deadbolt turned and the door was pulled open. 'Yes?'

Ella and Murray held out their badges. 'Are you Mrs Sal Rios?'

'I'm his sister, Nona,' she said. 'Is he okay?'

'So he's not home?'

The woman shook her head. She was in her late

thirties, Ella guessed, with dark hair in a bob and bright red lipstick. She wore jeans and a white shirt and sandals. Around her neck hung a gold chain and pendant. It looked expensive, even through the screen. 'And I don't know when he'll be back, sorry.'

'Your family owns a club in the city, is that right?' Ella said.

'My dad's part of a company that owns a few clubs and things like that,' she said. 'I don't know which clubs though.'

'Have you ever been to one called Rosie's, in the Cross?'

'Never.'

'But Sal works there?'

'I believe so,' she said.

'So he lives here, and you live here too?'

She nodded. 'And our father and brother. I moved back about eight months ago, after my marriage broke up.'

'Does your other brother work in the clubs?'

'He has cancer,' she said. 'That's partly why I came back, to help out with his care. Before he got sick he worked in sales. That's where I worked too, in jewellery.' She touched the gold pendant. 'Now I'm a full-time mother.'

Ella got out her card and wrote her mobile number on it. 'Could you have Sal call me, please, when he gets in?'

Nona unlocked the screen to take the card. 'Can I tell him what it's about?'

'We're trying to trace a phone call that was made

from Rosie's,' Murray said. 'We're talking to everyone who was there on that particular evening.'

Nona nodded.

'One more thing,' Ella said, taking out the airport photo of Thomas Werner. 'Do you recognise this man?'

Nona shook her head. 'I don't. Sorry.'

'No problem,' Ella said. 'Thanks for your time.'

Ella found a note on her desk when they got back to the office. *Call Wayne Rhodes.* She remembered her mobile battery was flat, and dug out the charger she kept in her desk drawer and plugged the phone in before calling him back.

'The plot is thickening,' Wayne said. 'Mrs Veronique Nolan, widow of Adrian who fell from the train, is a lovely woman. Yesterday afternoon she made me tea, fed me orange cake, and then proceeded to tell me that she thinks her husband has more money than he should have.'

'Now there's a statement I've never heard before,' Ella said.

'She said that Adrian always looked after the money, both for the warehouse and the household. Now she's having to do it, and fold up the warehouse besides, and she's found that while their accounts are more than healthy, the business was not, and she can't tell where the money came from.'

'Maybe they've got a really canny accountant,' Ella said. 'That's what we're looking into for our guy.' She told him what Rebecca Kanowski had learned about James Kennedy's bank accounts. 'You get your-self a whizz-bang accountant – especially in Nolan's case, with his own business – and who knows what you can end up with.'

'No, I reckon there's something weird going on,' Wayne said.

'Weird like what?'

'I'll tell you when I find out,' he said. 'Meantime, I've got an idea. Got a pen?'

He recited a mobile number and Ella jotted it down. 'Whose is that?'

'It's my guy's,' he said. 'I'm working on a hunch. I want you to run it through your guy's phone records and see what comes up. You got your guy's number there?'

'Are you checking because they died on the same day?' Ella said. 'Because Lauren went to both of them? And by the way, did I tell you I talked to her about the Nolan job? Perfectly straightforward, she said. Well, as much as it can be when a man falls from a train during a police pursuit.'

'Humour me,' he said. 'Tell me your guy's number.'

She found it and read it out with a sigh.

There was a moment's silence, then Wayne said, 'I should've made a bet with you on it.'

'You're joking.'

'Look at your guy's record,' he said. 'Look up the day they died. Four fifty in the afternoon.'

She found the entry. 'That's Adrian Nolan?'

'That's him. It was Nolan's last call.'

Goose bumps rose on her arms. Kennedy had

made one more call after that, then the log ended.

Dead men make no calls.

'Your guy rang mine the day before that as well,' Wayne said. Ella heard him shuffle through pages. 'And twice on the previous Thursday. This is too much to be just talking about courier stuff, and we haven't even gone all the way through yet.'

It was time to talk to their bosses, but before she hung up she read out the mobile number that was Kennedy's last call. 'See that anywhere on your list?'

'Not on a quick glance, but I'll keep my eye out,' he said. 'And do you agree now that it wasn't such a bad idea?'

'Only grudgingly. Talk to you later.'

She put the phone down and sat there for a moment, enjoying the feeling of a good clue cracked. The process of getting information through the phone companies was so time-consuming: first you requested the lists of incoming and outgoing numbers, then you looked for repeated ones, or calls at specific times, then you sent in another request for information on who owned the numbers and where they lived. They'd got the Rosie's number because they had a specific time and date and Detective Graeme Strong called in a favour from a mate in the phone company, but the lists they'd sent for the frequent callers for Kennedy's mobile would take a few more days at least. It had indeed been a good idea of Wayne's, if one that came from left field.

Ella looked around the office. Strong was out, so she couldn't ask him to ring his mate about Kennedy's final call. Jason Lambert was leaning against the doorframe talking to the poor long-suffering HR chick. Nobody was in earshot.

She grabbed the phone and dialled.

There was a moment of silence, then a woman's voice said, 'The mobile you are calling is turned off or out of range.'

So much for that.

Sal kicked at the screen. His fingers were going numb. He heard Nona coming, not in any big hurry, and he kicked the screen again.

'Okay! Jesus.' She unlocked it and yanked it open. 'You don't always have to bring it all in at once.'

'When you get the groceries, you can carry them in any way you like.' He lumbered to the kitchen and heaved the bags onto the bench. Something cracked.

'If that's my caviar you're going straight back out.'

He ignored her, shoving packets of cheese and sausages and a bag of apples into the fridge. She hunted through the shopping for the jar, pulled it out and ran her fingers over the bottom. 'Lucky.'

He didn't bother unpacking the bag of tinned goods and pasta packets, just shoved it full into the cupboard.

'It'd take you two minutes to unpack that,' Nona said.

'It'd take you the same.'

He couldn't believe he'd been involved in killing a guy for her. He must have rocks in his head.

She tossed the jar from hand to hand. 'A cop came looking for you.'

'Sure.'

'You think I'm making it up?' She shrugged. 'Okay. Don't call her back then.' She took a card from her pocket and waved it in his face.

He grabbed it from her. *Detective Ella Marconi, Homicide.* 'Does Thomas know?'

'He's gone to meet Tr–' She deliberately widened her eyes. 'Oops.'

Sal hardened his heart. 'Shut up and tell me.'

'How can I shut up *and* tell you?' But she must have seen something in his face then, and she put the jar down. 'She was asking about a phone call made from Rosie's, that you were there that night and they wanted to talk to you about it. They also had a photo of Thomas.'

Oh Jesus. 'What did you tell them?'

'What do you think?' she said. 'You'd better ring her back.'

'I should check with Thomas first.'

'He'll tell you to ring her as well,' Nona said. 'The longer you wait, the more chance there is that she'll just come back.'

Sal could work that out for himself. 'If I do the wrong thing he'll go nuts.'

'Yeah, and how pleased will he be if she's standing at the front door when he comes home?'

Sal secretly hoped they'd get the chance to find that out.

At that afternoon's meeting, Kuiper introduced the detectives who were looking for the leak. Bryan

Greer was a gangly man, all ears and jaw, his black hair like a bristle brush on his white scalp. Bethany Mendelssohn perched on the side of the table and smoothed her pale linen skirt. Her hair swung in a shiny ponytail over her shoulder.

Ella felt short and greasy.

'Here's what we know,' Bethany Mendelssohn said. 'Werner knew that Lauren Yates had made the statement that Kennedy identified him as his attacker, and Werner said so in a threatening phone call to her.'

This was indeed what they knew. Ella resisted the urge to roll her eyes.

'It would appear that the fact of our surveillance and phone tap has also been passed on, as there has been no approach by Werner or anyone else suspicious, in person or by phone, since those strategies were undertaken.

'The threatening call to Ms Yates has been traced to a mobile,' Mendelssohn said. 'We're currently awaiting the result of a request for the details of the phone's owner.'

It'd be good, Ella thought, to be able to do with that number what she and Wayne had just done. But where would you cross-check it? Not with Kennedy's or Nolan's numbers. They were well dead by the time Lauren was threatened.

'We've started our investigation with the auxiliary staff.' Bryan Greer handed out sheets of paper as he spoke. 'These are the names of the seven non-sworn administrative staff, two computer technicians and one air-conditioning maintenance man who were on these floors last week. We have two theories. Firstly, if it's a deliberate leak, it's most likely that it's down to one or more of these people rather than from one of the officers here now.' He looked around at them all. 'Second, if it's an accidental leak, then it's equally likely to have come from them or from somebody here.

'I want you to think about who you've talked to regarding this case, what you might have said even in passing. If you have even the slightest concern, you need to see us. Identifying the leak, however it came about, is a solid lead to finding Werner, because somebody at some point in that chain of knowledge knows him.'

The detectives were silent. Ella knew she hadn't spoken to anybody about it. She looked sideways at Murray, who was studying his list. He'd probably blabbed it all to his dad, but it was hard to imagine ol' Frank Shakespeare hanging down the local with his homey Thomas.

She looked at her own page. She knew some of these people by their first name, and others she didn't know at all. Toni Denham-Wilson was Radtke's assistant; Anna Thomas, Kuiper's assistant; Tracy Potter and Isabel Loftus job-shared the Human Resources position; Edwina Guilfoyle and Helena Cavendish and Michelle Spriggs were general admin staff; then there were the technicians' names. Ella couldn't recall having even seen any of the three men.

'Our investigation into these people is ongoing, but meantime let us know if you see any of these people – or anyone at all – appearing to take particular interest in the case or asking you for more details.'

Greer sat down. Ella knew there was more he could've said about precisely how they were investigating these admin people, but if anybody in the room was close friends with them, or god forbid in cahoots, there was the chance that the information would be passed on. It still might be, but with no specific clues it wasn't too helpful.

'Okay,' Kuiper said. 'Latest news on Deborah Kennedy is that the local police think they've found where she's been staying – in a ramshackle cabin on an isolated property about twelve kilometres west of Griffith. The owner knew nothing about it until he found fresh tyre tracks and then blankets and food in the building. He'd heard the reports on the radio and called it in, but Mrs Kennedy hasn't been back so it's likely she's moved on.

'Also, there's been a report of a suspected meth lab in another industrial area in south Sydney,' he said. 'That's to be raided sometime today, so we'll hopefully find out later if that's where Werner was working, if he's picked up.'

He paused. 'I've spoken with Detective Lance Fredriks about Lauren's new information on the Blake case. He wants to interview her again, tomorrow, 9am. You'll let her know, Marconi? And sit in on it if you want.'

Ella nodded.

'What's the Quiksmart link with this other homicide?'

Murray described the possible link with Feng

Xie and how Simon Bradshaw would be letting them know what he'd learned, and also about their checks on the Rosie's phone call people.

Ella then explained the phone link between Kennedy and Nolan. 'We still have to examine the rest of the record, but Rhodes is looking into it further from his end and keeping me posted.'

'Good work,' Kuiper said. 'Pilsiger, how did you go with the possible witnesses near Lauren's house?'

'I've had conflicting reports of partial number-plates on a blue sedan – some say Holden, some say Ford,' she said. 'I've been running them through the system in various combinations. Other than that, it's a generic description of a man of average height, average build, brown hair, bleeding, who kept his head down and drove off quickly.'

When the meeting was over Ella approached Bethany Mendelssohn. 'Excuse me.'

She looked up from her mobile phone. 'Yes?'

'I was wondering whether you'd tried calling the phone number from which the threat against Lauren Yates was made,' Ella said. The sheet of paper with the number on it lay at Mendelssohn's side.

'We're following correct procedure on this matter,' she said.

'Which is to wait until the records come back, I know,' Ella said. She wanted to say more, but Mendelssohn's gaze moved slowly over Ella's hair. 'Never mind.'

She went down the corridor and back to her

desk, feeling irritable and out of sorts. She rubbed her eyes and allowed herself to think about that bloody rock. Perhaps she could call Dennis and discuss it? But when she thought about what she'd say, it sounded so stupid. Imagine if somebody overheard: after all, they might have the lines tapped now, to try to catch the mole. Imagine if word got back to Kuiper that she was so frightened about a rock she had to shut it away in her microwave.

She just had to ride it out. Things would look better tomorrow, after a good night's sleep. She had to concentrate on the case, follow the leads.

Strong came into the office.

'Strongy,' Ella said. 'How's your mate in the phone company?'

'Gone on leave.'

'Know anyone else in there?' She waved Kennedy's phone records at him. 'Got a live one.'

'Sorry, we're back to official channels only until he gets back from the Sunshine Coast.' He picked up his empty coffee cup and went back out.

Ella frowned down at her desk. *Don't think about that rock. Think about the next task.*

She picked up the phone and dialled Lauren's number.

TWENTY-FOUR

They'd only been on board the moored ferry for a few minutes, but Lauren already felt sick. She looked out the salt-spotted window to where the Opera House glowed white in the afternoon sun. The water was dark green in the ferry's shadow and brighter and touched with light further out.

'So have you had this chest pain before?' Joe said to their patient, an English tourist in her seventies.

'Often.' She held the oxygen mask tight to her face with spindly fingers.

Lauren swallowed her nausea and unzipped the monitor's pouch, attaching the three leads to adhesive dots that Joe would stick on the woman's chest.

'When was the last time you had it?'

'Last week, I think, wasn't it, William?'

The woman's husband, a small man made smaller by the voluminous blue spray jacket he wore, nodded as he accepted a cup of tea from a member of the ferry staff. 'Monday night. Just after dinner.'

Joe took the leads from Lauren and explained to

the patient what he was going to do. Lauren tried to breathe deep and think about something other than the gentle swaying under her feet. The low afternoon sun filled the interior of the ferry with light, and people on the wharf peered in to see what was happening. She could see the stretcher behind them, parked hard up against a fence with the brakes firmly on.

Her mobile rang. She pulled it from her belt and saw it was Ella. ''Scuse me,' she murmured to Joe, then walked a few steps away. 'Hello?'

'How're things?' Ella said.

'No sign. Anything new there?'

'Nothing on that front,' Ella said. 'But they want to interview you again about the Blake case.'

Lauren's nausea worsened.

'It doesn't necessarily mean you'll be charged or convicted,' Ella said. 'It's just the first step in building the new case against Werner.'

Lauren's stomach was roiling. 'When and where?'

'Are you working tomorrow?'

'No.'

'I'll pick you up at half-past eight.'

'You'll be there too?'

'Yes.'

'Thanks.'

'No worries,' Ella said. 'Keep safe, and I'll see you then.'

Lauren walked unsteadily back to Joe and their patient, wondering if she would need to rush to the bathroom and throw up or if she could hold it until they got onto the wharf then back to the ambulance. Maybe once on solid ground she'd feel better.

Joe looked up at her. 'Pain's gone with O2 and aspirin, so I think we'll be right to walk to the bed.'

They helped the woman to her feet and across the ramp. The water was dark below them. She sat on the stretcher and they covered her with the blanket.

'Pain's still gone?' Joe asked her.

She nodded, watching her husband negotiate the ramp on the arm of the ferry staffer.

Joe and Lauren lifted the stretcher to its full height, loaded their equipment onto the back and sides, and started along the wharf. Lauren gripped the handles tight. *Nearly there, hold on.* Through the gates, held open by a smiling staff member, then onto dry land.

It didn't help. She tried to breathe deep as they lifted then pushed the stretcher into the ambulance. People gathered to watch, and Lauren felt their gazes. She was not going to throw up on the street. No way in the world. She yanked down the rear door after Joe had clambered in, then hurried the patient's husband into the front seat. She threw the gear into the rear through the side door and clambered in herself, pointing at the plastic vomit bags as she pulled the door shut and cut off the inquisitive gazes of the crowd outside. Joe, confused, handed her a bag and she got it up to her mouth just in time.

The patient tried to look around. 'You all right, dear?'

'She's okay,' Joe said.

The acid taste made Lauren's eyes water. She slumped in the seat behind the patient's head and took the paper towels Joe held out. 'Are you?' he asked softly.

She pressed a clean paper towel to her eyes, unable to answer.

Ella's email dinged. It was a message from Simon Bradshaw:

I disturbed your friend Daniel Peres's Sunday afternoon and got him to print out a list of possible matches for the Quiksmart barcode we found on Feng Xie's floor. Thought you might like a squiz. Got to rush, will be back in the office in the am. Talk then, Simon.

The attachment was a ten-page spreadsheet of numbers and addresses. She was printing it out when Murray came back from the bathroom drying his hands on a paper towel.

'What's that?' he said.

'Possible matches for the barcode from that drug flat.' She handed him half the pages.

The barcode numbers were nine digits long. The one found in Feng Xie's flat had begun with the numbers 632977 and the rest had been cut off. The Quiksmart computer had coughed out every possible match.

'God, there's hundreds of them,' Murray said.

'Try not to think about it.'

Ella ran her finger down the list of addresses. None of the deliveries had been made to anywhere near Chinatown. The closest was Leichhardt, and the rest were progressively further west – Marrickville, Parramatta, Blacktown, Penrith. However, Simon had italicised a number of the deliveries. The driver's name was Kennedy.

Ella tapped the page. 'Interesting.'

'But like Simon said, there are any number of ways a box could get from one of those places to a flat like that,' Murray said. 'Somebody gets it out of a skip behind a shop to move house with, then they take some stuff to uni, where Feng nabs it to drag some stuff home in.'

'And cut it in half and stuffed it in a hole in the wall of a meth lab,' she said. 'You think it's a coincidence that Kennedy's name shows up here too?'

'We don't know that the box was handled by him. There are eight other drivers listed there.'

Ella read through the list of goods. Cosmetics, medical supplies, toys, stationery, hardware. No chemicals that you might suspect would be delivered to a drug lab. But then would anyone be so blasé as to run an operation that way?

'Looks like Kennedy delivers to a cluster in the inner west,' Murray said.

'Makes sense,' Ella said. 'They'd save time and fuel by bunching the runs up.'

She turned to the next page where more deliveries were italicised, then a name jumped out at her from the receiver's list.

'Nolan.'

Kennedy had delivered boxes of toys to a Marrickville warehouse in the name of A. Nolan.

'Who's he?' Murray said.

'Wayne Rhodes's case. Guy died the same day as Kennedy. Hand me that highlighter?'

Murray passed it over, and Ella drew a wide stripe through the listing. She turned the page. 'Here he is again.'

'How'd he die?'

'Fell from a train during a pursuit by uniform, but Wayne's uncovering some odd stuff in his background.'

Murray picked up a highlighter of his own and started going through his pages. 'He gets a few deliveries.'

Ella finished with Nolan's name then took up a red pen to underline his deliveries done by Kennedy. Murray followed suit, and when they were finished there were stripes everywhere.

Ella sat back in her chair. 'So what's this mean? A box delivered by Kennedy to Nolan ends up in Feng's flat?'

'If it was one of those boxes.' Murray counted. 'Their deliveries look like a lot but they're only ten per cent of the total.'

'These are three guys who died within days of each other, two by homicide, one in unusual circumstances.' She tapped her finger on the spreadsheet. 'This means something.'

'But what?'

She got a handful of A4 paper and lined up different-coloured pens. Diagrams, she needed diagrams. On the first sheet she wrote KENNEDY in the top left corner, NOLAN in the top right. She drew arrows from each, coming together in the top centre of the page, where she wrote LINKS. Underneath that she wrote PHONE CALLS, then BOX.

'Question mark,' Murray said. 'You don't know what the box means yet, if it means anything. You need to add a question mark.'

She did so grudgingly, then wrote FENG in the middle of the page. 'Did Simon say whether Feng had a phone?'

Murray shook his head. 'And I didn't see one in the flat.'

Ella flipped back through her notebook to the pages she'd filled in after seeing Feng's flat. She'd written nothing about a phone.

Murray dialled Simon's number.

'I bet he's gone,' Ella said. The time on the email was more than an hour ago.

Murray listened. 'Voicemail.' He left a message then hung up.

Ella made a row of dot points next to Feng's name, listing the questions to ask when they did speak to Simon. *Mobile? Number? Recent bill?*

'Imagine if we find his number on Nolan's and/ or Kennedy's bills, or their number on his.'

'Because of a cardboard box?' Murray said. 'What's the likelihood?'

Ella didn't care. She drew a looping line between the three names on the page, with a big black question mark over the top.

Murray stretched and looked at his watch. 'What d'you say – want to call it quits for this arvo? Start fresh in the morning?'

'I might just ring Wayne, see if he's got anything

new,' she said, reaching for the phone. His number went to voicemail too, but she didn't bother to leave a message.

Murray was standing now, looking down at her. 'It'll all still be here in the morning, you know.'

'Maybe I'll just reread the list.'

He said, 'Anyone'd think you didn't want to go home.'

Ella parked the car in the drive and got out with her shopping. She was earlier than she had been the day before, and the sun's rays warmed her back as she stood there with one hand on the vehicle, the other holding the plastic bags, examining her house. She could hear the clack-clack of a skateboard down the street and a commentator calling the England–Windies test on a radio. In the distance somebody started a mower. They were the sounds of summer but today they seemed ominous to Ella.

There is nobody in the house.

She corrected herself. There were no *signs* that somebody was in the house.

She walked to the front door and inspected the lock before testing it. Locked. The windows to the side were intact and locked. She followed the path along the side, checking each window, then around to the back door. It too was locked. She went right around the front, examining Denzil's house too, because what if somebody broke into his place then cut through the dividing wall?

You're losing it.

She took her keys from between her fingers and unlocked her front door. She stepped in, put the shopping bags on the floor, closed the door behind her and locked it again. She listened. Silence.

Right. A quick survey, you'll see things are fine. Get changed. Take that fucking rock and go for a walk along the river and toss it out as far as you can. Put this entire matter behind you and—

She stopped short in the kitchen. The fridge stood open. The milk was on the bench, the top of the carton open, a lazy fly crawling along the edge. The box of Special K was next to it and a bowl and spoon sat in the sink.

Her breath came hard in her throat. She seized a knife from the drawer and bolted through the place, checking behind the armchairs and under the bed. She tested the windows and doors once more and pushed at the trapdoor with the knife blade.

Nothing.

She pressed against the kitchen cupboard as nervous sweat trickled down her back. She tried to be calm, tried to think like the detective she was. If she responded to a call like this from a member of the public, what would she say?

What did you have for breakfast this morning?

Those exact things: the cereal with milk.

Is there any chance you could have left them like that?

No.

Really? Are you sure? Do you have a lot on your mind? Is there any possibility at all that you may have forgotten?

She lowered the knife. It seemed unlikely, but she had been tired, and focused on that bloody rock . . .

She looked at the microwave. It suddenly felt like that would be the test. If the rock was gone, it meant . . . well, one thing. If it was there, it meant another.

She jabbed the knife point into the door-release button. The rock sat staring out at her, exactly where she'd left it.

She slammed the door in its face.

Dennis answered on the third ring.

'It's me,' Ella said.

'How's it going?'

'Pretty good,' she lied. She stared into the kitchen. She hadn't touched anything yet. She'd spent fifteen minutes trying to think what to do, who she might ring and what she would say. She'd practised saying, 'There's something funny going on at my house,' but now it wouldn't come out.

He said, 'How's the case?'

'Okay.' She heard Dennis's wife, Donna, speaking in the background. 'Are you busy?'

'We're going out shortly,' he said. 'Tim got a promotion and we're going to the restaurant to test him out.'

'Oh.' She'd thought she could ask him over, just show him without saying anything and see how he responded.

'Did you need something?'

'It doesn't matter. Have a good evening.'

When he was gone she went into the kitchen and stood close to the bench. Was it really possible that she'd left the things out and forgotten to shut the fridge in her rush to leave? She had been late, after all. She tried to think back, but routine actions like that you just did, you never thought about. It was like driving to work – suddenly you were there. You didn't remember every intersection and red light.

She stood as if making breakfast and went through the actions. Open the cupboard, get out the Special K and put it on the bench. Get out the milk. Pour both into the bowl. Eat, then put the bowl in the sink.

If you were rushing to get on the road, you might just turn away at that point and go to clean your teeth, put on your face and rush out the door.

The problem was the fridge. At what point could she have opened it then forgotten to both put the milk in and close it? And wouldn't she have poured the milk over the cereal then put the carton back in immediately?

She put her hand inside the fridge. It was warm enough to have been open all day. The milk sat in a puddle of water, a sign of the condensation that had collected on the outside then trickled down to the bench. The sides of the carton were now dry, the milk warm.

She stood there for a moment longer, then shut the fridge. She picked up the carton and tipped the contents down the sink, and threw the empty carton in the bin. She shoved the cereal box back in the cupboard. She turned the stereo on, checked the doors once more, got the new shampoo from the plastic shopping bag, and went to shower.

Sal woke with the neck-prickling knowledge that somebody was in his room. It was dark but he could just make out a black shape by the door. 'Mum?'

'*Mum?*' the shape mimicked in a high-pitched voice, and Sal heard the hope he'd put into the word. Embarrassment and disappointment flooded through him.

He snapped, 'You never dream?'

'I dream of having you off my back.' Thomas came further into the room.

Sal stood up and put the chair he'd been sitting on by the window between Thomas and himself.

'You seem afraid.' Thomas came closer still. 'But that makes no sense. Why would you be afraid of me? You've done nothing wrong – have you?'

'Of course not!'

'Nona told me you rang the police back,' Thomas went on. 'But you didn't do it till this evening.'

'I waited for you, I was going to check with you–'

'Don't you have a brain of your own?'

'Yes, but–'

'So why wait so long? They ask you to ring them, you fucking ring them.'

'I wanted to check with you.' He tensed his abs. 'Where've you been anyway?'

Thomas was right in front of him now. He grasped

the chair and yanked it from Sal's hands. 'Why are you sitting here at the window?'

Sal resisted the urge to fold his arms.

'You want a bird's-eye view when they come up to the door again?' A car passed outside and the glow of its headlights glinted in Thomas's eyes. His skin smelled of the chemicals and the soap he'd used to try to wash them off. 'What are you planning, Sal?'

'You said you'd take care of that paramedic,' Sal said.

'That's not an answer.'

Sal couldn't even muster a surreptitious lats flex. Thomas put his hand on his shoulder.

'This isn't right,' Sal said. 'We used to be friends.'

'You don't think we still are?' Thomas's fingers dug into his trapezius. 'Think for a moment about everything I've done for you. What about in that alley? Didn't I help you there?'

Sal tried to breathe deep. 'I know what you're capable of.'

'You think I'm reminding you to point that out? Sal, buddy, pal, you've got me all wrong.' Thomas slid his arm around Sal's neck and yanked him close. His breath was hot on Sal's ear. 'I'm just helping you remember what you owe me.'

Sal tried to pull Thomas's arm away from his throat. 'I owe you nothing.'

'You think?' Thomas tightened his grip, closing off Sal's airway. 'The way I see it, you owe me silence. And one way or another, that's what I'll be getting.'

The pressure built in Sal's head. He yanked at Thomas's arm but Thomas only squeezed tighter. Sal heard buzzing, and felt the pounding of his heart grow more intense. His lungs burned for air and he saw red flashes in the darkness. His legs grew weak. His fingers were slick with sweat and slipped off Thomas's arm. Thomas gave one final squeeze, then released him and walked from the room without a word.

Sal fell to his knees. His hands trembled at his aching neck. He couldn't believe it had come to this. They'd had fun in Spain, partying with the tourists 24/7, selling Es in the clubs owned by his cousins, although even then there'd been glimpses of Thomas's true colours – his at times all-consuming focus on money, the easy way he'd manipulate people when it suited him, the lack of conscience with which he could hurt someone. Then he was here, and things were okay, mostly, only really turning bad during Kristi's pregnancy – Sal still couldn't believe some of the things he'd said, like that Kristi was turning into a whale and he wished she'd got rid of it – and then, worst of all, when he went back to Austria without even seeing his daughter. He'd eventually worked in Spain again, with Sal's cousins, then got together with Sal's uncle and planned this business. Sal guessed Thomas saw it as his, being as how he started things off, but to Sal's mind it was more his family's than anyone's. It was Uncle Paulo's contacts in China they were using, it was through them that they'd got the cook; it was Paulo's friends here who were letting them use the plastics factory. Thomas was just one part of the whole, not king shit like he thought.

Sal sat on the edge of his bed. The frame squeaked with his trembling. He put his face in his hands and tried to think about something other than Thomas's threat, but his fingers were tingling and he was breathing too fast. He struggled to slow himself down. *In through the nose, hold it and count to five, then out through the mouth.* He'd read in the paper that this was part of what happened in panic attacks, as was the feeling of impending doom. But sometimes – like now – he feared that the feeling was less to do with the altered levels of carbon dioxide and oxygen in his blood than with how things were getting worse by the day, and how he knew deep down that it would all end in disaster, and soon.

TWENTY-FIVE

Ella picked Lauren up at eight-thirty on Monday morning and drove her into the Police Centre in Surry Hills. Lauren was nervous, shifting in her seat, feeling constricted by the seatbelt across her shoulder and chest. The wound on her back was hurting too. When she thought of what she'd have to say, a flush crept over her. It didn't make sense that she should be embarrassed or ashamed – Thomas had threatened her, and his actions since had proved that she was right to be afraid. But she wasn't habitually a liar and to apply that word to herself made her feel bad.

She glanced over at Ella, who looked tired and stressed. Lauren thought about that, how at least in her job the cases were usually over within an hour. They were longer if you worked in the country, of course, or when there were difficult circumstances. Cops on the other hand could go for weeks, months, even years, on the same case. It must haunt them, she thought, spending so long thinking about the same people and actions and situations, and trying to fit the pieces together and find the answer. Or collect enough evidence to lock somebody away.

Thirty minutes later they were in an interview room. To Lauren's relief, Detective Lance Fredriks was warm and friendly. He shook her hand. 'Have a seat. I hear you've been through the wringer lately.' He sat opposite her, a laptop open on the table between them. Ella sat next to him. Lauren folded her arms, then thought that might look defensive and unfolded them and put them under the table so she could lock her fingers together out of sight.

'When we get Werner into court,' Fredriks said, 'both your original statement and this one will be handed in as evidence. The defence will of course say that because you lied then, how can the court be sure you're not lying now, and so on and so on, but it's their job to cast doubt, and we have plenty to come back at them with. The main thing for now is that we get down what really happened that night. Everything else we'll worry about later.'

Lauren took a deep breath and thought back. 'I was working on my own. I'd just been to a fatal car accident, and waited around on scene there until the government contractors turned up, then I left. I got coffee on Broadway then was sent to Paddington, so I was taking the back way and was driving down Smithy's Lane when a man ran out in front of me.'

She could see it again, the flash of movement in her headlights, feel the lurching fear that she was going to hit him. 'Another man came out of the alley and fell over. He looked hurt so I called Control and told them what I had and asked them to send back-up. I lied in how I described that man too.' She flushed again. Her hands were sweaty. 'He was about eighteen, skinny, thin face, with acne. He had short spiked black hair. I think he was a prostitute. His shoulder had dislocated – he said it happened all the time, and usually to fix a thing like that the person needs to go to hospital. So the local hospitals probably have him on their records. He might've even walked into one that night.'

Fredriks nodded as he typed. 'That could help us.'

'He told me he wasn't going to get involved,' Lauren went on. 'I wondered after whether that meant he saw Thomas in the alley. I think there may have been somebody else there too. There was a car up on blocks, near the body, and there was a dark shape there, at the front of it.'

'I remember that car,' Fredriks said.

Lauren stared across the room, picturing it. 'I'd heard a noise when I was checking Blake's body for a pulse, and started down that way, then I saw that shape. I thought it was a person, huddled over, you know, and I was trying to shine the torch on it when Thomas made a noise behind the skip. I think he was trying to attract my attention away from it, because it wasn't an accidental kind of noise; he actually groaned.'

She couldn't hold back a shiver as she explained how he'd claimed to have chest pain, then feigned unconsciousness, and when she went close had grabbed her. 'When I was on my back and he was on top of me, with my shirt and jacket all bunched up hard under my chin, he said "Go".'

'Maybe telling whoever was hiding behind the car to get out of there,' Ella said. 'Did you hear footsteps?'

Lauren shook her head. 'All I could hear was Thomas breathing in my ear and saying that if I told the police about him being there he'd get us. He said he had contacts and he'd know if I told.'

'Get us,' Fredriks repeated. 'Us being . . . ?'

Lauren tightened her grip on her own hands. 'Me and my sister, Kristi, his ex, and their daughter, Felise.'

Fredriks typed this in. 'What happened then?'

'He made me roll over and he pressed my head to the roadway and told me not to move,' Lauren said. 'Then he got off me. I heard him running down the alley. I could hear the sirens coming. I took a moment to pull myself together, hauled myself up against the skip.' She breathed in, recalling the odour of wood and plasterboard, the coldness of the night air. 'I checked myself over and tried to think what to do. I knew the police would be there soon and I had to be ready with whatever I was going to say.' She looked at her lap. 'So I decided to do what he said.'

The only sound was Fredriks's fingers on the keyboard.

'I told the uniformed police I'd seen only the two men running away,' she said in a small voice. 'Then you came along and I told you the same thing. And I said it in court as well. And Thomas went free.'

She didn't say the rest; they all knew it.

And he killed again.

*

Ella dropped Lauren home then went back to the Homicide office in Parramatta to find the desks empty and the door to the meeting room closed. She knocked. The voices inside stopped, then the lock turned and Kuiper looked out. He held the door open to let her in, and she stood at the side of the room as there were no empty chairs.

'As I was about to say,' Kuiper said, locking the door again, 'the Griffith boys believe they're getting closer to finding Deborah Kennedy. They've received information from a local who believes he saw her and her daughter Tess with a man he identified as Paul William Roper. Roper lives in the region and works for a livestock agent. He grew up in Kempsey, which is where we've found Deborah Kennedy lived in her teen years, so it's possible they know each other from then. Officers are making contact with his friends in the area out there, so with any luck we might have her in the next couple of days.' He looked at Ella. 'Anything new from the interview?'

Ella told the group what Lauren had said about the young man with the dislocated shoulder. 'She said such an injury can happen repeatedly and needs medical treatment, so there's a good chance he's known to local hospitals and might even have presented that night.'

'Good,' Kuiper said. 'Strong, forget about your other task for now. Nip off to the hospitals this morning and see what you can find.'

Strong nodded.

'Okay, let's get to it.' Kuiper unlocked the door and people filed out.

'That's a good lead,' Murray said to Ella as they headed up the corridor. 'If we can find that guy we're not so reliant on Lauren's testimony.'

'Has Simon Bradshaw been in touch yet?'

'No calls, but looks like we've got a new email.' He sat at his computer. 'He says Feng did have a mobile, according to the professor. They haven't found it yet. Here's the number.' He read it out.

'That seems familiar,' Ella said.

'From where? Kennedy's list?'

'I don't know. Grab it and we'll see.'

While he was fetching the folder Ella dialled Wayne Rhodes's mobile. It went to voicemail. 'Hi,' she said. 'You're hopefully getting some great information from Mrs Nolan, but I've got another phone number for you to check when you've finished eating cake.' She recited it. 'Gimme a call, okay?'

Murray plonked the folder down. They took out the pages of the incoming and outgoing numbers and split them up.

Ella ran her finger down the list, her nail sliding over each number, her eyes fixed on the last three digits, looking for seven one two. Six eight three, four seven nine. *I've seen it, I know I've seen it somewhere.* Seven one one, two two four, seven one two. Her heart lurched. Did the rest of the number match? She slid her finger across.

It did.

'I've got one,' she said. 'Feng called Kennedy five weeks ago.'

'I've got one too,' Murray said. 'And another. And another!'

She grabbed the pages from him. Kennedy had called Feng Xie three times in the space of two days, almost three weeks ago. They'd spoken for between one and three minutes each time. 'I bet there's more too,' Murray said.

She had an idea. Her heart started hammering. She flipped to the last page. Feng's was the last number Kennedy had called before he died.

They stared at each other, Ella holding back a grin. 'Told you it was something,' she said.

Before Murray could answer, Ella's phone rang.

'This time Mrs Nolan fed me chocolate cake,' Wayne said. 'Mud. 'Twas lovely.'

'I'm pleased,' Ella said. 'But listen to this—'

'Just a second,' Wayne said. 'She also showed me a letter she got back this morning from one of the businesses she'd written to as part of the folding up of the warehouse. It was a post office box, and the PO had stamped *Not at this address* across it. She'd checked in the files – she even showed me while I was there – and Adrian, who was apparently a little anal when it came to paperwork, had noted that the address was current as of the start of the month, as he'd done with all of them. But when the envelope came back Mrs Nolan put on her investigator's hat. Seeing there was no phone number for them in the file, she went to the phone book. Finding nothing there, she called directory assistance. Zippo.'

'Silent number?'

'A business with no way of being contacted?' he said. 'That's like . . . like . . .'

'Okay,' she said. 'So what's your theory then?'

'Shenanigans of a criminal nature.'

'Nolan's got no record.'

'There's always a first time,' he said. 'I'm delving further into this DNP Holdings with their dodgy post office box at the Sydney GPO. Now, what's your news?'

She told him about finding Feng's number on Kennedy's list. 'Recognise it?'

'Can't say I do,' Wayne said. 'But I'll have a look when I get back to the office and keep you firmly posted.'

Ella put the phone down but wasn't entirely happy. Something about that number still niggled. *What?*

Lauren sat at the little table in the attic and watched Felise colour in. Every couple of minutes Felise would turn the picture around for Lauren to examine. 'You're an excellent student,' Lauren said. 'I think we're shaping up for a gold star here.'

Felise smiled and bent close to the page again, fingers white with the effort of staying inside the lines. Lauren looked past her out the small window. The sky was pale blue, the day warm. The interview with Fredriks hadn't been so bad in the end. If he thought she was an idiot for thinking she could keep the truth hidden, he hadn't shown it.

She wondered if they'd found the dislocated shoulder guy yet – whether they ever would. He might not have gone to hospital that night at all really. He might have managed to pop it back in himself.

They might all be in the same position as before, with just her word against Thomas's.

The air in the attic was stuffy and still.

'Are you hot?' she said.

Felise shook her head.

Lauren went to the window but it was already open as wide as it would go. She leaned on the sill and stared south, at the red roofs and blocks of flats and trees. Thomas was out there somewhere. Or so the police thought. She couldn't help but hope and pray he'd sneaked through the airport and gone home.

She heard the sound of the postman's motorbike. Felise leapt up. 'Postie!'

Lauren followed her down the stairs. Kristi sat on her knees on a chair at the kitchen table, frowning over some new mosaic design. 'That client rang me again,' she said. 'Got quite abusive.'

'You should just go and finish it,' Lauren said. 'Go this afternoon. I'm here with Felise. Nothing will happen.'

Kristi shook her head.

'This is your business,' Lauren said.

'Don't even start.' Kristi drew hard black lines on her sketch.

'Life doesn't just stop.'

'It almost did.'

Lauren turned away to the stairs.

Felise hopped from foot to foot at the front door. 'I didn't touch the lock.'

'Another gold star,' Lauren said. 'What if we run out of them?'

She checked the peephole and opened the door

as the postie's bike drew near. Their letterbox was fixed to the wall but Felise danced on the spot. 'Let me get it, let me get it!'

Lauren looked around the street then let her jump forward onto the step as the postie pulled up. He handed Felise three thin white letters and one fat brown one and she took them with delight then bolted up the stairs. Lauren thanked him, then locked the door and checked that it was secure before going up.

'Let me see,' Kristi was saying in the kitchen. 'Felise, give it to me now, please.'

Felise clutched the fat letter to her chest. 'Why can't I open it?'

'I'll count to three.'

Felise threw the fat letter on the floor and stamped away.

'Come back here and pick that up.'

Felise dropped onto the lounge and kicked her heels against the side.

'Do you want to spend the rest of the day in bed?'

Lauren bent to pick the letter up, then hesitated. The brown envelope bore twelve fifty-cent stamps and was addressed to her. She didn't recognise the stiff, stilted handwriting. She flipped the envelope over with the toe of her shoe. There was no return address.

'Well?'

Lauren looked up to see Kristi watching her.

'Who's it from?' Kristi said.

'It doesn't say.'

Kristi immediately went for the phone.

'Wait a minute.' Lauren flipped the envelope over again. 'See if you recognise the handwriting.'

'Yeah, that'd be what he wants,' Kristi hissed. 'Get us close to it then set off the bomb.'

'It's not a bomb.' Lauren kept her voice low. Felise was still kicking the lounge.

'You don't know that. He could be outside with a mobile phone, biding his time before he triggers it.'

'I'm going to pick it up.'

'Don't.'

'You saw how hard she threw it down – wouldn't it have gone off then?'

'Maybe that primed it,' Kristi said. 'How come you're so keen to get us killed? The detectives said if we got anything strange to call them. Why not just leave it there and ring?'

Lauren stepped back. 'Fine. Ring them. It'll turn out to be a sample of shampoo or something I forgot I wrote away for, and we'll have wasted more of their time.'

'Wasting their time I'm happy to do.' Kristi dialled the number. 'Ella, it's Kristi. There's a strange parcel here.'

'It's only a letter,' Lauren said.

'It's a big fat envelope with something inside, and we don't know the handwriting, and there's no sender's address,' Kristi said. 'Should we evacuate or – okay, yep, okay. Thanks. Will do. Bye.' She put the phone down. 'She's going to send somebody around. She said just leave it alone.'

Lauren sat on the lounge and caught one stick-like ankle. 'Enough kicking, Flea.'

Felise wrapped her thin arms around Lauren's neck. 'Can I watch Dora?'

Lauren looked at Kristi over her head. Kristi shrugged in a resigned way. Felise put the DVD in and sat on the floor.

There was a knock at the door. Lauren looked out the window. 'It's them.'

'Already?'

Kristi went downstairs and returned with two smiling uniformed police officers. They pulled on gloves and picked the envelope up off the floor. Kristi took a few steps back as they began to open it.

They looked inside. 'Hm,' the male officer said.

Kristi leaned forward. 'White powder?'

The female officer tipped up the envelope and let the contents slide out onto the table.

'Oh my god.' Kristi took a step back.

'It's just a toy,' Lauren said.

'With its head ripped off,' Kristi snapped.

The headless koala hand puppet lay crumpled up on the table while the head rolled in a slow arc and came to rest against her pencils. Grey fluff settled on her sketches.

'Get that thing off there,' she said. 'Get it off!'

The female officer checked inside the envelope before scooping the toy back in.

'No note?' Lauren said.

'Nothing.' She slipped the envelope into a plastic evidence bag.

The male officer said, 'We'll look for prints, and

try to track down where it was posted and when, but it was probably put in a street postbox – hence all the stamps – and not through a post office.'

'So no witnesses,' Lauren said.

'There could be prints,' he said again.

There wouldn't be.

'We'll let Detective Marconi know,' the female officer said. 'Are you all okay?'

'No,' Kristi said.

'Yes, we are,' Lauren said. 'I mean, we're on edge and upset, but there's nothing more that you can do.'

The officers exchanged glances. 'If you're sure.'

'Thanks.' Lauren took them downstairs, watched them to their car, then locked the door.

'We could've kept them here for a while.' Kristi grasped the banister, her voice full of hurt. 'What if he drops round to see how we liked his present?'

'That's what the surveillance people are there for.'

'But how do we know they're still out there? Have you seen them? Because I haven't.'

Lauren climbed the stairs. 'We can't even be sure it was him.'

'Are you crazy? Who else would send us that?'

Lauren didn't want to talk about it any more. To think that he was still here made her feel weak, sick. *Please let the police find him, through the shoulder guy or the leak or somehow.* Otherwise, there was no telling where he might stop.

TWENTY-SIX

Ella put the phone down. 'It was a soft toy with its head torn off.'

'Charming,' Murray said.

'They're trying for prints.' Ella frowned at her computer screen. The niggle about the phone number was still there in the back of her mind.

'Good luck,' Murray said. 'Hey, did you ring that guy back?'

'What guy?'

'There was a note on your desk earlier.' He pushed aside papers on her desk looking for it. 'Must be here somewhere. It was that Sal guy. The note said he rang yesterday evening. You didn't see it earlier?'

She shook her head. 'Feel like a drive back out there?'

'Nah. Got enough to do. Just phone him, then we'll go and talk to Simon.'

Ella found the sheet with Sal Rios's contact details and picked up the phone. While it was ringing she thought about the threats Thomas Werner was making. *Well, at least we know he's still here.*

'Hello.' The male voice was gruff, older.

'I'm calling for Sal Rios, please. It's Detective Marconi.'

The phone was dropped on a hard surface. She heard footsteps retreating then a voice bawled 'Sal!'

She waited. She wished she could work out what the niggle was about. She hated the feeling of the answer being just out of reach.

'Sal speaking.'

'This is Detective Marconi,' she said. 'We're looking into a phone call that was made from Rosie's nightclub on Wednesday the fourth. Paul Davids told us you were there that evening.'

'I work there,' he said. 'My family are part-owners. I keep an eye on things.'

'Did you make any calls from the phone on the bar that night?'

'You know how noisy that area can get? I'm surprised anyone makes calls from there.'

'This was before opening,' Ella said. 'Davids told us there were only seven or so people present. We know the call was made from there – we need to know who made it.'

'Wasn't me,' he said. 'Who was the call made to?'

'I can't discuss that,' she said. 'Did you see anybody use the phone? Or even go near it?'

'Nope. Everyone's got mobiles these days. I'm always saying we should can that phone. Save the line rental money.'

'Okay. Thanks for your time.' She hung up.

Murray said, 'Anything?'

'Nah.' Ella strained her brain. She was certain she'd seen Feng's number somewhere other than on Kennedy's list.

'Ready to see Simon?'

'Give me a minute.'

It was an itch she had to scratch. She grabbed the folders and started paging through the phone records. Murray huffed.

'One minute.' They'd already checked Kennedy's. She ran her finger down Lauren's. 'Bloody hell.'

'What?'

'Remember how Werner called Lauren and threatened to burn her house down? He did it from Feng Xie's mobile.'

Murray raised his eyebrows.

'See for yourself.' She handed the folder over.

His eyes widened. 'This is—'

'Huge,' she said. 'He's a triple murderer.'

'He might have picked the phone up in the street.'

'Yeah, right.' She grabbed her phone.

'You're sure?' Simon Bradshaw said.

'The call was made to Lauren last Wednesday,' Ella said. 'Feng was found in the water on Friday. You said the autopsy showed he'd been in there for a couple of days.'

'They think,' Murray put in.

She turned her back to him.

'This is huge,' Simon said.

Exactly, Ella thought.

'Can you send over a photo of Werner?' Simon asked. 'We found a couple of people who saw a man come out of the water in full scuba kit near Hermit Bay. He took some of it off and got into the passenger side of a late model blue sedan. With a bit of luck they might be able to pick out his face.'

She went into her email program. 'Sending.'

A moment later she heard his email ping. 'Bewdy,' he said. 'Okay. I'm going to see if I can get this confirmed. I'll ring you when I know.'

'Cheers.'

Murray had the diagram spread out in front of him and was writing under Feng Xie's name: *Phone used by Werner to threaten Lauren*.

'You know what the problem with all of this is,' he said in a conversational manner.

She nodded. 'We still can't find him.'

'The case against him gets bigger and bigger, but the jail cell remains empty.'

'I'm hoping Mendelssohn and what's-his-name are onto the leak and we'll get him that way,' Ella said.

She emailed Werner's photo to Wayne Rhodes with the message: *This is him – any recognition from your widow?*

After a moment's thought she wrote him another email, and cc'd Simon. *Can you send me pics of your guys and I'll see if Kennedy's girlfriend's seen them before?*

She hit send with her fingers crossed.

★

'Lemon tea cake,' Wayne told Ella on the phone later that afternoon.

'Never mind that. Did she recognise the picture?'

'She didn't,' he said. 'She apologised about it too. A nicer lady one couldn't hope to find. Get this: she says she wants me to find out what was going on because she needs to understand her husband's death. I told her that it looks like we're uncovering some bad things he was involved in, and she said that it didn't matter, so long as we worked out what happened.'

'So what have you found out?'

'DNP Holdings exists only in the books of Adrian Nolan's toy warehouse,' Wayne said. 'As I said, shenanigans.'

'So it's a dummy company?'

'It's not even that. It's basically just a name and address. Not even an address really.' He rustled papers. 'Nolan took delivery of stacks of stuff from various companies throughout the world, many of them Chinese, and much of it belonging in what we'll kindly call the lower end of the market.'

'Plastic crap.'

'In a word, yes,' he said. 'Nolan took this stuff, divvied it up and sold it on. DNP was made out to look like one of his customers. He shipped stuff to them on an average of every six to eight weeks.'

'To where?'

'It took a bit of hunting to find it,' Wayne said, 'considering Nolan's normally detailed record-keeping. But DNP's stuff went to 76 Hunter Lane, in

Chinatown. There's no such address. Nothing even close. But he's written that Quiksmart delivered it.'

Ella's scalp prickled. 'Kennedy.'

'That's my guess,' he said. 'Under-the-table-type deliveries, so I doubt we'll find proof.'

'Does it say what the goods were?'

'Snow domes,' Wayne said. 'Every single time.'

'How weird is that?'

'Not at all actually,' he said. 'Did you know there's a step in the crystal meth manufacturing process at which operations can be suspended, keeping the substance in a liquid form?'

'It was ice in the snow domes?'

'Pretty funny, hey,' he said. 'Ice, snow, get it?'

'Where did they come from?'

'I haven't narrowed it down yet,' he said. 'Looks like he bought snow domes from various Chinese companies, so which were the real thing and which were full of the drugs I don't know yet. I'm about to start a search on those companies, see what I can find out.'

'So,' Ella said, thinking it through, 'Nolan sent the druggie domes via Kennedy to Feng, who cooked it in his little lab there at the back of his craptastic flat. We need to find any witnesses who saw a Quiksmart van near his place.' She scribbled a note. 'And then what? Did Kennedy pick it up again? Did Feng drop it off somewhere?'

'Or maybe Werner went and collected it himself.'

Ella made another note. 'Have you got into the money side yet? Where it went, where it came from?'

'Still working on that aspect,' Wayne said. 'Did you get the pic of Nolan I sent?'

'Got one of Feng too. We're planning a trip to see Helen Flinders shortly.'

She felt excited and pleased by the developments in the case, but wished they were getting closer to the man himself. Maybe once they had all the links worked out between these three dead men, they'd see then what they couldn't see now.

'Talk to you later, okay?'

Murray drove them across to Helen Flinders's place in Double Bay. Ella knocked on the door next to the filigreed numbers. The corridor was bright with the late-morning sun.

The dog barked. They heard Helen Flinders's voice: 'Pepper, sit. Be quiet.' The dog kept barking. Helen Flinders opened the door with her hands full of silver wire in complicated-looking knots and pushed the excited dog back with her foot. 'Please, come in.'

She crossed the room to put the wires down as Pepper snuffled around the cuffs of Murray's trouser legs.

'We'd like to show you a couple of photographs,' Ella said. 'Could you tell us if you've seen these people before?'

Helen took the pictures. The first photo was of Feng Xie, and she handed it back with a shake of her head. The next one was of Nolan. When she looked up, her eyes were bright with tears. 'This is the man

I saw talking with James in the park on the night he died.'

'You're sure?'

'Yes.' Helen stared at the photo. 'Is this who killed him?'

'It isn't, I'm sorry,' Ella said. *But the pieces of the puzzle are certainly starting to come together.*

Ella rang Kuiper while Murray was driving them to Maroubra. She explained what Helen Flinders had said.

'Interesting.'

'I've let Wayne Rhodes know,' she said. 'He's looking into the Chinese companies that sent snow globes to Nolan. I spoke to Simon Bradshaw too, and he's talking to people in the vicinity of Feng Xie's flat about Quiksmart vans stopping by.' She took a breath. 'We're thinking we'll go back to see Sal Rios again. We believe he's worth another push. That call came from Rosie's that evening, and he was a bit thingy about the phone, talking about how it costs money. Perhaps he does take notice of who uses it and just needs a bit of face-to-face time to help him remember.'

'Let me know how you go,' Kuiper said.

They reached Sal's house in Maroubra twenty minutes later. Ella saw curtains move in a second-storey window. 'Someone's home.'

They walked up the path and Murray knocked. After a moment the door opened to reveal the sick-est-looking man Ella had ever seen. His brown eyes were sunken above sharp cheeks covered with paper-thin skin. Murray made a small and startled sound.

'Can I help you?' the man said.

Ella gathered her composure and introduced herself. 'Is Sal home?'

'I'll get him.'

He walked away into the house, leaving the screen door closed. Ella sneaked a hand up to test it. Locked.

When Sal appeared he unlocked it and stepped outside. He put out his hand then took it back, as if unsure what to do. Ella stuck hers out and they shook.

Ella said, 'We wanted to talk again about the phone call made from Rosie's.'

'I still don't know who made it.' He looked past her down the drive. She glanced that way too but there was nothing to see.

'We thought that as it's your family's club—'

'Only partly,' Sal said.

'—then maybe you did take notice of who used the phone, without even realising it, because after all the money's coming out of your pocket,' Ella said.

'What's a call cost? Forty, fifty cents? I'm not likely to be worried about that.'

'But it all adds up, doesn't it,' Murray said. 'My parents had a business too and every cent counted. Way better in our pocket than somebody else's, my dad used to say.'

Sal dug his hands into his pockets. 'We're not so fussy as that.'

'Maybe so,' Ella said. 'But you wouldn't mind having a look at this list, telling us what you know of these people? Whether you can recall them acting oddly that night?'

Sal took the page she held out. 'When was this again?'

'Wednesday the fourth,' Ella said. 'Six-thirty, seven, in the evening.'

Sal frowned at the page. 'I don't really have much to do with the staff.'

Ella remembered Paul Davids's words that Sal did little but sponge drinks for himself and his girlfriend. A thought struck her. 'Was your girlfriend with you that night?'

Sal started. 'I don't have a girlfriend.'

'Paul Davids told us you did.'

'I used to.' Sal's ears turned pink. 'We broke up. She hasn't been at the club with me for a long time, long before this night.'

Murray said, 'Of those people on the list, who do you know?'

Sal studied it again. 'Never met this Fonti guy, or Sommerson. I know Davids, of course. Known him for a few years. He doesn't say much. This guy Perante, I think he's a bouncer, big boof-headed bloke. He can be a bit of a prick. These other two, Lamond and Callaghan, they're bar staff, aren't they? He's friendly enough. She's a bit stuck-up.'

Ella thought he knew them rather better than he'd let on. 'Can you think why any of them might make a threatening phone call from the bar?'

'Threatening? To who?'

'Like I said this morning, we can't tell you.'

Sal shrugged. 'I have no idea.'

'How long has your family owned the club?'

'Part-owned,' Sal said. 'A fair few years. It's my dad's and uncle's thing really.'

'What are their names?'

Sal hesitated, just for a second. Ella's antennae quivered. 'My dad's name is Guillermo, my uncle was Paulo. He died last year.'

'Surnames all Rios?'

Sal nodded.

'Where's that from, out of interest?' she said with a smile. 'My background's Italian, so I'm always curious to know where people's families come from.'

'Spain,' he said.

'Oh right,' she said. 'Yeah, it does sound Spanish, doesn't it?' She looked at Murray who nodded dutifully. 'And the man who opened the door, that was . . . ?'

'My brother, Julio.'

'Ever heard the name Thomas Werner?'

'Don't think so,' Sal said.

'Recognise this man at all?' Ella held out the photo of Thomas at the airport. 'He's been seen in Rosie's.'

Sal shook his head. 'The place is so full sometimes, your own sister could be there and you wouldn't know. But I don't think I've seen him before, there or anywhere.'

'If you do happen to remember anything else, even something small and seemingly irrelevant, give me a call. You've got my card, right?'

He nodded, glancing down the driveway again. 'Will do.'

'Thanks.' Ella followed Murray back towards the street. She heard the screen door open and close behind her, and when they got into the car she looked back up the slope. 'He's still standing there, just inside.'

Murray started the car. 'Want me to wave?'

'Turn around slowly.' She put her sunglasses on and watched from the corner of her eye as they went past. 'Still there. And did you see how he kept looking down the driveway?'

'Maybe he thought his dad'd come home and he'd get busted for pinching drinks and allowing phone calls to go unpaid for.'

'You're so funny,' Ella said.

'It's a gift. What can I say?'

They grabbed lunch from Subway on the way back to the office, and when they got there Ella typed the surname Rios into the computer while Murray went to sponge barbecue sauce off his trousers.

Sal's father Guillermo had no record, and neither did his brother Julio or sister Nona. His uncle Paulo was a different story.

Murray came back dabbing paper towel at his thigh. 'How're they looking?'

'Uncle Paulo did three years for handling stolen goods, back in the early nineties.'

'Nobody else shows a flag?'

She shook her head. 'There's something off about Sal, though.'

Murray lifted the wet fabric off his leg and didn't answer.

'Don't you think?' she said.

'We can't go to Kuiper and tell him we have a feeling.'

'I never said we should. But we can keep in touch. Drop round at odd times. Call him up and say howyougoingmate. See what hatches.'

'I suppose,' Murray said.

Strong poked his head in. 'Meeting's kicking off.'

When everyone was in the meeting room, Kuiper closed and locked the door. 'First up, a few of you have asked whether there's news of the mole. I can't give you any specifics of the investigation's progress, but I can assure you it's moving along well.'

He turned to the whiteboard. 'Regarding Kennedy, fresh links have emerged to two other men who died that week.

'Adrian Nolan is a fifty-five-year-old man who has been identified as the man seen speaking to Kennedy the night that he died. Nolan also died that night. He was pulled over for running a red light and when the officers went to check his licence he ran. He made it to Redfern station and jumped onto a train. The officers almost had him when he apparently tried to climb up onto the roof. He fell and was killed.

'Nolan ran a warehouse in Marrickville. He imported fairly crappy toys and plastic goods. Marconi and Shakespeare discovered that he and Kennedy phoned each other frequently, including on the day of their deaths, and that Kennedy often delivered goods to Nolan. Also, both have had amounts of money deposited periodically in their accounts – money that Nolan's widow claims to know nothing about. We're looking into that further.

'The other dead man is Feng Xie, a twenty-year-old Chinese chemistry student. He was found underwater, in full scuba gear, drowned, just off Nielsen Park in Vaucluse. Investigators found evidence of a meth lab in his flat, and part of a cardboard box with a partial courier's barcode which has been traced back to goods delivered to Nolan's warehouse. Nolan would divide up batches of goods and send them on to retailers, one of which was called DNP Holdings. This company is nothing more than a false post office box and a non-existent street address, but examination of the records has shown that goods sent from Nolan to this supposed company were always delivered by Kennedy. The fake street address is two streets from where Feng Xie had his little operation.'

People scribbled notes.

'The goods sent to this DNP were snow globes, which we believe may have contained the liquid substance that is the halfway point of crystal meth-amphetamine,' Kuiper said. 'We've found none of these globes as yet. The lab in Feng's place was mostly cleaned out.

'Now, Feng had a mobile phone,' he said. 'This phone has been found to be the one from which Thomas Werner made the initial threat to Lauren Yates.'

'So we think Werner killed him too?' somebody said.

'He's certainly our strongest suspect,' Kuiper said.

Ella shivered. Blake, Kennedy, Feng Xie.

'Do we know why Nolan fled the traffic stop?' someone else asked.

'Not yet,' Kuiper said. 'We know he was driving a rented car, which he hadn't told his wife about. Possibly he was afraid of somebody, and saw the police officers as being a threat in some way.

'In other news,' he said, 'we think we're getting closer to Deborah Kennedy. Officers found a friend of Paul Roper, the man seen with her, who's spoken to him in the last few days. He told Roper they should turn themselves in. Roper told his friend that it wasn't how it looked; that Mrs Kennedy hadn't done anything wrong but was afraid of someone. The officers have Roper's mobile phone number now and are working to trace it.'

Ella drew pointy stars on her notepad. Nolan was afraid, Deborah Kennedy was afraid – of Werner?

'Werner has once again made his presence felt against Lauren Yates,' Kuiper said. 'In this morning's post she received a soft toy with its head torn off. There was no note. Scientific will do what they can with prints and so on, but they don't hold much hope.'

Ella cross-hatched around the stars. If they got Werner for the triple murder, a threat by mail was neither here nor there.

'Strong has located a possible match for the young man with the dislocated shoulder who Lauren saw the night that Blake was killed,' Kuiper said.

'Guy's name is Matthew Flack,' Strong said. 'He's had repeated Emergency Department visits for the shoulder, and also been assaulted a couple of times. Usually works on the Wall, going in men's cars to wherever they want. The hospitals have various addresses listed for him. It looks like he spends some time on the streets, then dosses down at a mate's for a while then out again. I haven't caught up to him yet, but I will.' Strong all but cracked his knuckles. Ella bit back a smile.

Kuiper nodded. 'What happened with the people present at Rosie's when the call to Kennedy's mobile was made?'

Detective Marion Pilsiger flipped pages in her notebook. 'Lambert and I spoke to Steve Fonti who was there as a DJ, Guy Perante who works as a bouncer, Tanya Callaghan and Peter Lamond who both work behind the bar. They all deny using the phone or seeing anybody else use it at that time. None of them recognised Thomas Werner's name, although Perante thought he looked familiar and felt he may have been in the club at some point but can't say when. He's worked there for over a year.'

Great, Ella thought.

'Shakespeare?' Kuiper said.

'We talked with Dan Sommerson who's the DJ's roadie. He knew nothing. Then we spoke to Sal Rios, whose family part-owns the place and who works there from time to time in a sort of supervisory role. He said he didn't use the phone and neither did he give permission for anybody else to use it.'

He glanced at Ella. If she wanted to say more

about Sal, this was her moment. She looked down at her notepad, and Murray shrugged. 'That's it.'

In the tiny kitchen afterwards he said, 'I thought you were going to mention your feeling.'

'You thought wrong.' She held up a cup.

He nodded. 'Thanks.' He drummed his fingers on the bench as she started to make the coffee.

Strong leaned into the room. 'Ella, your phone's ringing.'

She pushed the cups at Murray and hurried to answer it. 'Marconi, Homicide.' Still the little thrill.

'You like cake, don't you?' Wayne said. 'Veronique Nolan just rang. She tells me she's got some news.'

TWENTY-SEVEN

Lauren took the beer Ziyad held out. 'Thanks.'
'No worries.'

They sat on the Saleebas' back step. In the cubby-house Felise poured Max a cup of imaginary tea but he was too busy trying to pull down the tea-towel flag to take it.

'Looks really sick, doesn't he,' Ziyad said with a smile. 'I stay home for him and he miraculously recovers.'

They clinked bottles, and Lauren drank deeply. Kristi had grown herself a migraine after the soft toy thing and taken to her bed. Lauren and Felise went to play outside, then the rope on the tyre swing broke and Felise fell and started to cry, and Kristi had screeched something from her room, and Ziyad had heard the fuss and invited them over, and Lauren had practically hurdled the fence in her eagerness. She clinked her bottle against his again.

'So,' Ziyad said, 'how's the back?'
'Getting there.'

He fitted his thumb into the neck of his bottle. 'I'm sorry I didn't help clean up.'

'Hey, you did plenty,' Lauren said. 'You saved me.'

'You saved yourself. I just messed up your door.' He grinned. Down the yard Max managed to snag the flag, and wrapped it around his head like a bandanna, while Felise told off a toy bear. 'Tamsyn told me that Kristi was talking about an accident she'd been in, saying this brought it all back.'

'She said that, did she?'

'It sounded pretty bad.'

'It was,' Lauren said. 'Not so much for Kristi as for the other driver though.'

Ziyad picked at the label on his bottle. 'You sound angry about it.'

'Did she tell Tamsyn the guy died?'

'Apparently she said it was fatal, but didn't go into detail on that side of things.'

Lauren turned her bottle around and around in her hands and thought about the young man. She could hear again the bubbling of the blood in his lungs, see the paleness of his face in the glow of the headlights of passing cars and the contrast of it against the blood he coughed up. The sight through the windscreen of the other car, and Lauren's pain at knowing Kristi sat weeping behind the wheel there, arms around her pregnant belly, drunk and stoned and uninjured.

'I was working on my own because my partner had gone home sick.'

'Wait – you went to it?'

Lauren nodded. 'I recognised Kristi's car straight-away. I pulled up and went to her car first because it was closest. She wasn't hurt; she was sobbing and trying to get out. She was about eight months pregnant then. I told her to stay still while I checked the other car. I could see the instant I approached it that the driver was bad. His eyes latched onto me as soon as I got close. He was trapped, the steering wheel was against his chest. I managed to get his door open, and I crouched next to him with the torch, looking for how badly he was trapped, what we'd need to do to get him out.'

The young man – the boy, really he was just a boy – had reached for her. She'd taken his hand and kept shining the light over his lower body. She could smell the alcohol in his blood.

'The car was old and it'd just collapsed around his legs. The steering wheel was almost imbedded in his chest and stomach. His jeans were soaked with blood.'

The boy had cried, squeezing her hand. She'd had to pry his fingers off to go back to the ambulance and give a report, and get more equipment. Kristi had been crawling out of her car, sobbing and calling her name. Lauren had shouted at her again to stay where she was, not to move one inch. Kristi hadn't listened.

She blinked. 'I called for rescue and back-up urgently. If we didn't get him out soon he was going to die where he lay. And even if we did, when people are trapped there's a big risk that as you release the object pinning them down, their blood pressure crashes as the blood rushes to fill the crushed part, and toxins from damaged muscle flood from the injured part into the body and they can stop the heart.'

'So you already knew he might die?'

'Chances were that he would.'

Ziyad stared down the yard. 'I cannot begin to imagine how that must make you feel.'

'You think of what you can do to help, how you'll treat them and get them out, but there's this . . . feeling of panic . . . deep inside you. At the same time as you plan what you'll do, you're also seeing what is going to happen, that the person will go paler, deeper into shock, start to lose consciousness, their pulse will rise and their blood pressure fall, it doesn't matter how fast you're pumping fluid into them, and you can feel all the paramedics around you pick up their speed and the air goes tense and you're all waiting for the moment when the heart stops. You know it's coming and there's nothing you can do about it.'

Ziyad was silent for a moment. 'That's what happened to him?'

'After a while,' Lauren said. 'Rescue was cutting everything in sight. I was in the back seat talking to him.'

She saw the boy's ear, a spatter of blood on the curly cartilage, the lobe pushed up by the cervical collar she'd applied. She said his name, called him sweetie, told him he was doing fine, doing so well, he'd be out of there soon and, yes, his parents had been told and would meet him at the hospital. All of it was lies. She'd looked through the windscreen to see a paramedic helping Kristi onto a stretcher.

Kristi's face was turned their way, her mouth open. Lauren had stroked the back of his head and whispered that she was sorry.

'And then somebody said he'd flatlined.' She took a long drink. 'That's when you do CPR as best you can, and get them out without much regard for their lesser injuries.'

'So you yank them?'

'If you don't get them to hospital in minutes, they're dead. Losing half a leg doesn't matter in that context,' she said. 'We got him out and worked on him all the way to hospital.'

The boy's lanky body had rocked on the stretcher, up and down in time to Lauren's chest compressions, side to side as the ambulance tore around corners. His head had jounced on the mattress as they'd come over the bump in the hospital driveway and she'd said 'sorry' without even thinking about it. The doctors had whipped him off to theatre and Lauren had fought the urge to follow and stand outside the room while they worked on him, the feeling that she was responsible for him, that having been the first one to arrive she should stay with him throughout, and that he needed her near. Instead she'd gone out to the ambulance and started the paperwork, hearing other paramedics talking and joking, feeling that a moment's intense silence was needed, some sort of recognition for the fight that had been lost.

'But he died.'

Ziyad touched the back of her hand, the lightest touch. She turned her hand over and clutched the ends of his fingers in hers.

'Kristi had been taken to a different hospital, and when I went there we wept for that boy, and also for the fact that scans had shown that Felise wasn't hurt by the crash but had a heart defect.'

Alcohol-related, the doctor had said, stern-faced. Lauren had held Kristi close, their future one of court dates and uncertainty and fear over the baby's health and the knowledge that she'd require surgery if she lived.

'I didn't realise,' Ziyad said. 'From what Tamsyn said that Kristi said. I didn't know it was like that.'

'I never really went into detail about the boy for Kristi,' Lauren said. 'It was stuff she didn't need to know. And I think the way she perceives it now is a bit of a protective shell against the truth. I mean, she was charged, she went to rehab, she went to court and got a big fine and lost her licence, she heard everything that was said in court and she saw his family. I'm pretty sure she marks his birthday. She's certainly down when the anniversary of the crash comes around too. But I figured she didn't need to know about his actual final moments.'

Ziyad squeezed her hand. 'You're a good sister to protect her from that.'

Lauren looked at the kids waving from the cubbyhouse steps, and wished she'd been able to protect her even more.

The Nolans lived in Concord. The house was white-painted concrete, set towards the front of a large block. When so many Sydneysiders were subdividing their land, Ella was pleased to see nothing but lawn and garden behind the house and garage.

She followed Wayne up the wide curving concrete path. A currawong perched on the edge of a stone birdbath, giving them the eye. A shiny brass bell hung beside the door but Wayne chose to knock.

It opened just seconds later. 'Wayne, hello, come in.' The woman was thin, and in her fifties, Ella guessed. Her hair was bobbed, brown with streaks of grey visible at the part. Her eyes were overbright and a bit starey, as if her mind was completely somewhere else.

'Detective Ella Marconi, Veronique Nolan,' Wayne said.

They shook hands. Mrs Nolan's hand was bony and taut. Her skin was hot, as if she had a fever. 'Thank you for coming,' she said.

She led them into the living room and gestured to the lounges. Ella sank into the brown velour beside Wayne. Veronique stayed on her feet. She looked nervous.

'Are you okay?' Wayne said.

Veronique looked at Ella. 'You are working on the James Kennedy case?'

'I am.'

Veronique nodded. 'Wayne has told me about the ties between Mr Kennedy and Adrian.' Her French accent made it sound like *Adriennn*. 'I feel bad for everything that has happened.'

'None of it is your fault,' Wayne said.

She started to pace, then stopped herself. She crossed her arms and grasped her thin shoulders.

'What's the matter?' Ella heard genuine concern in Wayne's voice.

Veronique reached for a box of tissues, and dabbed at her eyes and blew her nose.

'Perhaps we should have tea first? And sponge cake?'

'What's upsetting you?' Wayne said. 'Is it this news you told me you had?'

Veronique looked at the floor then reached into the pocket of her slacks and pulled out a folded sheet of paper. She held it out to Wayne and he took it. Through her tears she gasped, 'Excuse me,' and hurried from the room.

Wayne unfolded the paper. Ella heard plates rattle in the kitchen. She moved closer to him and started to read.

Dear Ver, if you are reading this it's because something bad has happened.

'Oh boy,' Wayne said.

I want to first of all say sorry, and say that I love you and always will. I don't know how things finished but be assured I was not scared at the end because my final thoughts were of you.

I want you to give this to the police. Not just any of them, but one you have hopefully gotten to know a little. I have been made wary of police these recent weeks, and while what I've been told might not be true, I can't risk that the information isn't used except against you.

I am ashamed to tell you that I've done wrong. James Kennedy asked me to help and at first it seemed okay, not like anything too bad, it was just receive and dispatch like I do all the time. I didn't think about what was in the boxes,

I just sent them on. The money was good. I needed it, the warehouse wasn't doing so well and I knew I couldn't run it forever, and I wanted to take you back to France for that year, so you could experience the winter and summer of your youth again.

But Kennedy started telling me things, about the man he delivered the boxes to, about the men he worked for. The Chinese man told Kennedy what we were moving, what he was making. Ice started to be in the news all the time and I realised that our actions were part of the problem. We decided we didn't want to do it any more. Kennedy tried to tell them, but then one day, months ago, he brought the man in charge to the warehouse.

Ella grasped Wayne's arm. 'Thomas Werner was seen with Kennedy in his van back in May.'

This man made it clear that there was no way out for us. He said that at the very least we would be in as much trouble as him, we'd lose everything and go to jail for a long time. He said he had people in the police who would see to it that our information about him would go no further.

He also said that if necessary we would be silencèd, permanently, by these same people.

'Maybe that's why Nolan ran, and why Deborah Kennedy is still hiding,' Ella said.

That man's name is Thomas Werner, the note continued. *He's foreign, maybe German, from the sound of his accent. Kennedy told me once that he met him through some other cash-in-hand work he did.*

Ella thought of Benson Drysdale.

The final straw was when a friend of Kennedy's daughter almost died from using ice recently. We decided we'd really had enough. This time the Chinese man too wanted to finish.

He was at university and wanted to work a proper job and support his parents back in China that way. We thought if we used the amnesty they were all talking about, it might just work. But Werner was already threatening us about it. He called the warehouse a couple of times, telling me what he could do, reminding me about his police contacts, saying that as soon as my name went into their computer system, his mates would see and come for me, wherever I was.

'Nolan fled from the officers as soon as they took his licence back to their car,' Wayne said thoughtfully.

'Have you got those warehouse phone records?'

'At the office.'

It could be a long search to try to pin down where Werner had called from. Actually, she thought, it could be worse than that. It might be impossible. How could they know *when* he'd rung? They couldn't request caller information for every single number.

Veronique came in with a tea tray. The cups rattled as she moved and Ella saw her hands were shaking. She put the tray down with a clunk on the coffee table then sat opposite them on the very edge of a chair.

Wayne turned the page over. 'Where's the rest?'

'I don't know.'

Ella took the page from him.

. . . his mates would see and come for me, wherever I was.

We're trying again to get out. I don't know what will happen. I hope that things will be okay but

The page ended. Ella couldn't help but look on the back just as Wayne had done.

'There has to be more somewhere,' he said.

'I've searched and searched,' Veronique said. 'I cannot find it.'

'Where was this one hidden?'

'It was tucked in the envelope with our wills, in the safe at the warehouse. I can only think that in his fear he dropped the next page and didn't notice it.'

Ella glanced at Wayne. From what he'd said, Veronique had been more than forthcoming so far, but she had to wonder if the second page held information that the woman had decided was best kept to herself – maybe information that would stain her husband's name even further, or told where more money was hidden, or that might somehow incriminate her as well.

It was getting harder and harder for Sal to make the walk along the front of the factories to Preston's Plastics. It was bad for people to see him coming and going – not that he did it often – but it would be worse for them to see his car stopping out the front, and so he parked further down or further up, or in a side street, making sure to vary it each time. Thomas said it didn't matter, the street was so busy nobody took any notice, but that was from a man who didn't care that the cops had his photo and were asking people about him by name and kept coming back around to ask again.

Sal focused on his breathing. Two more places to get past. *Don't let me have a panic attack here.* In the front of a workshop a man paused in his welding and looked up, even raising his face shield. Sal tried to maintain his saunter. He carried two more fan heaters. That in itself must look strange, he thought. Fan heaters when summer was kicking in. Did undercover police know how to weld?

He glanced back. The man jerked his head to make the shield fall down into place and bent to his work again.

Sal kept on, but felt like his ears were pointing backwards, waiting for the running feet of Drug Squad and Homicide.

Inside Preston's he looked back out. Sounds of hammering and grinding, somebody singing tunelessly to the radio, hits of the nineties, people standing beside cars conferring over dents or paintwork or rust bubbles. The air smelled of hot plastic and the occasional whiff of paint fumes from the panelbeater's across the road.

'Whatcha looking for?'

Sal turned to find Colin Preston right behind him. 'I, ah, thought I saw somebody I knew.'

Preston peered past him, then looked down at the bags. 'More heaters?'

'Cold in there. The concrete, you know.'

Up close Preston smelled of Old Spice. His face was lined, and his blue eyes seemed to look right into Sal's soul.

'Comes up through your feet,' Sal stumbled on.

Preston sniffed and turned away, as if whatever he saw came up lacking. He crossed the room and switched on the radio. The voice of the Family Man echoed in the factory.

'—*Opposition spokesman for police, quoted in the papers today as saying "This amnesty has cost millions in advertising and man hours, as police have been taken from their regular duties on the street and told to man the phones then look into the claims made by these losers who would sell their own grandmothers for a snort of drugs. Meanwhile, the Police Minister cannot show us even one arrest produced by this hare-brained scheme." Listeners, we invited the Minister to speak today but his spokeswoman would only comment that arrests aren't reported because investigations are ongoing. Yes, folks, the same old double-speak. Hogwash, if you ask me.'*

Sal knocked at the steel door and glanced back at Colin Preston. He sat by the radio and watched Sal over the brim of a steaming teacup. Sal quickly faced the door and knocked again. 'It's me,' he croaked, wanting to get away from Preston's gaze and the Family Man's words.

Thomas yanked the door open. 'D'you get them?'

Sal pushed in past him.

'Open them and set them up,' Thomas said. He locked the door.

The room was hot. Four fan heaters ran at full speed on a makeshift bench. Thomas wore only jeans. His chest was tanned and sparsely haired and beaded with sweat.

Sal knelt to take the first heater from its box and unwind the cord.

'Do I look like I have all fucking day?' Thomas grabbed the second box and ripped it open. He yanked the cord straight then snatched Sal's heater and took both machines to an already overloaded powerboard. He shoved the plugs in but the second heater was too much load and the powerboard clicked off. Thomas swore. He pulled the lead back out and reset the overload switch. This time all five heaters ran, though not at the same furious rate as before.

Thomas threw the spare heater hard across the room. The plastic casing shattered against the concrete wall and the innards fell with a clunk to the floor.

'Hey!' Sal said. 'I could've taken that back.'

Tendons stood out in Thomas's neck. 'It's still not working.'

Sal looked at the burners and glass flasks. 'Really?'

'That useless Chinese imbecile probably forgot something.' Thomas glared at a handful of stained and wrinkled pages. 'His handwriting's fucking terrible too.'

It won't work! He'll have to leave! We won't have to sell anything and we won't get busted!

Thomas looked up at him. 'What?'

'What?'

'What'd you say?'

Sal groped around for a reply. 'Colin was listening to stuff about the amnesty out there.'

'So?'

'It's just, if he's listening to that, maybe he's thinking about it. About using it.' *It's so hot in here I can hardly breathe.* 'So maybe this is for the best. It might be safer to just quit now.'

'Is it him thinking about using the amnesty – or you?'

'What? No!'

'You're turning red.'

'It's bloody hot in here.'

Thomas came close and stared into his eyes. Sal struggled to hold his gaze. *Don't look away, don't look away, or he'll know for sure and you'll end up as dead as the others.*

He swallowed. 'Do you want me to try to read the recipe?'

'Do I want you to read the recipe, when you've already shown what you want by telling me over and over again to give up?'

'It was just a thought.'

Thomas turned back to the flasks. 'Just get out of here.'

Sal heaved the door open. The air in the factory was cool and easy to breathe. He took in big lungfuls as he heard the lock turn behind him.

Preston was still by the radio. The volume was lower and Sal could make out the Family Man's tone but not the words. Preston raised his teacup to Sal. 'See you next time.'

Sal ducked his head and hurried out into the light.

Wayne dropped Ella at the office and drove off. She wasn't going to wave, then changed her mind and turned back at the last second, but he stared out at the street and not at her.

She stalked into the lift and jabbed the button hard. When they'd left the Nolan house she'd voiced her concerns about what Veronique might be hiding and had practically seen Wayne's hackles rise.

'Wait, listen,' she'd said. 'Maybe she found the key piece of info that made her decide here's where the sharing stops.'

'I know this woman. You only met her today.'

'Cake doesn't mean a person's innocent.'

He'd shot her a look. 'I'm not even going to dignify that with a reply.'

The lift doors opened and Ella walked into the office. Murray wasn't at his desk. She threw herself into her chair. It was a totally legitimate suspicion to hold. Whoever heard of a person being *so* helpful anyway? Or telling a detective there was too much money?

She sat up at her computer and entered Veronique's name. She had no record.

Maybe she never got caught.

Or maybe Wayne was right.

Murray came in bearing a coffee. 'Oh, you're back.'

She pushed aside the thought of nervous Veronique and the uncomfortable feeling that she might have just spoiled something good with Wayne. 'Want to pay a visit to a certain young computer repairer?'

TWENTY-EIGHT

Murray brought his coffee with him. 'Drive smooth.'

Ella would drive any way she liked. 'How'd it go, being out with Strongy?'

'Tracked the guy to a squat in Surry Hills.' He raised the cup to his mouth, one hand braced on the door as if that'd help. 'Kids took off in every direction when we went busting in. We caught a couple and one of them fessed she knew him, said he went back to hospital just last night with his shoulder. We nipped around there but he'd only been in for a couple of hours and nobody knows where he is now.'

And he probably wouldn't be back at that squat again, once he got the word from his mates, Ella thought.

Murray said, 'So what's the go with Drysdale?'

She explained what Nolan had written about Kennedy's cash-in-hand job which led him to Werner. 'If we make like we're going to arrest Drysdale, that should shake his tree enough.'

'Have we got grounds?'

'I didn't say *actually* arrest him,' she said. 'Anyway, he won't know the difference.'

'He might.' Murray sipped carefully. 'They give away so much on TV now.'

She zoomed around a corner. 'I think we'll be fine.'

Benson Drysdale opened the door. 'Oh.'

'Hello to you too,' Ella said. 'Yes, we'd love to come in.'

He stepped back. One computer was on, its screen showing a whirling pattern of colours, and another was spread out in pieces on the table.

'Not working today?' she said.

'Had the early shift. Finished at two.' He pushed some computer manuals off a chair. 'Would you like to sit down?'

'We're fine.' She took her time, looking into the kitchen and the bedroom. 'Heard from Thomas lately?'

'Thomas . . . Werner?'

'How many Thomases do you know?'

'I don't even know that one.'

Murray stood by the TV with his hands in his pockets. 'We've been thinking,' he said. 'It was back in May that you said you'd seen Werner, but then you were able to describe him to us quite well.'

Drysdale frowned.

'If I meet somebody once, months back, I'm lucky if I remember that they exist,' Murray said. 'See my point?'

400

'Not really.'

'Perhaps you've seen him more recently.' Murray idly ran a finger through the dust on the TV. 'Maybe you actually know him well.'

'Then why would I tell you his name?' Drysdale said. 'Why wouldn't I just deny ever having met him?'

'Because you didn't know what we knew,' Ella said. 'And because a half-lie is easier to tell than a complete one.'

Drysdale shook his head. 'I don't know him. I only saw him once. I just have a good memory for faces.'

'Let's just take him in and be done with it,' Ella said to Murray.

'What for?' Drysdale said.

'I agree,' Murray said. 'We're not getting anywhere here.'

Ella said, 'You've got your cuffs?'

'Hang on,' Drysdale said.

'Here somewhere.' Murray felt along his belt.

'Hang on,' Drysdale said again. 'What do you want to ask me? You haven't asked anything yet. I'm not refusing to cooperate. How can I when I don't know what you want?'

Ella pretended to consider. 'I guess that's true.'

'Just ask me,' he said.

'How did Kennedy and Werner meet?'

'How would I know that?' Drysdale said. 'I wasn't there. I don't know anything about any of it. I only met Werner once, when he was sitting in the van.'

'Somebody told us that you know.'

'They're lying.'

'Why would they do that?'

'Don't ask me, ask them!'

'We'd like to, but they're dead,' Murray said.

Drysdale slumped onto his chair.

'Just tell us,' Ella said. 'How did Kennedy and Werner meet?'

'I honestly have no idea.' Drysdale's voice cracked. 'I never did anything other than sell some computers. Yes, James Kennedy helped me, but that was it. That was the end of our involvement. Whatever else he was up to I have no idea.'

Ella had a thought. 'How did your involvement with him begin?'

'What do you mean?'

'How did you come to ask him to deliver computers for you, and not some other driver? Why did you feel safe about asking him when you knew it would mean trouble if Peres found out?'

Drysdale pressed the sleeve of his T-shirt to his nose. 'When I'd just started working there, about three years ago, James brought in a couple of bottles of Midori. He said he'd been given them, he and his wife didn't drink it, and did anyone want them.'

'And?' Ella said.

'And my girlfriend at the time liked the stuff. I went up to him and asked how much he wanted for them, and he said again that he'd been given them and so I could have them. I said, wow, that's a good deal, who gave them to him? And he kind of looked around to see who was nearby, and said that it was an under-the-counter kind of deal from a customer.'

'A Quiksmart customer?' Murray said. 'A cash-in-hand thing?'

'Booze rather than cash,' Drysdale said. 'But yes, a Quiksmart customer.'

Ella said, 'Which Quiksmart customer?'

'I don't know.'

'That's handy,' Murray said.

'Hey, you wanted to know why I felt comfortable about asking him to take the computers. That was why.'

'Because he'd obviously done similar stuff for somebody else,' Ella said.

'Exactly.'

'What type of businesses does Quiksmart deliver booze to and from? Bottle shops?'

'Kennedy only ever drove a van, so if he went to bottle shops they would've only been small ones, or taking small deliveries, like specialty orders.' Drysdale thought for a moment. 'I guess it could've been for nightclubs too, and for sports clubs, and restaurants.'

Nightclubs.

'Ever heard of a club called Rosie's?'

'Nope.'

'You never heard Kennedy mention it?'

'Never.'

Murray was already headed for the door. Ella looked down at Drysdale. 'If you're spinning bullshit, we won't be happy.'

'That's all I know, I swear.'

★

They agreed that Sal, as sometime half-arsed supervisor and son of one of the owners, would be the place to begin. 'Plus he had that breakable vibe,' Ella said, powering towards Maroubra. 'I reckon we could get way more out of him than that Davids.'

'We should talk to the father this time too.'

The Rios house looked closed up tight. Ella knocked till her knuckles were sore. Murray looked up at the windows.

'Excuse me,' a voice called.

Ella saw one of the neighbours waving over the side fence. The woman said, 'Are you looking for the Rioses?'

Ella walked towards her. 'Do you know where they are?'

'Julio collapsed this afternoon and the ambulance took him to hospital,' she said. 'They all went to be with him.'

'Do you know which hospital?' Ella showed the woman her badge. 'It's important that we speak with them.'

'St John's in Randwick.' The woman lowered her voice. 'It's a hospice. Where people go to . . . you know.'

Ella knew. 'Thanks.'

'I don't know about this,' Murray said. 'If the guy's dying, we shouldn't be tackling his brother about stuff we're not even sure he knows about.'

'This is a homicide case.' Ella kept driving. Randwick was just a couple of suburbs away.

'We're not going to solve it today though, are we? It makes no difference if we leave Sal till tomorrow. He's hardly going to be cooperative if we drag him away from his dying brother's bedside, and we've got lots we can do in the meantime.'

Ella didn't slow.

'Let's go to Rosie's and talk to Paul Davids again, and see if we can get a look at their delivery records,' Murray said.

'He'll probably demand a warrant.'

'It's worth a try.'

They approached a big intersection. Right took them into Randwick, where skin-and-bones Julio Rios was slowly toppling from his perch while all the other Rioses watched. Straight on took them towards the city, to the Cross, to Rosie's, where implacable Paul Davids would hold out his hand for the warrant, his empty palm pink and lined and . . . empty.

Ella hovered along the edge of the right-turn lane then swore and accelerated forward.

Paul Davids's hand wasn't as pink as Ella had imagined – the creases were actually quite grimy – but it was every bit as empty.

They got back into the car. 'I'm still not going to that hospice,' Murray said. 'We should head for the office and type our reports, and make a start on the warrant paperwork.'

'I don't think we have enough to get one,' she said. 'We need to talk to the Rioses.'

'No way.'

'They might be persuaded into giving us access.'

'They won't.'

'They might,' she said. 'If they're fine upstanding citizens.'

'Is this before or after their son and brother dies?'

'Okay, okay.' Ella turned west. 'We'll go back to the office.'

'You are a good person.'

'Ha.'

It was almost peak hour. Traffic was sludgy. She crawled through a set of lights, thinking how after this the Rioses would be arranging the funeral and Murray wouldn't want to interrupt them in that. Then they'd be at the funeral, then recovering from it. She mightn't get near them for days.

This was the kind of task Murray loved. Ella watched him type merrily away while she hunched over her keyboard.

We should've at least gone past the hospice. Sal might've been outside getting some fresh air. He might've been climbing into his car, about to head home.

She put her forehead in her hand.

'Need some Panadol?'

'Huh?'

Murray was looking at her. 'You're holding your head. I thought you must have a headache.'

'Yeah, I do,' she said quickly. 'Maybe I'll go home. You don't mind, do you?'

He was already typing again. 'No worries. Take it easy.'

'See you in the morning.' She grabbed her bag from her desk drawer and headed for the door.

She turned right from the car park, heading citywards. It wouldn't matter if Murray was at the window. This was the way to home too.

Sal Rios wasn't in the hospice car park nor in the gardens near the front door. Ella hesitated on the steps, then went in.

A nun looked up from behind the front desk. 'May I help you?'

Show the badge or not? Ella chose not. 'I've heard that Julio Rios was admitted this afternoon. I was wondering if I might be able to visit him, please?'

The nun typed something into her computer. She typed faster than Ella did. 'He's on the third floor, in room nine. The lift is along the corridor there. Turn left when you get out, and the room is the third on your left.'

'Thank you.'

The lift was slower than the office one. Ella watched the lights change and told herself she hadn't just lied to a nun. The nun never asked if she was a relative or friend, did she? So she never needed to explain that she wasn't.

The lift doors hauled themselves open onto a brown lino hallway. Jesus on the cross watched her from the opposite wall. *You've lied to a nun, you may as well go and disturb a grieving family.*

★

Lauren balanced on the chair with one hand gripping the mulberry tree's trunk. With the other she lifted the old motorbike tyre on its rope, and it swung back and forth, hitting her in the knees. She wobbled and one of the chair legs sank deeper into the grass. She allowed herself a fast glance at the house. Kristi was still at the back door, one hand at her temple. *No, I still don't want your help.*

She took her hand from the trunk. The chair tilted a bit more. She hoisted the tyre and tried to fling the rope over the branch, then the chair tipped further and she dropped the tyre and stumbled to the ground.

'Lauren.'

'I'm *fine*.'

'Joe's here.'

Lauren stood up, brushing grass from her hands. Joe walked across the lawn. Behind him Kristi closed the door and disappeared from view into the house.

'Now this looks like an important task,' Joe said.

'Swing maintenance. Very important.'

He picked up the frayed-through loop that Lauren had cut off. 'I'd've thought Felise would be helping you.'

'She's in the bath.' Lauren climbed back up on the chair. Joe lifted the tyre so she could feed the rope over the branch.

'Might be too short now,' she said.

'Knot it up and we'll see.'

She had to use both hands to tie the knot and the chair wobbled again. Joe stepped closer, and put the back of his shoulder against her hip. 'Lean there.'

Lauren could feel the heat of his skin through his shirt and her jeans. She tried to focus on the knot. 'Busy day?'

'Not really. Just been playing squash with a mate in Dulwich Hill. Thought I'd pop in, see how it went this morning.'

His voice vibrated through the bones in his shoulder. Lauren scraped her knuckle against the bark. 'It went okay.'

He looked up at her. 'Are you in trouble over it?'

'They haven't decided yet.' Her fingers seemed stiff, numb. 'It sounds like I'll be charged, but because of the circumstances I could be let off, or just fined. Or jailed.'

He nodded, his face serious. They both knew that even being charged with a serious offence like that could see her kicked out of the job.

'With all your years of experience they'd be idiots to let you go,' he said.

'Let's hope they see it the same way.' She tugged the rope tight. 'There. How's that look?'

Joe let the tyre hang. 'How tall's Felise?'

Lauren got down from the chair and held her hand to her side. Joe crouched so his head was at that height and grabbed at the tyre. 'Should be fine.'

'Was probably a bit low before, come to think of it,' she said. Joe stood up and his knee, then his back, cracked. She smiled. 'You're such an old man.'

He smiled down at her, then suddenly put his hand on the back of her neck, and leaned in and kissed her.

For the first instant she was so stunned she didn't move, then she reached up to slide her own hand around the back of his neck and pull him close. His skin was warm and damp. His lips were firmer than she remembered. She opened her mouth, wanting to take all of him into her, and she started to press her body against his, but then he was pulling back, sliding out of her grip, breaking free of her lips.

'Joe.'

'I'm sorry.' Joe touched the back of his neck. 'I had a shower but I'm still all sweaty.'

'I don't care.' She reached for him again but he backed away, bumping into the tyre and setting it swinging. He looked up at the house.

Lauren looked up at the house too. Kristi was nowhere to be seen. 'Joe, wait.'

'Guess that's fixed.' He tugged on the rope, then looked at his watch. 'Shit. See you tomorrow night, hey?' He didn't wait for her answer but walked quickly across the lawn and inside the back door.

Lauren dropped onto the chair. She heard Joe's car start on the street and drive away. The windows of the house were empty, the pigeons sat along the gutter in the sun, and her gaze wandered past the roof to the blue sky.

What the hell just happened?

TWENTY-NINE

Jesus was still watching her. He was bigger this time, and stared down from the cream-painted wall in the empty waiting room. Ella sat against the opposite wall in a low chair. She'd heaved it right over near the entrance so she could sit and hold up a magazine and look past it down the corridor at the doorway of Julio's room, where Nona and an older man, who Ella guessed was the father Guillermo, and two young girls sat around Julio's bed.

Everyone but Sal.

The ward was quiet. A nun went past and Ella pretended to be reading. Where was Sal? Had he gone home? She'd waited fifteen minutes already. If he'd ducked to the bathroom he would've been back by now.

Jesus stared down from the wall. She stared back. She wondered if every room had one of these statues, what it was like to try to sleep under such close supervision. The hospital smell made her think of Netta. She'd phoned her a few times but hadn't been around to visit for a few days. She felt irritated by the guilt of not going, but knew the guilt trip she'd get when she was there would make her feel even worse. You'd think once you were over forty you'd be free of that sort of stuff. She was realising it never ended.

She looked down the corridor again. Maybe Sal had gone home. If she had his number she could ring and see if he answered, but she'd left all the paper-work at the office.

Another nun came past and pointed to the hot water system on the wall under Jesus's feet. 'Please help yourself to tea and coffee.'

'Thank you,' Ella said.

The nun went on her way and Ella watched her turn past a sign that said *Chapel*.

A-*ha*!

She followed the painted signs through a maze of corridors and came to one that was lit with fake candles and smelled marginally less hospital-like than the rest. Double doors with stained-glass inlays faced her at the end. One side was open, and she sidled up and peered into the gloomy chapel.

Sal sat alone in the third row from the front.

Ella stepped back to consider her approach. She could pretend she too had somebody upstairs on their last legs, that she too had come here for solace. He would no doubt recognise her, but that didn't mean they couldn't start to develop a bond based on their shared troubles.

She took a deep breath and went in.

The chapel had five rows of seats either side of a central aisle. She walked steadily to the front, thinking of what she'd seen on TV. You bowed now, right? No, wait, you did a little dip-type action. She'd never been a church-goer, so couldn't be sure. She paused there for a moment, looking up at the statue of Mary. Jesus was a baby this time, and snug in his mother's arms. Not so starey.

She turned to notice Sal. 'Excuse me. I didn't mean to disturb you.'

His cheeks were wet, shiny in the light from the fake candles set along the front of the chapel. Ella suddenly meant it about disturbing him.

'It's okay,' he said.

She didn't know what to do. She looked at the open door. She could go out and wait. That might be best.

'You're that detective.'

She focused on him. 'Yes.'

'Have you got somebody in here too?'

She hesitated. 'No.'

He was silent for a moment. 'You're here to see me?'

'Yes.'

'Are you religious?'

She shook her head.

'I saw you go up the front there.'

'You see it on TV; it seems like the right thing to do.'

He wiped his face. 'I'm not religious either. My dad was driving me nuts.'

'Oh.'

'You can sit down if you want.'

She sat in the row in front, a few seats along.

He rested his elbows on his knees and rubbed the back of one thumb with the ball of the other. 'My mum died in this place too,' he said. 'My family has bad genes for cancer.'

Now what could you say to that?

He switched thumbs. 'Is this about the phone call again?'

'How did you know James Kennedy?'

'Not well at all,' he said.

'So you do know him.'

'He's a courier. He delivered stuff to Rosie's. I was there a few times when he'd drop stuff off. I saw in the paper that he was dead.'

'What stuff did he deliver?'

Sal looked at his thumbs. 'Goods. Cargo.'

'That doesn't tell me much.'

'Whatever the club needed. Toilet rolls, cleaning products, paper serviettes.'

'Alcohol?'

'That too.'

'Dodgy alcohol?'

'Like what? Home-brew?'

'Like stolen,' she said.

'How would I know anything about that?'

'Because you're only there occasionally, in a sort of supervisor's role, right?' she said. 'So what do you know about?'

'I don't know who made that call. Though from everything you're asking I can guess it was made to him.'

Ella thought that was a reasonable enough deduction.

Sal switched thumbs again. 'I only knew James Kennedy well enough to nod or say hi to. Other couriers delivered to us too, you know. I'd nod and say hi to them as well.'

'We can get a warrant for your records,' she said. 'We can get forensic accountants to examine all the club's incomings and outgoings for the past ten years if we want.'

'Based on what evidence?'

Ella looked away to little baby Jesus. 'Why does your dad drive you nuts?'

'Because he likes Julio best.'

'How involved is your dad in the running of the club?'

'Not very. People annoy him.'

She studied him. 'Funny business to be in if you don't like people.'

'It was mostly my uncle's thing.' His eyes were dry now. He stared straight ahead.

'Paulo?'

He nodded. 'Died last year. He was single so Dad inherited his percentage of the company on top of his own.'

'Cancer?'

'That comes from Mum's side. Paulo had a heart attack while porking a girl in a massage parlour.'

'Oh.' That deserved a moment. 'He'd been in jail.'

'Yep.'

'Would he have been moving stolen alcohol about? Paying a courier with bottles of the stuff?'

'I don't know what he might have done,' Sal said. 'We were never close.'

'Did Julio ever work in the club?'

'Are you going to ask about everyone in my family?'

'If necessary,' she said.

'I could get up and walk away.'

'You could.'

He didn't move.

Ella decided to go for it. 'Sal, look at me.'

He turned his head. His eyes were dark in the dim light. He didn't blink.

She said, 'What do you want to tell me?'

He stared at her. He seemed to be holding his breath. The chapel was so quiet Ella could hear the electric buzz of the fake candles behind her. The air itself seemed to swell with meaning and consequence as he started to open his mouth.

'Uncle Sal.' The girl's voice shattered the stillness. Ella started and saw a gangly blonde of about twelve in the doorway. 'Mum says you have to come back now.'

Sal leapt to his feet. 'Is Julio . . . is he awake?'

The girl shrugged, her gaze on Ella. 'Mum just told me to get you.'

He hurried out of the chapel without a backward glance. Ella felt the air collapse around her. The girl swung on the door for a moment longer, staring at her, then ran off after Sal.

Ella looked up at the baby Jesus. *Did you engineer that?*

Ella eased the car over the kerb. It occurred to her that she was turning into her driveway more slowly each day. She saw her face in the rear-view mirror and frowned at herself. *What are you, a man or a mouse?*

She turned the car off and looked at the house. No sign of anything amiss. She opened the door and got out.

Sunlight glinted off the kitchen window that overlooked the side path. She went towards it more cautiously than she intended to, and tried to straighten her back. Muscle up! Nothing was going to be odd today. She'd checked and double-checked the fridge before she'd left that morning, and triple-checked the windows and doors.

She followed the path down the side and around the back of the house. The grass was as long as ever, the bins smelled, the windows were intact. The back door was locked and undamaged.

At the next corner she looked along the side of the house, seeing part of the front lawn. More intact windows. She could hear water running somewhere. A shower. In the neighbour's place?

Or closer?

She looked up at her own high bathroom window. The frosted-glass panels were closed. She couldn't see in. She reached up and put her fingertips on the glass, as if that would tell her something. It was neither hot nor cold.

She couldn't be sure.

What should she do? Her first instinct was to ring Dennis, but if he came round and they went inside together only to find it was indeed next-door's shower, she'd feel a right idiot.

If on the other hand she went inside to confirm

it first, and there happened to be somebody lurking there . . .

I'm meant to be able to handle shit like this. They pay me to do so!

She went to the next window along, one at the side of her living room. The blinds were down. She stood on her toes and pressed her ear to the glass but she couldn't hear anything clearly. It might be her shower, it might be next door's. She didn't know the neighbours and didn't fancy knocking on the door to ask about their current ablutions.

The water meter! She hurried to the front garden and flipped up the metal lid. There it was, in solid moving proof. The figures ticked over. Something in her house was hosing out water like a . . . like a hose.

'Orchard.' The line was crackly.

'Are you busy?' she said.

'Just heading home.'

'Would you mind coming via my place?'

'On my way.'

Glad Dennis hadn't asked why he was needed, Ella paced the footpath and stared down one side of the house then the other. Sweat prickled her armpits. Maybe the pipe had come off the washing machine. She'd heard that could happen. It could simply be the rush of water across the floor that she'd confused for the shower.

When Dennis pulled up she had to hold herself back from running over to him. He got out of the car. 'What's up?'

'I think I heard something strange in my house.'

He locked his car and walked to the path. 'Strange like what?'

'Like the shower running full pelt.' She felt herself start to flush. 'It's probably nothing. A pipe's come loose or something.'

'No sign of entry?'

She shook her head.

'But . . . ?'

'But the last two days there have been odd things.' She explained about the pizza flyer and the rock and the shampoo bottle, and the cereal and milk and fridge.

'Who have you told?'

'They're such pissy things, I thought I was doing them myself.'

He said, 'So you told nobody.'

'You can understand why.'

He looked at the house. 'What do you want to do?'

'Go and see ourselves.'

'You don't want the cavalry?'

'What if it's a pipe?'

He nodded. They started towards the house. Ella felt better having Dennis there, and almost certain now that it would turn out to be nothing.

At the front door he indicated the lock. 'Want me to do it?'

'That much I can manage.' She stuck the key in and turned it then pushed the door wide open.

'I hear it,' Dennis said quietly.

Ella heard it too, even over the drumming of her heart. Her shower was roaring. *Oh shit, oh shiiit . . .*

They edged through the house. The kitchen looked normal, as did the living room. The bathroom was along the short hallway. The door stood open. Ella had the sudden thought that they'd find a body in the shower cubicle – whose, she didn't know. Her scalp tightened as they crept to the door.

There was nobody in the bathroom, dead or alive. The showerhead vibrated with the pressure of the water blasting out of it. Water splashed high on the blue tiled walls and across the floor. It gurgled down the drain. The air was humid. It looked like the hot tap was cranked all the way around, but the spray Ella could feel was cold. *Tank's empty.*

Dennis motioned that they should search the rest of the house. Ella knew they had to leave the taps on for the crime scene officers, but hearing the rush of the water while they searched under her bed and in her cupboards put her teeth on edge.

'Everything else seems fine,' she said.

He looked around once more. 'We should wait outside.'

He made the call from his mobile while they stood beside her car. Ella folded her arms tight against her body. She felt she could still hear the rush of the water. She shivered.

'Cold?' Dennis said.

She shook her head.

He nodded at the house. 'Any ideas? Somebody fresh out of the clink? Or your current case maybe?'

'Maybe.' She told him about the case, about trying to find if Werner was here or overseas, about the attack on Lauren and the possible mole in the office. 'But what could they hope to achieve?'

'Put you off,' he said. 'He can't get to Lauren now, so he tries this.'

She was thinking. 'We should call a locksmith too. The mole must've got to my keys.'

'Did you ever leave them unattended?'

'They're in my bag in my desk drawer, but I don't take it when I go to see Kuiper or into a meeting or whatever.'

He nodded. 'Somebody could choose their moment when everyone's busy, get the keys out, make a wax impression, and all the while they know the lift will ding if it stops on the floor, and the stair door makes a noise when the fire seal closes.'

'And no doubt they'd have some good excuse ready if somebody did happen by.'

'I dropped all these files and was picking them up.'

Ella stared at her house. Soon the crime scene officers would be here, and Kuiper, and probably the detectives investigating the leak too. She didn't like the thought of Bethany Mendelssohn looking through her things.

'Don't stay here tonight,' Dennis said. 'Come to our place.'

'If I go, that's letting him freak me out.'

'Nobody's keeping score.'

'I'll be fine with new locks.' *I hope.* 'And if he's going to try for serious harm, wouldn't he have done it already instead of this kind of stuff?'

'They might be steps along the way.' He dug his hands into his pockets. 'If step A doesn't stop you, he goes to step B.'

'So, what, he wants me to quit?'

Kuiper's red sedan came flying down the street. Dennis pushed himself off the side of her car. 'Maybe it's all about distraction. You're working well on the case, and he knows it. He wants to put a worm in your brain and slow your thinking.'

He went to speak to Kuiper, leaving her to consider that.

If Werner thought she was doing well, that must mean she was getting close.

THIRTY

They went right through Ella's house in search of fingerprints, fibres, hairs, listening devices and bombs. Kuiper had people speaking to the neighbours, asking about cars in the street, people loitering about, workmen apparently checking wires or meters or pipes. Ella stood against her car and felt that she was the centre of a tornado – while action went on all around her, she was becalmed. Immobile.

Powerless.

Kuiper came over to her. 'Locksmith's on his way.'

'Good.'

'I'm going to put a couple of people in there tonight just in case he comes back.'

'I'll be fine.'

'You won't be here,' he said. 'Dennis said you can go with him.'

'I'd really rather stay.'

'Out of the question.' He looked across the lawn to where Bethany Mendelssohn and Bryan Greer conferred over a notebook. 'They spoke to you already?'

She nodded. 'Sir, I feel that if I don't stay I'm letting him control what goes on.'

'He doesn't control it; I do.' A uniformed officer came hurrying down the street. Kuiper said 'Excuse me' to Ella and went to meet him.

Ella slumped against the car, feeling more ineffectual than ever. She knew they were only worried about her safety, but she wasn't a little girl. She was a detective, for god's sake, yet they wouldn't trust her to be left with a few burly blokes to wait for a bad guy? It was her case, her bad guy. If he was going to come back, it wasn't fair that she didn't get to be in at the showdown.

As for Mendelssohn and Greer, they'd told her they were looking into three possible moles, and asked how much contact she'd had with Edwina Guilfoyle from Admin, Tracy Potter from Human Resources and Tony Ansible from some computer company. Edwina she thought she'd maybe spoken to once, Tracy she'd seen around the office a fair bit but had only spoken to a couple of times, and Tony never. She couldn't even conjure up a picture of him in her head. The detectives had nodded and jotted in their notebooks, while Ella wondered how much that'd help them.

She watched them walk over to Kuiper and the uniformed officer, and felt on the outer of her own problem. Other people decided what she should do and she didn't even get a chance to give her opinion. Well, no more.

When Kuiper came back she said, 'I'll stay at my parents' house.'

He frowned.

'How can he know where they live?'

'We don't know what he knows.'

'Well, he can't have keys. I keep them in the back of the pantry with a bunch of other old ones. None of them are labelled. Nobody could know what they're for.' She put everything she had into her gaze. 'I'll have two phones, and I'll get my gun, and the woman next door is an insomniac so even if all that fails, the second I scream she'll be on the phone.'

Kuiper rubbed the back of his neck. 'How about we find out the results of the canvass first.'

It was as good as she'd get for now. 'What did that constable find out?' she asked, nodding to the officer Kuiper had just spoken to.

'A woman four doors up watched a man walking slowly in the street two days ago. She thought he was looking a bit too closely at the houses. She sneaked out into her garden and watched him continue on down this way. She's certain he didn't come in here, but she said she saw him again today, about two in the afternoon, this time getting into a blue sedan. She managed to get the plate – we're running it now.'

The constable came over. 'Numberplate was stolen from a Toyota van in Alexandria last week.'

'Could she describe the man?' Ella said.

'Short dark hair under a cap in Broncos colours. He was white, and she thinks in his thirties. Average height and build, wearing jeans and a blue T-shirt. She wasn't close enough to see anything else.'

'I'll come and talk to her,' Kuiper said. 'Hopefully somebody else saw him too, plus was close enough to see his face so we can show them the airport photo of Werner.' He glanced at Ella. 'You stay here for now.'

She watched them walk up the footpath. *You stay here?* What was she, a puppy? That was really it.

'Honestly, I'll be fine.'

Dennis stood on the porch of Ella's parents' house and peered out at the street. Tree ferns obscured the view of their cars. The porch smelled of cold concrete and mulch. Lily was still near her fence, pretending to garden in the dusk. They'd already waved hello.

'Dennis,' Ella said. 'Are you listening to me?'

He turned from the street. 'Let me come in and check the house.'

She unlocked the door and turned on the hall light. The house was still and silent. Dennis went into the living room and examined the window locks. 'Are they all keyed locks like this?'

'And the doors are all deadlocked. Nobody can get in.'

He went into the kitchen and tested the back door. 'So there's just this and the front door?'

'Plus one at the side there, through the laundry.'

He went to see then came back. 'Bedrooms?'

She led the way first to her parents' bedroom, with its high bed, then to the one that had been her own. It was technically a spare now but Netta still told any staying visitors that they'd be sleeping in Ella's room.

Dennis checked in the cupboards and under the beds, then paused to look at a framed photo of her at eleven.

'Not one word,' Ella said.

He turned away grinning, but grew serious when they neared the front door again. 'Please come and stay with us.'

'I'm fine right here.'

He put a sad look in his eyes.

'Don't give me that,' she said. 'Go home. I'm okay. Nothing will happen.' She reached past him and unlocked the door. 'Donna will be wondering where you are.'

'She always knows where I am.'

'Yeah, at work,' Ella said. They smiled at each other. 'I'll see you in the morning.'

Dennis turned away, then stopped on the step and surveyed the street again. He went down the path to the low gate then to his car. Before getting in he looked up at her again. She flapped her hand. He motioned closing the door and turning the key. She did so, then stood inside, listening, as he started his car then drove off.

She scraped together a dinner of pasta and tuna, ate in front of the TV with her gun and phone by her side, left the dishes in the sink, showered and went to bed, all the while thinking about the case. If it was Thomas Werner who was doing these things, then, as Dennis said, it had to mean she was on the right track. Which was what?

She thought of her talk with Sal that afternoon. The timing seemed wrong though. If it was Werner who'd been seen in the street around two, her visit with Sal hours later could not have been the trigger. What else had they done? Spoken to Paul Davids again, talked with Benson Drysdale. How could Werner know what they'd been doing? The mole's supply of information had surely been severely constrained, if not completely cut off, with the clampdown in the office and Mendelssohn and Greer watching everyone like hawks. Maybe Drysdale or Davids had hopped on the phone as soon as they'd left. Weasels.

She rolled onto her side, watching the tree ferns alongside the window move in the night breeze, backlit by the light in Lily's house next door. She felt a buzz of excitement. It wasn't entirely logical; she knew she should be worried, maybe even frightened. But to think that they were getting close!

She doubted whether she'd sleep tonight.

The smashing of glass brought her bolt upright and groping for her gun and phone on the bedside table. The room was dark. Lily's lights were out. Gun in one hand, phone in the other, she moved quickly out of the room. She left the lights off as she hurried barefoot down the hall to the front of the house where she could see a glow coming in the windows of the front room.

She edged up to the curtain and peeked out, her thumb on the phone's keypad, her gun up and ready.

Fire. Something was on fire out the front.

It could be a trap.

She dialled 000 and asked for police, then told the call-taker who she was and what was happening. The flames were rising higher, casting a brighter glow on the porch. The next number she dialled was Lily's, to tell her to stay inside, but as she did so she spotted her running out the front with a hose. 'Dammit!'

Ella changed position at the window, trying to see through the tree ferns. She could make out Lily's outline against the fire, waving the hose about. She couldn't see anybody else, but a moment later the scene was lit with blue and red flashing lights, and police officers wielding fire extinguishers appeared.

One stepped over the low gate and came up the path to the door. She knocked. 'Detective? Are you okay?'

'I'm fine.' Ella started to unlock the door.

'DS Kuiper asked that you keep the door locked and stay where you are,' the officer said quickly. 'So long as you're okay.'

I'm not going to talk to you through a locked door like some hostage-taking crazy. Ella opened the door and looked out at the street. 'What is it?'

'A car.'

'Maroon Mazda?'

The officer looked away. 'Hard to tell the colour.'

Ella took the keys from the lock, stepped out and locked the door behind her.

It was her car all right. The fire was mostly out. Lily aimed the hose directly in a broken window while a heavy-set constable squirted an extinguisher under the engine. In the distance a siren wailed. Firies, Ella thought. She folded her arms against the chilly air, gun and phone and keys digging into her armpits, and watched her upholstery smoulder and planned her response.

The sun was almost up when Ella hammered on Sal Rios's front door.

Murray still looked half-asleep. She jabbed her thumb at the upstairs windows. 'See any movement?'

He blinked up at them. 'Nope.'

Ella pounded on the door again, making the screen rattle in its frame. 'Sal!'

Now she could hear footsteps. The lock turned and the door was yanked open. Nona glared out. 'What the fuck is your problem?'

'We need to speak to Sal.'

'Keep your voice down, I've got kids asleep up there.' She hadn't unlocked the screen. 'Anyway, he's not here.'

'Are you sure?'

'I just looked in his room.' Nona cinched her dressing gown tighter around her waist. 'Bed's not been slept in.'

'We'd like to come in and see for ourselves.'

'Our brother's dying. We've been at the hospital most of the night. Everyone's exhausted, and you are not going to start tramping through disturbing them. Anyway, Sal's probably with Julio now.'

'We've already checked,' Ella said. 'He hasn't been

in.' She stared at the woman through the screen door. 'You're sure he's not in the bathroom or garage or somewhere else?'

'I'm sure.' She put her hands on her hips. 'Anything else?'

'We'll be back later with a warrant,' Ella said.

'Yeah, that'd be right. Family's grieving, but you don't care.'

'Get Sal to call me, that might change things. Otherwise, see you then.' Ella headed down the driveway.

In the car Murray said, 'Have we got more evidence? Enough for a warrant?'

'We might have by this afternoon.' She looked up at the house. 'Did that curtain just move? The one second from the left?'

'I didn't see it.'

'I'll bet he is in there.' She started the car. 'He was probably lurking on the stairs, listening to every word we said.' *Weasel*.

They got breakfast on the way to the office. The food sat in Ella's stomach like a rocky island, the coffee a heavy surf washing around it. She was still trying to rub away the indigestion when they stepped out of the lift.

The office was empty except for Jason Lambert, who looked up, startled, from his monitor. 'You guys are early.'

'So are you.' Ella turned on her computer.

Murray said, 'The rest of them won't be far

behind us, I reckon.' He looked at Lambert. 'Did you hear what happened?'

'About what?'

Murray told him what had been going on with Ella. It made her embarrassed to hear it and she frowned down at her keyboard as he spoke.

'Wow,' Lambert said. 'You okay?'

'I'm here, aren't I?'

'She's her usual happy self,' Murray said. 'She's already had me out there this morning trying to kick down doors.'

'Are we going to start work or not?' Ella said.

Murray sat at his desk and flipped a pen between his fingers. 'Will you tell Lauren about what happened?'

'She's working tonight so she'll still be asleep.'

'It might be better not to tell her,' he said. 'Fire-bombing talk would make anyone nervous.'

'It was only a beer bottle full of petrol. Fire-bomb makes it sound like something from World War Two.' She pushed papers around on her desk, keen to start work. They couldn't get the folders yet because they were locked away and Kuiper had the key. She looked at her watch. It was just after seven. She hoped he wouldn't be long. She wanted to read back over things, see what she might have missed about Sal Rios.

He had *something* to tell her, of that she was sure.

THIRTY-ONE

Tired and damp, Sal let himself into the house. He hoped that the girls were at school, and Nona and their dad were at Julio's bedside, and Thomas was in the factory in Botany. He hoped he'd have the time and space he needed to think.

But suddenly there was Nona on the stairs, a basket of washing under her arm. 'Where've you been?'

'What do you care?'

She came down and dropped the basket on the floor. 'Cops wanted to know.'

He stuck his shaking hands in his pockets. 'And?'

'And they said they'd be back with a warrant if you didn't get in touch with them, and Thomas was upstairs listening in the whole time, and after they left he went off his tree.' She put one hand on her hip. 'He told me to tell you that, quote, if you fuck this up for him he will make you pay. End quote.'

'He's an idiot,' Sal said, then cast a panicked glance upstairs.

'He's not here.' Nona looked him up and down. 'I'm not washing those clothes, you know.'

'When did I ask you to?'

She grabbed the basket and headed for the laundry.

'How's Julio?' he said.

'Dad's with him. I said we'd be up later.'

The cops'll have someone waiting there for me. Sal shivered. If he didn't go, he wouldn't be caught. If he wasn't caught, and he didn't call, they'd bring a warrant and search the house, and find proof of Thomas.

He went upstairs to shower and think it through, dropping his damp clothes on the bathroom floor. The dew had been heavy in the park near Waverley Cemetery where he'd sat watching the sun come up. When the cemetery opened at seven he'd gone to his mother's grave. Her headstone had been cool and rough under his fingers. He'd scraped grime from the carved letters of her name with a twig, and pinched off the grass at ground level along the base of the stone, and pressed his fingers into the soil. A grounds-man had come past a couple of times but didn't say anything about him lying there. Sal guessed he was used to such things.

He didn't talk to her, either out loud or in his head. He just thought about his problems, and touched the grass, and hoped that help would come to him, in some way, in the end. And now it had.

The only problem was Julio. Sal tried to imagine himself in his position. Would he mind if his brother stayed away from his bedside in order to save them all from Thomas's madness? He didn't think so. Nona and Dad wouldn't understand, of course. But it would only be for today. Julio would surely hang on that long; the doctor had said it could be a while. Said he might even pick up a bit and come back home. Sal wondered if that was the effect of the herbal shit.

Anyway, by that afternoon the warrant should be served and cops'd be swarming all over the joint. He just needed to make sure they found what he wanted them to.

When he was dressed, he dug out an old street directory from the junk in his cupboard, opened it to Botany and circled the location of Preston's factory in red. He forced it into the back of his jeans, pulled his shirt down over it, then went to the top of the stairs and listened. The TV was on, some morning show, and he heard Nona laugh along with the studio audience. He edged along to Thomas's room at the end of the hall. The door was closed and he spent a long minute looking for hairs stuck in the frame as telltales if anyone entered. There were none. He pulled his sleeve down over his hand and turned the knob gently, then eased the door open in case there were more telltales of stacks of glassware or who knew what behind it.

'Thomas?' he whispered. No answer. He turned on the light and squeezed through the gap into the room.

The windows were closed, the blinds down. The air smelled of the drug chemicals. The bed was unmade and a pair of jeans hung off the end. T-shirts lay crumpled on the floor. Sal flung the street directory right up under the bed then looked around, wondering what else he could leave. A scrap of shiny bright blue fabric poking from under one of the T-shirts caught his eye. He hooked it out with his foot. Women's underpants. A pair he recognised from long ago.

Goddammit, Tracy.

'Sal!'

He booted a T-shirt across the underpants, hit the light switch and rushed from the room, pulling the door shut as quickly and as quietly as he could. Three huge silent steps and he was at the door of his own room. 'What?'

'There's a man at the door.'

'Who?'

Nona came halfway up the stairs. She looked apprehensive. 'You better come down.'

His first thought was that it was somebody from the hospice. But did they do that? When family members could just ring and break the news over the phone?

He followed her down to the front door. The screen was still locked and he had to go up close to see properly.

'Mr Rios?'

The man was Chinese. His face was round and plump, his black hair cut sharp across his forehead. He wore a suit of shiny blue that reminded Sal of the pants upstairs.

'Mr Rios?' he said again.

'Yes?'

The man held out an envelope. Out of his sight beside the door, Nona frowned and shook her head. 'Don't unlock the door!' she hissed.

'Just, ah,' Sal said. 'Can you put it on the mat?'

'I have to give it to you.' His accent was broad Australian.

Nona shook her head some more but Sal unlocked the door. The man handed him the envelope, then walked away down the drive.

'You're such an idiot.' Nona pushed Sal out of the way so she could relock the screen.

The man got into the passenger side of a silver Mercedes waiting on the street, then Nona slammed the front door and cut off Sal's view. 'What if he'd wanted to kill us?' she snapped.

He turned the envelope over. It was made of heavy white paper. Both sides were blank.

'You better not open that.'

He fitted his thumbnail to the corner of the flap.

'What if it's a bomb?'

Inside was a sheet of similar heavy paper, folded three times. Sal eased it open and saw five lines of blocky handwriting in black ink.

Feng Xie was our man. His family made us aware of his passing and the fact that the police are looking into the circumstances. Our arrangement with you is now at an end. You may not contact us. If we find any repercussions coming our way, you will be sorry.

Feng Xie taught you wrong, by the way. Your cook will never succeed.

Nona tried to read over his arm. He held it away from her. 'Are you Mr Rios?'

'You can be such an arsehole.'

'And you can be such a bitch.' *How on earth did I ever think I should hurt someone for you?*

She stamped upstairs, and a moment later shouted from the bathroom, 'Don't think I'm going to pick up these clothes.'

Sal tried to block her out and think. If he showed the letter to Thomas, it might make him give up cooking and book his flight home. And while he was waiting for that flight, he'd be hanging out here – a sitting duck for when the cops showed up.

In the car he mapped out the steps. Give Thomas the letter, and be prepared for the shitstorm. Remembering how he'd flung the heater across the room, Sal could imagine him trashing the place. So, give him the letter and get out asap, tell him Julio's crook as, sorry mate gotta go. Then hide out somewhere for the rest of the day. The movies! He hadn't been to the movies for ages. He liked the thought of sitting in a cosy dark place, large Sprite in the armrest, popcorn oil on his fingers, while the hours ticked by and the detectives got sick of waiting and went to get their warrant and smashed into the house. He'd see movie after movie, and emerge blinking at dusk to get into the car, put on the news, and hear that the murderer Thomas Werner was now behind bars.

It'd be nice to be able to explain to Julio, but he just had to hope he hung on.

Wayne Rhodes burst into the office. 'Are you okay?'

'I was before you gave me this heart attack.' Murray clasped dramatically at his chest.

'Not you.' Wayne was sweating and pale.

Ella felt a not-unpleasant flush creep over her. 'Better have a seat.'

He grabbed the closest chair. 'I only just heard.'

'And what'd you do?' Murray said. 'Run in from home?'

'Up the fire stairs.' Wayne loosened his shirt from his shoulders. 'Lifts're full this time of day.'

'Just to see if she's okay.' Murray smirked.

Ella's skin was tingling. She kicked Murray under the desk.

'Hey, I'm just saying,' he said.

'Where's the coffee machine around here?' Wayne said.

Ella said, 'Murray'll get you one.' She looked pointedly at him. He heaved a sigh and left the room.

'It's just,' Wayne said, 'I like to keep an eye on my friends.'

Ella looked down at the diagram on her desk. 'Thanks.'

'And I wanted to say, maybe I overreacted a bit about Mrs Nolan.' He picked at the vinyl on the arm of the chair. 'I felt bad when I heard this morning, and thought that was how we left things.'

'I'm the one who should stop accusing people,' Ella said. 'I think you're right – she wants to get to the bottom of things, and the next page of that letter did go missing somehow, but not because of her. Because if she'd wanted to keep it a secret, why not hide the whole thing?'

Murray brought the coffee. 'Kuiper just arrived. Rushed straight into his office looking all serious.'

He put the cup down in front of Wayne and turned to Ella. 'Maybe they caught him. Maybe he came back to your house with an axe and they nabbed him good.'

'Murray,' Wayne said.

Kuiper rapped on the door. 'Meeting room, now.'

'I'd better go.' Wayne got up. 'Talk to you later?'

'Indeedy.' Ella smiled.

When everyone was in the meeting room Kuiper shut the door. 'The net is almost over Deborah Kennedy. The local officers believe they've located her and we're just waiting for confirmation now. Hopefully she'll be interviewed by the end of the day.

'Closer to home, however, we've had some significant developments.'

He told the silent group about what had been happening in Ella's house. She kept her gaze straight ahead as he spoke. It sounded stupid now that she hadn't reported the first incidents, but who could've been sure what was going on? It was always easier with hindsight to know what you should've done. At least Mendelssohn wasn't here, swinging her smooth ponytail as she listened.

'The canvass produced a few descriptions of a man seen in the street in the last few days,' Kuiper said. 'One man seen apparently studying the houses near Marconi's is described as white, average height and build, aged in his thirties, wearing jeans and a blue shirt with a Broncos cap over short dark hair. He was seen twice, most recently yesterday afternoon, at which time he got into a blue sedan, with plates which turned out to be stolen.

'The other two witnesses described a similar man in vaguer terms. Average build, dark hair, white, wearing jeans. One saw this man two days ago when she was backing out of her garage and he walked behind her and she almost ran him over because he was looking across the street – the direction of Marconi's house. The other saw him the same day, from the end of the street, as he went into a property that was either Marconi's or very close to it. None of these witnesses could identify the airport photo of Werner as the man they'd seen.'

All well and good, Ella thought, but it didn't amount to much. They'd be lucky to get charges for any of it, unless prints were found, which she doubted, because Werner wasn't a complete idiot and you only had to watch a bit of TV to know how to avoid leaving them.

Kuiper went on to describe the arson attack on Ella's car outside her parents' house. 'This happened just after four this morning. There were no witnesses to the actual incident but a taxi reported nearly being hit by a blue Ford sedan close to the location. He got a partial on the plates, which we believe match another stolen pair.'

'Car's pinched too, no doubt?' Murray said.

'Probably. Twelve blue Ford sedans of the Falcon type that the witnesses describe have been stolen in the past month alone.'

'Do we know how he got access to Ella's house?' Marion Pilsiger said. 'How he knew where you lived?'

'As best we can figure, the mole probably copied her keys at some point when they were in her bag here in the office,' Kuiper said. 'All our addresses are in databases here, and we're thinking she may have been tailed to her parents' house, or as they're in the phone book with only a few others of that surname, that Werner checked out the locations and recognised her car.'

'Where are we up to on that mole?' Pilsiger asked.

'Mendelssohn and Greer are following a number of leads,' Kuiper said, looking at Ella. She looked right back. She knew better than to leak the names of the three targets. 'That's all I can tell you for now.'

Ella glanced down at her pad full of doodles and wondered how it was all going to end. Maybe Deborah Kennedy's information would be the key. Or maybe following the trail of the mole would end with Mendelssohn marching Werner triumphantly into the office.

Or maybe, she thought, *it'll be me, working on Sal, with help from Wayne.*

The letter was folded up in Sal's pocket and a corner poked him in the thigh with each step that he took past the little factories and workshops. He didn't mind, like he didn't mind people glancing his way or happening to raise their welder's masks or pausing in their conversations to ash their smokes as he went by. Today was the last day he'd be walking down to Preston's Plastics and the knowledge made him feel strong again. He'd give Thomas the letter, and Thomas would trash the place then go back to the house to plan his return to Austria. He'd be on the lounge, probably, watching crap afternoon TV and eating toast and dropping crumbs down his front when the cops came hammering on the door.

Sal crossed the Preston's Plastics forecourt with a smile.

Inside, Colin Preston worked a machine that was doing something noisy and making a hell of a smell. He glanced up and nodded at Sal. Sal nodded back then knocked on the door at the back. 'It's me.'

Thomas opened the door. Suddenly a little nervous, Sal dug the letter from his pocket and held it out.

Thomas motioned for him to come in.

'I have to go,' Sal said. 'Julio–'

'Come in so I can shut the bloody door.'

Thomas yanked him in by the arm. The noise of Preston's machine was cut by half as the door clanged shut, and Sal's courage wavered. The heaters whirred. The room was hotter than ever, and Thomas's bare chest ran with sweat.

Sal tried to slow his breathing. 'A Chinese guy brought it to the house.'

'It's already been opened,' Thomas said.

'He asked for Mr Rios.'

Thomas took out the sheet and let the envelope drop to the floor. It seemed to Sal that the sound of the letter being unfolded was louder than Preston's clanker outside. Thomas walked away from him as he read it, and Sal saw that he had a metallic blue hand-gun stuck in the back of his jeans. *Oh shit*.

'That little Chinese fuck.' Thomas stuck a corner of the letter into the flame of one of the burners and held it up.

Sal saw the flames lick up towards his fingers. *Is he crazy as well?*

But at the last second Thomas let the fragment of paper fall to the concrete floor where it smouldered and died. 'There's nothing else to do now,' he said.

Relief washed through Sal.

'I have to kill those paramedics.' Thomas pulled the gun from his jeans.

Sal froze. 'What?'

'I have to kill them.'

'No, you don't,' Sal said.

Thomas racked the slide. The sound chilled Sal's blood. 'Hey, no, wait,' he said, as nervous sweat ran down his back. 'Why don't we, instead, find somebody else who knows how to cook, and we add in that step that we missed? We can still make that money.'

'Stuff's fucked.'

Thomas aimed the gun at Sal's head. Sal couldn't speak, couldn't move. He thought of his mother, how she'd feel losing two sons in such a short time, though it made no sense to think that way because she was already dead.

The inside of the barrel was so black.

Thomas lowered the gun and stuck it back into his jeans. He looked at the mess on the benches.

Sal edged to the door. 'Julio's in, um, hospital.' His voice was high and thin. 'Nona's waiting for me, so

I better, um.' He found the handle by feeling behind him. He slid the lock around, then eased the door open. 'I'll see you later,' he croaked, and got the hell out of there.

THIRTY-TWO

Lauren stayed in bed till midday, trying to sleep ahead of her night shift, but mostly thinking about Joe. By the time she got dressed and went out to make lunch, she'd decided: that night she would tell him how she felt.

In the kitchen she could hear Kristi and Felise talking in the attic. 'I'm up,' she called. 'You want lunch?'

'We've eaten,' Kristi said.

Lauren made herself a sandwich and sat at the table, thinking about what she'd say. *Joe, we need to talk.* That sounded too grim. Like a break-up conversation.

What about, *Joe, can you tell me how you feel?* Or perhaps, *Joe, I'd like to tell you how I feel.*

She'd say it when they were driving, so they didn't have to look at each other until they were ready. It was hard putting your heart out there and asking for a response.

Kristi came downstairs and busied herself at the sink.

'Felise been on the swing yet?' Lauren said.

'No.'

'Joe reckons it's just the right height.'

'So I believe.'

'Are you okay?'

'Why wouldn't I be?'

'Is this because Joe helped me do the swing yesterday after I told you I didn't want help?'

'How petty do you think I am?'

Lauren put down her sandwich. 'He was just there, okay? I didn't ask him, we were talking, I was putting the rope over the branch and he held the tyre up.'

'I know.'

Lauren looked down at her plate. *Just because we didn't see her at the window doesn't mean she wasn't there.*

'You know he's engaged,' Kristi said.

'Der.'

'So what were you doing kissing him?'

'He kissed me.' *He kissed me!* Lauren couldn't help the little shiver of excitement that ran through her. *He really did it.*

'I can't believe you,' Kristi said. 'With all the stuff that's going on, you start up this thing with him?'

'Nothing's been started.' Lauren threw the rest of her sandwich in the bin. 'Anyway, what do you want me to do? Sit here and worry all the time? Be so frightened I can't leave the house?'

'I'm doing the best I can,' Kristi snapped.

'I wasn't having a go at you. I was just saying.' Lauren put her plate in the sink. 'Sometimes things happen at odd moments.' *You don't get to choose when you fall in love.*

'Just tell me you're going to sort it out.'

'I am.'

Tonight.

Ella sat at her desk with the huge file of statements in her lap. Rereading these things was like digging an enormous pit for gold. A nugget might pop out at you any second – or it might not.

Across the office Lambert talked in a low voice on his mobile, Pilsiger frowned at her computer screen, and Murray laughed at something Strongy said.

Ella sighed and turned to the next statement. Jules Cartwright. Ah, yes.

Scanning the lines of text, she remembered sitting on the woman's lounge as she described Thomas Werner arriving at her place and expecting to stay, and how she'd let him bunk down for a few days. She read, *We met on holiday in Spain.*

Spain.

Hm.

'Murray!'

He came over. 'What?'

She held the folder out, her finger on the spot.

'And?'

'Sal Rios comes from Spain.'

'His name comes from there,' Murray said.

'His family did at some point.' She started to hear how absurd this idea was but forged on anyway. 'Maybe Thomas knew him then. Or his family.'

'Your family comes from Italy but that doesn't mean you know all other Italians.'

Sal had almost told her something at the hospice; a bit more gentle persuasion and who knew what he'd cough up. Ella picked up the phone and checked her voicemail, then called switch to make sure she hadn't missed any calls.

'He's probably with his brother,' Murray said.

'Let's go and see.'

'Now?'

'Yes – no. Let me check something.'

She entered Sal's name in the computer database and checked for registered cars. He owned a white 2005 Honda Accord. She jotted down the plate number, then entered Nona's name. She owned a gold Toyota Avalon. Ella wrote down this number too. A search of their father Guillermo's name produced nothing, then on a last-minute gamble she typed in Julio.

'Blue Ford Falcon,' she read. 'Same car that's been around my place.'

'Same type of car,' Murray said.

Ella wrote down the numberplate. It didn't match any of the whole or partials noted by witnesses, but if Thomas was using this car to do dodgy stuff he might be switching plates regularly.

She turned off her computer. 'Let's go.'

Murray stood back from the Rioses' house and watched the curtained upstairs windows. 'Nothing.'

Ella banged on the door again. She resisted the urge to press her ear against the crack. 'Now?'

'Not so much as a twitch,' he said.

Ella went slowly down the drive, periodically looking back. She'd thought that morning that Sal had been in the house and heard her warrant threat. What did it mean now that he wasn't ringing her back? Perhaps he knew they didn't have enough evidence to get one. Or perhaps they were all just focused on their brother.

Traffic was light and they were soon at the hospice. They shared the lift with a nun carrying a stack of *Who Weekly* magazines, then stepped out onto the third floor. Ella looked at the opposite wall. *Yup. Me again.*

'Which room?'

'Third along.'

They walked slowly along the corridor, both glancing in as they passed Julio's room. Ella caught a glimpse of Julio's sunken and yellow face, Guillermo like a big bear hunched over his hand, Nona standing by the window.

They went into the waiting room. 'Now what?' Murray said.

Ella thought for a moment. 'Let's do a stake-out for a while. You stay here – comfy chair, nice cup of tea – and spy down the hallway. I'll go back to the house and sit in the car. He's bound to show up at one place or the other soon.'

Murray looked about the room. 'Okay.'

Ella went via the chapel, finding only an old woman kneeling at the altar. She walked away silently and hurried out to the car.

★

Ella parked across the street and two houses up from the Rioses'. A couple of azalea bushes with patchy foliage let her see the front and garage doors while protecting her from being seen from most of the windows. She got out of the car and walked along the street and up the oh-so-familiar drive, watching the curtains as she went. Nothing. She knocked on the door. More nothing. She turned and went back to the street and climbed into the car. She checked her watch, got out her notebook and jotted down the time.

She turned back a page to where she'd written the Rioses' plate numbers and left it open on the passenger seat, then texted Murray. *Nothing here.*

The reply arrived quickly. *Nor here.*

She settled down into the seat. If worst came to worst, school would be out in a couple of hours, and the kids Nona had referred to would arrive home at some point after that. Ella thought of the blonde girl at the chapel door. *Somebody* would either be here for them, or come to get them and take them to visit their uncle.

Surely.

On the screen, somebody shot somebody else, and the popcorn stuck in Sal's throat. He took a gulp of Sprite but it seemed like it couldn't get past and foamed back up into his mouth, making him cough. The man three rows ahead looked back with a frown. Sal's eyes watered and he gasped for breath. The popcorn was still there. He thought he could feel it when he pressed on the spot in his throat. He took smaller sips this time, and slowly and painfully the lump worked its way down.

It was no good. The movie was shit, the seat was uncomfortable, and why did people have to sit so close to him? He couldn't stop thinking about the round eye of Thomas's gun and the look on his face when he said he was going to get the paramedics. Let's not colour it, he thought. Kill. He said he's going to kill them.

He felt sick. The soundtrack was too loud, but even above that he could hear the woman along his row rustling plastic constantly. He stared at her for a long moment but she didn't even notice, just kept shovelling whatever it was into her mouth.

Finally he got up and pushed past her and left.

The afternoon sunlight was bright after the gloom of the cinema. It was after two already. He wondered if the cops had been yet, if it was all over. He walked a lap of the mall, trying to occupy his mind looking into windows, watching a kid play a video game in a computer shop. He walked a lap going back the other way. The place was huge but too soon he was back where he'd started.

He thought of the paramedics.

He felt sicker than ever.

Murray texted again: *Nothing*.

Same, Ella replied.

Meeting's on soon.

I know.

She sat holding the phone and staring out through

the shrubs. This wasn't how it was meant to go.

A car came slowly past and she slid lower in the seat. It was a red Corolla and it turned into the next driveway along from the Rioses'. Ella recognised the driver as the woman who'd told them the Rioses had all gone to the hospital with Julio. She grabbed up her notebook, shoved it and her phone into her bag, and got out of the car.

The woman was just about to go into her house, hands full of green enviro shopping bags.

'Excuse me,' Ella called. 'May I speak with you?'

The woman shouldered the screen door away so she could see her. 'Oh, hello. Let me just put these down inside.'

Ella waited by the step, looking across at the Rios house. She could see some of the side from here, and noticed a window in the garage.

'Sorry about that,' the woman said.

Ella got out her badge. 'I'm sorry I didn't introduce myself earlier. I'm Detective Ella Marconi.'

'Lottie Tuxworth.' The woman's hand was soft. 'Did you find the Rioses at the hospice?'

'We did, thanks,' Ella said. 'I was wondering what you could tell me about Sal?'

'He's a nice young man, very polite. Took it very hard when his mum died, you know.'

'Do you see him coming and going much? Does he have friends dropping by a lot?'

'He doesn't seem to have a lot of friends,' Lottie said. 'There was a Chinese man talking to him this morning, but he might have been selling something. Although he didn't come to my door.'

'What did Sal do after that?'

'Well, a little while later I heard him go out in his car, and then Nona went out in hers.'

'Sal's still got the white Honda?'

'Is that what it is?' Lottie said. 'It's the same white car he's had since he moved back, that's all I know.'

'And Nona was in her gold Toyota?'

Lottie nodded. 'She carts Mr Rios around a lot, because he doesn't drive any more. Between him and her kids, she spends half her life in the car. Have you seen those bumper stickers? *If a woman's place is in the home, why am I always in the car?*'

'I've seen them,' Ella said. 'What about Julio? Do they still have his car?'

'Oh, yes,' she said. 'They take it out pretty regular. I guess to keep the battery in good shape. Nona's boyfriend takes it out a bit.'

'Who?'

'The other man who's there at the moment,' Lottie said. 'I assume he's Nona's man friend.' She lowered her voice conspiratorially. 'You know what these divorcees are like.'

'Hm,' Ella said.

'Not a real friendly chappie though, if you ask me. I said hello to him once and he just put his head down and walked away. I don't know that he'd make a good dad to those girls. He never spends time playing with them in the yard.'

Something stirred deep in Ella's chest. 'What does he look like?'

'Average type of fellow,' Lottie said. 'Short brown hair, normal size, height and weight, you know.'

'And you've seen him driving Julio's blue Ford.'

'That's right.'

'How long's he been there?'

'Hard to say,' she said. 'A few months, I'd think.'

'I'd like to show you a photo.' Ella fumbled in her bag, almost dropping it in her urgency. Where was it, where was it? Notebook, phone, wallet, keys, scraps of paper, but no photo. Back at the office. *Damn*. 'Will you be home all afternoon?'

'I think so.'

'I'll be back soon.' Ella wrote her mobile number on one of her cards and gave it to Lottie. 'If you see the Rioses come home, especially Sal, or if you see this boyfriend, don't say anything to them but just call me, please.'

'Will do.'

'Thanks.'

Ella went back to the street, glanced around, then hurried up the Rioses' driveway once more. This time she pushed through a couple of spindly grevilleas and along the side of the garage, then moved a couple of bits of timber so she could stand on them and peer through the window. The blue Ford was parked closest to her, and the other space was empty. She couldn't see the plates on the car. If that car was here, did it mean Thomas was inside?

She went to the front of the garage and tugged surreptitiously on the roller doors. Both were locked. At the front door she took a deep breath, touched her gun and knocked.

Nothing.

She hurried back down the drive with a strong

feeling of being watched, jumped into her car and dialled Murray. 'Anything?'

'Nope,' he said.

'I'm coming to get you.' She started the car. 'Be waiting out the front. No, wait. On second thoughts, stay there. Don't step a foot away from that room. Ring if they leave or use a phone. I'll fill you in later.'

'But—'

She hung up on him and peeled rubber.

THIRTY-THREE

'It's like this,' she said to Kuiper. She laid out everything she knew. She counted the points on her fingers and drew links in the air. She explained what they needed and why. Then she waited.

Kuiper ran his thumb over the stubble on his chin. 'Murray told me about Julio Rios. A nun said he could die any time.'

'Well, yes,' Ella said. 'That's why he's in a hospice.'

Kuiper aligned two black pens on his desk. 'I don't know that we have enough evidence to justify disturbing a family at a time like that.'

Had he been sitting with his fingers in his ears?

'Yes, we can look into the immigration records,' he said. 'You can certainly ask Sal Rios in for an interview, but if he refuses you don't have grounds to arrest him. We don't have enough for a warrant to search their house or examine Julio's blue car, or for a phone tap either.'

'What if the neighbour identifies the photo of Werner?'

'Then come back and see me again.'

Back at her desk she phoned Maroubra station and asked for Detective Chris Frame, who she knew from a training course a few years back. 'If I email you a photo, can you show it to a woman who lives over there?' she asked him.

'Not a prob,' he said. 'Hey, what's this I've been hearing about somebody attacking your house?'

'It's complicated.' She pinned the phone between her shoulder and ear and sent the photo of Werner across. 'I'll tell you about it later. Has that arrived yet?'

'Let's see.' She heard the clicking of keys. 'Got it. You want me to go now?'

'If you could, thanks.' She told him the address. 'This man might be staying next door. Nobody answered when I knocked but there's a car in the garage.'

'I'll keep an eye out,' he said. 'I'll talk to you soon.'

She put the phone down and glanced at her watch. Ten minutes to get out of the station and drive over there, five minutes to talk to the woman, ten minutes to drive back. Sooner, if he rang from the scene on his mobile. She imagined getting the confirmation, going back into Kuiper's office, the team swinging into action. Lovely.

She got a cup of coffee and tried to read more statements but couldn't concentrate. She set her watch beside the folder so she could glance at it, but soon realised she was simply staring at the second hand go around. At the twenty-minute mark she checked her voicemail, in case the phones were playing up and Frame couldn't get through. She did it again at the thirty-minute mark. Her untouched coffee had gone cold.

She turned the page and tried to focus on the next statement then the phone rang. She snatched it up. 'Marconi.'

'She's not sure about the picture,' Frame said.

Ella couldn't believe it. 'She had a good look? She didn't just glance at it?'

'That's what took so long,' he said. 'She really studied it. She wanted to recognise it, I could tell. But in the end she just couldn't say it was him.'

Ella put her head in her hand.

'No sign of anyone in that house either, and the neighbour said nobody had been around,' he said. 'Sorry.'

'Thanks anyway.'

When Frame was gone she stared into space, trying to work out what to do next. Sal Rios hadn't called. They didn't have enough for a warrant on the house. Nona and her father would not be receptive to an approach asking about the identity of their lodger, and anyway she doubted Kuiper would give the okay. Not that she checked with him for every-thing, of course. But he was right about the evidence they had: it really didn't amount to much at all. They'd already shown Nona the photo of Thomas Werner and she'd denied knowing him, and while Ella had a feeling she was lying, that's all it was for now – a feeling. And while Kennedy had delivered goods for them, possible dodgy ones at some time, he'd also delivered to hundreds of people across the city.

She needed to speak to Sal.

An hour later she walked up the hospice corridor. Murray sat in the chair with a magazine on his lap, texting. He stood up as she approached. She looked sideways into Julio's room as she went past and saw only Guillermo, dozing in a chair with his mouth open. Julio appeared asleep too.

Murray said, 'I was just texting to say Nona and the kids left. I'm surprised you didn't see them in the foyer.'

'Dammit,' Ella said. 'I wanted to ask her where Sal might be.'

She'd already asked the same question of Paul Davids at Rosie's, who said he had no idea and then stepped back to let her check the place and confirm that he was indeed alone.

'Maybe we should call it quits for the day,' Murray said. 'We can talk to Nona in the morning if Sal hasn't turned up by then, but I think he will. He's got to eat and sleep somewhere.' His stomach rumbled.

'But maybe he works somewhere else that we don't know about, and he'll come by to see Julio this evening,' she said. 'I mean, he's not going to stay away the whole time, is he?'

'Well, you can sit around and wait if you want, but it's almost dinner time and I'm starving.' Murray started down the hall. 'Call me if something happens, otherwise I'll see you tomorrow.'

She sat down in his chair and picked up the magazine. She would wait. Even if Sal didn't turn up, at some point Guillermo would leave, or at least go to the bathroom, and she could ask him then where Sal might be. She looked up at the Jesus statue. That was fair, wasn't it? She wasn't waking him up, she wasn't hassling him in front of his dying son.

Her mobile rang. She didn't recognise the number on the screen. 'Marconi.'

'Hello, this is Lottie Tuxworth.'

Ella sat upright. 'Yes, Mrs Tuxworth. What's happened?'

'Well,' she said, 'that man friend of Nona's must have come back to the house some time this afternoon, because a few minutes ago I saw him run out and get in a yellow car that pulled up in the street. I think a woman was driving.'

'Could you see the numberplate of the car?' Ella said. 'Or the make or model?'

'Nothing like that,' Lottie said. 'Only that it was small, and yellow.'

'But you're certain it was that same man.'

'Definitely,' she said. 'I'm sorry I couldn't say if it was him in the photo. But listen, Nona came home with the girls just now, so she might be able to tell you.'

'You haven't spoken to her about any of this, have you?'

'No, no, she went straight into the house.'

'Please don't mention it at all, Mrs Tuxworth,' Ella said.

'No, I won't,' she said. 'I promise.'

'Thanks. I might be in touch again soon.'

Ella hung up then scrolled through her contacts list to find Kuiper. Just before she pressed the call button, movement down the corridor caught her eye. A woman came out of a room further along than Julio's. She wiped her eyes with the back of one hand as she shakily thumbed a mobile with the other, then put the phone to her ear. 'It's me,' she said. 'Mum's just passed.'

Ella sat perfectly still and silent.

'Yes, just now.' The woman's voice cracked and broke. She put her hand across her eyes. 'No, not since yesterday. But I don't think she knew I was there even then.' She slumped back against the wall as if her legs weren't coping. She was crying now. 'I'm okay, really. She's out of pain, that's the main thing.' She glanced up and saw Ella sitting there, then turned and went back in the room and closed the door.

Ella looked at the floor, thinking of Netta. She hadn't called her or her dad in a few days now; she couldn't even recall the last time. Three days ago or four? They'd probably been calling her house and worrying that she didn't answer. Oh god, what if they'd rung Lily and she'd told them about the firebomb? Netta would be furious that she hadn't heard it from Ella herself.

I should have rung them, at least. What's that take, five minutes?

She would ring them tonight. Soon. After this.

For now she called Kuiper. He answered curtly. 'I'm flat out here. They've tracked Deborah Kennedy to a house west of Griffith but she's refusing to come out. I'm trying to get more info.'

'What's she want?'

'She won't say,' he said. 'She's got her daughter and that bloke with her, everyone's apparently unharmed, but she won't talk or leave the house. They're sending more officers plus a negotiator now.' The phone went muffled for a moment then he came back on the line. 'I have to go.'

'Just before you do,' Ella said quickly, 'the Rioses' neighbour called to say she saw that the man who we suspect is Werner leaving the house with a woman in a small yellow car. No make, model or plates.'

'Okay.' He sounded distracted. 'Are you knocking off now?'

'I'm still looking for Sal—'

'Keep me posted,' he said, then he was gone.

Ella sat with the phone in her lap, thinking about Deborah Kennedy and her daughter and friend holed up in a farmhouse. Why would she behave like that? Had she gone crazy with grief? Down the corridor she could hear the bereaved woman sobbing. She thought of Sal in the chapel, telling her that his mother had died here too. She thought of Lottie saying how devastated he was at her death. She looked up at the statue and had an idea.

She scrolled through her phone to the received calls, chose one and pressed to dial. 'Mrs Tuxworth,' she said, 'Detective Marconi again. Can you tell me where Mrs Rios is buried?'

Dusk was falling when she arrived at Waverley Cemetery. A man was stooped over locking the gates.

'Excuse me.' She showed him her badge. 'I'm looking for a man who might have spent quite a while here today, and maybe recently, at one grave. He's in his early thirties, brown hair, brown eyes, on the slim side, average height, and drives a white Honda.'

'There was a guy like that who we had to ask to leave so we could close,' he said. 'I think I saw him get into a white car out on the street there.'

'When was this?'

'About fifteen minutes ago.'

'Do you know which grave he'd been at?'

'He was walking around in the southern side there,' he said. 'That's all I can tell you, sorry.' He bent to the gate again.

Ella went back to her car. She got in and stared out the windscreen. *Fifteen minutes.*

I should've thought of this sooner.

Joe turned another page in the newspaper. 'This is nice, isn't it?'

'What?' Lauren said.

He gestured at the station living room, them with their boots off and feet in socks on the coffee table. 'It's not often we get to sit about like this. I could get used to it.'

It felt eerie to Lauren. They'd come in, checked the truck, and eaten dinner. She'd lifted the phone a couple of times, even going so far as to actually call Control and make sure they were on the roster. The officer had laughed. 'It's just quiet,' he said. 'Although now I've said the Q word, that should put an end to that.'

It hadn't though. Lauren turned the TV on and flicked through the channels then turned it off. 'Let's go for a drive.'

'Can't we enjoy our downtime instead of going out looking for work?'

'I'm bored.' *And I need us to be in the truck, side by side, so I can talk to you.* Now that she'd imagined it like that, she couldn't conceive of it happening any other way.

'Check the drug expiry dates if you want something to do.' He focused back on his newspaper.

She got up and walked into the muster room. She felt antsy and unhappy. Kristi had had another shot before she'd left home that evening, saying she had to sort things out before they went too far.

'I will,' Lauren had said. 'I will, okay?'

Kristi had watched her put her metal buttons and paramedic epaulettes on her shirt. 'And be careful tonight.'

'With Joe?'

'I'm serious,' Kristi said. 'I've got a weird feeling.'

Everything feels weird lately, Lauren had thought. 'I'll be fine.' She'd kissed Kristi's cheek. 'See you in the morning.'

Now, adjusting the magnets on the whiteboard, she had to admit she felt weird too. It's just because of the slow start, she told herself. Almost two hours without a job – this must be a record in the history of the station.

The phone rang. She grabbed it up. 'The Rocks.'

'Told you I'd jinx us,' the Control officer said. 'For you I have a man crying.'

Lauren's hackles rose. 'Are you kidding me?'

'Nope,' he said. 'Called in by a neighbour. The address is Unit 7, 19 Betts Street in the 'Loo. Cross is Victoria. Save a life, wontcha?'

Joe came in, hopping as he pulled on a boot.

'Man crying,' she said.

'Not him again.'

'Different address.'

She yanked her own boots on and followed Joe to the ambulance. She felt sick with apprehension. *It won't be the same guy. You're here with Joe, and everything's fine.*

'So where is it?' Joe drove out of the station into the night.

She told him the address. 'Clear this side.'

'Stay there, little yellow car.' Joe accelerated out of the driveway across the path of traffic. 'I'm going for girlfriend trouble this time.'

Woolloomooloo was only minutes away. Not long enough to even start to tell him. 'I'm going for boyfriend trouble.'

He laughed.

'Clear this side,' she said.

The block of flats at 19 Betts Street was new and clean and tidy. An elderly woman was waiting for them under a streetlight, holding the tails of a black-and-white scarf out of her face as the wind gusted. 'I'm sorry to bother you,' she said.

'No problem at all.' Lauren felt better already. This was completely different from the ice addict job. *Nothing bad is going to happen.* 'Do you know the man at all?'

'He hasn't long moved in,' she said. 'I keep meaning to introduce myself but haven't had time. Can I carry one of those bags for you?'

'Thanks, that's fine.' Joe brought the stretcher around and Lauren piled the Oxy-Viva, drug kit and monitor on top then topped it off with the first aid kit.

The woman hurried to get the door. Joe wheeled the stretcher past her and into the lobby. Lauren hit the lift button and they all squeezed in together.

The elderly woman looked up at Joe. 'Aren't you a nice young man?'

'He is, isn't he?' Lauren grinned. Joe tried to kick her under the stretcher but she shuffled out of his reach.

The lift doors opened and they filed out. The woman pointed to a door numbered seven. Lauren heard a faint thump from inside.

'He wouldn't answer me when I knocked before, but you might have more luck. Or I can see if the caretaker's home yet?'

'Leave it with us for a few minutes,' Lauren said. 'Thanks for your help.'

'I'm right in here if you need me.' The woman went into her flat and closed the door.

Lauren knocked. 'Ambulance. Can you hear me?'

A low grunt. She knocked again and put her mouth near the crack. 'Ambulance.'

Joe tested the doorknob. 'Locked.'

Lauren pounded on the wood with her fist. She listened, and thought she heard moaning. 'Maybe we should send her for the caretaker. Could be post-ictal or anything.'

Joe knocked on the old lady's door and she was quickly on her way in the lift.

The caretaker was a brusque man in black jeans and a cream jumper. 'Can you confirm for me that there is a medical or other emergency taking place within these premises which require me to allow you use of the key to access said premises?'

'I can confirm that,' Joe said with a straight face.

The man handed over the key. Joe fitted it to the lock and the caretaker backed away to the lift. 'I'll, uh, leave you to it. I'm not good with blood and that.'

Good, Lauren thought. Go.

Joe opened the door wide and they looked in. The only light came from the fridge but it showed a man lying on the kitchen floor. Lauren hit the living room lights and looked around as she went in. 'Can't see anyone else here.'

Joe asked the old lady to mind the door then followed Lauren with the stretcher and gear. Lauren turned on the kitchen lights and expected the man to look up at her blinking, but he stared vaguely around the room. Half the contents of the fridge were pulled out and on the floor, and when she took a step forward she felt stickiness under her boot. 'Honey.'

'It's all over him,' Joe said.

Lauren crouched by the man. His skin was sweaty where it wasn't honeyed. Honey was smeared on his jeans and shirt too. 'Looks like a hypo,' she said. She squeezed his shoulder. 'You're a diabetic?'

He grabbed at her, putting honey handprints on her arm and shirt. Unable to focus or speak, he pulled at her arm.

'I know, it's okay,' she said. Even through her gloves she could feel how wet and cold his skin was.

'Jabber's ready,' Joe said.

'Find something to wipe his hand or the honey'll send it off the Richter.'

Joe ran a tea towel under the tap and squatted on the other side of the man. 'How you doin', buddy?' He caught the man's hand as he reached for him. Lauren kept hold of the other. Joe wiped the honey from the man's fingers then held that hand still as Lauren pricked the man's index finger and let a drop of blood fall onto the glucometer stick. The man put his free hand on the side of her head, smearing her ear and cheek and hair with honey.

'Aw, crap,' she said.

Joe giggled.

The machine beeped. 'Low low low,' Lauren read.

'Let him pat your hair some more while I set up the dextrose.'

Lauren held both the man's hands in hers. He was crying and trying to speak. 'It's okay,' she said. 'Sugar's on the way.'

Joe used the wet towel to wipe a clean patch on the man's arm, then cannulated a vein. He taped it down securely, flushed it with normal saline, then screwed the nozzle of the fifty ml syringe of dextrose into the cannula. 'Twenty-five grams of sugar, mainline hit.' He depressed the plunger slowly. It was thick, sticky stuff that was hard to inject. 'Ooh, that feels good, doesn't it?'

Within a minute the man was blinking and trying to focus. 'Sugar,' he croaked.

'We just gave you some,' Lauren said. 'Can you understand me?'

'Diabetic,' he said. 'Ambulance.'

'That's us.' She squeezed his hands, and he focused and really saw her. She loved this bit, as they came back to full consciousness from their hazy and confused hell.

He looked up at Joe, then around the trashed kitchen. 'Oh, wow.'

'What's your name?' Lauren said.

'Kieran Scott.' He touched the front of his shirt. 'Is this all honey? Oh, man.'

'Can you remember what happened?'

'I went to the gym, then came home and showered when I usually have a snack first. I remember feeling funny, and knowing what was happening, and coming into the kitchen. Then I must've gone too low to know what to do.'

Lauren took his pulse and blood pressure and checked his blood sugar again, while Joe made him a sandwich to build up his reserves. The old lady came in and introduced herself. 'Are you okay now?'

'Did you call for help for me?' Kieran said. 'Thanks so much. Can I offer you a cup of tea?'

'Let me help you clear this mess up first,' she said with a smile.

Down at the ambulance Lauren and Joe wiped

down the handles of all the equipment they'd used. Joe said, 'True neighbourly love. Good to see.'

'It is.' Lauren spread clean sheets on the seats to keep the honey off the upholstery. She could feel the stuff drying in her hair. She called Control on the radio. 'Thirty-four's complete at this scene, post hypo covered in honey, substance now transferred to both officers. Request to return to station for major clean-up, please.'

'Go ahead,' Control said. Lauren heard the smile in his voice and somebody in the background laughing.

'It was pretty funny.' Joe pulled out. 'Especially when he started patting you.'

Lauren collected herself. *Now, do it now!* 'Joe,' she said.

'Hey, I just thought of something.' He started to laugh himself. 'That might've been the bad thing Claire was so worried about. Wait till I tell her.'

'Joe,' Lauren said again.

He looked over at her, smiling. 'What?'

Ella was hunting for a park near Rosie's when her mobile rang. She saw it was Kuiper, and ducked into a no standing zone and flicked on her hazards as she answered.

'Deborah Kennedy gave herself up,' he said. 'She waited until there were a number of officers, including senior ones on scene, then asked the negotiator to meet her in the garden so she could explain every-thing. Kennedy was killed over drugs.'

Ella clenched her fist. *I knew it!*

'He was working with Thomas Werner and the Rios family, and with Adrian Nolan and Feng Xie too, just as you suspected. When the amnesty came along, they all decided they wanted out, but Werner had them so frightened with his threats they didn't know what to do. He told them he had police working for him, and he sent Kennedy and Nolan photos taken of their wives out shopping or in their cars. He threatened to get Feng put into detention then deported. Kennedy told his wife all this, and they set up a code system so he could let her know if there was trouble and what she should do.'

'The line of poetry in the dying declaration,' Ella remembered.

'Yes,' Kuiper said. 'She also said he told her Feng Xie had told him that Werner had made him teach him how to cook the drugs, and that he'd been instructed by the syndicate back home to leave out a step so that the process would never succeed.'

'Protecting their investment,' Ella said. 'If Feng was out, then so were they.'

'Also, Mendelssohn and Greer have identified the mole. Tracy Potter works part-time for Human Resources. They were checking the phone records of the suspects and found multiple calls from her mobile to one belonging to Sal Rios. They went to her place but she appears to have done a runner.'

'That's maybe why I can't find Sal too,' she said. 'They're probably hiding out together.'

'There's more. One of Potter's neighbours described a male visitor and remembered the numberplates of Jason Lambert's car. We're looking for him now.'

'Dorky Lambert?' she said. 'She had both of them on the go?'

'And she drives a yellow car.'

Holy crap.

'We're in the process of getting the warrant for the Rios house now,' Kuiper said. 'Meet us on scene in twenty.'

Ella dropped the phone on the passenger seat and gripped the wheel. It had all happened just like she'd thought. The amnesty was the trigger. Nolan and Kennedy were in cahoots, they'd tried to get out together with Feng Xie, and Werner's threats kept them from acting then eventually came true anyway. Nolan's desperate flight from the uniformed officers who pulled him over made perfect sense. *Wait till I tell Wayne!*

She drove towards Maroubra. The orange sodium lights on the highway made all the light-coloured cars appear yellow. She was trying to see the occupants of each one that passed her going the other way when her mobile rang.

'Marconi.'

Silence.

'Lauren?' she said.

'It's Sal Rios.'

Ella almost drove into a pole. 'We've been looking for you.'

'I need to tell you some things.'

'Hold on,' she said. 'Let's meet and do this face to face.'

'It can't wait.'

'Just tell me where you are.'

'No, listen,' he said. 'I know Thomas Werner. I saw him today. He's got a gun and he said he's going to get the paramedics.'

THIRTY-FOUR

Lauren took a deep breath. 'I have to tell you something.'

'That sounds serious,' Joe said.

'It is.' *Come on, say it!* She shut her eyes tight. 'I love you.'

Silence. She glanced over. He was staring straight ahead. She held her breath.

Suddenly a small yellow car shot around them and darted in front, the occupant waving a hand for them to pull over. Joe stepped on the brake. 'What's this wacko up to?'

'Joe,' she said.

He gestured at the car. A young woman scrambled out of the driver's seat. 'Let's see what she wants, okay?'

The woman rushed up to his door. 'It's my brother.' She was crying, and clutched at the side of the truck. 'He rang me, he's going to kill himself, can you help me?'

Joe was all business. 'Where is he?'

'I don't know the exact address, I only know how to get there.' She flapped a hand down the street.

'Show us then.'

She rushed back to her car and shot away. Joe followed, and Lauren picked up the radio microphone. 'Thirty-four to Control.'

There was a burst of static. She waited a moment then tried again.

'Black spot,' Joe said.

'Not usually around here.' They were heading into the Darlinghurst backstreets.

'Try when we get there.' Joe's words were clipped and short.

He's angry, Lauren thought. Have I offended him? Or could he be fighting with his feelings? *Now you sound like a bad romance novel.* 'Can we talk?' she said.

'Let's just do this job, okay?'

Lauren stared out the windscreen. Of all the responses she'd imagined, this wasn't one of them. Thrilling wonderful acceptance she'd dared dream of; gentle let-down she'd told herself to expect. Not anger.

The yellow car turned into an alley, then into another narrower one. Lauren couldn't recall having been in any of these streets. The buildings were old and partly demolished. Joe slowed to get around a skip bin. Lauren tried the radio again but only got more static.

The alley was dark, the one streetlight broken. The sliver of moon was no help. The ambulance headlights cast eerie shadows.

The yellow car stopped and the woman leapt out. 'He's in here!'

Lauren and Joe got out of the ambulance. 'Why's he in there?' Joe said.

'He's homeless, it's a squat,' the woman said. 'Bradley, we're coming!' she shouted into the open doorway.

Lauren suddenly felt sympathy for her and anger at Joe. 'Get the torch.'

'I'll just phone Control.'

Lauren stamped around and grabbed the torch and the Oxy-Viva and the first aid kit. The woman had already started into the building, sobbing her brother's name. 'You coming or not?' Lauren said to Joe, heading for the black doorway.

He put his phone away, took out the monitor and drug box, locked the ambulance, and followed her in.

Kuiper said, 'Slow down, you're getting garbled.'

'We need to see where the tracker is,' Ella barked. 'I've just spoken to ambulance Control and they haven't heard from them since they left a job in Woolloomooloo. They were meant to be returning to station but aren't answering the phone there. I've tried Lauren's mobile but get no answer, and they said they get the same with Joe.'

Kuiper shouted an instruction to somebody else in the office then came back on the line. 'Sal doesn't know where they might be?'

'He has no idea. He's told me everything else,

about how he saw Werner kill Blake, and that Werner drowned Feng Xie and took the drugs to finish the cooking, so I can't see why he'd hold out on that.'

'Where are you now?'

'Darlinghurst,' she said. 'Looking.'

'Okay. Let me call Control, get the rego of their ambulance, put out an alert. I should have the tracker location in a couple of minutes.'

Ella threw the phone down and concentrated on her search. She put her lights on high beam and drove down every alley and laneway, even if it was too small to turn around in and she had to reverse out. She squeezed the wheel. Lauren was her responsibility, and she felt that this was now somehow her fault, as if she'd been too focused on tracking down Sal and Thomas and in the process forgot about protecting the innocent.

And she *was* innocent too. Sal had told her how Thomas had tricked and attacked Lauren in the alley the night that Blake died, while Sal himself hid trembling behind the dumped car. It had happened exactly as Lauren had described.

Her phone rang. Kuiper said, 'The tracker's somewhere just off Desmond's Lane in the 'Loo.'

'I'm right near there,' she said.

'I don't have to tell you—'

'Sorry,' she said, and hung up.

Desmond's Lane was thirty seconds' drive. Ella was almost hit by a yellow car screeching past her as she turned a corner. Tracy fleeing the scene of the crime, she thought, seeing the plate in her rearview. Or sneaking off to an arranged location to pick

Thomas up once he'd done a rat-run through the backblocks of the 'Loo. She couldn't worry about her now.

She turned another corner and her high beams flashed off a reflective strip on the back of the ambulance. She flicked her headlights to low and crept forward. Her skin prickled. This was dangerous. She should back out, wait for the cavalry, let them storm the joint in all their protective gear.

She got out of her car and eased along the side of the ambulance. The cabin was empty. There was no sign of the officers in the alley. Ella could hear only the traffic on the street and her own rapid breathing.

The doorway into the dilapidated building was black as pitch.

Lauren's phone beeped that another message had been left on her voicemail.

'You're a popular girl,' Thomas said.

'And you're an arsehole.'

'Keep walking.'

She stumbled forward in the darkness. Joe was behind her, his fingers tucked into her belt. Thomas was behind him, the muzzle of a gun pressed into the back of Joe's neck.

Lauren wanted to tell Joe she was sorry, this was all her fault, he was right, they should've rung Control, they should've lingered a moment, she'd got all snippy and rushed in here because she was angry at him, and the woman's concern for her brother

Bradley sparked memories of her own brother Brendan, and when Thomas had stepped out of the darkness and said, 'Thanks, Tracy,' Lauren saw she'd been led into the entire mess like a pig to a fucking trough.

He'd taken their torch, made them drop their gear and forced them to walk deep into the abandoned building. It stank of decay and urine, and Lauren kept tripping on the broken concrete and exposed reinforcing bars. She could hear the scuffle of little ratty feet, and beyond that the sound of traffic on the city streets. She listened for sirens. She had the tracker. The number of calls on her phone surely meant they'd realised they were missing.

She tried to think positively, told herself that they'd survived the ice addict, they could survive this too.

But this was different.

She gulped back a sob. She felt Joe's hand move a little, and his thumb stroked her back, just once.

It gave her courage. 'You know they'll all be here soon. I've got this tracker. They know *exactly* where we are.'

'It's not that accurate,' Thomas said. 'But it'll help them find your bodies.'

'You know this won't fix anything,' Joe said.

'Shut the fuck up,' Thomas said. 'Stop there. Turn around.'

Oh Jesus.

They faced him. Lauren was shaking. She felt the steady pressure of Joe's arm against hers. 'You should let Joe go,' she croaked. 'It's me that—'

'Shut up,' Thomas said again. He held the torch low, and he looked gaunt and crazed in the poor light as he aimed the gun directly at her.

'Police! Drop your weapon!'

Lauren was suddenly knocked flat. A gun went off, the sound deafening. The torch hit the floor and blinked out.

She pressed herself against the rough concrete. There was another shot, then another, and she held her breath as her heart galloped in her chest and her skin crawled with the expectation of the punch of a bullet at any second.

But it didn't come. The room felt still. She couldn't hear anything through the ringing in her ears. She felt tentatively around for Joe. Her fingers touched something soft. Skin. An arm. It was warm but didn't move. She felt her way up it, her breath coming fast in her throat. She found the edge of a sleeve, the round ambulance patch. *Joe, it's Joe.*

She slid her hand to his chest and felt a rush of relief at the movement of his breathing. *Alive, but unconscious.* Further across she found wetness and warmth. He was bleeding from a chest injury.

Shot.

Shot!

Get the gear and save him. Get the radio and scream for help. Find the torch, get it working, see what you're doing, could be a tension pneumothorax, could need decompression, you can save him, you can. You can.

Somebody grabbed her leg. She leapt away in fright – *It's Thomas, oh god* – but then Ella said, 'Help me.'

481

Lauren put out a trembling hand. Ella's fingers seized hers. 'Help,' she said again.

'Shh.' She pictured Thomas lining them up in the dark, working off their voices.

But she could hear the bubbling of blood in Ella's lungs. *That is it. She and Joe could die. You have to move, right now.*

Ella wouldn't let go of her hand. 'Help me.'

'Shh.' Lauren prised her fingers off, feeling the slick of blood.

'Don't leave me.'

'I'm coming back.'

Lauren scuttled across the floor, groping for the torch, sure she'd find a gun barrel pressed against her forehead instead. She fumbled around a pile of rubble then her hands closed on the torch's round plastic body. While Ella coughed wetly behind her, Lauren pressed the button on and off then shook the shit out of the thing. The beam came on and she swung it in an arc across the room.

In the flash she saw Ella clasping her chest with her left hand, her gun wavering about in her right, and Joe flat on the floor.

No Thomas.

Ella pressed desperately against the hole in her chest as blood slid oily and warm between her fingers, soaking her shirt. She watched Lauren dart back across the room towards her, drop the torch, and ease Joe onto his side. She saw her feel at his neck for his pulse, put her hand on his chest to check his breathing.

She fought against the sensation of simultaneously drowning and being consumed chest-first by fire, and hung on for as long as she could. After all, he was the worse of the two of them, he was unconscious, he needed more care, but finally she could hang on no longer. 'Can'tbreathe.'

Lauren scrambled over. She moved Ella's left hand from her chest and slid her shirt up to see. Ella fought to hold her right arm up, to keep her gun ready in case Thomas appeared, but somehow the gun came to rest on the filthy concrete floor.

'Press your hand flat here again.' Lauren put Ella's hand back on her chest. 'Press it.'

'I am.'

'You're not. Press.'

Ella tried her hardest.

'Better. I'll be back in a sec.'

'Don't leave me.'

'I need the gear.'

'Dontleaveme.' Ella let go of the gun and grasped Lauren's trouser leg.

'I can't look after you properly without the gear.'

'Holdmyhand.'

Lauren knelt beside her. Inexplicably, Ella smelled honey. She thought of heaven, and Netta.

'Let me get the stuff,' Lauren said.

'Holdmyhand.'

'I am.'

But Ella couldn't feel it – she couldn't feel anything.

THIRTY-FIVE

Lauren sat perfectly still in the chair beside Joe's hospital bed. Before he woke again she had to make up her mind.

She didn't have long, either. Claire was on her way, and once she blasted in Lauren knew she'd be out on her ear.

She frowned, trying to concentrate, but Joe's hands lay on the outside of the blankets, his tanned skin a stark contrast to the white cotton. The urge to grasp his fingers was almost overwhelming and she shifted her gaze, only to find herself staring at the bruise where he'd hit his head on a pile of concrete rubble and knocked himself out.

He pushed me out of the way.

She blinked back tears and focused on the IV bag hanging above the bed, dripping in fluid and antibiotics to treat the wound that had luckily missed his lung. *Count the drops per minute, don't think about how he almost died for you. That's his instinct to protect life, it doesn't matter whose. It doesn't change your decision one little bit.*

When he'd been awake before, they'd smiled at each other, and he'd asked if she was okay, and asked about Ella and Kristi and Felise, and Thomas, and there'd been not a word about her declaration before he'd sunk back into his morphine dreams.

So.

The way she saw it, she had three options.

One: if he had forgotten what she'd said, did she really want to bring it up again? The memory of his angry response was all too clear, and if that was how he truly felt then saying it again wouldn't achieve a thing.

Two: if he had full memory of it but was deliberately not saying anything, hoping it would just go away so he didn't have to actually reject her, then she should accept both his kindness and the fact that she should bloody well put it behind her.

Three.

Three was tricky. Three insisted that whether he remembered or not, she should say it again. She should put it out there. She should be bold and daring, she should remember his thumb stroking her back, and the shove out of the way, whatever his reason . . . and she should remember his kiss by the mulberry tree.

Because that was what it all came back to, right? The thumb and the shove you could maybe attribute to his nice-guy compassion, but that kiss was something else.

She put her face in her hands, feeling like a coward for her inability to decide. What did she have to lose? So what if he rejected her – was she going to shrivel up and die?

She started when the door squeaked open.

Claire stopped short in the doorway. 'You have some nerve.'

Could she be any louder? 'He's asleep,' Lauren said.

'You almost get him killed,' Claire hissed, 'and then you dare sit around here like you're important in his life?'

'We're friends.'

'Not for much longer if I have anything to do with it.'

'I think that's up to him.'

Claire folded her arms. 'Nobody cares what you think.'

Anger boiled up inside Lauren. If she stayed much longer she was going to punch the bitch. 'I think it's time I left.'

'What took you so long to realise that?'

Lauren touched the blanket near Joe's hand and headed for the door.

The corridor was empty. She went to the window and looked down at a bare courtyard where the wind was driving dead leaves into a corner. Her chest hurt and her mouth was sour. She should've spoken up when she'd had the chance, when Joe was awake that first time. She should've grabbed his hand just now, before Claire came back, and woken him, and asked him for his answer.

Claire came out of his room, frowning at his chart. She saw Lauren and pulled the door firmly shut behind her. 'I want you away from here.'

'Free country,' Lauren said.

Claire stared at her. 'You're disturbing people.'

'Who?' Lauren looked up and down the deserted corridor.

'If you go in there again I'll have security kick you off the hospital grounds.' Claire stormed away with the chart flapping in her hand, glaring back once before flouncing around the corner.

Lauren looked at the closed door. She had to see him, just one more time. She turned the handle, checked down the corridor, then went in.

Joe lay in the same position as before, his eyes closed, his breathing slow and even.

'Joe.'

No response.

She bumped the bed with her leg. 'Joe.'

He stirred but didn't open his eyes. She bumped the bed again, harder. Claire would be back any second. 'Joe!'

Nothing.

She knew ways to make him wake: she could rub her knuckles along his sternum, or push her thumb into the bony arch above his eye, or press a pen against his fingernail. But they worked because of the pain they caused, and he'd been through enough.

She stood by the bed. Voices approached along the corridor and she quickly bent to kiss him. She saw the curl of hair by his ear and the pinkness of his skin, and his breath was a rush of warm air against her neck as she pressed her lips to his cheek.

The door flew open. Claire snapped, 'What the fuck did I say?'

Lauren turned around. 'I'm going.'

Claire gestured to the nurse she'd brought with her. 'Call security.'

'I said I'm going.'

'I'll have you banned,' Claire said. 'I'll put in a complaint, I'll tell them about the tube, I swear; I'll get you kicked out of that job.'

Lauren looked back at her from the doorway, then past her. Joe was awake. Claire stood oblivious and ranting. Joe's gaze was fixed on Lauren, and she thrilled at the gentle smile on his face.

'Get out!' Claire shoved her out the door, but not before Lauren caught a glimpse of Joe raising a shaky hand.

She stumbled into the corridor as Claire slammed the door. Lauren didn't look back. The sun broke through the clouds outside and made the windows glow, and lit Felise's hair as she turned the corner into the corridor with Kristi. They each carried a bunch of flowers. Felise started to run when she saw Lauren, and Lauren knelt in the sunlight and caught her in her arms.

Ella came to slowly. Hearing was first: there was an annoying rustling sound, but she couldn't open her eyes to see what it was, and couldn't speak to protest.

Pain came next, colouring her chest and side and back an angry red.

Not dead. In hospital?

She forced her eyes open, and tried to move to ease the pain. Something tugged at her arm.

'Whoa,' a voice said. 'Don't grab at that.'

Ella didn't realise she was grabbing at anything. She turned her head to see the source of the voice, but the light was bright and she had to squint, and even then could only see a shape.

'Hang on, I'll close the blinds.'

The brightness went away. She blinked.

'How's that?'

'Wayne,' she croaked.

'That's me.'

Sweet warm honey spilled into her veins. *Wayne*.

He sat down in the low chair and put a newspaper on the floor. 'How're you feeling?'

'Crap.' She felt her side, found a tube there.

'That's a chest drain. It's stitched in so don't go yanking it.'

'Ugh.'

'You should see what's coming out.'

She dozed for a moment then woke with a start. 'Lauren?'

'Fine.'

'Joe?'

'On the mend,' Wayne said. 'In a room down the hall.'

Her mind was fuzzy. Anaesthetic, she thought.

Another thought. 'Thomas?'

'Dead. Tried to do the bolt through the building in the dark, skidded, fell, and skewered himself through the neck on some busted reo.'

She nodded slowly. 'Justice.'

'The final kind.'

She searched her foggy mind for another name. 'Tracy?'

'We caught her near the scene,' Wayne said. 'She'd been waiting for Werner at a pre-arranged spot on the other side of the building. We think that's why he walked Lauren and Joe so far in, so his escape run would be short. She fessed all, as did stupid Jason Lambert.'

Ella thought she was hearing him wrong. 'Lamby?'

'He was so desperate for a bit of action that he'd taken whatever she deigned to give him in return for information she couldn't get herself,' Wayne said. 'She'd flagged down the ambulance and led them into the trap, but also stuck a doover on the side of the truck to block their radio signals, so they couldn't tell anyone where they were.'

Ella struggled to take all this in.

'Deborah Kennedy told everything, but you know that already. Umm. Sal Rios sent a message asking how you are. He's at his brother's bedside but with an officer outside the door. He'll be facing a few charges but is cooperating fully, in the hope of leniency I guess. Doesn't seem too bad a guy actually.

'Oh, and Kuiper came by before, with the Commissioner, to tell you what a good job you'd done, but I said you were washing your hair and couldn't be disturbed.' He smiled. 'Your mother keeps phoning, and your aunt and father are on their way.'

Ella tried to smile, tried to relax back into the bed, but she ached in both body and mind. She clumsily wiped her eyes with the back of her wrist.

Wayne squeezed her knee through the blanket. 'They reckon you'll be out in a week.'

'I thought I was dying.' She put out a trembling hand. 'I thought I was gone.'

Wayne took her hand in his. His palms were broad and warm. He turned her hand over and smoothed his thumb over the pads of her fingers. 'For a while they didn't know.' His voice was tight. 'We were all waiting to hear, you were in theatre for fucking hours, and I thought, if . . . I thought . . .'

She closed her eyes, so tired, so warm, so safe, and fell asleep as he folded her hand gently into his.

AUTHOR'S NOTE

I'd been an ambulance officer for ten years when a writing teacher told me to think about drawing my experiences on the job for my fiction. It took another five years before I could see the value in this advice and realise that right there in front of me lay a world brimming with drama, a world full of conflict and fascinating stories, and from the years I'd spent doing it, I had the sort of knowledge that can bring a story to life. After all, I've scrambled down cliff faces in the rain to reach people screaming in wrecked cars. I know the waxy feel of dead flesh, the sound of a dying man's last gasps. I've breathed the odour of alcohol-rich blood at a car crash in which the driver lay dead. I've broken into houses to get to patients who've collapsed. I've caught babies born on stained lounge room floors. I've done CPR until my back screamed and my shirt was soaked with sweat. I've held a mother's hand and looked into her eyes and told her that her daughter was dead. I've cared for bashing victims in the middle of brawls.

I've pressed desperately on haemorrhaging wounds while the blood ran off the stretcher, drenched the floor and escaped under the back door of the speeding ambulance. I've been abused, assaulted, bitten and threatened. I've wrestled a knife from a deranged teenager, and run away from violent psychotics. I've testified in murder cases. I've even done my absolute best to resuscitate a dog whose owner thought the two of them were better off dead.

Trouble was, the years of trauma and shiftwork had really taken their toll, and the first ambulance scenes I tried to write bore all the emotion of the cases I'd recently done and came out as little more than rants. It wasn't until I quit that I was able to get some perspective: it took six months of being out of the job for me to understand how far from normal I'd actually been. I slowly started to realise that *this* was how I should feel, how normal people felt, not the fatigued, depressed, emotionally strung-out person that I had become. I realised that not everyone is dying; not everyone's life is full of trauma.

The more time went by, the better I felt, and the scenes I wrote were no longer rants. I found that I was able to use in a controlled way everything I'd felt and seen and done, and give those experiences to the paramedics in my story, also giving a bird's eye view of ambulance work to the reader.

They say that nothing comes without a price. I guess for me, perhaps the price of publication was those years of emotion and pain. At the time, going between doctors, psychologists, sleepless nights and miserable days, it was hard to see that any good could come of it all. But I wouldn't change my life for the world – not only because the experiences in the job brought me the fodder for the books, but because they taught me to take nothing for granted, and because seeing so much of both the best and worst of humanity, in others and in myself, has made me a better writer, and, I hope, a better person.

Katherine Howell, 2006

Visit **www.panmacmillan.com** to read more about all our books and to buy them. You will also find features, author interviews and news of any author events, and you can sign up for e-newsletters so that you're always first to hear about our new releases.